I0633734

Knightshield

Wayne Basta

Published by Many Worlds Fiction, 2025.

KNIGHTSHIELD

First edition. October 1, 2025.

Copyright © 2025 Wayne Basta.

ISBN: 978-1958159149

Written by Wayne Basta.

Also by Wayne Basta

Seraph
Seraph's Gambit
Seraph's Bind
Seraph's Break

Standalone
Knightshield

Watch for more at waynebasta.com.

Chapter 1

The sound of the bullets echoed off the narrow walls of the alley. While an unnerving sound, the plink of the bullets ricocheting off my shield made me smile. They couldn't touch me.

I'd caught these goons assaulting some poor human woman in an alley and dropped in to intervene. That had allowed the woman to get away and I considered just leaping away. But now that they had pulled guns out, any slight hesitation I had to send these goons to the hospital evaporated. Any asshole who opened fire deserved what they got.

With a defiant yell, I rushed forward, keeping my shield up and intercepting the barrage of fire. I slammed into the first goon at full speed. Unfortunately, even running all out, the mass of my tiny uvoy body compared to the goon's large grunde body only made him stumble backwards into a trash can, instead of going flying, like I'd envisioned in her head. That didn't mean I'd waste the opportunity though.

Pivoting to keep my shield arm facing the other goons, I slammed my steel-toed boot backwards into the goon's crotch. I followed up with an elbow to his nose and abdomen and then another kick to the groin for good measure. With the goon bent over double, I reached my arm around his neck. Spinning around, I leapt up to race along the brick wall and used momentum to flip the goon into the trash can where he stayed, groaning quietly.

The gunfire from the other two goons had paused when I'd grabbed the first. I had to give them some marks for at least caring enough about each other enough to not fire indiscriminately at their buddy. That compassion didn't extend beyond their little gang though.

I deflected a fresh barrage of gunfire and then heard the distinctive click of empty magazines. Seeing my chance, I loosened the strap on my shield and tossed it at the goons. The shield clipped the one on the left's gun hand as he fumbled with a new clip. It then continued its arc and took out the right one's gun as well.

I didn't have much time to act now without my shield to protect me. I dashed forward and threw myself into the air, grabbing the bottom of the fire escape above the two goons. My momentum carried me forward and swung a foot into each ones head, knocking them to the ground. I let go of the fire escape at the end of the arc and landed on the right one's chest.

With a quick hop, I came up and down, smashing my full body weight into the goon's prone chest again. While us uvoy aren't very big, we can jump quite high, so I had a fair amount of speed when coming back down. To finish him off, I bent over and rained two fists into his face, careful to avoid the tusks sticking out. He let out a groan and his eyes rolled, unfocused. A smile started to form but faded in an instant when I felt the spike of pain as a knife blade sliced into my left shoulder.

I let out a grunt of pain but managed to keep my wits enough to rotate my body in the direction of the knife's cut, easing the force of it driving in. The blade slipped free of my attacker's hand, leaving it embedded in my padded clothing, only the tip partially digging into my shoulder. Probably for the best as it would help staunch the bleeding. Unfortunately, the goon had also gotten ahold of my mask and pulled it off my head as we twisted, exposing my face.

"Brilliant, Kali. The other goon was down but not out. You're getting sloppy." I thought to myself as I turned to face the final goon.

We circled around each other in the narrow alley. This final opponent towered over me by almost a full meter. That meant he might even be double my mass, even though my small frame sported a decent amount of muscle for its size. I was at a decided disadvantage in a straight fight, which compounded more since I had to end this quickly. The other two were already starting to stir. There might even be more of their buddies nearby.

"You may have gotten the drop on us little girl but that won't help you now." The goon said with a sneer. "You picked the wrong people to mess with. Do you know who we are?"

"Yesterday's egg salad left out in the sun to long?" Kali asked. "You smell about the same."

"Cute, kid."

"You know, you're right. I am a cute kid. Still going to kick your ass." Kali said.

Before the goon could issue another retort, I rushed forward, but slower than necessary. As soon as the good reached out, his height forcing him to bend down to reach me, I leapt. I landed one foot on his outstretched arms and then stair walked the other onto his head before flipping over his back in a cartwheel. On the way down, I grabbed the goon's shirt collar and pulled it with me, leveraging my momentum to yank him backwards.

I didn't have the force to pull the goon all the way over but did get him bent backwards at an awkward angle. Dropping onto my undamaged right shoulder, I propelled myself into a slide, back under the goon's legs, still holding onto his shirt collar. He tumbled down and I narrowly avoided having him land on top of me. I slammed fists down into the goon's exposed crotch and then pummeled his kneecaps. A sickening crunch announced there had been some lasting damage.

Around me the three goons lay moaning in pain. They were alive but wouldn't be a threat, at least not right away. I surrendered to the exhaustion and pain for a moment. My body still surged with the adrenaline, but I could feel it already starting to fade.

"You have no idea what you've started. Blood Daggers do not forgive and forget." The goon with the broken knee said through his moans.

"Neither do I." I said but couldn't suppress a shiver of worry creep down my spine. I hadn't known these guys were Blood Daggers when I'd gone after them.

Not wasting any more time, I picked herself up and raced over to where my shield had landed. I wiped some gunk off the emblem at the center of the blue and silver pattern. The flicker of lights from alleys entry way alerted me to someone approaching. I tensed to run away but relaxed when I recognized the silhouette of the distinctive hat of two constables. With them was another shape I took to be the woman these goons had been harassing.

As the lights approached, I pulled my mask back over my face before raising my unhurt arm to wave, "Right on time, Constables. These guys are all..."

I didn't get a chance to finish my sentence as all sound was drowned out from the echo of a pistol shot. Fortunately, I had been resting my shield against my chest and the bullet deflected off that instead of going right through my chest. I dropped on instinct, getting as much of my body behind the round piece of metal as I could and moved to make myself harder to hit.

"What the hell?!" I shouted. Behind the constables, the woman screamed and added her voice to mine, "She's the one that saved me! Don't shoot!"

"Keep your damn green-skin mouth shut, you whore!" The constables with his gun smoking said. The other one had his gun out but looked frozen unsure what to do.

I crouched beside a garbage bin and called out again, "Come on, I'm the good guy here. Put the gun away, asshole!"

I probably shouldn't have added that last part. But I really didn't like it when people shot at me. Coppers should know better. My dad's deputies had drilled into them. Guns were always a last and terrible resort. A lesson I wish I had taken to heart earlier.

"Throw down your weapon and put yourself on the ground!" The constable shouted. "I won't give you another warning!"

"You didn't give me a warning the first time. Why should I take this one?" I shouted back. "You put your damn gun away and then I'll come out."

"Your funeral." The copper said, hints of a smile visible in the faint light.

With a sigh, I coiled up, compounding the dense muscles of my legs. Uvoy muscles can work a lot like springs with the right amount of training. I'd been training in some fashion almost every day of my life. Part of me was excited that I finally had a practical use for it but mostly I was just hoping I didn't screw this up and die.

I sprung upward, arcing over the constables before they could react. I came down behind them in an instant and swept my shielded arm out into the backs of their vulnerable human knees. My shoulder flared in pain, but I ignored it. As they crumbled, I smashed my fist into the back of the asshole's head, then my shield down on both of their gun hands, making them drop the weapons. The asshole groaned but didn't get up and the other one just looked at me terrified.

I kicked the guns away and then grabbed a pair of handcuffs from the downed constable and slapped them on the still groggy grundes. They probably could have gotten up by now but had given into their bodies desire to not move. Made this part easier for me.

"Thank you." The woman said as she backed away from the scene. I finally was able to get a good look at her and saw she was human, but several years older, well into her middle years as opposed to my barely out of my teens.

"Any time." I said. "Too bad these clowns were more eager to shoot me than do their jobs, or none of this would have had to happen. Do they not train you guys at all in the city?"

The one who hadn't shot me, shook his head, "It's my first week. I was just doing what I was told."

"Shooting innocent people?"

"You had a weapon." He stammered.

His partner started to sit up and I decided I didn't want to have to explain anything more to him. I tipped my head to them before jogging around the alley's corner and back onto the street. I took a cloth out of my pocket, winding it around the shield, obscuring the colored metal. I removed my mask, revealing my dark green skin, and then set the shield on my head like the traditional wraspisa it resembled. Now, I was indistinguishable from any other uvoy woman you'd see on the street. If you ignored the knife still wedged into my shoulder. With luck, that wouldn't be very obvious under the shadow of my wraspisa.

The flow of pedestrians at this late hour was small but the streets weren't empty. I walked close enough to another pair of uvoy so that, at a casual glance, you might think we were all one big family. Once the pair turned into a pub, I picked up my pace to get around the next corner and stopped in the doorway of a closed shop. I waited a good ten minutes but saw only regular people pass by. Finally, I breathed a sigh of relief and let myself relax slightly. Just enough to once again feel the full pain of the dagger in my shoulder.

Moving more quickly now, I headed for home. The outside of Nerpi's Cycler Garage wasn't a pretty place, but it had become home. I unlocked the entry door as quietly as I could, careful to keep the bells from jingling and waking anyone else up. Unfortunately, my key wouldn't work on the next door but luck was with me as Allora had left her adjourning clinic unlocked for a change.

Rifling through the storage cabinets, I searched for bandages and alcohol. Every place I looked was packed with bottles of herbs and colored liquids, all labeled in a shorthand I couldn't interpret. Fortunately, most of the liquids were colored and alcohol was not and I managed to find a bottle.

Gingerly, I unfastened my jacket and tried to pull my left arm out of the sleeve. Every movement caused the knife to wiggle and I couldn't move my arm enough to get it free of the sleeve. With gritted teeth I decided it was time for the knife to come out. A sharp yank pulled it free and blood began running down my back.

Quickly, I pulled the jacket and shirt off exposing the wound. I poured the bottle of alcohol onto the wound and couldn't stop myself from letting out a squeal at the sudden sting on top of the agonizing pain. I tried to staunch the blood flow with a bandage but couldn't reach with my other arm in order to apply enough pressure.

When the lights came on, I was sitting there, dripping in blood, in my sports bra, and helplessly flailing at my wound with a blood-soaked bandage. I locked eyes with the tall, dark haired, middle-aged evian woman who stood in the doorway. Her light blue skins, long floppy ears, and brilliant violet eyes were the main distinctions between evians and humans. Fortunately, or not, almost all species on this planet shared similar facial expressions so I could easily read the disapproval etched on her face. We stayed frozen for only a second before the woman rushed in and grabbed a fresh bandage.

"Kali Estuta! What the hell happened to you?" Dr. Allora Ren asked. While her voice was gruff and stern, her hands were gentle as she cleaned the wound. "Is this a knife wound? You're going to need stitches girl."

I withered under the scrutiny. I hadn't known Allora long, I hadn't known anyone in the city long, but I had tried to keep my nighttime escapades separate from my day job. While technically that didn't include Allora, she did rent space from Nerpi for her clinic and lived in a room on the second floor just like I did.

"Um...yes it was a knife."

"And why did you come here? You should be in a hospital, reporting this to the Constabulary."

I let out an audible laugh. "Seriously? Isn't it you whose always telling me the Constabulary only solve crimes that are easy or they've been paid off to 'solve'? Knife in my back, must be my fault. I'm not human."

"Sure." Allora said in reply. The next stitch was decidedly less gentle than the others had been. "So, you were just minding your own business and someone walked up and stabbed you in the back?"

"You know what it's like out there. Streets are full of thugs and goons who'd just as soon stab you as say hello."

Allora continued to work, muttering something quietly under her breath as she did. I assumed it was some kind of curse directed at my actions but as I listened more closely it didn't have the right cadence for that. I couldn't make out the exact words, but it sounded more like a litany chant than actual words.

"Are you chanting?" I asked and felt the older woman stiffen behind me and the temperature in the room dropped.

"What? No." Allora said.

"You were. I thought you called the Church a controlling, autocratic, cesspool of assholes?"

Allora sighed, "I did. They are."

"You grumble and complain every time Nerpi makes us all go to Church."

"I do. I don't even technically work for him. And speaking of that, don't you need to be up in, oh a few hours, to go do that?"

I narrowed my eyes. Allora had deflected the questions. But then, so had I. A draw felt like an acceptable result after my night so far. I nodded accent and then gave a final wicked smile.

"Don't you mean, don't WE need to be up for church?"

Chapter 2

I woke the next morning to someone rapidly shaking me. I punched out and rolled away from my attacker before my brain could come awake. My bare feet hit the floor beside my bunk and with the bed between us I took a second to catch my brain up on what had happened. Across from me, the shop's receptionist, En DeSkies, a human with a black goatee and shaggy hair, sat on his butt rubbing his jaw.

"Shit, Kali, why you gotta do that. Every time."

I sighed. "Sorry, En. I've told you not to wake me like that. Call out to me. Don't touch me while I'm sleeping."

"I keep forgetting. I feel like I gotta be quiet when someone's sleeping." En said and stood up, still rubbing his jaw.

I glanced at the clock on the wall hanging above the door and sighed. It was barely past dawn. "Why did you wake me so early?"

"I didn't want too. Nerpi told me I had too. You have a wicked right cross, but he's still scarier than you. You know how he gets about us being seen in church when Turmlin's gonna be there."

I rolled my eyes. Nerpi was about the least threatening boss I'd ever worked for. Granted, I gathered En came from a very different background than I did. Turmlin though, En had a valid point about. Our garage's biggest customer definitely had gotten his hands dirty before, and unlike Nerpi, not with engine grease.

"Yeah, all right. I'm up. I'll be down in a minute." I glanced at the clock again, "Make it fifteen. I need a quick shower."

"Sure, sure. Just remember to wear the dress this time. Nerpi says we have to look the part. All worshipful and stuff." En said from the safety of the stair well before disappearing at full speed.

9

I ran myself through the shower, only bothering to scrub the dirt, grime, and blood off my hands and head. No one would see the rest of me. Because there was no way I was wearing that stupid dress. Not even to help Nerpi keep this place open. My regular overalls would do just fine. They were clean.

When I emerged downstairs, I made sure it was time for us to leave. I found Allora and En sitting in the break room. En had on a fashionable suit that cost way too much for what Nerpi paid him. His hair was immaculate, despite having been punched in the face not twenty minutes ago. Allora sat beside him in a frumpy old dress that did nothing to mitigate her reputation as a curmudgeon. But her hair too was done up in a fancy braid. I felt fortunate I didn't have hair. It looked like a real pain in the ass to manage.

Unlike Nerpi. My boss paced back and forth across the room, his brown and white eowian fur freshly cleaned and brushed. He wore a tattered suit of a style older than me. But I had to give him this, unlike every other piece of clothing he owned, it didn't have a single grease stain on it.

With a growl of frustration Nerpi stalked over to me. I had to glance down to look him in the eye. I'm slightly below average for a uvoy and we are one of the shorter species on Akka. But eowians make us feel like giants.

"We can't be late. Turmlin's in town and he can't see us skipping service." Nerpi chittered.

I gestured up to the clock on the wall, "And we're not going to be late unless we stand here badgering me. This is when we always leave."

"Because one of you is always late getting ready." Nerpi fumed.

"Because none of us want to go."

"Neither do I." Nerpi said. "But I'm always ready on time. Early even."

"That's because you're a wonderful and respectful person." I said and ruffled the fur on the back of his head.

He batted my hand away and led the way out the door. We walked down the street toward the massive building that dominated the central square at the end of the street. Very few other people were out at this early hour with us. Only the sad workers from the new Mega Mart that had just opened down the street.

"See, we're not the only ones going to church service." Nerpi gestured.

"Attendance is mandatory for all Mega Mart employees. My da...uh...I heard from some guy I don't know that their CEO is very religious." En said.

"Right. But in a way far more sinister way than Nerpi's demand." Allora said quietly.

"I don't force you to go." Nerpi said defensively.

"What would you call it then?" Allora asked. "I don't even work for you and yet here I am."

"It's highly encouraged. You all know how important these meetings with Turmlin and his company are."

I patted Nerpi's shoulder, "We do. That's why we're all here."

"Then why didn't you wear the dress? Everyone else is dressed nicely." Nerpi said.

I glanced down at my overalls. They were clean and I had a long-sleeve shirt on underneath at least. I even had all the buttons done up for a change. "I love you Nerpi, but not that much. That dress clashes with my skin and it's all rigid and stiff. I can't move in that thing."

"You don't need to move. Just sit and look worshipful."

"I can do that and be comfortable."

"Not according to the acolytes. Only true suffering is a sign of honest commitment to Akzad. But only for some people." Allora mumbled.

I frowned over at the doctor. She said things like that sometimes. I couldn't tell what she meant by them, she clearly didn't like the Church. But then, out of all of us, she was the only one who ever actually paid attention during services. Including Nerpi. He made a good show, but I knew him well enough to tell he was running through engine schematics in his head.

We reached the church and all went inside. Waiting at the main doors stood two of the acolytes in their fancy blue robes. This was the part I hated the most. One by one, we knelt before the acolyte and repeated the catechism while looking up. Ostensibly, we're supposed to be looking up to Akzad, but we were effectively on our knees looking up into the smug face of a human while he leered down at you. That's another reason I never wore the dress. My shirt was snug but covered me, the dress was way too loose in the chest.

Fortunately, I ended up kneeling before Acolyte Benthic, a relatively kind old man. While I'm sure he leered down plenty of dresses in his days, he was too old to show any interest these days and just smiled warmly. Acolyte Hishu, on the other hand, I had avoided punching his groin by only the slimmest of margins.

The service went the same as they all did. Long and boring. I've been to dozens but I honestly couldn't tell you what happens. You stand up. You sit down. You kneel. You bow. You intone some bullshit. You get lectured at. I only pay close enough attention to know when to stand. Despite all his talk, Nerpi sat beside me doing the exact same thing.

En, however, got really into it this time. Normally, he slouches and practically snores. I guess this week he's playing the part of a devote follower of Akzad? That would make the rest of the week annoying. When he made tweaks to his character, he got really into it, to the point of being insufferable. But that's to be expected. He'd been playing the part of a lowly garage receptionist for a few months now without breaking character.

When the service neared its end but before we all trudged along to the reception hall, the only cool part of the service happened; the Manifestation. I'm no religious scholar but I can tell you this much about the Church, it was founded on Old Magic. And not fanciful storybook magic either. Genuine magic.

The Manifestation was one of the few examples of it left in our world. We all knew it had been real. Afterall, how could a half dozen different species all end up living together on the same world? The new science of genetics had proven we all had come from different places. How had we all gotten here if not magic? Some kind of boat that could travel through the emptiness of space? Come on.

Anyways, besides our origin, the only bit of magic left in the world are holy relics and Manifestations. The Church High Acolytes are the only ones who can summon a Manifestation. Now, I've never seen a Relic manifest any magic (despite my grandpa claiming the shield I wore as a wraspisa was one), but I had seen the Church Manifestations. I thought they had to be some kind of parlor trick, but damn if it wasn't a good one.

The acolytes stood around the alter before empty bowls. I noticed one of them, a young human, was new and wore the robes of a trainee. He was cute, for an human, and his nerves were evident. I would be too if I had to summon magic for the first time in front of a room full of people.

The High Acolyte began the incantation and we all dutifully followed suit. This was the only one I knew, most of, the words too and didn't just mumble something. "We are the vessels of Akzad. We are his instruments on the physical plain. The power of our faith will shape the world. We give this power because together we are strong. Our will is Akzad's will."

As we neared the climax of the chant, the empty bowls before the acolytes gave off a faint blue shimmer. The shimmer slowly coalesced into a full collection of fruits. We'd all get to eat a piece after the service. I felt a little bad for the trainee whose bowl only yielded a single pear.

You might be wondering why I'm so hard on the Church if I accepted the claim of magic existing in the world, and saw the Manifestations with my own eyes? Well, because it was boring. And the acolytes were skeevy. But mostly because that's all they did.

There were hungry people all through this city. Half the people in attendance today didn't get regular meals. Yet, all the Church could do was summon up a few small bowls of fruit, once a week, to share with the rest of us. In exchange for that benevolence, we all were expected to bow to them, listen to their stupid rules and tithe ten percent of our earnings. That was the world's most expensive fruit, even at my meager pay rate.

As usual, there were a few gasps of shock throughout the congregation. Everyone had to have a first time seeing the Manifestation. The Church would have a few more devoted minions for awhile. But for every new person who saw the light, there were two more like me who saw past the light to the bullshit underneath.

Finally, the service ended and the real work began. Now we had to mingle. And be seen. And, uh, talk to people.

We shuffled along next door to the reception hall and joined the queue for our piece of Manifested fruit. I managed to wedge myself in behind En and in front of Allora so I didn't have to talk to anyone while we waited. The line moved with practiced efficiency. The acolytes clearly wanted to be done with their weekly moment of pretending to care about others as quickly as possible.

One of the weirder things about the Manifestation was that the bowl of fruit contained a huge variety of samples. Despite the High Acolyte being human, as well as most of the other acolytes, their was fruit from all the different inhabitants of Akka. Fruit that we had brought with us from wherever we had each come from Before.

I ended up with a kelva, which I eagerly traded to Allora, as I couldn't stand the taste. She gave me an apple, a human fruit, which I pawned off on En for a melba. I bit into it and savored the sharp, tart bite of flavor. I'll give the church this much. Scam or real magic, the fruit they handed out was always perfectly ripe.

We all stood together near one of the exits, quietly enjoying our fruit. Except En. He talked animatedly with anyone who came close, waxing poetic about the blessing we'd received and the importance of the acolyte's lecture. The more he talked the harder it was to not crack up laughing.

Finally, *finally*, the whole purpose of today's production ambled into view. Mikail Turmlin, owner of the League One Turmlin Racing team, Nerpi's biggest client. He commissioned us to do some refurbishment and repair work on some of their racing cyclers. Not the main ones, just the team's practice and transport models. Plus, occasionally, some more off-the-book type jobs.

"Ah, Nerpi, excellent to see you here. I know I can always count on your devotion." Turmlin said with an oily human smile.

"Of course, of course. Nothing but devotion in my garage." Nerpi said.

I pasted a fake smile on my face and stood behind Nerpi. I normally didn't have to say anything, which was good. Speaking got me into trouble with types like Turmlin.

"And I see you've even managed to persuade your reluctant subletter to join you. I am glad to see you opening your heart to Akzad, Doctor."

Allora gave a weak smile in return, "Nerpi is relentless and I'm starting to see the light."

"Excellent, excellent." Turmlin said, cast his eyes over the rest of briefly. He then stepped in closer. "I'm glad to find you here. I have need of your...special...services. Someone had the gaul to break into our garage last night. Go see Garret Ryncol today on some pretext. He'll give you the details of what happened. I need you to find our lost property and retrieve it. I don't care what happens to those that stole it, so long as it can't be traced back to me."

Nerpi nodded absently. I could see the disappointment in his shoulders. He always hoped that forging this relationship with Turmlin would lead to a better contract, maybe even getting us on the racing team. But it always went down like this.

Chapter 3

We stood outside the Turmlin garage and I marveled at the sight. This wasn't a local repair shop like Nerpi's, but across the street from the big arena in town. You didn't come here to get your oil changed but to supe up your cycler for professional races. The outside was clean, colorful and the street didn't have garbage littered everywhere. There was still the stale smell of piss though.

"Nerpi, ah, good to see you. I have those, ah, parts for you to repair." A middle aged and overweight evian man called from the open garage door. Garret Ryncol, the floor manager for the Turmlin racing team was our main business contact. Nerpi tried to cozy up to the owner during church services, but it was actually Garret who gave us all of our legitimate work.

Garret gestured for us all to follow him inside. Everyone else had changed clothes after we left the church. I hadn't seen the point since I was already in what I normally wore. Another point for comfort. Nerpi now wore his usual grease-stained coveralls and Allora had a very simple blouse and pants. En had put on a trench coat and fedora despite there being almost no chance of rain today.

Inside the garage was quiet. No races on service day so very little for the team to do. The only other person present was Niels, the security guard. He sat on a couch, dried blood on his uniform and an ice pack held to his head. Allora immediately went over to him and inspected the wound.

"Have you been to see a doctor?" She demanded.

"He's seeing one right now." Garret said, his tone defensive and a bit whiney.

"I'll send you my bill." Allora grumbled before rummaging through her bag.

"Now, we'll need to see where the crime happened. And all of your clues. Chop, chop my good man." En said, his voice deep and commanding. He took a magnifying glass from his pocket and began inspecting random objects around the room.

Garret stared for a moment but turned back to Nerpi. He'd had enough encounters with En to know to ignore him. He gestured for us to follow him and we walked over to where one of the team's racing cyclers was in the middle of a rebuild.

"They took an experimental turbo booster we had designed for our bikes. It was going to give us a huge advantage in the rest of the upcoming races this month. Without it, we're toast."

"You think a rival team took it?" I asked. Nerpi bent down to inspect the array of parts, softly mumbling to himself. He was trying to figure out what made this booster special no doubt, oblivious to the questions at hand.

"Undoubtedly." Garret said, "But, just like us, their, uh, extra-legal activities are done through third parties."

I glanced up and looked around the garage and then walked out through the big door and scanned the outside walls of the building. I spotted what I was looking for and shook my head. Security cameras. Those things weren't cheap. Fancy new bike parts, cameras, Mr. Turmlin was investing quite a lot in his racers.

"Your fancy camera see anything?"

Garret shook his head, "No. An empty street and then they stopped recording. Whoever these guys are, they're good."

I looked around the street some more, trying to see how someone could get to the cameras. They were placed high up on the wall. A ladder would certainly do it, but not without being seen by another camera. You'd have to get them both simultaneously. I looked up to the top of the building above the garage, several stories above us. To come from above you'd have to suspend down several of them. A uvoy like me might be able to get up their easily enough, but getting down to the cameras would be quite difficult.

"So, they both cut out, at the same time? No hints of anything in the last few frames?"

"Nope. They just go out. I watched both films several times."

I frowned and looked at the garage door and the person sized side door. "How did they get in? Anything busted?"

"Nothing. They probably picked the lock. With the cameras down they would have had time."

I walked over to the side door. Since the thieves didn't steal any of the cyclers, just a component, there would have been no reason to open the main garage door. I inspected the lock but saw nothing out of the ordinary. It was in good condition. No scratches. "But you have a guard. Doesn't he do patrols?"

"Yeah, every half an hour or so. I guess we rely on the cameras to much."

"But he'd hear the door opening right? The office is just inside."

Garret shrugged, "I suppose. He told me he didn't see anything. Someone conked him on the back of the head."

I walked back inside to where Allora was stitching up the guard's head wound. En had finished his diligent examination of everything and had come over to stare down at the guard, who fidgeted uncomfortably. He kept glancing up at En and then away.

"Hey, Nerpi, I want you to look at something." I called out.

Nerpi broke away from his inspection of the disassembled vehicle and came over to join us. "En, give him your magnifying glass. Nerpi, check out the door locks. I want to see if your skilled eye sees what I saw."

We stood there in silence while Allora worked and Nerpi inspected the door. When he returned, he shrugged, "Not sure what you wanted me to look at. The locks look fine. They're in good condition. Work well. No damage. Lock securely."

"Do they look like they've been picked?" I asked.

"Nope. There would be some scratches on the metal from the tools. An amateur might even break the lock mechanism. A professional might be able to do it cleanly but I'd think there would have to be some scratches."

I turned back to look down at the guard. Before I could say anything else though, En leaned in real close to the guard and started snarling. "It was you! I can smell a rat. You stole it. You're going to be thrown into a deep hole and never again see the light of day."

To my, and everyone else's, complete astonishment, the guard broke down and started crying. "I did. I'm sorry. They promised to pay off my debts. I didn't want to. But they said it would be easy. Just open a door and turn off the cameras."

En stood up, a smug smile on his face. "Well looks like my work here is done. Case closed. Another mystery solved by the Detective Brill Yant."

"No, it's not." Garret growled, a dark look on his face as he stared down at the guard. "Who was it?"

"I don't know their names! I met them in a pub down on Jumaker. That's all I know. I swear!"

Garret cursed, "Well, you all know where to look for our booster. I'll take care of this sorry piece of shit."

The way Garret said 'take care of' sent a chill up my spine. I shared a glance with Nerpi but he shrugged. We'd argued before about what kind of people these Turmlin guys were. He felt strongly that, if we were the outside muscle they were hiring for their illegal jobs, then they couldn't be that bad. And he had a point. If they didn't want to get their hands dirty chasing down people who had robbed them, they weren't going to murder their own employee. Even if he had betrayed them.

The four of us left the garage, Allora handing Garret an invoice for her medical services. We boarded our cyclers, Nerpi hopping into a side car attached to En's, and made our way over to Jumaker street. The avenue was quite narrow for a main traffic way, it wouldn't be wide enough to allow two quadcyclers to pass each other. We weren't too far out from the city streets, only needing to accommodate horses as engines were only a few years older than me. Fortunately, traffic was light and cyclers weren't much bigger than horses.

We cruised down the whole length of the street and I didn't spot any obvious pubs. When we stopped at the end of the street Allora called out, shouting to be heard over the sound of the engines, "I didn't see a pub, but I did see a bunch of cyclers lined up in an alley. That has to be the place."

I frowned at her, glancing down at my cycler, "That seems like a stretch. We all ride cyclers, we don't visit pubs."

"But, Kali, did you forget? We are going to a pub." En said with complete sincerity and not a hint of malice. Allora and Nerpi laughed. I had walked into that one.

We turned around and went back to the alley Allora pointed out. En started toward the door, but Nerpi grabbed hand. "We shouldn't all go at once. Filter in so we don't look like we're together. Allora, you go in first. Then Kali and I. En, you, you stay here and guard the bikes."

"Right on. Detective Yant has to come in last, to save the day. Good thinking, Nerpi." En stroked his non-existent beard and nodded sagely.

I stood around, surveying the alley way, looking for hiding places and exit points. The emergency escape ladders on the side of the buildings were all up but I could make the leap up to the first floor without trouble. Trying to get my cycler out of the alley, jammed in as it was with all the others, would take precious time. If I had to run, I'd go up.

When it was our turn to go in, I followed Nerpi. All the eyes in the place had turned down to see the little, furry eowian. While I wasn't much taller, it did give me a second to survey the room without any eyes on me. A group of three grunde males sat at a booth to the left. None of them had earrings or rings on their head horns, which struck me as odd. Earrings on grunde were as ubiquitous as wraspisa were on uvoy. They did all wear sleeveless shirts and had matching tattoos on their biceps of a dagger dripping blood that stood out against their greyish skin.

At the bar, a tall grunde stood with a deep frown on his face. His horns and ears were more typically decorated with gold jewelry. He set a mug of something in front of Allora and called out to us, "Three strangers in as many minutes. Must be my lucky day."

"I guess so." Nerpi said as he climbed up onto a stool, "We saw the lady there stop and figured it must be a place to get some food."

"You don't want the food." The bartender said.

"I don't? Isn't this a pub?" Nerpi asked.

"Technically. You could order some food. But you wouldn't want to eat it. I just have a menu to keep my license."

"Ah. Well then, I'll have a mug of...." Nerpi said, standing up on the stool to see over the top of the bar, "The Butterman's Ale."

"Sure thing." He filled a mug with a brown liquid and set it in front of Nerpi. He then set a bottle of soda in front of me, "On the house sweety."

I frowned at his back and heard chuckles from beside me. I swiveled to see one of the guys from the booth had moved to sit beside me. "You can have a sip of mine if you want to. You're not too young in my book."

My scowl deepened and I weighed the advantages of decking him. It might start a bar fight, which would be bad. But it would feel good, which would be good. And if this cretin was one of the thieves we were looking for, maybe beating him up would get him to confess.

While I debated, he smiled and wiggled his eyebrows before leaning in closer to me. His smile dropped and his face scrunched. "Do I know you?"

I blinked, confused. I had never met this man before, had I? His face was puffy, as if swollen and the way he stood suggested he was favoring one leg. I glanced down at his arm. He bore the same tattoo as the others. A bloody dagger. My mind raced as I recalled the other night. I hadn't paid to close attention to which ally I had followed those thugs down. It could have been here as well as anywhere. But that dagger, now so close, shown like a beacon. I had a matching one back at the garage that Allora had taken out of my shoulder.

The door to the pub suddenly slammed open. Everyone turned to look and En stood in the doorway, his chin raised and his shoulders squared back. He strode in confidently and then said in a deep, commanding voice. "Step away from the lady, you piece of scum. Or I'll have to teach you a lesson."

Silence hung in the air for a second before it was broken by the characteristic sound of a shotgun shell being chambered. I swiveled to look at the bartender who now stood with a heavy barrel pointed toward En. Unrestrained hatred scowled his face.

"We don't serve your kind here, human."

En blinked, popped off a little wave of his hand and twirled around. He sauntered right back through the door, only pausing long enough to pull it closed behind him. Beside me, Nerpi chuckled. "They must be fans."

"Sorry about that." The bartender said, lowering the shotgun. "I'm sure you can appreciate my desire to keep humans out of my establishment."

I nodded gingerly but a hand landed on my shoulder and spun me back around to face the thug who had been trying to pick me up before. "I do know you. Boss, it's the girl from the alley."

The bartender had been about to set the shotgun back onto its rack below the bar, but he stopped. Slowly, he straightened back up and held the gun in two hands, threatening but not yet pointed at me. "Is it now? How fortuitous. I've wanted to meet you."

Chapter 4

All eyes in the pub fell on me. Fortunately, I didn't have to experience that kind of scrutiny for long. As soon as the thug's statement registered in my brain, I decided I needed to act. No amount of bullshitting was going to turn this situation around.

I launched myself up from my stool and at the bartender. With one hand I grabbed the shotgun barrel and slammed the other into his face. My wrist clipped his right tusk opening a slight gash in my skin. The pair of us tumbled down to the ground. I ended up on top, which gave me enough leverage to yank the shotgun away.

With the gun out of his hand I wanted to waste no more time in keeping him down and out of the fight. Unfortunately, he was quite a bit bigger than I was. He shoved me away and grabbed my injured wrist in the process. I choked off a cry of pain as he dug his hand into my wound. This pause in my assault allowed him sit up enough to get his other arm free and hurl me down the length of the bar. I slammed into a rack of bottles, shattering several of them. My back and shoulders were now covered with liquid, either alcohol or blood, I couldn't tell.

My first attempt to stand back up failed as my hands slipped on the pool of liquid forming below me. I couldn't regain my feet before the bartender had fully regained his. He wiped my blood off his face before retrieving a second shotgun from underneath the bar.

"That was a mistake, missy. Beating up my guys was going to get you a beat down. Seeing how scrawny you are, and yet took down so many of them, we wouldn't have left any permanent injuries out of respect. But now you're not walking out of this bar. I can't have someone disrespecting me in my own place."

While the bartender talked, I hastened to get my shield off my head. There was no time to unwrap it, which left the cloth dangling but I did manage to get it secured on my arm before he pulled the trigger. The blast from the shotgun echoed through the small room. Bottles shattered all around me as the buckshot deflected off my shield.

I managed to pull myself to my feet, keeping the shield raised between me and the bartender as two more blasts were fired. I didn't have enough space to build up any speed so when I slammed into him again, he barely wobbled. But I was now inside the effective range of the shotgun and he couldn't bring it to bear on me.

I swung my shield in an upward arc, knocking the edge of it into the bartender's chin. This caused him to reel back. I slammed my other fist into his stomach several times, while I smashed the shield back into his head. He continued to stumble back but tripped on the first discarded shotgun. As he went down, I grabbed his legs and shoved, causing him to fold over instead of just land on his back.

With the bartender momentarily neutralized, I took the time to survey the rest of the scene. Allora stood with a broken mug held to the throat of the thug who had recognized me. The others were in the process of standing up from their booth but hadn't gotten very far. Their hands held weapons but they hesitated, their eyes on Nerpi who now stood on top of the bar.

The little guy had a lit lighter held out his hand, extended over the bar. He bore a wicked grin that scared me a little, "I drop this, the whole place is going to go up in flames. There won't be time to do anything to stop it. Alcohol makes a wonderful accelerant."

I looked back down to the bartender who was trying to untangle himself to get back up. I kicked both shotguns away and behind me so that he wouldn't be able to pick them back up. A quick scan of the rest of the underside of the bar showed no other weapons.

"I'd listen to him gents. Little furball likes fire." I said menacingly. It was a lie though, Nerpi was crazy safety conscious and never let anyone have open flames anywhere near the garage. "Now, we didn't come here to pick another fight. We just need some information about something you stole last night. A piece of tech from the Turmlin garage."

"We didn't steal nothin'." One of the thugs said. "We're just ordinary people that you beat up in an alley and then trashed our place."

"Oh please. You were ganging up on a poor woman on the street. No doubt looking for a little celebration after your big score earlier." I said.

"Be lucky it wasn't me that found you doing that." Allora snarled "A little flick of my wrist, and your buddy here bleeds out in about fifteen seconds. That's more than he deserves. Return the item and we walk away. No fire, no bloodshed."

"We don't have it." The bartender said with a resigned sigh. He kept his eyes solidly on Nerpi's lighter as he spoke. "We were hired by Nil Rady to get the part. We already handed it off to him."

I recognized the name of Nil Rady. A major competitor for Turmlin's team, there was no love lost between them. This wasn't the first time either side had used go betweens to cause the other trouble.

"Okay, we've got what we came for. We're just people trying to make a living. Same as you. There's no reason this has to go any further. Let's all back away and we never have to see each other again." Allora said, her voice measured and calm, "So drop the guns, and I drop the knife, then we all go home."

The bartender looked between each of us and his guys before settling on me, "You two can go. This girl stays. We have some unfinished business."

I narrowed my eyes and lowered into a fighting stance, "Your guys got taught a lesson about harassing people, especially women who can't defend themselves. If they learned that lesson, then our business is done, and as the good doctor says, we can all go home. If you're telling me they haven't learned their lesson I'm more than ready to give them another one."

We all stood there in silence for a few seconds, staring each other down. Then, everything happened at once. I honestly am not sure what happened first. A gun went off. Nerpi dropped the lighter and the bar went up in flames. The bartender kicked out and threw me across the room. And En burst through the front door riding one of the thug's cyclers. It careened across the room before smashing into the booth the thugs had been sitting at. The ceiling above them collapsed, sending the lot of them to the floor.

After hitting the wall and slumping to the ground, I struggled to find my feet. Heat flared at me from my left and dust rained down on me from above.

The ceiling and walls creaked ominously. I lost sight of the bartender and his thugs in all the dust, smoke and flames. Fortunately, Nerpi kept his head. I felt a furry hand grab mine and pull me toward the door.

Once outside, a fresh gust of air, as fresh as you can get in the city anyways, helped clear my head. I felt relief at finding Allora and En there with us. Shouts came from inside. They were panicked orders of people trying to fight a fire, rather than desperate pleas for help. Punks got what they deserved so I didn't feel any guilt as we all hopped onto our cyclers and sped away as quickly as we could.

We didn't try to talk on the ride home. It's quite noisy and I think everyone else also appreciated the time to think and sort through what had just happened. Up until now, I'd mostly been able to keep my nighttime vigilante escapades secret from my friends. The other night hadn't been the first time Allora had patched me up, though it had been the most severe and unexplainable. It had never interfered with any of our work, legitimate or otherwise.

Once we were all safely back inside the garage, I braced myself for the incoming tirade. I wasn't sure how Nerpi would take it, but I started considering alternative places to sleep tonight when he fired me. Allora would definitely lecture. She already did that but now would have more ammunition.

Fortunately, En once again saved the day. As soon as the door closed, he became the center of attention. Allora laid into him the loudest, "What in the hell were you thinking? Riding a cycler into a building? For the love Akzad, you missed running me over by centimeters! You could have killed someone!"

"I was saving the day. Detective Yant never lets a perp get away with hurting innocents." En replied, tilting his head up and squaring his shoulders.

"Who is Detective Yant?"

"Uhh...I am...I was...to solve the case..." En stammered, slipping back into his usual persona.

"En, you went right through a door! You couldn't see where you were going. You probably tore up the wheel on the cycler and permanently messed up the steering. Though, smashing into the wall would have done more damage. But that's beside the point." Nerpi said, his voice started out high pitched and faded down to his more usual volume.

"Yeah, but did you see the looks on their faces? Totally unexpected. I took them by surprise. Check mated." En said, nodding his head self-confidently again.

While they yelled at En, I slinked away, trying to get to the stairs before anyone noticed me. I could use a shower and needed to bandage my hand. With the way I had slammed into two walls, I felt sure the stitches in my shoulder wound had probably ruptured too. Though I couldn't sort out that particular pain from the rest of my aching body.

"And as for you," Allora said and I froze in place, "See what your escapades have caused?"

"Um..." I stammered.

"I have no doubt they deserved what you did to them. But you can't just go around beating people up. I've been meaning to talk to you for awhile." Nerpi added.

"Uh...you know about that?"

"Dude, of course." En scoffed, "Who doesn't? Wait, what do we know?"

"Kali's the Knightshield." Allora sighed.

"The who?" Both En and I asked at the same time.

"That's what people are calling you anyway. Hopping through the night defending people with that shield you pretend is a wrapisa." Allora said.

"Speaking of that, I've been wanting to ask if I can see it. The rumors all said you had stopped bullets with that thing and I never believed them until I saw it with my own eyes. It must be incredibly uncomfortable to wear something so heavy on your head." Nerpi said.

I blinked in confusion at Nerpi, "It's not heavy at all. Lighter than some wrapisa I've seen before even."

"Really? What's it made out of?"

Resigned, I took the shield back off my head and handed it to Nerpi. He braced himself as if to receive something heavy and looked genuinely astonished when he was able to hold it in one hand. He turned it over a few times, tapping it and scrapping it with his fingernail.

"Kali, this is aluminum."

"Okay. So?"

"Aluminum can't stop a bullet. At least not this thin. Hell, this should crumple if you sat on it. Well, not you. Or me. But someone real heavy could."

I cocked my head, "It must be something else. You've seen it stop bullets. I would be dead a dozen times if it couldn't."

"But it shouldn't..." Nerpi said quietly.

"Whatever it's made out of is irrelevant. Kali needs her wounds tended too and then we all need showers." Allora said. "We can talk about what happens next in the morning. I doubt that's the last we'll see of those bloody daggers."

Chapter 5

I awoke the next morning, sore and aching everywhere. Despite having showered the night before, I crawled myself into the bathroom again before anyone else was awake. I'd been last the night before and the water had been practically ice cold. I wanted heat now.

I let the water wash over me for far longer than was strictly fair. We all had to share this one bathroom, though there was another toilet closet off Allora's clinic downstairs at least. When I finally made myself get out, the room had filled with steam, and I had to wipe the mirror off with my damp towel. I noticed the bandage on my shoulder had gotten messed up in the water so I removed it.

In the foggy mirror, I tried to look at my wounded shoulder, but I couldn't see the wound. I twisted as much as I could, thinking maybe I wasn't able to see it at that angle, but when I felt around with my hand, I found where it had been. A patch of skin had scarred over. It was definitely tender, but it hadn't been two days since the injury. There was no way it should have scarred over this fast.

I unwrapped the bandage around my hand and looked at the wound there. It didn't look as healed as the one on my shoulder, but given I had gotten it last night, it looked far better than it should. The skin had already grown back over the cut.

Seeing no need to replace my bandages, I dressed in my usual tanktop and overalls and went down to the main garage. I found Allora getting her clinic ready to open. I held my hand up to her. Her mouth twitched for a moment before settling into her customary flat expression.

"Why did you take your bandages off so soon?" She demanded.

"They came off in the shower." I said, already feeling defensive, "But look at them. They don't need a bandage anymore. That doesn't seem right."

"That's because it isn't. Just because they have started to heal doesn't mean you should remove the bandage yet. It needs time to heal without danger of reopening or getting infected."

I twisted my body around to show her my shoulder, "This is practically completely healed. I've gotten deep cuts before. This should take weeks."

"You're young." Allora said with a dismissive wave of her hand. "You heal quickly."

"Not this quickly."

She turned away from to rummage around in a cabinet. "It also wasn't as bad as you thought. The dagger was barely in there."

Before I could argue with her more, Nerpi called my name. I sighed and gave up on getting any more of an answer out of Allora. In the garage I found Nerpi had already opened the main door. I went over to the tool chest and did a quick inventory, one of my responsibilities. I wasn't much of a mechanic, I normally served as Nerpi's assistant, but I had learned a few of the basics. I knew what each of the tools were and what they were for and could do simple maintenance tasks.

As was becoming custom, I found all the tools except the 10mm socket wrench. Everyday, I put the tools way, including that one and almost every day, it vanished. I sighed, "We're missing the 10mm again, Nerpi."

"It will turn up." Nerpi said with a shrug. He shuffled over to a quadcycler parked in the garage and lifted the hood.

As we worked, I asked, "So what's the next move, boss? We didn't get the part back. Turmlin's not going to be happy."

"No, but we do know where it is. I need to go talk to them to see what they want the next move to be."

"Get it back, I would expect."

"Naturally. But I have a few ideas they might like." Nerpi gave a mischievous smile before turning back to the quad. "Huh, looks like I'm going to need that 10mm after all."

I opened the toolbox and gestured to it, "Well, you're going to be out of luck then."

Nerpi bent over the toolbox and then held up the 10mm wrench, "You might need to get Allora to check your eyes."

I frowned and decided I needed to get more sleep. We worked the morning as usual, finishing up that first quad and then proceeded to sit around most of the morning. Our customer flow had never been what anyone would describe as steady. A few people each morning would come for a check-up with Allora and a few would get us to change their oil or something else we could do in five minutes. We had one guy need a new alternator. But for the most part, sitting around.

At lunch time, Nerpi closed the garage door and put out the Be Back sign. He told me to go down the street and get us all some sandwiches while he had En drive him over to the Turmlin garage so he could talk with Garret. That gave me a little extra time to kill as it would take them far longer to go and come back than it would take me to get sandwiches.

I strolled down our street, Lesshon, enjoying the slight breeze and the sunshine. With all the tall buildings, the sidewalk was in shadow much of the time, except around midday. We were getting into summer so this nice fresh, cool breeze wouldn't happen much longer. But my mind wouldn't relax and just focus on that.

Nerpi's words from the other night kept coming back to me. He thought my shield was made of aluminum, which now that he had said it outloud, I couldn't disagree with. It was way to light for steel or any of the metals that you'd think about stopping a bullet.

What really bothered me though was that there were no marks on the shield. Last night, I hadn't had time to unwrap it, yet the cloth covering I wore to disguise it as a wraspisa, hadn't been damaged. No holes in the fabric. No blemishes on the metal. Even if it were bulletproof, there should be something.

I pondered this while waiting in line at Sanja's Shop. The MegaMart across the street had no line and was cheaper. But I, like every other local, knew where to get the best food in the area. Sanja, an old uvoy that could have been my great-grandfather he seemed so ancient, had apparently been running this shop since the street had been made of dirt.

When I got to the front and gave my order to Sanja, an impulse struck me. I took my shield off my head and unwrapped it. Across the counter, working on my order, Sanja raised an eyebrow at me. Among us uvoy, it was considered impolite to remove your wraspisa in front of non-family. That tradition was dying out in some places due to practical reasons, but the middle of a shop wasn't one of those places.

"It pleases me that you think of my shop as your home young, Kali." Sanja said, his tone turning his kind words into a rebuke.

I ignored that and held the unwrapped shield up to him, "Sanja, my father always used to tell me that this was an ancient Relic, from the days of magic. I never questioned him before, but now I'm curious. Do you recognize the emblem there in the center? Could he have been right?"

Sanja set down his knife and reached out for the shield. He studied it, turning it all around. After a moment, he handed it back. "That is the symbol of Clan Uta. They were a powerful family at one time. Some stories say they lead us during the Cataclysm to come here. Others that they were the cause of the Cataclysm back on our world. But all stories associate them with powerful magic. If this is one of theirs, it could indeed be a Relic."

I frowned and started rewrapping the shield. "Is there anyway to tell if its authentic?"

"You should speak to an acolyte. Acolyte Benthic is the head of the Office of Relic's. Or was. He might be able to answer more questions."

I managed to keep myself from sighing audibly at the mention of the acolytes, but Sanja did see my eyeroll, "I know what you youth think of the Church. But without the Church we would have fallen to anarchy long ago. It is because you young people turn away that we are seeing so much crime now. That and we've let grunde run amok in the city."

"Okay, that's enough grandpa." Anisu, Sanja's grandson who worked the shop counter, said. He gave me an apologetic smile and handed me my sandwiches, "Remember, you were the one to tell me not to talk about politics with the customers?"

I took the bag of sandwiches from Anisu gratefully and made a quick exit. Sanja was mostly a sweet old man. Mostly. He had some questionable opinions about a few things if you let him get started. Though, after my run with those Blood Dagger grunde, it was hard to disagree with the sentiment.

I checked the clocktower over the church and figured I still had awhile to kill before En and Nerpi returned. I thought about what Sanja had said.

Benthic was one of the less skeevy acolytes. He might know something that could tell me more.

I headed to the church. I'd never been there outside of a service day. Going in without having to bow down to one of the waiting acolytes was nice. The worship center felt expansive without all the people, its sloping rows of pews clicking in my head for the first time. It was shaped like a hexagonal bowl, just like the one the acolytes Manifested the fruit into. I'm sure there was some kind of symbolism about that but I didn't care to think about it too much.

I did take a few minutes to walk around the room and admire the stonework. I'd seen it all before, often staring at it quite intently to alleviate my boredom, but I'd never had the chance to get a closer look. There were stone carvings of scenes out of church lore. I know I'd heard all of these before but couldn't tell you who was who beyond a couple of the most popular. But the main draw were the six statues.

Giant figures stood at the vertices of the hexagon. Each one represented one of the church founders, the Unifiers. These were the legendary figures that founded the Church after we all came to Akka from wherever we had been before. Each Unifier was from one of the six species; Saliu the uvoy, Wishe the eowian, Talesh the evian, Munnir the grunde, Juan the human, and Judik the nudra. They each were surrounded by children and had a hand raised to the sky. If you followed their hands your eyes would fall on a carving at the apex of the curved ceiling. This was the image of Akzad, the supposed benevolent god who ruled over us. Akzad had traits of all six species; uvoy feet, eowian arm fur, evian ears, grunde tusks, human nose, nudra scales. And was, of course, depicted as a man with his shirt off.

"Admiring the magnificence of Akzad, child?"

I jumped at the sound. I'm normally fairly good at noticing people sneaking up on me. And in a giant stone room like this, there should be echoes everywhere. I turned around and tensed up even more when I saw Acolyte Hishu. His oily smile radiated creepiness. I nearly bolted from the room right there, but I decided I had come here for a reason. I wasn't going to let him thwart me so easily.

"I'm looking for Benthic." I said.

Hishu gave me a stern look, "Acolyte Benthic? He is busy with important religious matters. How can I help you, child?"

"You can tell me where to find Benthic." I repeated, deliberately not using the title this time.

"Very well, come with me." Hishu said and turned toward one of the many doors. I'd only ever used the main entrance and the one that led to the reception hall. I knew there had to be much more here. As big as the worship center and reception hall were, the building was even more massive than that. We entered a long corridor with many doors. It bent to follow the hexagon shape of the worship hall, with branches leading further away at different points. Many of the doors were open and I glanced in to see classrooms, or meeting rooms, storage closets. But mostly bedrooms. Which, I suppose, made sense. The acolytes had to live somewhere.

We stopped at one of these bedrooms and Hishu gestured for me to go inside. "You may wait here while I go and get Acolyte Benthic."

Looking at the small room, I realized it looked different from the others I'd seen. Most resembled a jail cell more than a real bedroom. They'd contained only a cot and a small dresser, with no decorations on the stone walls. By contrast, this one had a giant painting of Akzad hanging along with golden sconces burning scented candles. The beds sheets looked comfortable.

I knew I did not want to go into this room. "Um, nah, I'll wait out here. I, uh, wouldn't want to intrude in Benthic's room without his permission."

Hishu frowned at me, "That would be unacceptable to do such a thing. That is why I took you to my room."

Of course he did. "How considerate of you. But I couldn't impose. I'll wait here in the hall. Or back in the worship hall. Or outside."

"I could not permit that. No one but an acolyte is allowed to be unescorted in the Church except as a personal guest of an acolyte."

The way he said 'personal guest' sent another shiver up my spine. Hishu was technically bigger than me, almost all non-eowian or uvoy were, but I felt confident I could break him if I had too. As satisfying as that might feel, I knew there would be major consequences, and not the kind I could run away from easily.

"I'm just going to go. This was a mistake." I said.

Before I could start back down the corridor, Hishu moved to cut me off. He flashed a wide, predatory smile, leaning in close from above me. "Nonsense. It would be irresponsible of me to let a wayward daughter of Akzad leave without getting the...counseling she needs. Please. Step into my room. I insist."

I tilted my head down, grateful for my wraspisa covering my head that would prevent Hishu from seeing my expression. I'd probably be labeled a heretic on the basis of that alone. If he didn't move, my scowl would become the least of my issues. Fortunately, I was saved by having to make that call by the sound of a new voice behind us.

"Is there a problem here, Brother Hishu?" Benthic called out. I turned and saw the old human and another acolyte, the trainee I recognized from the last service, approaching down the corridor. I let out a sigh of relief, something I'd never expect to do at the sight of a priest.

"No, of course not, Brother. I was just escorting this young lady to see you." Hishu said smoothly.

"And so you have found me. Thank you, Brother. You may come with me and Brother Claren, child." Benthic said.

Eagerly, I fell in behind Benthic and the other acolyte as they continued down the corridor but before we got far Hishu called out, "Are you not forgetting something, child?"

I turned and saw Hishu extending his hand out as the priests did when we were made to kneel before them before services. My eyes narrowed and my limbs tensed. His hand rested far closer to his own crotch than was necessary and he smiled, knowingly. I glanced at Benthic and the other acolyte for help. Claren, looked annoyed. Benthic rolled his eyes but didn't say anything. Apparently, his timely arrival would only save me from so much.

Reluctantly, I removed my wraspisa. I squatted down, keeping my knees off the floor, and only lowering my head just enough to come down to Hishu's belly. "Bless me holy one, so that I may receive the touch of Akzad."

Hishu had to raise his hand to set it on the top of my head but he made sure to stroke my cheek as he did so. I shuddered but held myself still until he spoke. "Go forth, child of Akzad, with his love."

As soon as the words we out, I bolted upright and rejoined Benthic. Disapproving frowns stretched across both of their faces but were directed at Hishu rather than myself. Apparently, there were limits to what acolytes could get away with, at least when in the presence of other acolytes.

I followed them quietly. Claren cast several glances at me as we walked. He tried to give me a comforting smile, but I wouldn't meet his eye. When we reached an exterior door, he leaned in close to me and whispered. "Hishu is an ass."

I jerked my head up and looked at him. He nodded his head, "We all know it. But we're not supposed to say anything."

Louder, he said farewell to Benthic before continuing down the corridor. Benthic then led me outside into a small garden on the church's exterior. I had seen this garden several times passing through the city. He led me to a bench in the shade underneath one of the big trees.

"Now, tell me, child, what brings you see me?" Benthic said smiling.

With all that had happened with Hishu, I almost forgot why I had come. I glanced up to the tower above us and saw hardly much time had passed. I could leave but I still had time. And unanswered questions. I set my bag of sandwiches down on the bench but didn't sit myself.

"I was told you were an expert on Relics. Head of the Relic office or something."

Benthic beamed, "I was. Brother Hishu now leads that office. But I have made the study of Akzad's Gifts a lifelong pursuit. What do you wish to know?"

I blinked. What did I want to know? I couldn't just ask him if my father's shield was a Relic. I fumbled for words before starting with something simple, "How are Relics made?"

"A relic is a Manifestation of Akzad's blessing. A Gift from him."

"You mean like the fruit, at service?"

"In a way. Those truly touched by Akzad had the ability to create things. Most existed only temporarily to fill a need. The greatest of them could Manifest these gifts into permanent objects that retained the powers of Akzad upon their deaths, ensuring the blessing would persist past their lifetime."

"So, anyone can use a Relic to do magic?"

Benthic laughed, not unkindly, "Oh, heavens no. Gifts are not magic. But yes, any believer can wield the power of the Gift."

"What kind of things can Relic...uh Gifts do?"

"Anything Akzad wishes them too. The Candle of Joub will burn forever without melting. The Mask of Grettle allows you to breathe in the acidic air of the marshes without burning your lungs. You know the story of how Grettle saved the children of her village right?" Benthic said eagerly.

"Umm, yes, of course." I said not wanting to hear another proverb, "But they weren't all benevolent were they? There are weapons? Swords. Armor...shields?"

"Oh yes. There were many heathens that fought against the believers of Akzad when we first came to this world. Despite Akzad's blessing bringing everyone, many refused to believe. So, there were wars. And Akzad found the need to bless some believers with weapons of destruction." Benthic shoulders slumped as he talked now.

"What could these things do? How were they different than regular items made by crafters?"

"Like all Gifts, they were each unique. Though, given their intended purpose, they do share a much smaller subset of abilities than most Gifts. Swords never went dull, and some could cut through anything. Some could he summoned back to the hand of their wielder if they were ever disarmed. Likewise, Gifted armor would protect the wearer from any blow."

I perked up, "So they were invulnerable?"

"Heavens no. All Gifts are only as strong as the faith of the wielder. While any believer can use them, those that have doubts can see the Gift fade. Which is why we have lost so many of the Gifts over the years. Their power has faded when those of weak conviction wielded them for evil purposes."

I frowned at that. I didn't consider myself much of a true believer, but my shield had stopped plenty of bullets. But maybe it could actually do much more than that. "How can you tell if something is a Relic or not? If you don't know what its Gift is that is?"

"That is tricky. Many fakes crop up over the years. Sorting those out is the job of the Relic Office. When they fail to demonstrate a power, is it because we don't know what it is? Or because an unbeliever tainted the Gift? Or is it just an unsavory character telling lies?"

I nodded. I'm not sure if this helped me any but it did give me something to think about. I glanced up at the clock and picked up my bag. "Thank you, Acolyte."

I started to bend down by Benthic waved his hand, "That is not necessary, child. But before you go, tell me, is someone trying to sell you a Relic?"

"No, nothing like that." I said quickly.

"Then why the sudden curiosity?" Benthic asked.

"Stories my father used to tell me. I found myself missing him and thinking of them." I said, which wasn't entirely a lie and I found I didn't want to actually lie to this kind old man, even if I also didn't want to tell him the whole truth.

"Of course. May the blessings of Akzad be with you."

I nodded and started to walk away but Benthic called out one more time, "Be warned about Brother Hishu, child. He is a favorite to ascend to a high acolyte and has a reputation for always getting what he wants. With his position now with the Relic Office, if you do find yourself involved with a lost Gift, tread carefully."

Chapter 6

Nerpi and En took far longer than I anticipated to return from Turmlin. I ended up eating my sandwich without them and had to reopen the shop after our lunch hour on my own. Fortunately for me, nobody came in during that time asking for anything I couldn't handle. And by that, I mean we had one customer who needed to buy some wiper fluid.

When Nerpi did return he hopped out of En's sidecar and chattered away excitedly to himself. He carried a roll of paper with him and hastily cleared space off of the workbench. I stood beside En and he gave me a mischievous smile and bobbed his head eagerly. Something had excited the two of them.

Neither of them said anything, Nerpi busy starting some project and En standing there looking jazzed. I sighed and asked, "So, what happened with Turmlin?"

"We're going on a heist. I've always wanted to do a heist movie. This will be great research." En said.

"A heist? Of what?"

"We're going to steal the thingymajiggy back." En said. "Ninja style."

"Not unexpected, considering our job is to retrieve it. Though that does run a lot of risks. I assume we're taking on all those risks rather than Turmlin?"

"Um." En said. "Nerpi?"

"Yes, yes it will be dangerous. But Kali, I got them to give me the schematic! The schematic!" Nerpi chittered.

"Um, okay...How does that help us?"

Nerpi waved a hand, "I can build one for our racing cycler. They think I'm just building a mockup to switch out for the one Rady stole, so he won't know we stole it back. But with the schematics I can build a real one for us too! We'll have a real chance at winning the Munsa Classic!"

"Great." I said flatly. We hadn't entered Nerpi's custom cycler in many races but when we did, I always had to be the driver. Nerpi loved to build them but was terrified to drive himself. En said he couldn't risk damage to his marketable face and Allora had just laughed at the suggestion. That had left me. I hadn't hated it, and truth be told I didn't completely suck, but it wasn't something I looked forward to doing.

"So, the plan is to switch out a fake part for the real one without Rady being aware? How are we going to do that? They keep their own garage away from the arena. How are we going to get in unnoticed?"

"You're in charge of that. I have parts to machine." Nerpi said.

I glanced at the door to Allora's clinic and dismissed the idea of asking her for help. What shenanigans she agreed to participate in always left me baffled, but I knew a long boring stakeout wouldn't be one of them. With a resigned sigh, I looked to En.

"Come on, En. We have work to do."

"Right on. Stakeout!"

We gathered a few supplies and headed across town. I opted not to take our cyclers in order to keep a low profile. Cycler racers would naturally notice any cyclers they saw, and I couldn't risk us being noticed. Turmlin hired us because we were nobodies. We couldn't risk losing our anonymity this way. Having the Blood Dagger thugs notice me was bad enough.

The Rady Racing garage was in a seedier district than ours, and much seedier than the arena. Which struck me as odd. They weren't as successful as Turmlin on the race circuit, but they weren't bottom tier either. Though, I supposed rent was probably cheaper here than near the arena. And if their primary means of advancement was through thievery, having some separation was probably a benefit.

The garage itself was the bottom floor of a long, squat building. A large garage door took up much of the street facing side. No alley separated it from its left neighbor. The only way you could tell they were separate buildings was the different brick exteriors. On the building's other side stood a construction site. They looked to be midway through tearing down an older structure for a new one. Judging by the state of the exterior wall facing the construction site, the garage and the old building had shared a wall. Ducts and wires left gapping holes in the wall.

"I wonder if we could get in through the exposed wall by the construction site. If they shut down at night it should be quite easy." I mused.

"No worries, Kali. Detective Brill Yant will find out."

"No!" I yelped. "En, we can't have anyone thinking the Constabulary are sniffing around anything. It will put everyone on alert."

"Riiiight. Good catch." En said. "Well then, Mr. Joe Schmoe will have to inquire about work at this rugged establishment. He needs to feed his wife and four kids after losing his last job of twenty-five years to a crooked foreman."

"En, nobodies going to believe you're in your forties."

En held up a finger in a symbol to wait while he pulled out several things from the big bag he had hauled with us. My bag contained some binoculars, a canteen, and a few snacks. His looked like he could travel for a month. Indeed, it proved to contain a makeup kit and several different pieces of clothing. He quickly tried on a few shirts and settled on a red and black checkered shirt, which he left half untucked. Make up was not a thing I had ever messed with, it was a very human pastime, so I was unprepared when he turned to face me again. His face now looked more worn and tired and he had wisps of grey in his hair.

"Wow. That...that...how old are you anyways? I always assumed just a few years older than me but now I have no idea."

"That's the magic. Movie magic." En said and then strolled away, right for the construction site. His gate changed from the casual saunter of an arrogant slacker to a firm, but beaten gate of a desperate man. I watched him talk to a guy at the gate and then get shown into the temporary building that had been setup, presumably as an office. After a few minutes he came out with another person and they walked around the site.

"Well, he'll be a little while. Guess I should check things out myself." I said to myself.

The garage door was closed and it had no windows so I figured I couldn't learn anything that way. But the building next store probably shared a wall. Maybe I could find a way through. The building was dirty and run down. It had windows on every floor facing the street, which made it look like a residential building. Many of the windows were broken and covered over. If it was abandoned, that would make things much easier.

I walked across the street as casually as I could. No one came out of the Rady garage precisely at the moment I walked past their door. That would have been a very welcome coincidence but luck didn't shine on me. I made it to the door of the apartment building without interacting with anyone. This time luck was with me as the front door had no lock so I slipped right inside.

A single dim light bulb left the lobby in heavy shadows. A second bulb flickered on occasionally adding to the eeriness. A set of mailboxes covered one wall, half of them had been smashed open. There was an empty office behind the boxes. The rest of the ground floor led to a handful of closed numbered doors and a set of stairs.

"Don't go up the creepy stairs alone, Kali." I told myself right before I did the opposite. They wound up along the back of the building all the way up the three stories. I climbed to the top but was disappointed to discover no roof access. Reluctantly, I moved into the corridor on the top floor. Only a single hallway extended off from the stairs, six doors leading off it to apartments. Most were closed and locked, but again luck shined and I found one on the correct side with a busted door.

Inside, the apartment had bits of trash and debris scattered around. But despite the garbage, it looked lived in. Most of the trash was relatively fresh and the furniture wasn't covered in dust. I hoped whomever came here didn't make it a regular visit.

I explored around the exterior wall and found a brick layer as I expected. You could hammer through it to get into the Rady building but not quietly. I next looked up at the ceiling and spotted the vents. I pulled the rooms table over underneath the vent and climbed up. I pried the vent off and found it led to a spacious duct. I had to jump up in order to grab ahold but I didn't feel any give from the duct as my body pulled down with all my weight. I hauled myself up to peer inside and smiled. The duct extended through the exterior wall into the Rady building next door. We had our way inside.

"Hey, what are you doing on my table?"

The sudden voice startled me and my hands slipped. I dropped from the ceiling and smashed onto the table, shattering it. I lay there winded and unfocused for far too long. Had the voice belonged to someone hostile, they would have had an eternity to finish me. When I did manage to pull myself back to my feet, I found a young evian standing in the doorway. They wore a ruffled and dirty school uniform and despite them being to young have formed their first gender, they stood stubbornly with their hands on their hips, staring me down.

Relieved to find a child and not a giant thug I smile meekly, "Sorry about that. I didn't know this was your house. The door was open."

"I don't live here." They said fiercely, "This is my secret castle. You're not supposed to be in here."

"A secret castle huh? That must mean you're a legendary hero." I said recalling my youth playing as the heroes from the legends. We would all play as one of the Unifiers, those legendary figures who possessed powerful magic and the church deified. Regardless of their connection to church doctrine, their stories were epic, especially as a fantasy to play when young.

"I am Talesh, slayer of evil!" The child said with a smile proving some things never changed between generations.

"Well, Talesh, do you think me and some friends could hide in your castle later? We want to fix your table."

"Hmm." They said. "If you're coming to my castle for protection, that makes me your liege lord."

"Of course."

"And you have to tithe to your liege lord a share of your worldly goods. Otherwise, I won't be able to protect you from the bandits."

I grinned, catching onto the child's game. They weren't dumb. I couldn't fault them either. Living in a place like this meant this child had started out life with a shitty hand. If we could get what we needed and make their life a little better, that wouldn't be such a bad bargain.

I felt through my pockets until I found my wallet. It was depressingly light, but it probably held more than they had ever seen. I withdrew a couple of coins and handed them over. "A small sum now, and more when we return."

Their eyes went big at the pile of coins. "And you'll fix my table too?"

"Of course."

"Very well, then I grant you the protection of my realm." They said imperiously.

When I left the apartment building, I saw no sign of En so I returned to the garage. He sauntered in a few minutes after I got back. He bore a self-assured smile and slapped a piece of paper down onto the table before me. I picked it up but couldn't figure out what the series of lines were supposed to be.

"What am I looking at, En?" I asked.

"That is a highly detailed floorplan of the place we're going to rob."

The highly detailed floorplan consisted of a dozen or so boxes and a few scribbled words I couldn't decipher. Now that I knew what it was supposed to be, I started to make it out. Once I determined the word for 'garage' I was able to orient the rest of the floorplan. It had a lot of unidentified space but did show the basic layout for the building.

"How did you get this?" Nerpi asked, looking at the map over my shoulder.

"I did it myself. From memory." En said.

"From memory? How can you remember a place you've never been?" I asked.

"But, Kali, I have been there. After getting a job at the construction site..."

"You got a job at a construction site?" Nerpi interrupted.

"No, Joe Schmoe got the job." En said matter of factly. "Anyways, after getting the job, I went over to Rady's garage and told them I had something to discuss with them about the construction next door. They showed me inside and I copied down where everything was."

I stared dumbfounded for a second. "That's...that's actually a brilliant idea. I'm impressed you came up with it."

"Well, the foreman did ask me to go over there after hiring me."

"And there it is." I said. "No, matter you got a look on the inside. Any guards? What kind of locks?"

"Yeah. There were two mean looking guards right in the front door. One of them took me back to the offices and I spoke to the manager. The offices open into the main corridor and into the garage. Then there are some stairs here. I gather that the staff all lives there on the upper floors."

I thought about my plan to sneak in through the ducts from the neighboring building. If everyone lived there, going in at night wouldn't be a good idea. Crawling through the ducts wouldn't be quiet. I shared what I had and Nerpi nodded in agreement with me.

"What about just breaking into the garage door at night?" Nerpi asked.

"If there are guards in there, as En saw, they would have a full view of the front of the building from inside. That entrance juts out a little from the garage door. There were also light fixtures all across the front of the building. Much of the rest of the street, half the lights look broken. But not that building."

"Umm. In order for this to work, we can't be noticed breaking in. They can't know anything has happened."

"What about a distraction?" Allora said from behind us. I hadn't realized she had come in. "Something to get all of the people to go outside?"

We thought about that for a moment and then I recalled the construction site next door. There were several pieces of pipe stacked up near the fence. "En, you said you got a job at the construction site? What did you tell them?"

"Joe Schmoe has kids to feed and needs work. He spent years building for their competitor. Knows the ins and outs of everything. They hired me to run their crane."

"Do you know how to run a crane?"

"Can't be that hard." En said with a shrug.

I turned and looked at Nerpi. "I think there's going to be a distraction whether we wanted one or not."

Chapter 7

Nerpi and I returned to the abandoned apartment a short time before En was supposed to start his first shift as a fake construction worker. We didn't find the evian child waiting for us, something I had half expected. But then, I hadn't known when to tell them we'd return.

"Before we go up there, we need to repair this table." I told Nerpi.

He studied it and then pointed to a broken dresser against a wall, "We could stand on that instead. Its doors are falling off but looks sturdy enough to support our weight."

I shook my head, "No, I made a promise we'd fix the table if we used this place. I kind of broke it."

"So that's why you wanted me to bring the wood glue and clamps? I'm a mechanic, not a carpenter." Nerpi said.

"Neither am I. But I helped my dad do some stuff around the house. It won't be pretty but we can clamp the pieces back together while we do our crime and grab them on the way out. Also, we need to leave a gift of some kind."

"Fixing the table isn't enough?"

"No."

"All right, fine, let's get on with it. We need to be in position whenever En breaks whatever he ends up breaking."

We did our best to hold the broken pieces of the table in place and glued them together. Our clamps weren't big enough so we contented ourselves with flipping the table over and letting gravity hold everything in place. It would have to do. Nerpi was right about one thing. We weren't carpenters.

With that done, we moved the dresser over and I climbed on top. It wobbled a bit but held. I reached down and pulled Nerpi up and he climbed up onto my head, using my wraspisa to stand on. I felt glad we uvoy had such strong neck muscles, I couldn't imagine doing this with a human's scrawny little neck.

The two of us standing stacked together proved enough for Nerpi to easily climb into the duct. Once he was clear, I leaped up and pulled myself in after him. The space was cramped and I had to take my wraspisa off and push it ahead of me. We went slowly, me pushing my shield and Nerpi pushing his big toolbag, trying to make as little noise as possible. It was daytime, so presumably everyone was down on the ground floor doing their jobs, and even without En's coming distraction, the construction site made a lot of covering noises.

After we'd crossed between the buildings, Nerpi called a halt. "The room below us looks empty."

I nodded silently and scooched forward to the vent. The screws weren't designed to be remove from this side, which we should have thought about. Nerpi tried to squeeze his hand through the vent slats and use the screwdriver. He managed to get one screw undone before dropping the screwdriver. Fortunately, this was Nerpi and he always had a spare tool in his kit. He got two more screws out before dropping the second screwdriver.

It proved enough though as were able to bend the vent grate open enough to slip through without breaking it. How we were going to reattach it after slipping back out I had no idea. But just to be safe, we put the vent back in place as best we could before leaving the room.

Outside we found a narrow hallway, just like the one in the building next door. We crept through it quickly and into the stair well. The further we went now, the closer we would be to our destination, but the more likely we were to run into someone. With silent agreement we decided speed later would be best so went all the way down to the ground floor.

Carefully, I pulled over the stair door and glanced through the slit. Several doors lined a corridor. I could see daylight coming in from the end of the hall, through the front entrance door. There would be several people in that room. The garage was to the left of that.

Getting daring, we went into the hallway and peered into the first half open door. It showed an office. A ledger lay open on the desk and filing cabinets lined the wall behind. The sound of footsteps echoing sent a chill up my spine. It had been stupid to move beyond the stairs. Hastily, Nerpi and I went into the office and closed the door behind us. Hopefully, whoever was walking around wasn't coming back here.

I crouched behind the door so I would be out of sight if the door opened again. Nerpi, however, wasn't so circumspect. He climbed into the desk chair and studied the accounting books open there. He let out an impressed whistle.

"Looks like Rady just found themselves an angel investor. A sizeable sum of funds were recently deposited. Someone called ECG must really like cycler racing."

My heart skipped a beat at Nerpi's words. I thought back to my last few weeks at home. ECG had been the name of the company that had destroyed my town and my family. "Say that name again."

Nerpi gave me a concerned look, "ECG. Are you all right, Kali?'

I closed my eyes, suppressing my rage. My theory had been right. They were based out of the city. I had searched for them when I first came to the city but the address from city records led to an abandoned mailbox. I had started to despair that I would never find another lead on them. But here it was.

The whole building shuddered and a penetrating sound reverberated through everything. Dust shook from the ceiling and the lights flickered. An eerie silence followed and Nerpi and I exchanged a look. Another loud crash echoed and the building shook again.

"That's our distraction." I forced myself to forget the ledger and opened the door to peer into the hallway. Several people came out of other offices and raced to the front door, which people were pushing out through. "Now's our chance."

Nerpi and I ran down the corridor but slid to a halt part way. One of the offices on the side with the construction site had a crumbled pile of bricks where the wall had been. We stared at the hole for a long moment.

"Shit, when En makes a distraction he doesn't go half way. I thought he was going to knock over those pipes and make a bunch of noise." I said.

"Come on. They won't be outside forever." Nerpi said but his eyes didn't move away from the gaping hole either.

We turned left at the end of the hall. I peeked into the garage and was relieved to find nobody in there. Several cyclers were lined up in the center of the garage. This was where good fortune ran out. I had been expecting whichever bike Rady was going to install the new part too would be separated, undergoing the upgrade. I hadn't counted on their mechanics being done already.

"Which cycler is it in?" I asked.

Nerpi frowned and then closed his eyes. "Rady will put it in his personal one. His has a red streak down the side, so he stands out from the rest of his team."

I didn't pay much attention to races but knew Nerpi did. I looked over the four cyclers, they were painted in the same style, but he was right. One of them did have a bright red streak down the side that the others lacked.

"How long will it take you replace this?" I asked nervously.

"Ten minutes." Nerpi said.

"Seriously? I don't think we'll have that much time."

"It should take thirty if I wanted to do it properly."

I sighed heavily. At the garage, Nerpi had said he could do it fast. Apparently ten minutes was fast. I left him to his work and went across to the entryway next door. I would be more of a hinderance than a help to Nerpi while he worked and couldn't see if anyone came back from here. I moved over to the main entry room to watch the front door. Fortunately, it had a window I could peer out from.

An eternity passed while I waited. I could see the shapes of people out through the entryway windows. They were standing in the street, watching the construction site. One of them, was yelling animatedly at someone else. That was good. An altercation would keep people focused.

I glanced down the hall back toward the office we had hid in. I had time. I could go and grab those records. Maybe there would be more information about ECG in them. An address. Or a name. Anything to give me a clue of where to go next.

I could do this quick I decided and started down the hallway. Before I reached the door a distinctive bang echoed from outside. Gunshots. Apparently, someone was really not happy about what En had done. With a growl of frustration, I unwrapped my shield and pulled my mask up over my face.

The quickest way outside would be through the brand-new hole in the wall. I paused long enough to assess the situation outside. En stood at the base of the construction crane, cowering behind the big treads. The crowd that had been gawking at the disaster were screaming and running away. A very angry human stood holding a pistol toward En.

I readied myself and sprung out the opening and landed on top of the control cab for the crane, then leapt down. I put myself between En and the man, shield raised to cover both of us. A fresh set of gunshots echoed, followed by the plink as they deflected off my shield. I hoped no one in the crowd was hit. Normally when this happened it was just me and the people shooting at me, with narrow alleyway walls to absorb the ricochets.

"Put the gun down!" I bellowed with as much authority as I could muster. It wasn't much but I guess it proved enough because the human lowered the gun. He stared at me, a look of bewilderment on his face.

"Where did you come from?" He asked.

"I came when I heard your gun. That's a vile weapon. How dare you fire it off. At a person. Surrounded by innocent people." I growled, my voice unable to dampen the anger I felt.

Around us the crowd had stopped backing away and I could hear gasps. A faint whisper could be heard from them. "It's the Knightshield. He's real." That name Allora had pegged me with the other night. Apparently, my friends weren't the only ones who had heard rumors attached to my evening escapades. And everyone assumed I was a he. Double perfect.

Quietly, I whispered behind me. "Run you idiot."

En didn't wait for another opening and took off, running around the crane to get as far away from the shooter as he could. The human raised his weapon when he saw En run, but I moved to keep myself between them. When he couldn't get a shot, he lowered his weapon and his shoulders slumped.

"We're ruined. That idiot destroyed us."

Sensing this wasn't quite over, but the immediate danger had passed, I lowered my shield some. "The crane guy?"

"Yeah. I took a chance on him. He sounded like a real hard luck case. Was willing to accept a low wage. Thought we could stay on budget. But I never checked him out. And now we're ruined. He destroyed the work site. We're not going to be able to recover from this."

Shit. I looked around but didn't see too much damage. The building under construction here looked unaffected. Those pipes were scattered all over the place and there was the hole in the wall to Rady's building. But what did I know about construction?

"Did anyone get hurt?" I asked, praying for the answer to be no. Fortunately, he shook his head and I smiled, though he wouldn't be able to see that under my mask. "No one got hurt. Everything else is recoverable. What would have happened had I not shown up? A murder in broad daylight would have been a different story."

The human glanced down at the gun as if seeing it for the first time. "I don't know what came over me. I was so mad. I keep this to protect myself when making runs to the bank or for supplies. I never wanted to use it. Damn. What have I done?"

I sighed. Anger still flared inside me but what could I say? I'd been in almost exactly the same place. No one had intervened in my case though.

"You made a mistake. As I'm sure did the man you were shooting at. You said he sounded hard up. When we're desperate, we all do stupid things. It's hard to think straight. But nothing's happened yet that can't be undone. So, let's put the gun down and figure out how to move forward."

He nodded and put the safety back on before setting the pistol down on a barrel next to him. I moved to stand beside him and went one step further by stripping the weapon and emptying the chambers of bullets. You could never be too careful.

As I put the disabled weapon back down, a shout rose from the crowd. A group of constables were pushing through. Given what had happened the last time I had run into the constabulary, and that I wasn't exactly innocent in these events I decided I didn't want to stay to answer questions.

I got a running start and then leapt up over the security fence and into the crowd on the street. The constables shouted at me to stop but I wasn't about to do that. I leapt again, this time across the street and up onto the next buildings balconies, before leap frogging up them to get to the roof. From there, I could move quicker. My only obstacle would be other uvoy bouncing across the roof tops as messengers.

Before leaving, I glanced back down to the crowd. I scanned it hoping and then let out a held breath. Nerpi waved to me from the street, holding up a wrapped package. Our little adventure had been a success.

Chapter 8

The next day, Nerpi returned the recovered part to Turmlin and then proceeded to spend almost all of the money they paid him on material and some specialty machined parts. We all got a cut, of course, but I think we would have been better off spending that money on the shop. The front of the store needed a repaint and the chairs in the waiting area were falling apart.

Even though my injuries were healing at an unnaturally fast rate, I gave myself a few nights before I went out hunting for wrongdoers again. With the revelation that ECG was indeed operating in the city, I also had to contend with the shame of having given up looking for them. I had let myself get distracted by my life at the garage and hunting down criminals. While it was satisfying to mess with thugs, it wouldn't help me reach my goal. I had to bring down the people who had destroyed my town. I couldn't do that beating up hooligans.

Unfortunately, the only thing I was really good at was beating up thugs. I decided to play to my strengths and set out back toward the Rady garage. I climbed up a fire escape in the alley across the street so I could get a good view of the garage. The hole En had made in the wall was covered by a big canvas tarp. That would make getting back in a lot easier at least.

I waited outside for a good half an hour, hoping to catch one of the workers coming back after a late night out. I had no such luck there so I dropped down from my perch and crossed the street. I did it a fair ways down the street so the guards who watched from the front window wouldn't be able to see me. From there it was a simple matter to leap over the fence around the construction site and over to the tarped wall.

I stood quietly for another several minutes, listening to the other side of the canvas. The only sounds I heard were faint hints of distant conversation from the guards and the hum of the city itself. Carefully, I pried the lower corner of the tarp loose and let it flap in the wind. No one appeared to inspect it and I risked peaking my head inside. Luck returned to me and I saw no one in the wrecked office.

Gingerly, I crept inside, careful not to disturb the rubble that hadn't all been cleared away. The office door had been left open and I could hear the voices of the talking guards clearer now. They were fully engaged in some banal topic so I felt comfortable slipping into the hallway. They wouldn't be going anywhere for awhile.

I found the office Nerpi and I had hidden in before. The ledger book hadn't been left out on the desk this time but the storage cabinets had no locks. I flipped through several of them. I didn't understand finances very well but could do basic math. Rady's funds had been steadily declining for months until a sudden infusion of cash.

Why would a business group that, I had thought, bought up mineral rights, give money to a mid-level cycler racer? Unfortunately, the ledgers didn't include any handy background text. There were tons of other papers filled in the cabinets but going through all of that, hoping to find a clue, would take me the rest of the week.

The only way I was going to get any answers would be to ask some questions. I considered taking down the guards and asking them. I had only heard two voices and I felt reasonably certain I could take two with surprise on my side. But employees pulling guard duty probably wouldn't have the answers I needed. Someone comfortably asleep upstairs would though. Rady himself would be the best bet, but I couldn't risk opening every door looking for his room.

I opted to head for the room Nerpi and I had entered from the ducts. It was on the top floor, which meant there was one less neighbor to overhear things. Also, the vent was probably still loose and would allow for an alternative escape route if I needed one. Plus, I had already seen the layout so would be less likely to bump into random furniture in the dark.

I crept up the stairs carefully, not wanting to get caught by someone in there. While it wouldn't be the worst thing to find someone awake and on their own, any sound I made subduing them would echo on the bare concrete. No one came though and I made it to the top with just my heartbeat echoing.

The upstairs hallway also proved empty. I don't know why it continued to surprise me when I ran into nobody. It was late and most people would be in bed. I opted for speed anyways and ran down the hallway to the door I wanted as quickly as I could. When I reached the door, I tentatively tried to turn it and to my surprise, it turned. Why wasn't it locked?

Gently, I pushed the door open. The room beyond was hidden in darkness, the only light source the weak bulb behind me in the hallway. I quickly closed the door behind me as I didn't want to be an obvious silhouette, but that left me temporarily night blind. I took several slow deep breaths to calm my nerves and keep myself still. It's quite hard to sit patiently in the dark when you're breaking and entering.

With infuriating slowness, I began to make out shapes in the room and matched them to my memory. This room had been set up like a living and dining room. A small kitchen was on one wall and a door went off to my left to the bedroom. That room was snuck up against the next building and where we had entered from. I cautiously opened the door and peered inside. A lumpy shape lay on the bed. Someone was there but I couldn't tell anything else about them.

I stared at the sleeping figure, paralyzed. I had been in many brawls since leaving home. The big one that got me sent to prison. In prison. All of the thugs I beat up on the street. Despite that, this felt different. Those had all been fights I was forced into or at the very least in response to someone hurting someone else. This time, I was invading someone's home while they slept.

"Come on, Kali. This is a bad man. He's in league with an evil corporation. He sent a bunch of thugs to rob his competitor." I said to myself. "You know, kind of like said competitor sent us to do. A competitor that, let's be honest, probably takes money from groups just as evil."

I talked myself in a circle for a moment and then the figure on the bed rolled over. He sat up and groggily stared at me. I stared back and neither of us moved. I saw the sleep drain from his face as he realized he wasn't dreaming anymore. Not wasting more time, I dashed forward and grabbed him around the neck, yanking him to the floor, with me on his back.

"Don't call out." I hissed. He struggled for a moment, and I put pressure on his neck. Now that I had him, I could feel his tusks, telling me he was grunde. Always them, and always so much bigger than me. I felt my grip slipping already. I had held on to big guys before, and this one wasn't of particular note. But for some reason my arms felt weak and strained already. Fortunately, the pressure on his neck proved enough to persuade him and he gave up before my arms did.

I took a deep breath, feeling winded and tired. But I managed to get enough air to speak without sounding out of breath. "I'm going to ask you a few questions. When I'm done, I leave and you go back to bed and forget this ever happened. Understand?"

He nodded and I smiled. "We'll start simple. What's your name?"

"Jermain." He whispered.

"Good. Nice to meet you, Jermain. Okay, now, you recently got a large influx of cash from someone. Tell me about them."

"What? I don't have any money. Why do you think I live above the garage?"

I sighed, "No, not you personally. The company."

"Oh. This is about that money? I don't control it. I'm not the accountant. I'm a promoter." Jermain hissed.

"Answer the question." I said and put a bit of pressure on his neck to emphasize my point.

"Okay, okay. Someone gave us a bunch of money. I don't know the details. They made the deal directly with Rady."

"Why did they give you money?"

"An investment? I don't know what Rady promised them. But since then, our riders have been training harder and Rady has been adamant that we win the next race. Says if we do our money problems will be over. He's been spending like crazy too."

"Spending on what?"

"Parts. Ads. I've been told to get our name on the tip of fan's tongue. We have to make an impression."

I frowned. Rady wasn't an obscure racer, not the biggest name to be sure, but not obscure. If he already had a big investor, why spend a bunch of money to get more people interested in him? Especially if he was so obsessed with winning. Winning would do all of that for free.

"What else?" I asked.

"We also had to start going to church and thanking Akzad for everything."

"Akzad? Not your investor?" I asked.

"No. We're not to mention them."

"Why would someone give you money and not want their logo plastered all over everything?"

"Look, I don't know. Please don't hurt me."

The pleading in his voice made my arms go slack. Not for sudden sympathy but because they felt even weaker than before. He was giving me good information. I couldn't wuss out now. I had to know how to find them. As my determination hardened, my grip weakened.

I had nearly lost my grip on him when I heard a muffled sound. At first, I bolted upright, expecting someone to come bursting through the door. Nothing happened and I stood there, ready for a fight and my only opponent was already cowering on the floor. Then I heard it again. The sound came through the wall connecting us to the next building. I moved over closer and listened.

"Get out of my castle!"

"Come on kid. Give it up. Don't make us hurt you."

The kid! Someone was threatening them and it was probably my fault. Rady goons trying to figure out how I got in before. But no, they didn't know about that. As far as they knew, this was the first time I had been here.

In the end, it didn't matter who they were or why they were there. Someone was threatening them. I looked away from the wall to where Jermain still lay on the floor. He stared at me uncertain. There was still so much more I could learn from him. I would never get another chance. My shoulders slouched and I felt weak and defeated. But I had a duty to carryout. For my father. For my town.

A muffled scream reverberated through the walls. I growled, deep and angry. I looked at Jermain. "Give me a boost."

"Um...what?"

I pointed up to the vent in the ceiling. "Give me a boost so I can pry that off."

He continued to lay on the floor, staring at me dumbly. I barked an order, "Get up! There's a child in trouble."

Either my words or my tone got him moving. He stood underneath the vent and then tentatively cupped his hands together. I put my foot in his hands and reached up to the vent. I yanked it and the loose reattachment we had done gave way with ease. I tossed my wraspisa up inside and grabbed the edges of the duct to pull myself up.

Moving quickly, I made no attempt to muffle my sounds. I reached the vent that led into the other room and tried to assess the situation. I couldn't see much from my angle. But there were at least three grown evians. I heard Talesh scream again and saw one of the adults struggling with something.

I kicked the vent in and it crashed to the floor below. Grabbing the edges of the duct with one hand, I dropped down. With my other I tossed my shield at the nearest person. It smacked into the head of one of the adults, ricocheted off and into the head of another one, before doing the same and smacking the one holding Talesh. They all wobbled, stunned, one with a bleeding nose.

I pulled my legs down through the duct and swung myself in an arc toward the closest target, slamming my feet into her face. She toppled backwards and I dropped, landing on her stomach. She grunted and I heard the air come out of her.

As I got a closer look at the situation, I realized, adults wasn't quite the right descriptor for them. They were all old enough to have developed their first genders, but you would be hard pressed to call them adults. They probably weren't only a handful of years younger than me if I'm honest. But one of them was holding onto Talesh quite forcefully.

"Let them go and pick on someone your own size." I growled.

"What in Akzad's name? Where did you come from?" One of them stammered.

"Last chance." I said and fixed my gaze on the one still holding Talesh.

I tensed my muscles, ready to lunge at him when he released the child. Talesh dropped to the ground and kicked him in the shins. They then ran to get behind the newly repaired table, putting it between them and the thugs.

"Now, you can leave here under your own power or get carried out by medics. Your choice."

They shared a look between themselves and then started backing away toward the door. I hopped off of the one I had landed on so she could get up. They all watched me nervously as they left but were soon through the door and gone.

I let out a heavy sigh and let myself relax. The adrenaline had kicked in and I no longer felt physically weak like I had when holding down Jermain. But I did feel a heavy weight of exhaustion at everything that had just happened.

"Are you all right?" I asked, turning to look at Talesh.

They smiled broadly, "I am, good Knight! You saved me!"

I smiled back, "Of course, my lord. A knight must answer the call of her liege lord. Who were those thugs?"

"They think they're a gang. They saw the money you gave me and decided they wanted more."

I felt my smile fade as I realized the broader implications of what had just transpired. This had been my fault. It may not have been Rady thugs to come after them, but it was still my fault. And Rady would be coming now.

"I am afraid your castle has been breached, my lord. You must abandon it."

"But you protected it and drove them away." Talesh said excitedly.

I shook my head, "For now. But worse will be coming. See where I came from? The people in the building next door are going to be following me. They cannot find you here."

"They are no threat to me. They have holes in both sides of their castle." They said with a laugh.

I wanted nothing more than to enjoy the joke but I forced myself to remain serious. I knelt down to get to eye level with them. "I am serious. You cannot come back here. Not for awhile at least. Promise me."

The smile faded from their face, replaced by fear. They nodded timidly and then vigorously. I forced a smile back onto my face. "Good. Now go home."

The kid ran from the room. It was about time I did the same, before anyone did show up looking for me.

Chapter 9

I decided to avoid hitting the streets anywhere near the Rady garage for the next week. There wasn't anything else I was going to get from them, not after my stunt and alerting them to my interest. But I hadn't learned anything of use. ECG gave them money and had some rules for them. That didn't tell me how to find them or why they did it.

Fortunately, for my peace of mind, I didn't have time to dwell on it much. We had the Munsa Classic coming up and it became the only thing anyone else wanted to talk about. Nerpi had finished fabricating his copy of Turmlin's compressor design and installed it in my racing cycler. I had been hoping his manufacturing efforts would take too long and he wouldn't be done before the race. But that just ended up meaning I had no time to test it out.

We arrived at the arena early on Restday, which was when all big races were held. The arena was the biggest structure in the entire city. And that's saying something considering how big the temples are. A giant oval of bleachers stretched around an open dirt area. As big as it was, when you're riding a cycler at full speed, it wouldn't take that long to cross. I think it had originally been used for horse races or something slower. Now the race course weaved in a twisting pattern all throughout the center space, extending the course much further than just racing along the perimeter.

We could only race in the minor league, so our race happened first. On the plus side, I wouldn't have to try my skills out against the likes of Turmlin or Rady, which I was glad for. Not that I thought my skills were lacking but, well, honestly, my skills were lacking. I only did it because that's what Nerpi had originally hired me for. He wanted to build racing cyclers and to do that, you needed a racer, otherwise they were just fancy regular cyclers.

I lined my cycler among the other racers and Nerpi and I began a pre-race check. We weren't the only ones having to do this out on the raceway. Many of the minor league racers were small, amateur groups like us. But not all. Most of the big racers had a team entered in the minor league, sort of their next up and coming racer. If they did well, which they usually did because they trained with the professionals, they would join the main team.

I exchanged pleasantries with the other racers but mostly focused on my cycler. This wasn't my first race, but it was the biggest. Whomever won would be invited to race in the next major league season. I didn't think I had any hope of winning, but Nerpi was convinced the new compressor would give us an edge.

As we worked, I felt a presence and then a shadow fell over me. My back stiffened and I stood up quickly. My eyes narrowed and a scowl took over my face. I glared down at the eowian standing before me.

"What the hell do you want, Mallis?"

"Just wondering why you're here again. I thought I told you; women were not allowed to race."

Mallis, an eowian, was the commissioner for the minor league. I wasn't sure if his special harassment of me was because he hated women or he hated Nerpi. Probably both. But I had learned to ignore him a long time ago.

"Yeah, and the rest of the commissioners voted you down after we pointed out that the current record holder for the track is evian and is currently a woman." Nerpi said.

"And I conceded the point, since she is not currently racing. But you are not evian. You have one gender your entire life. Racing is no place for women."

"Lay off, Mallis." Hann, one of my fellow minor racers said from nearby. "There's no reason she shouldn't be allowed to race. She's better than you ever were. Besides, she's not going to beat me."

I gave Hann a sneering smile and he winked good naturedly. Mallis ruined the moment by putting his finger in my face. I almost ripped it off his hand in response.

"She better not. The major league won't let her race, regardless of what the rest of the minor commissioners decided." Mallis said and then flipped around and stalked off.

"What flew up his butt?" Hann asked. As a grunde he towered over me, but it was nice to not feel threatened by one.

I shrugged, "I have no idea."

"He has always hated me. And you're associated with me, so he hates you." Nerpi said, poking his head out from the other side of the cycler.

"Oh, hey Nerpi." Hann said, "What did you do to him?"

"Nothing. Everything." Nerpi said noncommittally.

"Great story. Look, could you take a look at something? One of my cylinders keeps skipping at medium RPMs." Hann said.

"Of course. Come by the shop. Tomorrow." Nerpi said and plastered a wide grin on his face. "Now, Kali, you'll want to get in near Hann here during corners, when he's trying to maintain speed. If you can keep him there, his engine will stall out."

"Not cool, Nerpi." Hann said but the smile on his face betrayed him.

A loud tone rang throughout the arena signaling festivities were about to get started. At the center stage, the pre-game newsreel movie started playing. I rarely had the time or money to afford to go to a movie and the tech had never made it out the Outskirts when I was a kid, so this was my only chance to see one. They were normally kind of boring topics, news around the city and some ads for products I also couldn't afford, but they were still fascinating. The current one was about an upcoming movie and as I watched I stopped paying attention to the plot and focused on the actor who must have been playing the lead.

"Doesn't that guy look like En?" I asked Nerpi.

Nerpi closed the engine compartment on the cycler before looking up. "Yeah, he kind of does. Weird." He then patted me on the shoulder and rushed from the raceway. He'd watch the race from the sidelines with En and Allora. The newsreels ended and I put them out of my mind. Now I had to get to work.

I took my wraspisa off my head and secured it to the front of the cycler. While it was curved, and made a good airfoil up there, on my head it would just catch the wind in uncomfortable ways and try to rip my head off. I had learned that the hard way. Instead, I donned a helmet and goggles like everyone else around me.

With several slow deep breathes I tried to focus on what was coming. While I didn't show up wanting to win, after my interaction with Mallis I now kind of did. Just to rub his face in it. That would feel good.

After I went through my pre-race calming routine, I looked around and saw everyone else still standing beside their cyclers. Normally, we were all strapping in about to go. What was taking the announcer so long today?

I turned toward the stage in the center of the arena. I had been ignoring the announcements, assuming they were your standard fair nonsense. Instead, a robed figure stood on the stage with their arms stretched wide. Around me, the other racers had their heads bowed and were looking at their feet uncomfortably.

"What nonsense is this?" I asked to no one in particular. "This isn't a service day. Why the hell is an acolyte lecturing us at a race?"

Beside me Hann shrugged, "I dunno. Giving some kind of blessing from Akzad. I won't turn down help. Even invisible kind."

I listened more closely to the words the acolyte was saying and I felt my spine stiffen. The oily voice of Hishu echoed over the arena's speakers. "Today Akzad looks down on you, racers, champions of the people, as you push your bodies to their limits. He blesses you and offers you strength. Those who are worthy will feel his power flow through you. Whoever of you is the most devout will feel his gentle hand guiding you across the finishing line. Give thanks and praise!"

"Well, now I have to win." I snarled. "Just to prove that Akzad didn't do it."

Hann and a few of the other racers laughed but more than a handful glared at me. I know some of them thought like Mallis about woman racers. Apparently, more than a few also thought Akzad was going to help them race today.

Ignoring them, I climbed aboard my cycler but didn't start it up. As disdainful as I was of the sermon, I knew how to follow the rules. The announcer would signal engine start all at once. That was part of the challenge. If you had an engine that took a while to warm up, you were at a disadvantage.

Eventually, Hishu finished rambling and the announcer returned. His voice excitedly echoed through the space and the watching fans cheered. In the booming chaos of the screams, I almost missed the call for racers to start their engines. But the groan of the ones next to me clued me in and I pulled the ignition cord. The cycler rumbled and coughed, threatening to not start for an agonizing second before coming to life. It settled down into a smooth hum, where normally it chugged and belched. If nothing else, the new part or the work Nerpi had done installing it, had one benefit.

The announcer's voice was now lost to us racers among all of the engine noise. I turned my gaze to the tower that stood by the start line. A tall evian stood waving a signal flag, this one telling us to start engines. I felt tension build around me as they switched to a new flag and held it high in the air. When the flag dropped, the sound became deafening as two dozen cyclers took off at once.

I leaned down as close to my cycler as I could, getting my face beneath the lip of my wraspisa to block at least some of the dirt cloud. My eyes were protected by goggles but that didn't mean I could see, and it didn't do anything to help me breathe. An actual windshield would have been nice but also no racer wanted a large section of glass right near their face should they crash. Which happened quite often.

I felt more than saw the first turn coming and leaned myself to my right to ride through the curve. As soon as I came back into a straightaway, I gave the engine full power and felt myself surge forward. The crowd of racers had spread out some by this point, as people accelerated differently and had different risk tolerances for going around the corner.

Now in the straightaway, I had the advantage. My relative small size, being female and uvoy, meant my cycler had to devote less power to pull my mass along with it. It was a miniscule difference, all cyclers out weighted even the heaviest riders by a lot, but every little bit helped. I also felt the improved engine performance from the new compressor. The engine heat gauge climbed into the red much slower so I was able to give it more acceleration.

I surged forward, passing several people. The further ahead I got, the clearer my vision became as less and less dirty filled the air. I wasn't in front now, but I had to be in the top three or four. Unfortunately, the hardest turn was next and I had to slow down.

I eased back on the accelerator, and leaned to my left, trying to cut around the curve as close to the inside as possible. The hard part came next. Right after the curve, a series of humps made up the next portion of the track. I came out of the curve slowing down but had to accelerate quickly or lose a lot of ground on the uphill portion. I also had to do this without slipping in the dirt and crashing.

The first mound loomed before me and I gunned the engine in preparation. I shot up the mound of dirt faster than I was prepared for and instead of cresting the top and popping into the air only slightly before rolling down the other side, I flew into the air as if launched. I gained enough height that when I started to come back down, I fell twice as far due to the mound slopping downward with me. My wheels didn't hit dirt again until near the bottom.

I almost fell over right there but my reflexes were faster than my brain. I wobbled as I started up the next mound but didn't fall. Without giving it anymore power, I had enough velocity to reach the top, but only just. This left me rolling over the top at a snail's pace, which after the unexpected launch I didn't mind much. But it let those I had passed earlier gain some ground. I could feel them nearing.

Fighting down my nerves, I sped up into the downhill and up the next mound. I wanted to keep my speed down to avoid launching myself again but recklessness set in. This time I accelerated as much as the cycler would handle. When I came off the top of the next mound, I flew through the air and cleared the bottom of the slope, landing on the upslope of the next mound.

This surge regained my lead and I accelerated down this final mound, preparing for the final sharp curve of the course. I leaned hard into it, trying to shed as little speed as possible. I could see the leaders ahead of me. They probably weren't all that far but the distance felt enormous. Once clear of the curve, I gave the cycler all the power it could handle. We had nothing but straightaway and a single, far gentler curve around the perimeter of the arena to go before the end.

Unfortunately, my anticipation of the final curve being gentler than the others caused me to come into it faster than I should. I lost control and started to slide. I skidded through the dirt across the track and almost crashed into the wall. I got close enough to see the startled expressions of the people in the stands.

I recovered without crashing but it was now too late. I'd lost more speed than I would have had I slowed down to do the curve properly. By the time I got myself righted and accelerating again, the leaders were too far ahead. What's more, the group I had left behind on the last section had almost caught up. I raced ahead for all my cycler was worth but only barely beat them across the line, bringing myself in as a distant third.

Chapter 10

When I pulled my cycler off the track, I fumed at myself and my mistake. I had been so close. Within my grasp and I missed. It didn't matter I hadn't cared about winning before the race.

"Nice job there, Kali. Guess Akzad had a hand in things after all." One of the racers laughed as he walked past me.

"Oh shut up. I beat you." I snapped.

He didn't get a chance to retort because everyone's attention shifted to Hann, who had taken the win, rolled his cycler in. We all clapped for him, as everyone liked Hann, even when he beat you. He took the praise with grace, both acting like he'd earned it and didn't deserve it.

When he walked by me, I offered my congratulations and he smiled, "I thought you might have had me for a moment there. I saw you go into that last curve. If you hadn't slipped, you had the acceleration to catch me. Good thing for me I get to move up to the majors and don't have to race you again."

"Not until next season anyways."

He smiled broadly, "Oh, you think you'll catch me by then?"

"Nah, an old man like you won't be able to hack it. You'll be booted back here after two races."

He placed a hand over his heart and pretended to fall over, "Ouch, Kali, straight to my heart."

Hann winked and went about receiving praise from the others while I attended to cleaning up my cycler. Dirt got all over it and I didn't want to have to scrub it off later. A cheer went up behind me and I turned to see En, Allora, and Nerpi standing there with big smiles on their faces.

"You all look happy." I said. "You bet on Hann?"

"Well yeah, of course." En said and Allora slapped him on the back of the head.

"That was an amazing race, Kali! Third! The compressor really made a difference, didn't it?" Nerpi chittered.

Reluctantly, I nodded, "Yeah, it did. I'll give you that. Almost a little too good."

Nerpi waved a hand, "You'll get used to it. Now that you've had a race under you, the next one will be better. I can fine tune some things and you'll have some time to practice."

While we talked, the others helped dust off the cycler. By the time we were finished, a human in a fancy looking suit approached us after extracting himself from talking to Hann. I frowned at him reflexively. Fancy suits had no place in a garage.

"You must be Ms. Kali Estuta, correct?" The man asked.

"Yeah, whose asking?" I said flatly.

"And that would make you, Mr. Nerpi, owner of this fine racer?" The man continued, ignoring my question.

Nerpi stood up straight, missing the implication of the man's words. "I am indeed."

"Excellent. My name is Grant. I represent a corporate group interested in financing a racing team. Your performance today puts you at the top of our list of candidates. Might we speak for a few minutes?"

I saw the images of money flash through Nerpi's eyes as he stepped away with the suit. I almost thought I had escaped when Nerpi gestured for me to follow. With a sigh, that I made no effort to suppress, I followed them over to a quieter place. Grant smiled way too much at us before he began speaking.

"We were very impressed with your performance today Ms. Estuta. Mr. Nerpi's bike is clearly an excellent machine and you handle it like a pro. It's a shame you weren't able to get the victory, but I hope to turn that into a win for both of us. My clients are looking to finance up and coming racers and help guide them into the big leagues. Winning today's race isn't the only way to make it. Just the only way without big supporters, like my clients."

My spine stiffened as he talked. I didn't like the implication of what he said about big supporters. I hated even more that he was kind of right. My performance today was proof of that. Without that compressor I never would have been able to do as well as I did, and we never would have gotten that without our work with Turmlin, even though I didn't think this was the same kind of "support".

"We've managed to do fairly well for ourselves so far." Nerpi said surprising me. He had talked about the need to get a big bank roll. It was half the reason we kept doing work for Turmlin.

"No doubt. A marvelous achievement. But you want to go further don't you? Make a name for yourselves. Race in the big races."

As Grant talked, I watched Nerpi wiggle slightly and his fur stiffen. He was losing the battle with himself to stay cool. I felt sorry for him but that's why I liked working for him. Hard as he tried, he would never be a ruthless businessman.

But he surprised me again by asking the question I had been about to blurt out, "I'm sure there would be some conditions for this help. Nothing comes for free."

"Naturally. My clients are investors after all. We would expect a portion of all proceeds. Additionally, we would expect endorsements of select products and events from Ms. Estuta once her name carries enough weight."

"So, you want me to slap a logo on our cycler and smile in some ads?" I asked.

"Nothing so course. My clients prefer to remain anonymous so there will be no logos. Just targeted marketing."

Something clicked in my head. Anonymous investors. Just like the ones funding Rady. Could I be so lucky that the very people I was looking for had come to me? I doubted it but knowing more about the shady world of anonymous donors might give me a better lead.

Gritting my teeth, I smiled back, "He makes a compelling argument, Nerpi. Maybe we should consider it."

Nerpi practically beamed at me, "Yes, yes, we accept. Um...that is...we will consider accepting."

I interjected quickly, "How can we get in contact with you again to get more details? Do you have an office we could visit?"

"Oh, don't worry. You take a few days to think about it. I'll be in touch." Grant tipped his hat and strode away.

"Well, that was cryptic." Nerpi said.

"And frustrating. Now I'm going to have to follow him." I sighed.

Nerpi grabbed my arm, "You're what?"

"Going to follow him."

"Okay...wait! Why are you going to follow him?" Nerpi asked.

I shrugged, trying to look nonchalant. "I found it fishy that he wouldn't tell us who he worked for. Who knows where his money comes from."

"Since when would you care about that?"

"Since always. I don't want dirty money." I said flatly.

Nerpi held his arms to the side and stared at my disbelieving. "We're criminals, Kali. Thugs. Miscreants. We take money and say, now what. We burn down other gang's bars. You beat people up in the middle of the night. It doesn't sound like you have any more of a moral compass than the rest of us."

My eyes narrowed and I leaned in close to him, "Don't pretend like either of us is a cold-hearted thug. We're no angels but we don't hurt innocent people. That bar belonged to rapists and muggers. The people I beat up are just as bad. The people I'm looking for killed my parents and all but enslaved my entire hometown. I don't know if that suit works for them but I'm going to find out."

I swiveled on my heel, grabbed my shield off the front of my cycler, and headed after Grant into the crowd. Turns out, I didn't need to hurry. He went up to the stands and took a seat. Of course, he would watch the rest of the races. With no seat, but not wanting to lose him if he decided to leave early, I spent the rest of the morning leaning against a rail with a bad view of the arena floor.

My boredom got the best of me, and I didn't notice when Grant finally got up from his seat and walked away. I had a moment of panic as I looked through the crowd of people and couldn't find him. Fortunately, the final race was in full swing and there weren't a lot of people moving around. I ignored the stands and swept my gaze over the walkways. I spotted him headed down a set of stairs.

Hurrying after him, I wondered why he would be leaving in the middle of the final race. This was the big one for the day, the top of the league. If he wasn't interested in seeing them race, why had he stayed so long?

We made our way down the stairs and into a section reserved only for racing personnel. The guard at the door let Grant pass without a comment which I found odd, but I probably shouldn't have. He had been in a restricted area when I had met him.

When I tried to follow him down, the guard stopped me. "Sorry, kid, only racers allowed."

I gestured down to my dust covered overalls, "How do you think I got covered with this shit?"

"Playing in the dirt with your friends?" the guard chuckled.

I sighed and dug into my pockets for my ID. It took me longer than it should have. I only wore these when racing, so there wasn't a lot in my pockets. It just happened to have quite a few and I had to check all of them before I found it.

"See? I'm a racer. Now I let me through." I said but didn't wait for the guard to acknowledge me before pushing past him. I rushed down the stairs as quickly as I could only to find myself having to stop at the bottom. Grant stood in the main garage, where he had met me before, and where all the current racers would pass when exiting the arena. Of course. He was looking for clients in my league. He probably had some or was also looking for some in the major league.

Once again, I hunkered down to wait. This time, it didn't feel like a waste of time though. The first thing Grant did when the racers came into the garage was speak to Rady. That confirmed it for me. He worked for ECG.

In the confusion of the incoming racers, I slipped into the garage and worked my way toward Grant and Rady. I pulled down the top part of my coveralls and let it hang down, exposing my sweaty shirt underneath. While I knew who Rady was, he'd never met me and Grant had last seen me without my wraspisa on and with my arms covered. Hopefully this would prove enough of a disguise to avoid being noticed.

The downside to the crowd was the noise. Many of the racer's cyclers were still idling. They were all shouting at each other, jokes and insults mostly. This forced me to get uncomfortably close in order to hear anything.

"...my engine stalled out. That's why I came in last." Rady voice had a sharp edge to it.

"Are you sure your mechanic installed the part correctly?" Grant asked.

"Of course, I'm sure. Are you sure you didn't get played by Turmlin?"

Grant shook his head, "He's not that clever. You said you had a break in. Some thug roughed up your PR guy? Maybe there was more to that."

"No one came near our garage. We had guards." Rady hissed.

"Can you be certain? Someone got in. Whose to say they didn't go and sabotage your bike before going to threaten your man."

"Fine. I can't say for certain. But you want to know why they were threatening my PR guy? They were asking about you."

I had been looking away, trying to avoid notice but I glanced over at that comment. I wanted to see Grant's face. There was a genuine spike of fear in his eyes. He smiled unconvincingly and tilted his head, taking a long, silent moment before replying.

"No one is supposed to know about my client's relationship with you. What did you man say?"

Rady shrugged, "Nothing. The thug jumped into the air ducts and slipped away real fast. It was weird."

"Are you certain they said nothing?" Grant said leaning in close to Rady.

Rady leaned back, away from Grant. I couldn't see his face but I felt he probably looked uncomfortable. "Yeah. Of course. He didn't say a word."

Grant face went neutral and he looked down at Rady. "We may have to rethink the nature of our relationship. My clients can't work with people who don't know how to keep their affairs in order and their mouths shut."

"He didn't say anything. And you can't back away now. We need those funds. Especially after this humiliating loss."

"You're no good to us at the back of the pack. No one listens to what losers have to say. Your influence is what we buy. If you have none, we have no use of you."

"It was one loss. We're not in danger of relegation. I can remove that part you gave me and get back on track. Remember, this is as much your fault as mine."

Grant's eyes narrowed, "You're playing a dangerous game, Rady. Think carefully before our next meeting."

With that, Grant turned and headed out of the garage. I had expected him to speak with other racers. Hoped really. That would have told me how far his influence spread. But he stalked right out of the garage. It took me a split second to remember that was what I had originally wanted.

I rushed toward the exit but a voice brought me up short. "Kali! Come here!"

I considered ignoring the shout. It was a busy room, conceivable I might not have heard. But I made the mistake of glancing over my shoulder and saw Garret, the Turmlin manager, waving me over. Now if I ran off it would be a deliberate snub. I glanced back toward the exit but turned away. I had already lost sight of Grant and could see the stream of spectators flooding the street. I hadn't a hope of finding him again.

With a sigh, I went across the garage way. Garret nodded appreciatively at me. "You ran a good race today."

I blinked at the unexpected compliment. I never imagined anyone from the major teams would have watched the amateurs. "Um, thanks. You guys too." I said though, honestly, I had no idea how Turmlin had done. Better than Rady I would assume.

"Tell Nerpi his advice worked out perfectly. I'll be sending two of our cyclers down to his garage for a full tune-up. Can't let ours end up choking like Rady did today." Garret said with a mischievous grin directed toward Rady who was not far away.

Rady swiveled and strode over, pushed me aside and got into Garret's face, "Did you have anything to do with this, Garret? You did, didn't you."

Garret grinned, "I don't know what you mean, Rady. I'm not the one sticking second hand parts into my cyclers. Maybe you should be more careful."

Rady's eyes narrowed, "You don't know what you started here, Garret. Tell your boss, he's made a powerful enemy."

"Turmlin's never been scared of you, Nil."

"I'm not talking about me either. You better watch yourselves. You and your little gang of thieves." Rady waved a finger at Garret and then turned it to me before stalking off. I'd be lying if I didn't feel a chill run up my spine when I saw the fear in his eyes.

Chapter 11

The next day, Garret sent over the cyclers as he promised. That kept Nerpi and I busy all morning. While we worked, I tried to broach the topic of Grant and Rady by explaining what I had overheard in their conversation.

"Yes, I agree, they definitely had a relationship. And yes, it does look very suspect. We know those thugs who stole the compressor from Turmlin in the first place were hired by someone, and maybe it was Grant. But that's no reason not to do business with him." Nerpi said in response.

"What? Why would we want too? He hired thugs to steal from Turmlin in order to give Rady a boost. Do we really want to work for someone like that?" I asked.

Nerpi leaned back from the cycler we were working on. He wiped some grease from the fur on his face and looked at me seriously. "We already do. But right now, we're the people who get hired to do the dirty work. Wouldn't you rather be the people who get things stolen for them, rather than the people who do the stealing?"

I shook my head. "We're still going to be the ones getting our hands dirty."

"No, they want to fund our racing. They want to use us to sell stuff. To do that, we need to win races, and we need to appear clean and upstanding citizens. They won't ask us to do shit like we had to do in that bar or at Rady's garage."

"That doesn't mean our hands will be clean." I huffed and threw the wrench I had been using down into the toolbox for emphasis. "Those guys in the bar, they were a real gang. I mean, not like us. They were into real bad stuff."

"And we burned down their bar." Nerpi said. "That makes us the good guys in this story how?"

I fumed, disagreeing with him but not sure how to explain it. "I've told you what ECG did to my hometown?"

"Yes. It's deplorable but not a unique story. Lots of companies treat people like disposable resources. Especially in the outskirts." Nerpi said and I started to raise an objection, but he held up a hand to cut me off, "We don't even know if these are the same people. We only have one mention in Rady's books that mention ECG. That could mean anything. Grant never gave us his full name. ECG could be his initials and it's just a coincidence."

"Quite the coincidence." I crossed my arms.

"What's more likely, a company that runs mines in the outskirts also happens to be funding racing in the city or that a couple letters are similar?" Nerpi asked.

I had to admit he had a point. But I didn't say it out loud. Fortunately, En arrived with sandwiches from Sanja's for lunch. My stomach gurgled audibly, and I hurried to wash my hands off. I hated it when grease got on my food.

As I dug into my sandwich, Nerpi held his hand out to En. "The change this time. The extra isn't a tip."

"Yeah, yeah." En dug around in his pocket and handed the change over and then asked. "Did you all hear about the fire?"

Nerpi and I shook our heads looking at En expectantly. He shrugged, "Well, there was a fire."

"Yeah, burned down almost a whole city block." En said. "Much like the one we caused on Jumaker street last week."

I blinked at him, unable to speak with my mouth full of sandwich. I swallowed quickly. "That bar fire burned down a whole block?"

Allora came out of her clinic and gave En an exasperated look, "No, it wasn't caused by us. Much of the block did burn though. But it happened a few days later. We didn't cause it. But they did burn down deliberately. All the older, poorer buildings burned down. But coincidently the rich buildings were saved by the fire brigades."

"How does that make it deliberate?" En asked through a full bite of sandwich, bits of sauce running down his chin.

"Fire brigades are funded by local taxes. Poor neighborhoods can't afford them. Hence the poor building burned." Allora said flatly.

"What started the fires? Was that deliberate?" I asked. I hadn't heard about the Jumaker fire as I had been avoiding the area. Despite Allora's claims it and the bar fire were days apart, I felt they had to be related.

Allora shrugged, "Unlikely. People don't burn down their homes and businesses on purpose."

"They do sometimes. For insurance money. Meteor Studios had several movies go over budget so my Da...their financial backer burned the sets down for the insurance money." En said.

"Poor people can't afford insurance." Allora told En.

"I wish I could afford insurance." Nerpi set his sandwich down and looked around the garage slowly.

"Where was this latest one?" I asked, mostly to fill the silence.

"Somewhere on Bleecher I think." Allora said.

I pursed my lips and thought. "Isn't Rady's garage on Bleecher?"

"Well, it was." En chuckled.

My mind flashed back to the conversation I had overheard between Rady and Garret. Rady had been trying to threaten Turmlin's manager but had looked more scared himself. Now there was a big fire on his street. That didn't feel like a coincidence.

I stuffed the last bit of sandwich into my mouth and headed for the open garage doorway. Nerpi called after me, "Where are you going? We still have two more cyclers to finish!"

"Need to check something. Be back." I mumbled through my sandwich but didn't turn back to look. I hopped onto my racing cycler and shot out of the garage. I normally walked everywhere, often using the uvoy highway on the tops of buildings where there were less crowds. But it was daylight and I wasn't trying to avoid being seen.

Turning off our street onto one of the major thoroughfares through the city, I was surprised by the number of vehicles. Cyclers had been around for quite a few years and seeing people use them for transport was fairly common. The recent introduction of four wheeled version that could be used to transport cargo had begun to replace the once ubiquitous carriages.

The combination of the two proved disastrous for anyone's ability to get anywhere.

Fortunately, this street was wide enough for a lane for cyclers to operate in between the bigger vehicles. As I raced down the street, I almost felt like I was on the raceway, doing an obstacle course rather than a straight race. It kept my mind focused on that task at hand rather than what I feared I might find.

When I turned off the main road, traffic thinned out and I slowed down. Now I had to contend with people walking in the street more than other vehicles. As I slowed, I immediately noticed the smell of char and soot. I parked my cycler near the construction site next to Rady's garage, as it appeared untouched. In fact, workers still were busy putting up the new building. En's interference looked to have caused no lasting trouble for them, despite the foreman's fear.

I walked along the street and came to a small crowd. They blocked my way and my view beyond but I could already tell something was wrong. I should have been able to see building tops over the crowd's heads. And I did, but they were from buildings much further away. Pushing through to the front, I gaped at the sight.

The line of multistory buildings were gone. The one containing Rady's garage still partially stood, but had been gutted. Of the building next door, only a partial shell. My heart thudded in my chest as I thought of the little evian child who had called themselves Talesh. Their home was gone. A darker thought crept into the pit of my stomach then.

I turned to one of the people in the crowd. "Was anybody killed? Did the people make it out of those buildings?"

The grunde male shrugged silently but another beside him answered. "The building was supposed to be condemned. Of course, people were living in it. It varied day to day sometimes so we're not sure."

Desperately I asked, "There was an evian family. With a child about ten. Did they make it out?"

The big grunde sighed and gave me a compassionate smile, which was difficult to do through their tusks. "I think I know the family you mean. Very bright child. I haven't seen them unfortunately. That's not definitive but I'm not hopeful."

I stumbled away from the grunde without another word. I had to get out of the crowd. Desperately, I pushed through, but they proved too thick. Finally, in a wave of panic, I leapt upward. I arced just enough to grab ahold of the fire escape on one of the nearby, surviving buildings and collapsed on the first-floor railing.

I don't know how long I sat there, that familiar feeling of panic closing around me. I'd felt it far too often in my life. When my mother died. When my father died. My first day in prison. I didn't think I would feel it again, especially for a child I had barely known. But this, like the others, had been my fault. I had involved Talesh. I had broken into Rady's garage.

A familiar voice interrupted my self-chastisement. Nil Rady looked up from the street below. "Come to admire your handywork?"

"My...? I didn't do this." I snarled, despite feeling the exact opposite.

"You may as well have. You and your group of punks. You stole my part. Beating up poor Jermain. And now he's dead."

I blinked and looked down at Rady. Jermain had been the PR guy I had interrogated the night I broke in on my own. "He's dead?"

"Yes. I expect because he talked to you. Ms. Knightshield."

"Um...I'm not...who is that?" I stammered.

Rady waved a hand. "Don't play coy. Your little stunt, saving the incompetent construction worker made quite the scene. I had my suspicions but seeing you jump out of the crowd confirmed it. At least for me. You uvoy are good jumpers but that's above and beyond the norm girl."

I didn't have a response to that. I hadn't tried to adopt this Knightshield persona but everyone loved a story. Arguing with Rady didn't seem like a worthwhile use of our time. I needed more information from him. So, I ignored his accusation instead.

"What happened here? Who killed Jermain?"

"The same people who stole the compressor from Turmlin I expect. Despite what you might think, that wasn't us. We just got the part."

"Advanced piece of cycler tech just shows up on your doorstep out of the blue? Sounds legit." I said.

"Of course, it was stolen. But we didn't steal it or know where it had come from. That should have been the end of it. Then you had to come and steal it from us. And seriously piss off some gang in the process. They had a lot of questions about you."

I stared at him. "They killed Jermain and burned down the neighborhood to find out about me? Or because you lost yesterday?"

"No, I suspect the burning down the neighborhood was always going to happen. It was highly suggested I leave our cyclers at the arena last night. Which I did. I guess that's how they're paying for our new garage." Rady said, gesturing to the construction site. "But the questioning and the murder. That was because someone crossed them."

"What did you tell them?" I asked.

"I didn't tell them anything. I was far away from here last night. But some of my people who were here say they asked Jermain a lot of questions."

"What did he tell them?"

Rady shrugged, "Who knows? The others were told to flee and they did. They aren't fighters. Or costumed vigilantes. But what could he tell them? We had no idea who had broken into the garage. It wasn't until yesterday, at the arena when Garret acted all smug, that I put two and two together that he was involved. And that meant your little group of thugs. I doubt Jermain had any idea."

My heart pounded and I considered this. Presumably, the people who had burned down Rady's garage, and killed Talesh and Jermain, were the people whose bar we had burned down. That part had been an accident but I doubted they cared. It showed what they were capable of though.

"What are you going to tell them now?" I asked.

Rady gave a dark laugh. "What kind of person do you think I am? You robbed me but that doesn't mean I want you dead. Jermain's death is my fault as much as it is yours. I shouldn't have gotten involved with these people. I knew what kind of people they were. But the money...I needed the money."

Gently, I swung over the fire escape railing and dropped down to the street beside Rady. I got a good look at his face for the first time. His eyes were puffy and red. The stress and worry were evident. Humans were so expressive.

"Who are they?"

"Who? The thugs? I don't know."

"No, the people who hired them. The people who gave you money. ECG." I pressed, leaning in closer to him. He was a bit taller than me but I knew my wide, dark uvoy eyes made humans uncomfortable.

Rady had been trying to look away but jerked toward me at the mention of the letters. "How do you know that name?"

"Where can I find them?" I asked.

"You don't find them. They find you." Rady hissed. "I don't want anything more to do with this. I won't rat you out. I couldn't live with any more deaths on my conscious. But that won't protect you much. Consider moving."

With that he pushed away from me and walked down the street, back toward the crowd. I could have grabbed him and hauled him into the alley way nearby. Maybe even before anyone else saw. But I found myself believing him, that he didn't want anyone else to get hurt.

I gave one last look at the burned wreckage and ran back for my cycler. I had my friends to protect.

Chapter 12

When I returned to the garage, Nerpi was still working on the Turmlin cyclers. I quickly braked mine and ran over to him. I explained what had happened to Rady's garage. By the time I finished, En and Allora had joined us.

"We need to get out of here." I finished desperately.

"We should go to the constables." En said.

Allora scoffed, "And tell them what? A gang of thugs is out to get us because we burned down their bar and Kali's the masked vigilante they're so eager to arrest?"

"Wait, what? They want to arrest me?" I asked, shocked.

"Of course. You beat people up in the dark. Why wouldn't they?" Allora said, her expression stern.

"I beat up bad guys. I stop them from hurting others to committing crimes. I'm one of the good guys."

"Good guys don't beat people up, Kali." Allora said sternly but not without compassion.

"We can discuss that later." Nerpi interjected. "The important bit is no cops. They wouldn't help us even if they weren't after Kali. It's all hearsay. And we're not important enough. We also can't afford to run and let our home get burned down or trashed. We'll have to defend ourselves."

I shook my head desperately, "You don't understand the kind of people these guys are. They killed a guy to get information out of him. They burned a whole block down, killing innocent children."

"Exactly. These are the kind of people the Knightshield is supposed to stand up too." Nerpi said defiantly.

"I'm not the Knightshield! I'm not some kind of crusader folk hero." I cried, "I'm just an angry girl whose trying to get revenge."

"Revenge works too." Nerpi said flatly.

"Yeah, revenge is a good motivation. Like Gensu in the Gladiator of Bens. That was my best part." En said.

"Revenge is why these guys are coming after us." I said.

"They may not even know who we are. They probably don't." Allora said. "Rady only figured it out because of a coincidence. They wouldn't have been able to learn anything last night so we should be fine."

"That's your plan?" I asked incredulous, "Just assume they can't possibly know who we are and go on with our lives?"

"Of course not." Nerpi said. "We are going to take precautions."

As it turned out, precautions turned out to mean rigging some alarms. I was skeptical at first, but Nerpi demonstrated with a little bit of wire he could rig all the doors and windows to trigger a loud speaker if any were opened. The noise was quite deafening so I didn't doubt it would wake us up.

But I wasn't content to trust our lives to a bunch of wires. I sat up at night, in full gear, watching the street. When morning came, and nothing had happened I collapsed into bed. After that, the others volunteered to take shifts with me. I doubted how well they watched, especially En, but I did need to sleep sometime. Which was fortunate, because nothing happened until four nights later. Had I tried to stay awake that whole time I wouldn't have been able to do anything.

Allora shouted us all awake and I rolled out of bed, having slept in my suit. I grabbed my shield and met the others at the big front window. Down the street, a fireball flashed, emerging from one of the buildings. We stood there dumbstruck. We had been expecting an attack. Was this it or a regular fire?

Another fire flared to life down the street. The flash of life illuminated the pair of grunde thugs on a cycler. They hooted and cheered, thrashing their heads around wildly. The light faded but the image of their ecstasy at their mayhem had been burned firmly into my head.

"What the hell is going on?" Nerpi whispered.

"Retribution." Allora said.

We all looked at her and she looked downcast. "They must not know which building we're in. So, they're going to burn the whole neighborhood down."

I turned my head back to watch the gang. In the flickering light of the fire, I couldn't see them as clearly has I had in the initial flash. Even then I had only been able to make out their species, but not any facial details. But I suppose, evian's do have better vision.

"How can we be sure?" Nerpi asked.

"Does it matter?" I spat. "They're assholes and need to be stopped."

I lifted my shield and without another word, took off at a run down the street. People all around were poking their heads out of their apartment windows above their shops. All stared transfixed by the gang of thugs throwing firebombs. I wasn't going to be like them, staring helplessly. I had to do something. They had come for me and again, innocent people were getting hurt.

The thug on the back of the lead cycler howled and pointed a fist at me. He slapped the back of the driver, who gunned the engine and accelerated directly at me. The cycler rushed down the road, closing the time I would have to spend running to get to them. I smiled.

A few seconds before they would have run me over, I tossed my shield ahead of me as hard as I could. At the same moment, I leaped sideways and landed on one of the light poles that ran down the center of the street. My shield rocketed toward the cycler and pegged the driver's arm. I couldn't hear anything over the roar of the cycler engine, the fires and the shouts of the rest of the gang. But in my head, I heard the crunch of bone as his arm crumbled. The shattered arm caused him to lose control over the cycler and it jerked sideways, crashing into the front window display of the Mega Mart.

I paid no more attention to those two thugs, instead looking for my next target. My vantage point on the lightpole gave me a better view of the thugs and I saw that there were two groups of them for the first time. One group that we had been watching and another new group approaching from the opposite end of the street. This new group hadn't yet started any fires so it explained why we had missed them until now.

I shouted a warning to Nerpi and the others before leaping down to where my shield had landed. I kicked it up with my foot and back onto my arm. I turned to face the oncoming cyclers but stopped when I saw the unexpected.

I had missed a group of them in the dark and they were almost on top of me. But Allora stood behind them. She raised her stethescope up toward them as it were a weapon. There was a brief flash of light and then the two thugs collapsed. I heard faint snores emanate from one of them.

Unfortunately, I didn't have time to ruminate on what had just happened. More thugs were approaching. They had seen Allora take out their companions, I knew what they had planned. With a burst of speed I didn't think I was capable of, I rushed forward and leaped in front of Allora. I held my shield before me and immediately heard the metallic twang as bullets bounced off the shield.

With the shield covering us, I glanced back at Allora and just stared questionably at her. The look she sent back made it clear now was not the time to ask, a sentiment my curiosity didn't like but I had to agree with. My shield could only protect us from one direction and it wouldn't take them long to decide to flank us.

I risked peering over the top of my shield to see they had already come to that conclusion. My only option was to rush forward now, before they got too far, and hope I could get close enough. That's when I received my second surprise for the night.

Nerpi and En had stayed in the garage when the second group had been spotted. I had thought it had been for safety but I was mistaken. They both came back out carrying weapons. Nerpi had his favorite wrench and En held the dagger that had once been partially embedded in my shoulder. Where he had found it, I had no idea. I had assumed Allora had disposed of it.

The pair yelled and charged at the nearest thugs and started swinging. Nerpi managed to kneecap one of them but En tried to swing the dagger like it was a sword. He even gave it an impressive looking twirl but the only thing he accomplished was giving the goon time to step aside. It wasn't long before En was on the ground and the goon was holding the dagger.

"Where did you get this, boy?" The goon asked, holding the dagger up into the light.

Nerpi and En's had succeeded in putting themselves into danger but they had caused a momentary distraction. The other members of the gang had stopped shooting for a moment. That was all the time I needed. I pivoted around and threw my shield up toward the street lamp. The twinkle of shattering glass and then darkness followed.

Moments of chaos followed as everyone lost sight of everyone else. There were other lights on the street, it wasn't pitch black, and there was light from the nearby fires so it would not take long for eyes to adjust. But for the moment we were blind. Fortunately, while evian's had much better eyesight than uvoy, we both had much better night vision than grunde.

I came upon the first shadowy shape in the dark and didn't slow my approach. I kicked out ahead of me and tripped the goon. The shape fell and I leaped up, landing straight down on his stomach. The goon groaned but didn't try to get back up.

From the first, the rest weren't far. I moved faster than I had ever moved before. If I didn't, they would reach the others before I brought them down. Allora had whatever she had done to those first two goons but I didn't know if that was repeatable. Plus, this was only half the problem. The rest of our neighborhood continued to burn while we fought here.

I played dirty, going for knees and ankles, whatever I could to get them down and out of the fight as fast as possible. That wouldn't incapacitate them long term but if they couldn't move well they wouldn't be able to do much damage. A few times I was able to kick guns away when they fell but I knew I didn't get them all.

It turned out to be enough though. Before I knew it, my eyes adjusted enough for me to see none of the thugs were still standing. Allora and Nerpi stood over two groaning goons. En looked shaken but unhurt. I bent down to retrieve my shield and also picked up the danger En had tried to use.

"En, get their guns before they get back up." Nerpi ordered and proceeded to do the same.

"All right." En said his carefree tone clearly forced, "Now we'll have firepower."

I yanked the weapon out of his hands and ejected the magazine and stripped the barrel. "No guns. Disable them and then let's move on. There's still more."

To emphasize my point another fireball bloomed down the street. Cheers and roars of laughter followed the spectacle. The gang launched another fireball to more cheers. I had assumed they were using some kind of firebomb but they clearly had something more elaborate. All the more reason to move quickly.

With the guns disabled, we started down the street toward the rest of the gang and the raging fires. The first place we reached was Sanja's sandwich shop. The window had been smashed and a fire burned, though the place had not yet been completely engulfed.

"There's people in there!" Allora shouted. "Help me get them out!"

The three of them went inside but I stayed behind. I checked the street nearby, but the gang had already moved on and would be no immediate threat. The gang appeared to have stalled their advancement down the street and were standing in a cluster. As I watched, a figure emerged in the center of the group. He held a candle of all things in his hand. The flickering flame shone on their face and the sight made me stumble.

My mind flashed back to the night my mother had died. Venti, the man who had pulled the trigger stood before me, illuminated in the night.

Chapter 13

I felt reason drain away at the sight of Venti. While in my more logical frame of mind, I had devoted myself to finding the people in charge, the leaders of ECG. They were the ones who had sent him to massacre my family. They were the ones who had wrecked my town for their profit. But that didn't mean I didn't have a score to settle with Venti himself.

There were six goons with Venti. As I watched, Venti gestured with his hand and the group parted. He then held the candle before his face as if to blow it out. Instead, as he blew, flame billowed out from the small candle into a rushing fireball. The fire flared against the windows of the nearest building, shattering it and igniting the curtains just inside. The group of goons chortled in feverish excitement.

Venti had a Relic. That was the only explanation for how he had just done that. Despite my antipathy toward the Church, it turned my stomach to think of a man like that defiling holy items. Now I had even more of a reason to bring him down. But it also meant, aside from avoiding getting shot, stabbed or beaten up, I had to avoid getting burned.

As I approached the group, I passed directly under a streetlight and someone in the group spotted me. I'd love to say my ferocity scared them but in truth, I think they were just dumbfounded by the sight of me. At this point I probably had blood and grime all over me, yet I was still a girl much smaller than them holding a shield.

Their surprise allowed me to get close but not land the first hit. The closest goon recovered himself and he reached out to grab me. I had to twist to avoid it and slammed my shield into his stomach before swinging it up to smash it under his chin. He started to tumble backwards but I felt a blow to my back from his companion who had been standing next to him.

I threw myself backwards to get inside his reach and hopefully make him stumble. I failed at that second part but I did end up pressing his arms against his body so he couldn't punch me again. With a grunt he shoved me but I was ready for that. I launched myself away, using his shove as added momentum and went flying.

I sailed over the top of a nearby cycler, grabbing the machine as I did. Between my momentum, and the fact that they aren't particularly stable when parked, I pulled the cycler down with me and it crashed on top of another goon standing beside it. She let out a cry of pain as it crushed her legs. I took the time to slam my shield down into her gut and kick her gun out of her reach before leaving her alone.

That only left me facing off against five more total opponents. All of whom, by this point, had identified me as a legitimate threat. Several of them drew their guns and started firing. The sounds of the gunshots only inflamed my anger as the memory of that final family dinner floated fresh in my mind. I somersaulted behind another cycler and put my shield up to cover my side. Several bullets bounced off before Venti's voice broke through the carnage.

"Stop shooting you idiots! That's my cycler!"

I smiled at the thought of his precious cycler getting shredded by his own bullets but that faded quickly. It wasn't a very good protective barrier. Cyclers weren't bullet proof. And they had plenty of gaps in the wheel spokes and struts that wouldn't even deflect or slow bullets.

"I recognize you. Kali was it?"

"Fuck off, Venti." I shouted back.

"Quite the mouth on you. I see prison didn't do much for your manners. Or your temper. But you've got spirit, I'll give you that. And I'm feeling generous. This has been a fun night. Walk away now. Before you are unable to walk. Like your cousin."

My anger flared. I saw a gun I had kicked laying on the ground near me. I picked it up without thinking but as soon as I had the grip resting in my hand, the memory of what had happened the last time I held one of these hit me like a gut punch. I felt nauseous and my body shivered with chills.

But all that didn't banish the anger and hate. I just had to get rid of the gun. I ejected the magazine, emptied the chamber and then lobbed the empty gun in a high arc. It sailed through the air before coming down on one of Venti's goons. I heard a cry of pain, a thud of a body dropping at least to a knee and then the clatter as the gun bounced across the street.

"Should I take that as a sign of your surrender?" Venti asked.

"You should take it as a sign I'm going to kick your ass." I said, but weakly, as I still was trying to clear the taste of bile from my mouth.

"Have it your way. The rest of you, take the candle and continue with the job. We still don't know which one of these buildings her companions live. Burn them all down to be sure no one comes out of it."

A new sense pushed away my lingering revulsion at holding a gun again. Why were these goons doing this? Were all these homes and shops burning because they were after me? Just as vengeance for what we had done to their bar? That seemed like an amazing bit of overkill.

My mind raced and I missed the first sound of an engine starting up. The remaining goons, including the one that had been pinned under her own cycler, were getting ready to depart. That left just me and Venti alone in the street. Better odds I thought with a vengeful smile.

Then my mind clicked back to where the goons were going. They had the Relic now. To use to burn the rest of the buildings on the street. My friends were helping get people out of Sanja's shop. There was no one else to stop them.

I glanced over the top of the cycler and saw the keys were still in. I could steal it and follow, leaving Venti impotent and alone. He was several meters away. I should be able to get on and start moving before he could reach me. He'd probably try and shoot me but I could angle my shield toward him. I could do it.

But that would mean leaving him to get away. Again. I had gone to prison for what I had done after my mother's death. He hadn't. He had gotten away with it. Even testified against me in my trial.

Hatred flared. I had to end him. Now while I could. Then I would go after the others. I'd have time. It was a big street. But I wouldn't have time to take him out after that. He'd be gone, slipping away like the scum he was. I had to make him pay.

A snarl on my face, I stood up. We stared at each other across the dark street, just lit enough for us to see each other's face in shadow. He smiled at me which made me even more mad, which, honestly, I wouldn't have thought possible.

I let out a mad scream and leaped over the cycler. I charged at full speed toward him. He had only seconds to react, but he was ready. I saw his arm go up, a gun in his hand. I ducked my head and held my shield up, covering my body. I heard the gunshot echo but not the distinct ring of the bullet bouncing off my shield. Then my legs gave out and I collapsed.

I found it hard to breathe and I felt a wetness on my chest with my shield hand. I lifted my arm and saw fresh blood on my fingers. My blood. And behind my arm, a hole dead center in my shield. The bullet had gone right through. Exactly as Nerpi said it should.

The light disappeared as Venti stepped over me, obscuring the streetlight. I wanted to get up and attack, but my body wouldn't respond. His smiling face was the last thing I saw before the pain and difficulty breathing overcame me and the world faded out.

Chapter 14

When I finally came back to my senses, I didn't find myself lying on the street in a pool of my own blood. Instead, I woke up in a reasonably comfortable bed. I still found it hard to breathe but not as bad as those last moments before I lost consciousness. The rest of me was sore and stiff but responded when I tried to move it. When I tried my arms, I discovered the most disconcerting thing, my hands were bound by a metal ring.

This sparked a bit of panic, and I started thrashing around, trying to get free. I hadn't opened my eyes yet, as they still felt heavy and didn't want to open unless I forced them. Now I forced them open and saw what I feared, handcuffs connecting my arms to my bed. Not only was I injured, but I was also trapped. This didn't improve my ability to breathe.

"Easy there, Kali." A familiar voice said.

I froze, not realizing I wasn't alone. Cautiously, I took in my surroundings. It was a very boring looking room, beige bare walls, tiny windows. The only thing that stood out was a chair to my left with an evian woman sitting in it. I let out a sigh of relief as I recognized Allora.

"What the hell happened?" I snapped, not meaning to be so harsh but overcome with confusion and fear.

"You were shot." Allora said flatly. "Bullet punctured your left lung. I couldn't treat that in my clinic so we took you to a hospital. You'll live."

"I could figure that part out on my own." I said, "I mean how am I not dead in the first place? Venti was standing right over me."

Allora shrugged, "I don't know anything about that. We found you alone in the street, bleeding. The Constabulary had just shown up and the gang flew or were being arrested."

I frowned, trying to piece together why he let me live. He had shot me in the chest, which would eventually kill anybody. Maybe he thought I was dead or unsavable. I doubt he knew there was a doctor nearby.

But that wasn't my only point of concern. I held up my restrained arm as best I could, "Why am I chained up?"

Allora grimaced, "The Constabulary arrested you."

"For what? Bleeding on the pavement?"

A small smile crossed Allora's lips but it didn't last long, "For vandalism. Arson. Destruction of property. Assault. You name it."

"What?! I wasn't the one burning down the neighborhood." I spat.

Allora held up her hands defensively. "I know. I know. They arrested everyone they found. The actual criminals and the ones trying to stop them."

"Why?"

Again, Allora shrugged, "To look like they are doing something, I guess. They've always been quite useless. But this was the fourth neighborhood to burn in the past year. I suppose, we're fortunate ours was just down the street from a church."

Confused, I asked. "Fortunate?"

"Yes, actually. While the constabulary ignores us, except when harassing us, they do patrol near the church. They saw the fires and summoned help."

A cold chill overcame me. I must have looked like I was dying because Allora grew concerned and leaned over my bed, "Kali? Are you all right? What's wrong?"

I didn't say anything for a long minute and Allora repeated her questions. If the Constabulary hadn't come, I would be dead and the rest of our neighborhood would have burned down. I could have stopped them, but I hadn't. I hadn't even tried.

After an eternity of self-recrimination, I had to ask the question I didn't want to hear the answer too. "Did anyone die?"

The look on Allora's face told me the answer. "Several people. At least four buildings are ash and we don't know how many people were inside. But that's just the unknowns. Sanja, from the sandwich shop, died from smoke inhalation. The rest of his family made it out okay though."

"Talesh." I whispered and Allora raised an eyebrow. I didn't know the child's real name. They had only given me the mythical figure of Talesh, the evian founder god. First an innocent child and now Sanja. I saw him almost every day. He was kind, if a bit old-fashioned and a little racist. We were the same species even. The death of anyone is a tragedy but this felt worse than that. Like both their deaths were my fault.

I lay there, seething in silent rage for several minutes and Allora let me. She probably assumed my anger was toward the gang, which was fine. While I was more focused on myself, I had plenty of rage to spare. Eventually I needed to distract myself from it, if only to suppress the pain for a time.

I turned back to Allora, "If the constabulary arrested everyone, including girls bleeding in the street, how are you here? Did you and the others avoid it?"

She cast her eyes down before she said, "No, Nerpi and En got locked up with everyone else. They're being released now though. Same with most of the others. I...I was able to avoid it due to some special considerations."

"Like because you're a doctor?" I asked.

"Something like that."

I decided not to press this clear avoidance for the moment because what I really wanted to know I asked next, "And me? When are they going to uncuff me?"

If anything, Allora looked even uncomfortable, "They probably won't. Nerpi had the foresight to drop your shield at the shop, which survived the fires by the way, before we took you to the hospital. But we couldn't do anything about your outfit. They're convinced you're the Knightshield vigilante. Plus, it seems you have a criminal record, so the inspector is convinced you're involved."

I felt my cheeks flush at that but only for a moment. Allora didn't ask but the implication was there. She wanted to know about the criminal record. I had avoided talking about this with my friends.

"The record is true. Though I'm surprised they know about it. It's from the outskirts. And I was a juvenile." I said defensively, though, I wasn't much older than a juvenile now.

Apparently, I wasn't forthcoming enough because now Allora looked directly at me and asked the question I feared she would. "Did you kill someone, Kali?"

I involuntarily shuddered and pulled the blanket as close to me as possible, which wasn't much since I had such little free arm movement. I could only nod in response, not wanting to voice the truth out loud. But nor did I want to hide from my guilt. So, I took the cowards way out.

"I did. But it was technically only involuntary homicide. I didn't kill the person I intended too. He's the one who shot me tonight. He killed my mother. Shot up our house in a drive by, just as we sat down to eat."

Allora gasped and put her hand on mine. I cringed at the sympathy, it actually hurt me more than the recrimination would have if I had told her the full truth. But I still didn't.

"Kali, I'm so sorry. I knew your parents were dead, but I had no idea they had been murdered."

The irony of her misunderstanding, while also being completely correct, almost made me burst out laughing while crying. I didn't but I think mainly because it already hurt to breath and laughing would have been pure agony. Though, I might have deserved that.

Eventually, I pressed forward, "How do I get out of here? I didn't burn those buildings down. There are ample witnesses for this."

"The truth doesn't matter for the constabulary. They have their eyes fixed on you. They're calling you getting shot as just bad blood in the gang."

I nodded, not wanting to argue with Allora. My father had been our sheriff. I knew not all of them were as bad as Allora claimed. But she did have some points. I had to wonder if I would be chained up like this if I weren't uvoy. "Then you need to get me out of these cuffs. I'll be okay on my own."

Allora vigorously shook her head, "No, you won't. You were just shot. I think you'll fully heal. You are in good shape. But not overnight. You can't leave yet."

"Okay, fine. Then when I'm healed but before they haul me away."

"They're going to haul you away before you're healed. They don't care. But I have an alternative option. One you are not going to like."

I spent the next few hours agonizing over my decision to let Allora proceed with her plan. Before she left, I hadn't agreed to it, just to listen more, but I didn't see much of an alternative. I didn't want to go back to prison. On the bright side, I didn't agonize over it much as I did a fair bit of sleeping, which also saved me from the pain.

When Allora returned, she had a large bag holding my shield, and an old man. Acolyte Benthic smiled sympathetically at me when he came in. I nodded in response, not pretending to be pleased but I tried to keep my unease at his presence off my face.

"How are you doing, child?" He asked.

"I've been better."

"But you will live, and Sister Allora says you should make a full recovery, true?"

"That's what she tells me too. Though, recovering just to get thrown in jail doesn't sound like much of positive."

An amused smile crossed Benthic's face which surprised me for some reason. "Yes, Sister Allora has shared your plight. I am not sure what I can do to help, unfortunately. We acolytes have no control over the constabulary or local government."

"Bullshit." I snapped, annoyed that I had waited for him to come here to play some game, "Acolytes are always interfering to help rich donors or what not. We can't have a government leader whose not endorsed by the church. Don't tell me you don't have influence."

Rather than looking angry at my indictment of the church, instead looked saddened. "All behaviors I regret to be true. But because I do not condone them, I cannot participate in them."

I flopped my head back on my bed, "So you're telling me we've found the one priest too honorable to use his power to help out an innocent woman?"

Benthic frowned, "I did not say that. While I personally cannot intervene in the constabulary's work, I can offer you an alternative."

"Go on." I said.

"If you were to join the church as an apprentice, you would fall outside the jurisdiction of the constabulary. The church sees to the punishment of its own members. It is how Sister Allora avoided things. The same rule would protect you."

I stared dumbfounded at the pair of them for a solid minute, not sure what had floored me more, the offer, the hypocrisy, or the news about Allora. I settled on the last bit.

"Wait, what do you mean about Allora?"

Beside Benthic, Allora averted her face, refusing to look at me. It was left to Benthic to speak. "I was unaware she has hidden this from you. My apologies. I will say no more, as that is her place. But, if you were to join, you would be protected from this incident. And, other, more severe, crimes."

"What do you mean, more severe crimes?" I said with a cold dread.

"Possession of Holy Relics is blasphemy for all but acolytes. While the crime, if the relic is unknown, is minor, using the powers of such an item to wage a street war on criminals is not something the church could ignore. But, if an apprentice were to use one, the punishment would be far less severe, and may even lead to her education in their use." He shifted his look to encompass Allora as well as myself, "We have so few acolytes who can unlock the true potential of the Holy Relics and Akzad's Gift."

"Damn it, Allora! You said he could help me! But now I'm going to be tried as a heretic on top of going to prison for helping people!" I snarled. The irony churned inside me. Here I was facing punishment for stopping criminals and using a Relic to do so, while Venti ran free after using a Relic to burn down our neighborhood.

"I didn't say anything." Allora said.

"She is correct." Benthic interjected, "We have been searching for the person known as the Knightshield for some time. The rumors of the magical shield were too consistent to all be exaggeration. Testimony of the locals after last night's events have revealed your identity. Allora's coming to me was most fortuitous as it allowed me to be the one to speak to you first. But I assure you, if she hadn't, we would have come before much longer, and it would likely have been Brother Hishu who came."

I shivered at the thought of Hishu coming into my room while I was chained to my bed. That didn't make the predicament any better but at least I knew it could have been worse. That always helped, right?

My mind raced for what to say, a way to get out of this. I then recalled what had happened and how I had been shot. "I don't know anything about this Knightshield person. I saw people trying to burn down our neighborhood, so I intervened. I wear my father's old heirloom as my wraspisa. It's metal so I tried to use it as a shield. As evidenced by my gut wound, it is not magically able to stop bullets or anything like that."

The corners of Benthic's mouth rose in amusement, "That, no doubt, is because you are untrained. Only a person fully dedicated to Akzad can wield a Holy Gift to its full potential. If your faith and devotion is not pure, the Gift can be withdrawn."

I could only blink in reply. My shield had been bullet proof. Otherwise, I would have ended up in a hospital a long, long time ago. I hadn't believed Benthics warning from our first conversation that Relics could lose their power. Had I done something to cause that? I had never been a devoted follower of Akzad so I doubted that was it. Or had I just been lucky before now?

"Then how do you explain the Relic the thugs were wielding to burn everything down?" I asked.

Both Benthic and Allora stared at me confused so I reluctantly explained. "The leader of those thugs, guy named Venti, was using a candle that when you blew on it, like you were blowing it out, it instead through up a fireball. Tell me that's not a Relic and if he can use it to destroy stuff, why would one I've been using suddenly fail me? Theoretically, of course, as I'm not saying I ever have."

Benthic looked disturbed by my question and wouldn't meet my eyes for a second. Finally, he said, "How did you know the name of this criminal? Venti you called him?"

"Yeah. We have history. You're avoiding my question."

Benthic forced a smile onto his face. "Yes, of course. Relic's are Manifestations that persist without being sustained by an acolyte. The Gift can be wielded by anyone. But Akzad can withdraw that Gift. His Protection, as granted to an item like a shield, will not be granted if the actions of the wielder go against his teachings. Unfortunately, the powers of destruction, are not as fickle."

"So, you're telling me, anyone can use god's power to kill people but if you use them to protect people, you're at his fickle mercy?"

"It is more complicated than that. We all carry his greatest Gift, that of Choice. This Gift he will never withdrawal. We can choose to destroy at any time, whether we have a Relic or not. Only with his Gift can we do other, what many call magical, things."

I started to object again but Benthic held up his hand, "I understand you have many questions. If you become an apprentice, we will be able to train you to better understand how to wield Akzad's Gifts. All apprentices must learn to summon the Manifestation to be elevated to full acolyte. But only some receive Akzad's full blessing. That you have been wielding this Holy Gift without training suggests he has already blessed you. That the shield failed, suggests he may be withdrawing that favor because you have not devoted yourself to his cause."

I wasn't sure if I bought that last bit but the idea of learning how to control the Relics did sound appealing. Learning to Manifest food would be damn useful. Joining the church sounded like a world of trouble. But apparently Allora had done so and gotten out, at least somewhat. Maybe it wouldn't be so bad.

So, I said yes.

Chapter 15

My first day out of the hospital, the first thing I did was return to Nerpi's garage. Breathing was still troubled so I wouldn't be doing any vigorous exercise for awhile yet, but I could move on my own. Even this amount of recovery had taken me a week to reach. So, I was a bit amazed to only find Allora there.

I packed a bag of a few personal possessions and stepped into the doorway to Allora's clinic, "Where's everyone else?"

Allora let out a heavy sigh, "En got released the same day you met with Benthic. Some rich guy bailed him out. Haven't heard from him since. Nerpi is still awaiting processing."

"Still?! It's been a week!" I said.

"I know. But he hasn't been charged with anything yet either."

"If he hasn't been charged, they have to let him out."

Allora shrugged, "Sure. Everyone in jail gets out. Eventually."

I stood there dumbfounded for a moment. But in my present state, both injured and about to have to turn myself into the church, there wasn't anything I could do for Nerpi. I hoped I he would be all right though.

We stood there, silently, for several moments, contemplating everything. I had so many questions for Allora but I didn't know where to start. We hadn't talked about the incident or the revelation about her connection with the church.

Finally, my shoulders slumped, I just said, "What the hell, Allora?"

She smiled, "I'm sorry, Kali. This isn't going to be easy for you. When I first joined the church, I was male. After my change came, things were different for me there. More difficult. Evians change genders so even when we're female, the misogyny isn't as bad. You won't have that benefit."

I slumped back against the wall and stared down at the floor. "Then why would they even agree to take me?"

"The church's core message is supposed to be one of unity. They can't turn you, anyone, away because of their gender or species. Not openly. Especially when you have a power they want. Never lose sight of that. That's why they took you."

I shrugged, "Okay. But I can just leave right? Like you did?"

Allora bowed her head, "Technically I am on sabbatical. To pursue my medical studies. I should have returned after my graduation. But for evians, it's an unspoken rule that these sabbaticals can last until our next change."

I nodded my understanding, "But you don't even like the church. You come with us to services every time Nerpi makes us, but I can see your disdain. Why did you ever join?"

"I thought differently then. Before I saw it from the inside. You're going to have a harder time. You don't like it now. But there is good there. It's corrupt and run by assholes. But its purpose for being remains a good one. To unite all the people thrown together on this planet. Without the church we would have wiped each other out in wars a long time ago. Most of the people in it understand that message. You can do some good things if you work with people like Benthic. Just..."

Allora stopped for a moment and collected herself. She looked up at me with concern in her eyes, "Don't take the vow of celibacy as your first right."

I frowned, "Why would I? I'm not giving up sex for them."

"As one of the few women there, many will see you as available. You will have many trying to get your attention and get you alone."

I cocked my head, "So shouldn't that mean it would be better to take a vow of celibacy? Wouldn't that warn them off?"

"That vow is an optional one. If you take it, you become unavailable. The good ones will leave you alone. The ones you actually should be worried about will become more interested. You'll be forbidden fruit."

"They're welcome to try." I growled.

Allora leaned forward in her chair to look me directly in the eyes. "I know you can take care of yourself. But that's what I'm most worried about. You beat up a senior acolyte and it won't be prison you'll be facing. It will be condemnation and execution."

Uncomfortable, I stood up and started pacing the small clinic. "Sounds like I should not go. I'll go tell Benthic I quit or go sabbatical or something."

"You are awaiting trial by the Council of Acolytes. If you complete your studies and become a full acolyte, you will pass and be free to make that choice. Until then, if you leave, you lose the protection of the church."

I shrugged, "So what? The constabulary only wanted to arrest me because of my past record. Give it a little time and they won't care about me anymore. You say they're corrupt but I've known cops my whole life. What they really are is lazy."

Allora shook her head vigorously, "The church will make sure that they care."

"Sounds like a wonderful solution you found." I said being sure the sarcasm was apparent.

"I know. And I'm sorry, Kali. It was the only thing I could do at the time."

I sighed and slouched against the door frame, "I know you did. And I appreciate it. Really. You know what they say, no good deed goes unpunished. Guess we're both seeing the truth of that."

"Indeed. Here, I'll walk you to the church."

"And you can tell me about that stethoscope that can knock people out."

Allora stumbled to a stop and looked at me with a stern expression, "That you can never mention again."

"Why not?"

"I was granted its use as a medical tool. It can render people unconscious for surgery. It was never supposed to be used as a weapon."

"How exactly does a stethescope go about doing that? It's for listening to hearts right?"

"Your shield is made of aluminum and shouldn't stop bullets. Relics don't follow any rules but those of Akzad. If the church knew I used mine as a weapon, or that I had learned a new way to use it, my time away would be over. Promise me you won't mention that?"

I nodded vigorously, "They won't hear a peep from me. But they already knew about me and my shield before you brought them to me. Who knows what else they know."

"The only ones who saw it were you, Nerpi, and En."

"And a bunch of goons."

"The ones who did won't be telling anyone anything."

I shivered at Allora's simple statement. I wasn't sure she was right. People had been watching the events of that night from their windows or as they fled into the street. But I didn't want to press her on this.

We walked down the street the rest of the way in silence. As we passed the burned down buildings I marveled at the damage. I hadn't yet seen it in daylight. The sandwich shop was gutted but the rest of the building still stood. The one next to it, however, had completely burned down. The goons had gotten to it before we even knew what was going on.

As we got closer to the church, I was surprised to see how close the destruction had gotten to the church grounds. Yet, they had remained untouched. I guess even these goons didn't want to risk holy damnation. But here I was walking into this place they feared, and I'd probably been more blasphemous.

To my relief, I saw Benthic and Claren, the young acolyte I had met last time I'd visited, waiting for me rather than someone like Hishu. Allora squeezed my shoulder and turned away before I crossed the street. I would have to face this alone after all. Summoning my courage, I crossed over and went up the stairs.

Benthic smiled kindly at me and Claren gave me an odd look before glancing down to his feet. "I see your recovery is going well. That alone attests to the blessings Akzad has bestowed upon you."

That I still ached everywhere and had a hard time breathing if I exerted myself even a little bit didn't make me feel particularly blessed. But then, the doctors at the hospital had also gushed about my quick recovery. None of them had said so to my face but the impression I had was they never thought I would walk out of there.

"Yeah, okay, I guess." Was all I could manage to say in response. I followed the two acolytes up the stairs and into the private areas of the church. I had only ever been there once before so wasn't very sure where we were going. I tried to pay attention so I could find my way out again, but the hallways were surprisingly bland. The main worship center and reception halls were lavish. Hishu's personal quarters had been luxurious. But the hallways bore nothing but flat panels and muted tones.

We arrived at a door that looked like all the others. Once inside I found a large room with about a dozen cots lining the walls. A small chest was tucked up next to each. Three small windows up near the ceiling on one wall provided the only light. No electric bulbs hung nor any holders for candles.

"This is the Chamber of Apprentices." Benthic explained, "You will sleep here. Claren will show you where to store your items and then take you to Chapel and to afternoon lessons."

I nodded mutely to Benthic who seemed to be waiting for something. I grumbled and started to bow to him, but he shook his head. "Acolytes, even apprentices, do not bow to each other except during services to the High Acolyte of our church or to one of the Arch Acolytes."

I nodded, a little surprised. But I guess it made sense. They put themselves above the regular people, but not each other. How magnanimous.

"Our ways are not that mysterious, child. You will learn quickly. Now, settle in. You have a few minutes yet before Chapel."

Benthic left me alone with Claren. I glanced at the young acolyte and he hastily cast his eyes elsewhere. Unlike my time with Hishu, I had no unease being alone with him. He didn't set off any warning bells, but I couldn't read him either.

"So, how many apprentices are there?" I asked, gesturing to the dozen cots.

"There are only four at the moment, including you and me." He answered.

"Huh. Figured there would be quite a few."

"At the start of each season, the beds are always full. But the calling to serve Akzad is a hard one. Many find they are destined for a different form of service."

I rolled my eyes while my back was turned to him. "So, which one is mine? It sounds like there are plenty of options."

Claren pointed to a cot closest to the exterior wall. I resisted the urge to ask who was on either side of me. I'd find out soon enough. I focused on trying to stuff everything from my bag into the small chest. I didn't have much, but even what I did have wouldn't fit easily into the small chest. Especially with the voluminous robes already in it. With a reluctant sigh, I took the robe out and put it on.

The room lacked a mirror so I couldn't see what I looked like. The robe was way too big for me, obviously sized for someone who wasn't uvoy. Claren didn't impart a lot of emotions into his expressions, but he did cringe a bit when he looked at me.

"We'll find you something that fits a bit more. But later. We will be late for Chapel if we do not go now."

I nodded and closed the lid on my chest. "So, what's this Chapel?"

"It is a worship service."

"But it's not service day."

Claren gave me a bewildered expression. "Acolytes worship every day. There are four services each day."

I felt the blood drain from face and my heart sink. Four times a day?

Chapter 16

To my immense relief, the four per day chapel services didn't turn out as bad as I feared. They were not over an hour like the weekly one I had been used to attending, only lasting maybe fifteen minutes. There was still plenty of bowing and intoning drivel. They also didn't appear mandatory. At least for full acolytes. Each session had us four apprentices and then a handful of others but never the full conclave. Even Benthic often failed to turn up. Though I felt confident if I failed to show up, it would be noticed.

Claren introduced me to the other two apprentices after that first chapel. To my surprise, only one of them, Jensen, was human. The other, Mateto, was a nudra. I had never interacted with a nudra before that day, as they were the most inclusive of the six species of Akka. When I shook his scaled hand, it felt very warm in mine. I was tempted to ask if the rumors that nudra could breathe fire were true but, fortunately, I stopped myself. I was a country yokel, but I didn't want to be that country yokel.

"Is it true uvoy wear those hats because the top of your skull is soft?" Mateto asked. Apparently, he was that type of country yokel.

"What? No. And it's not a hat, it's a wraspisa."

"Oh right. Sorry. Forgot you people were so sensitive about that. So, your skull isn't soft? Why wear those big hats...err...wraspisa's then? They look heavy."

I stared, dumbfounded at Mateto, not even sure where to start. My hand reached up to feel the wraspisa on my head and its unfamiliar weight. I had gotten used to hiding my shield as a wraspisa and the aluminum shape was a bit lighter than the standard style. With the Church having confiscated my shield, I was back to wearing my old one. We uvoy have strong necks but Mateto's questions made me realize how heavy the thing actually was.

I don't know how long we stood there, me frozen between a couple of different responses. Part of me was insulted by his bluntness. Part of me was mad because I had almost done the same. But mostly I didn't have a good answer. I wore the wraspisa because I had always worn one. It made some sense out in the sun, we did sunburn easily, but I wasn't a farm hand.

Finally, I went with what I had always been told, "Akzad gave them to us when we came to this world to protect us from the harsh sun."

"Ah. That makes sense." Mateto said with a nod, accepting the answer better than I had as a kid. But then, he was training to be an acolyte so would probably accept anything that followed after 'Akzad did it'.

The other one, Jensen, had remained quiet throughout all of this. I tried to offer him a friendly smile, after all, I would have to spend a lot of time with these three, might as well try and keep things friendly. While I wouldn't categorize his response as hostile, I also wouldn't have called it welcoming.

Claren led us from the chapel room to a room I immediately recognized as a classroom. A large chalkboard covered one wall and a lectern stood beside it. There were no individual desks like I had seen in city schools but long tables with benches that felt more familiar. My town hadn't been your stereotypical one room schoolroom type. We'd had two. But the tables were similar.

We all took seats at one table, the emptiness of the rest of the space felt ominous to me. Even if the whole dozen Claren had mentioned before had been here the room would still feel empty. I voiced this question and Claren smiled. "This isn't just used to train apprentices. Full acolytes also study here and attend lectures. Sometimes the entire Conclave."

My shoulders slumped, "They keep going to school after graduating?"

"The pursuit of knowledge is a core tenant of Akzad's teachings. Even a newbie should know that." Jensen said dismissively.

I bit back a retort. I supposed he was right. That was one of the chants we had to do every week. Service. Community. Obedience. Knowledge. Unity. Which made Allora's sabbatical to learn medicine make even more sense. It wasn't just because she was a woman now. But still mostly I bet.

The door nearest the chalkboard flew open and a frumpy looking human acolyte waddled in. He was pudgy and looked even older than Benthic. Not the distinguished style of old but just old old. He set a heavy book down at the lectern, opened it, and immediately started reading.

I glanced at the others and they had all drawn out notebooks and were writing things down as the acolyte spoke. I hadn't been given any kind of notebook or had any idea what he was droning on about. But at least this was familiar to me.

After a minute, Claren noticed me sitting there looking lost and he raised a hand. "Brother Joh?"

With an annoyed huff, Joh looked up from his book. He cast a withering look at Claren but then blinked as his eyes took me in. "Oh. Oh yes. We have a new student today. Of course, of course. Please stand-up child."

Reluctantly, I did so and he gave me a smile. "I am Brother Joh and this course covers the history of the Holy Order of Akzad. Commonly just known as the Church. We are already deeply into the history so you will have to do some catch-up reading on your own. I can give you some books after class. For now, you can find notebooks in the chest at the back of the room. Do your best to follow along."

Without another word, he turned back to his book and began reading again. I stood there uncertainly for a few seconds before going to look for the chest he had described. Inside, I found several half-used notebooks and spent several minutes debating between one already half full of notes or one mostly empty. As the fuller ones appeared to not cover any single topic, I opted for as empty one as I could find.

I returned to my seat without Joh having slowed or made any change to his lecture. Coming back gave a vantage point to read over the shoulders of my fellow trainees. I had first taken them to be studiously writing notes, but I now saw that Jensen and Claren were playing some kind of word game. Mateto did appear to be trying to pay faithful attention to Joh though.

A lot of my lecture time went like this. We had several lectures throughout the day, and most were fairly boring. Claren explained that we were expected to spend much of the rest of our time studying and reading the materials covered in these classes. He admitted he learned most things from that. I had never been a big fan of reading, especially old stuffy books, so was not looking forward to that.

But not all our lessons were this way. Some were even worse. As it turned out, the only topic I had any real interest in was taught by Hishu. He swaggered into the classroom and fixed his lecherous eyes on me. I tried to sit as low in my chair as possible and for once felt glad to be wearing the big formless monk robe.

"I see a new student has joined us. Welcome." Hishu said with a smile. "Mateto, please explain the fundamentals of this class so she can catch up."

As Mateto stood up, his tail knocked his chair backwards. He grimaced and turned around to pick it up, this time knocking his tail into Jensen and sweeping both notebooks to the floor. I had seen him answer questions in other classes before and he had never acted like this. I felt pity for him, despite my general dislike of his obsequious attitude toward the acolytes, and crawled under the table to retrieve his notebook.

When I sat back up, he gave me a toothy grin of thanks. With everything put back the way it had been before he stood, he opened his mouth to answer the question but before he could start speaking, Hishu cut him off. "Clearly you are not ready to answer even this simple question, Mateto. Sit down before you break anything else."

Mateto deflated and slumped down into his chair. I felt a fury at Hishu that built on my already existing dislike of the man. I narrowed my eyes in hate at him, but fortunately, we uvoy had large eyes and humans tend not to notice when we do that. I could glare at him all I wanted and I doubted he'd notice.

"Claren, would you like to try?" Hishu asked.

"Yes, sir." Claren said, standing up. He gave an apologetic side glance to Mateto before continuing, "The art of Manifestation is the greatest gift of Akzad. With it he bestows upon us his fundamental self, the power to create. With it, the first peoples of Akka were able to create food to plant and grow in order to survive after the Cataclysm cut us off from our original homes. It is the most tangible example of his love."

"Very good, Claren. What is required to create a Manifestation?" Hishu asked.

"Akzad's Blessing."

"Excellent. You may sit."

Claren sat back down, his shoulders loosening in clear relief. Hishu appeared satisfied with his answer, but I wasn't. Nothing Claren had said told me anything I wouldn't have gotten from a regular worship service.

"Now, today, we will begin discussing the elements of a service and how they call upon the blessing. For in a short time, you will each take a turn in the main ceremony and will need to demonstrate your ability to Manifest. This is an important step along your path to becoming a full acolyte. While, as an important member of the senior acolytes, my position during a worship service has prevented me from directly observing your attempts, reports say all of you have managed to achieve a full Manifestation during a service. This is good but as Brother Claren demonstrated when he failed his first attempt during a service, it is not always as easy when before the watching congregation."

As he talked, Hishu paced around the room, including behind us. I didn't like the idea of him being behind me, so I had to shift uncomfortably in my chair to follow up with my eyes. "Jensen, explain for our new apprentice how to receive Akzad's Blessing of Manifestation and why she might struggle in class to do so."

Jensen stood up. "To receive Akzad's Blessing, you must open yourself up to love. To do this we recite his Mantra and draw upon the prayers of the devout."

"Excellent. And the Mantra?"

"I am the vessel of Akzad. I am his instrument on the physical plain. The power of the faithful is mine to shape. I deserve this power because my faith is stronger. My will is Akzad's will." Jensen intoned reverently.

As he spoke, I shifted to look at Jensen. I couldn't keep a look of contempt off my face. That was what the acolytes were muttering during a worship ceremony? I had always assumed they were saying the same thing as the crowd. I couldn't remember all of the words, I was always watching the bowls, but I knew it was similar but not the same.

"It seems our new apprentice has found a fault in your recitation." Hishu's amused tone made me flinch. "Tell us, what did Jensen do that was so egregious?"

My cheeks flushed and Jensen gave me a dark stare. I was doing a great job making friends so far. I decided to go fully apologetic. "Nothing, Brother Hishu. That I am aware of. As I am just learning. So have no idea."

"There must have been something. You were clearly disturbed by his performance. I must know what he did to pain you so."

I swallowed and tried to think of a diplomatic way to say this. "I was surprised by the words is all. They aren't the same as what's said by the congregation."

"You are correct on that point. The words for the servant are different than that for the master. They offer their faith up for us to shape."

"And that doesn't disturb you? We out there think we're offering a prayer to Akzad but the priests think they're using that faith for their own power? I mean, that's clearly how it works, but I honestly didn't think you all were up here saying that part out loud to yourselves."

The room went deadly silent. My attempts at diplomacy hadn't lasted very long. The three apprentices each stared at me with differing expressions. On the positive side, they weren't all annoyed. Hishu, however, did not mask his displeasure.

"Well, it seems you have much to teach our newest recruit. Extra practice sessions will help you. Private lessons in my quarters starting on Restday after midday chapel."

I squirmed in my seat at the pleased look Hishu gave me. I didn't know how I was going to get through that without getting myself arrested again.

Chapter 17

Dreading the idea of being alone with Hishu, more for his safety than my own, I tried to come up with a way to avoid it. I decided the only real option I had was to appeal to a higher power. I figured Akzad would side with his priest, and I didn't know the High Acolyte which left Benthic. The old man had helped me out already by keeping me from prison so I didn't want to impose on him, but I couldn't think of another solution.

Fortunately, I had a few days before Restday, which ended up being important because I didn't see Benthic for several days. It took me the first few to adapt to my schedule and figure out when I might have time to go to his office. It was a busy schedule, filled with classes, prayer chapels and a surprising amount of dreary paperwork. Each apprentice was assigned to a different department, doing grunt work for the junior and senior acolytes.

My job ended up involving tending the gardens. Not only was I terrible at it, but I also had to endure the jokes from the human acolytes about how I should be great at it because I, literally, had a green thumb. What made it worse was they weren't jerks about it aside from that corny expression.

Finally, the day before Restday, I managed to grab Benthic after a chapel service. He greeted me warmly and asked how I was settling in. "Better than I expected at first. It is weird being the only uvoy around."

"We do not see many of your kind who answer the call." Benthic said.

"Nor nudra, grunde, or ewokian."

"That we do not do a better job of reaching out to those communities is a failing of the acolytes, I would admit."

"Or it could be the way they are treated when they are here." I said. "Brother Hishu is especially hard on me and Mateto. He is expecting me to attend a private tutoring session tomorrow."

"That is very kind of him." Benthic said, his tone reproachful, "You have a lot of catching up to do with the rest of your apprentices. Devoting his personal time should show his devotion, not the opposite."

I cursed myself. I had come about this from the completely wrong angle. Now, instead of getting Benthic's sympathy, I looked like a whiny child. I had to do something to recover from this.

"He wants me to meet him in his personal quarters. Alone."

"That is where many of us spend our Restday. That is the purpose, to get away from the office or classroom." Benthic said, somehow completely missing the implication.

"Have you not noticed how Hishu treats women?" I asked, deciding I was done with tact, as I wasn't very good at it. "He wants me alone near his bed."

"Come now, young Kali, you are letting your fears get the better of you. Brother Hishu has taken the vow of chastity. He would never do something untoward." Benthic said, but his words lacked reproach. "If you were to make these accusations to any other acolyte, they would tell you that your impure lust for Brother Hishu has clouded your judgement and you are transferring your feelings to him. They may even offer to help you, ah, purge those thoughts from your mind."

I couldn't help shivering at the implication, but I didn't know what to say in response. I got the message loud and clear that I wasn't going to get help from anyone else and probably shouldn't mention it. That just riled me up so fortunately, Benthic threw me a final lifeline.

"There has been a discussion among the senior acolytes that, should it happen, would require your presence elsewhere on Restday's. But that is for the future. I caution you to attend your session tomorrow with an open mind for that future and to not do anything to jeopardize that."

After that, I had to get to my next class. The meeting with Benthic had gone about as well as I could have hoped. I mean, sure, he hadn't done anything to help me, but he had given me vague promises of help in the future, which was all I had actually expected. It would probably be enough.

The time of my meeting with Hishu arrived and I reluctantly went to his quarters. I knocked and was directed to come inside. The room was just as gaudy as I remembered it from the last time he had tried to get me inside.

Hishu sat at his desk, a book open on it. He swiveled in his chair and gestured toward the bed.

"You may sit there, Apprentice."

"I'm good to stand."

I thought he would argue with me but instead he just shrugged. "Suit yourself. Now, let us start at the beginning. What can you tell me about Relics?"

A wave of relief washed over me. He at least was going to do what he said and tutor me. And we weren't starting with the mantra, which I assumed would be the focus. "Relic's are examples of Akzad's Gift that persist past the life of the acolyte who made them."

"A simple but accurate answer." Hishu said. "Why do Relic's persist? Why does not anything gifted by Akzad last like they do?"

I shrugged. I wanted to know that answer myself. "I don't know. None of the reading I've been given so far has a clear answer."

Hishu frowned, "You would do well to remember you have access to the full library. If you don't know something, you have the resources to enlighten yourself. But, that admonishment aside, there is some debate as to the true answer. Some feel it is driven by necessity. In our early days on this planet, after the Cataclysm, our needs were greater, so Akzad gifted us more power. Others argue that our faith in Akzad is weaker now than it was. It takes an entire congregation to Manifest fruit during a service. There is yet another, smaller group of scholars, who believe the stories of Relics are mostly embellishments."

Hishu stood up and started pacing around, like he did in class. Despite my loathing of him, I had to admit he had a real passion for this topic. "There are records of countless Relics but none that have ever been found. The Staff of Jundon, Emerelas Candle, the Blanket of the Long Night, and on and on. Your shield may have been one of them. Demantra's Shield was said to be impervious to damage. Yet, you were clearly shot through it. My testing to date has not shown anything conclusive."

"You have my shield?" I asked eagerly.

"Of course. I am the director of the Relic office. We are studying it to see if it's Gift can be restored or if you ruined it. Or even if it ever was truly a Relic. Given that it is supposed to save the user from lethal damage, I am uncertain how to test it safely."

My mind started reeling with possibilities. I knew the Church had taken possession of it as part of Allora's deal for me. I didn't know what they were going to do with it. Lock it up in a vault I had assumed. If they were testing it, maybe I could get it back. Maybe I was the only one who could use it. Or, maybe, I really had ruined its power somehow.

While I pondered that, Hishu stopped pacing. He looked at me in a neutral way before saying, "It is getting hot in here isn't it? Feel free to remove your robe if you need too, I will not be offended."

He then proceeded to take off his robe, revealing he had only tight shorts and a shirt on underneath. For a few moments I had started to think I could make it through this without having to hit him. I am sure he would suggest I sit down on the bed before suggesting again I take my robe off too. I would like nothing more than to take it off because it was warm in here thanks to my having worn my overalls underneath the robe. But even though I was fully clothed underneath, I didn't want to give him the satisfaction.

Akzad must have been on my side for once though because before Hishu could finish disrobing, a knock sounded at the door. He gave a dark look before pulling the robe back on and opening the door. Claren stood in the hallway. My fellow apprentice carried a book in his hands and bowed his head low before pushing his way inside.

"My apologies for being late, Brother."

Hishu continued to frown, "Late? Late for what?"

"Your remedial studies class."

"This is a private session. Besides, you don't need remedial studies."

"But you said I did, sir. After my failure to Manifest during a service. My time for testing for full acolyte is coming up. I do not want to fail."

I jumped at the opening, "I don't mind if he stays. I could benefit from his example. There's an open seat for him on the bed."

Hishu looked like he would argue but then thought better of it. His pretext for inviting me here would fall apart if he turned another student looking for help away. He beckoned for Claren to sit down, and he did without a glance in my direction. Maybe Benthic had come through for me after all, sending Claren here. I doubted he had made this decision on his own because Hishu was right, he didn't need extra lessons.

The rest of the extended lesson proceeded ponderously. The spark of enthusiasm Hishu had demonstrated at first vanished and he was far more snappish and impatient with my lack of knowledge. I left the session with a large list of books I needed to read in all my copious free time.

When we departed, I expected Claren to head away to do whatever he normally did on Restday that he had been forced to put aside. I wasn't sure if I should thank him for coming. If Benthic had sent him, he might not know why or there was at least a small chance he had genuinely felt he needed the extra lesson. Instead, he stopped in the hallway and turned to me.

"I am meeting Jensen and Mateto for dinner. Would you care to join us?"

I had eaten with the three of them several times since coming to the Church, we had the same narrow window for meals. But I had never been invited to join them before. I'm not sure I would have chosen eating with them, Jensen was far from my favorite person and I still wasn't sure how to felt about Mateto. If I said no, it wouldn't be a good way to repair his gesture though.

"Sure, that would be great."

We went down to the dining hall where all the acolytes regularly ate. Jensen and Mateto were already there, both with books open before them. Despite very few formal duties this day, we all had lots of things to do. Jensen let out a loud sigh and slammed his book close as we approached.

"Took you long enough. I hope Brother Hishu really gave it to you hard for making us wait." He said with an annoyed grin. I honestly couldn't say if the innuendo was intended or not because he was looking at Claren when he said it.

"The tutoring session was most...enlightening." Claren said. "But yes, I have worked up quite an appetite. Let's give thanks and then eat."

By this point I had been forced to accept that I wouldn't be able to eat without saying a prayer first. It annoyed me at first but in truth it never took that long. Only when one of the acolytes felt the need to show off did it drag on. Those times they also said their prayer out loud when, fortunately, it was often done silently.

If there was one thing I couldn't complain about here at the church, it was the food. Now, I wasn't the worst cook in the world, but I've never been able to make anything half as good as my mother used too. The head chef here, Auran a fellow uvoy twice my age, put even my mother to shame. I smiled at her through the kitchen window as I took the first bite of the dish and then let my day's worries vanish for at least a few moments.

"So, what did Brother Hishu say when you showed up begging for more lessons?" Jensen asked between mouthfuls.

"You were right. He did not think I needed to be there." Claren replied and then gave me a sheepish look, "Said I was not to return next week so he could focus all of his attention on Kali."

I paused with my fork in my mouth for a second in surprise. I had missed that exchange as we left Hishu's room. I suppose part of my good feeling had lay with the idea that Claren would be with me for future sessions. I recovered without saying a word. That would be next week's problem. I had plenty more to sustain me until then.

Chapter 18

M y second week at the Church went about as well as the first. And by well, I mean tortuous yet also not as bad as my imagination always assumed it would. It was mostly just boring. Of course, I had another private session with Hishu to look forward to which took up the majority of my brain's capacity for worry.

When the next Restday finally arrived, it started with an unusual summons to Benthic's office. A small spark of hope emerged as he had alluded to something he might be able to do to get out of these private sessions. With a skip in my step, I went directly to his office. My elation ran into a brick wall when I arrived. Sitting there in a chair across from Benthic, was Grant, the shady race sponsor.

I entered the room cautiously. Finding Grant in Benthic's office had been the last thing I had expected to find at this meeting. I glanced between the two men unsure how to proceed. Both gave friendly smiles and Benthic invited me in and toward the empty chair next to Grant.

I hadn't seen Grant since that day at the arena and had never been able to follow up on my suspicions. While the group of thugs who had burned down Rady's garage and many buildings in my neighborhood had been led by Venti, I hadn't been able to verify he still worked for ECG. He was a hired thug after all. He might work for multiple different unsavory companies. I also had never verified how Grant was related.

"Please, have a seat, Sister Kali." Benthic said with a smile. "This is Mr. Grant. He has come to us with a proposal."

I kept my expression flat, "We've met."

"Excellent. The Church has hired him to set up a Cycler team sponsored by the Church. We want to reach out to more of the people and bring them back into the fold." The tone in Benthic's voice did not carry any of the sarcasm I would have inserted into that sentence but nevertheless it lacked his usual earnestness.

"That's right, Brother Benthic." Grant said with a wide, insincere smile, "Our research has shown that people derive a lot of their opinions from those they look up too. Cycler Racers. Actors. Musicians. All the new popular entertainments now available to the masses thanks to the glory of film. It's my job to connect people who want to share a message, with people others will listen too."

"You think the Church sponsoring a race team will get more people to go to church?" I asked.

"Brother Hishu proposed the idea, and it was approved by the High Acolyte." Benthic said and I caught the hint of amusement in his eyes. Well, at least someone else thought this was a ridiculous idea.

My mind warred with itself over focusing on the ridiculousness of the idea or the fact that Grant was sitting right here and involved. Benthic knew nothing about what had happened to Rady, in my hometown, or the possible connection between them. In truth, I wasn't fully sure of what Grant's connection was. Had he been hired by ECG to work with Rady, and knew nothing about Venti's group of thugs, or was he more intimately involved?

I decided I needed more information. "What does this have to do with me?"

Benthic spread his hands out, "As you can imagine, there are not many within the Church who have much experience racing cyclers. We could hire a team, but the High Acolyte likes the idea of the racer being one of our own. He feels it would humanize us more to the people."

I narrowed my eyes. "You do realize I'm not human."

Benthic bowed his head, "I apologize. A poor choice of words, Sister."

"I think you'd make an excellent spokesperson. You're young. Attractive. Energetic. An excellent connector to today's disconnected youth. It was the reason I was prepared to sponsor you and Mr. Nerpi. In fact, I hope we can renew your association with him and Mr. Papadopoulos." Grant said.

I blinked. "I'm sorry, Nerpi and who?"

"Arron Papadopoulos. I believe you knew him as En DeSkies."

"Right." I said, recalling the movie trailer I had seen in the arena. I had forgotten his real name but Allora at least shared my belief En and the actor were the same person. "I'm afraid I haven't had a chance to speak with Nerpi or En for several weeks. I'm not entirely sure they ever got released from prison after the thugs you hired burned down half the buildings on this street."

I hadn't meant to blurt out that accusation so directly, but I was annoyed at him trying to rope my friends back into this. While I missed them, if they were away from me, they were safe. I had a habit of bringing darkness down on those around me.

"Kali!" Benthic spoke in a stern voice I rarely heard him use, "That is an outlandish accusation to throw at Mr. Grant."

Despite Benthic's defense, Grant put up a moderating hand, "I'm afraid Ms. Estuta has a right to be weary. I previously represented a client and connected them with another cycler team owned by Nil Rady. Unfortunately, my client thought his interests would be better served if Mr. Rady was seen as a champion and proceeded to pursue efforts to ensure he won, no matter the cost. This ended up involving a gang of street thugs who have since been arrested for arson, among other things."

Grant leaned in closer to us, "Let me put your mind at ease. I knew nothing of these events prior to them transpiring and I have since severed my relationship with said client. That's not how I like to do business. In this case, my client would be the Church, who I think we can all agree would not be inclined to use such brutal methods."

I assessed Grant, trying to gauge the sincerity of what he said. Unfortunately, I got the impression he would use the same flowery tone of voice whether he was lying or telling the truth. It was one of the reasons I didn't trust anything he said when we first met. But that also didn't mean he was lying now.

"Who was the client?" I asked.

"I'm afraid that is privileged information. I am bound by a non-disclosure agreement which I must honor. My current clients must know they can trust my confidentiality." Grant said.

"So, these guys hired arsonists and you have to stay quiet? What about the Constabulary?" I pressed.

"Of course, I would cooperate fully with any legal requests made by the Constabulary. But you, nor even Acolyte Benthic, are members of the Constabulary. I hope you can appreciate my conundrum. I don't always have the luxury of knowing the true intentions and heart of the people who hire me. That's one reason I am so excited by this opportunity to work with the you and the Church."

Damn if he wasn't good. There was just enough pained expression and faux outrage mixed into his tone that I couldn't be certain of what he said. I doubt he would have said anything different whether he was guilty or innocent. I hated this man even more for that.

Instead, I decided to try his tack and deflect, "I'm afraid my course of study is too great to be able to devote time to racing anymore."

"That will not be a concern, Kali. Brother Hishu has agreed to release you from your additional duties." Benthic said, his tone stressing the point. "This was originally his idea after all. That you joined us may have helped convince some of the member of the Council that it was worth pursuing."

"So, I don't have a choice?" I asked incredulously, not sure if I should be angry at being roped in or elated that this would get me out of any more private sessions with Hishu.

"Of course, you have a choice." Benthic said though his tone implied the opposite.

"I would encourage you to speak to Mr. Nerpi before you make your decision." Grant said. "Without you, I was forced to cancel our deal with him. I believe he would be very eager to renew it."

"Why, what's happened to Nerpi?" I asked with growing apprehension.

Fortunately, Benthic gave me leave to depart the Church in order to speak with Nerpi. I hadn't left the confines of the grounds since I had arrived for my training. That I hadn't seen Nerpi or Allora at either of the Worship services had been disappointing but until now I had been mostly jealous they could get out of it.

My walk back to the garage came at almost midday. Despite this, the street was almost deserted. The burned-out apartment building nearest the church had already been torn down by construction crews. It looked like they would have a lot of work ahead of them as the next several buildings were also gutted.

The fires had been contained mostly to one side of the street yet many of the businesses across the way were closed. Which, I guess made some kind of sense. Most of the people who would have worked or shopped there had lived in the destroyed buildings. To my disgust, the Mega Mart looked to be the only place still doing much business.

I passed by this depressing sight to find a more depressing one. Allora's clinic looked packed. She had always had steady business as the only doctor on the street, and the only one who charged a fair price within the greater neighborhood. I expected to see a bunch of burn victims but then, it had been several weeks since the fires. Most burns would have either killed a person by now or healed to a state they didn't need constant treatment. Everyone here just looked defeated.

I had hoped to talk to Allora as well on this trip but did not want to interfere with her line. If I needed too, she was the one person I felt the senior acolytes wouldn't deny me trying to reach out too. Without any more reason to delay, I went through the side door into Nerpi's garage. Our set of cyclers, including my racer, sat in one corner, covered in a tarp. The closed main bay door kept the room dark and haunted. The rest of the bay sat empty, devoid of repair work. It was unsettling not finding Nerpi in the middle of tinkering with something.

"Nerpi?" I called uncertainly.

"We're closed." Nerpi's voice said from a corner.

"Why would you be closed in the middle of the day? Getting lazy?" I asked, trying to add some levity to my voice.

"Kali?' Nerpi said and I heard a crash as he tripped over something in his excitement to get up from where he had been curled up. "It is you! That was a very quick training. Or did you drop out already?"

I gave a sheepish smile, "No, I haven't dropped out. Allora said I can't do that until I get made an acolyte or I'll get arrested as a blasphemer, which is apparently worse than getting arrested as a vigilante."

"Oh. Right. I guess you're not here to go back to work." Nerpi said with a dejected shrug. He stepped out of the shadows, and I saw the sling holding his left arm.

"What happened to your arm?" I asked. When last I saw him, on the night of the fire, he hadn't been injured. Allora hadn't mentioned anything about him getting hurt when they were helping people from burning buildings.

"Oh. This. Some of the constables at the jail didn't appreciate my attitude. Allora says it will heal up okay though. Does make it hard to work on cycler repairs with only one hand though."

Anger broiled in my stomach. First held on baseless grounds for weeks and then beaten? What the hell kind of justice was this? I thought my time in prison had been bad but I at least had been locked up for cause. Nerpi had never even been charged with anything.

"That's awful. Did you get a name? I'll find that asshole..."

"Please, no, Kali. No more vengeance. We've had enough of that." Nerpi said and sighed, slumping down against his work bench.

"This wouldn't be vengeance. It would be justice."

Nerpi shook his head. "There is a difference but that isn't it. What you did, when you would go out at night. That was justice. You saved people from direct harm. What we did to stop those thugs from burning down even more of the street was justice. Why they attacked us. Why I was arrested. Why you went out at night. That was all vengeance. Vengeance has always made things worse."

I thought back to that night. I had faced a choice between getting vengeance against Venti and stopping the rest of his gang. I had chosen vengeance and gotten shot as a result. I still didn't understand enough about Relics but Nerpi's words made me consider how much that played a role.

"Well, maybe instead of beating up a prison guard, I could help you out in another way." I said. I hadn't intended to come here and tell Nerpi about the offer from Grant. I just wanted to know why he thought Nerpi would be so keen on taking it. But now I knew. He hadn't been able to work for a month now. I doubted he could afford to keep paying the rent on the building for another month. Then he too would be out on the street. "The church wants to sponsor a race team. To spread the good word or something. And they want us to be that team."

Nerpi sat up, a new bit of spirit in his shoulders. "Really? Us? Why?"

I shrugged, "They want the racer to come from within their ranks. Which apparently includes me. And they know how devoted you are and thought you would be worthy to represent them." That last bit had been a lie but if it made him feel good, who cares. The next bit was truth that I had to include. "Plus, they hired Grant to do the marketing and he told them about our super-fast cycler."

Nerpi's fur flattened, "Grant? He was the one who worked with Rady and you thought were in-league with those people you've been hunting? The church is in business with the same people?"

I held up my arms in a wide gesture, "I don't know. Grant claims he works for a lot of different people. He also claims to have severed ties with whoever was sponsoring Rady. Won't tell me who they were."

"Do you believe him?"

"I don't know if I can trust anything that man says. Which means, maybe I do believe him. He's the kind of shady figure who would work with an evil business rather than running an evil business himself. He's greedy and amoral but not immoral. If that makes any sense."

Nerpi nodded, "It does. He wouldn't stab you himself but he's happy to take money from a guy who would if no one is looking. I guess that doesn't help you find who you were hunting."

"It might. Just because he hasn't told me anything yet doesn't mean he won't later. Another reason to keep him close."

Nerpi smiled, "So I guess we're going back to the racetrack."

Chapter 19

The day of my first race approached faster than I would have liked. My last one had been at the end of the previous season. The gap between seasons had steadily grown shorter each year and this one only lasted a little over three months. I had spent most of that time recovering from my injuries and then training as an acolyte. That had left me very little time to get ready, as I hadn't been on a cycler nearly that whole time.

Between my continued duties as a trainee and the training regime Nerpi pleaded to let me do, I came into the day already exhausted. Yet, it was a good kind of exhaustion. Being busy kept me from worrying too much about everything.

Unfortunately, my day started with a visit from Hishu. He stormed into the apprentice barracks and demanded I get up immediately. As this was Restday, the only day of the week that we apprentices got to sleep in, I received a number of dirty glares from the others. Hishu ignored them and dropped a garment bag onto my bed.

"You must get up, get dressed and eat. The Church is counting on you to show the people the power of Akzad." He declared haughtily. "Don't let us down."

He left as quickly as he had come in. I reluctantly opened the bag, not eager to see what kind of racing uniform Hishu had picked out for me. It was colored in the greens, whites, and golds of a typical acolyte's vestments, rather than the dull brother of an apprentice. Unsurprisingly, the costume looked skintight. There was padding but not in any places that would provide comfort. And there was a gapping hole in the chest, which also happened to be where a fair amount of the padding resided.

I hated it.

But I couldn't refuse to wear it. That Hishu would design the uniform had been a fight I had lost a long time ago. I had been expecting something a lot worse and had been prepared to argue against whatever he brought on the grounds it was impractical. Unfortunately, the formfitting aspect to it was a necessity. The cleavage hole was the only really objectionable part but my chest would be pressed down against my cycler during the race so that wouldn't actually catch any wind. Reluctantly, I donned it.

When I emerged from the bathroom, Jensen whistled. "You clean up nice. Makes me wish our regular acolyte robes were more...shapely."

Mateto also let out a low hiss that sounded similar. "Yes, I too enjoy the shape of your body and am given unholy thoughts of mating. This will help the people have positive feelings associate with the church."

I gaped at the pair of them. My look of astonishment was mirrored by Claren and, surprisingly, Jensen. We all just stared at Mateto for a moment before he realized what was happening. He slouched down at the onslaught.

"Did I do it again? Say something that was to remain unspoken?" He asked.

His look of shame reminded me of how he cowered during Hishu's classes. I didn't like Mateto's fawning devotion to the church, especially bullies like Hishu, but I also didn't like how the humans treated him just because he was nudra. It was the same way they treated me because I was uvoy.

"Yes, you did. But maybe that's not a bad thing. Because you're absolutely right. That is exactly why Hishu wanted me dressed like this." I said.

"Brother Hishu. We must respect our elders." Mateto squeaked and my moment of supporting him, despite his words, evaporated.

"I'm going to breakfast." I said in order to end the conversation.

Because I was up so early, the dining hall sat empty. The rest of the acolytes were taking full advantage of their chance to sleep in. The cooking staff had just begun preparing the morning meal. They looked surprised to see me when I went into the kitchen.

"Don't mind me. Just need to grab something to eat." I said by way of apology.

"We can prepare whatever you need, Holy One." Auran the cook said meekly.

I turned to the uvoy woman. She had to be twice my age yet she kept her eyes downcast and almost bowed before me. I had barely met any of the staff here, just eaten the meals that were prepared. In truth, I had originally thought cooking would be one of the apprentice's duties, and when it wasn't assumed, some of the acolytes did it as their form of service. When I had learned there was serving staff, I hadn't given it much thought, something I immediately regretted.

"You don't need to call me that. I'm just an apprentice." I said, and then kicked myself. It shouldn't matter that I was only an apprentice. "Just a regular uvoy like you."

"Begging your pardon, Sister, but you are blessed by Akzad."

"I'm really not." I said flatly but decided I wasn't going to win this argument. Not without ruining this poor woman's day. "I'll take whatever is easier. Sandwich. Porridge. Whatever you have one hand. I apologize for being up so early."

"No need to apologize." Auran said, her body loosening and her tone improving, "It is I who must apologize to you. We knew of your race today but failed to account for it with our preparations. We had Brother Hishu's meal prepared but he did not mention we should prepare anything for you."

"He wouldn't." I said under my breath. "No need to apologize. In truth, and no offense, but I would have preferred to go by Sanja's shop. If he was still alive and it was still open."

I suddenly felt very sad. I had missed the funeral for all those who died in the fires, having still been in the hospital. It would be a stretch to say any of them had been my friend, but I had seen and spoken to Sanja or his grandson Anisu almost every day. The smells of the fresh baked bread coming from the shop every morning had been a nice relief from the industrial smells in the garage.

"Oh, my dear, me too." The cook said, looking me in the eye for the first time. "Sanja was a dear friend. It is such a tragedy what happened. You were there that night. You and the others from the garage. You saved Anisu."

My cheeks flushed. The others had saved Anisu. I had gotten shot trying to get vengeance. They were the real heroes. But I didn't know how to explain that to this woman.

"My friends did yes."

"Now I remember. You were the one who got shot. Oh, my poor dear." Auran said and then snapped her fingers, issuing orders to the staff around her. The change in attitude in the kitchen was palpable. Before, there had been weariness and unease. They had been around a figure they considered holy but out of reach. Now I felt more like one of them but if anything, more worshiped.

I chatted with the cook while I ate a delicious egg sandwich. It was better than anything I had ever gotten from Sanja's, but I wasn't going to admit that out loud. It turned out most of the people working here had lost their homes in the fire. They were now either crammed into rooms with friends whose buildings hadn't been hit by the fires or had to move several blocks away.

"So, the Church took you on as an apprentice because of what you did to protect us?" Auran finally asked. I knew it would come up eventually.

"Um...something like that." I hedged but then shook my head. I hated half-truth BS. "In truth, joining as an apprentice was the only way to avoid going to jail. The Constabulary wanted to lock me up as one of the gang who set the fires."

"Typical." Auran said, "My nephew had to join the army to avoid going to jail. One of my cooks spent six months locked up for being robbed. Most of the people here could probably add their own stories."

Auran's resigned tone reminded me that my experience was hardly unique. The most dramatic to be sure, but nowhere near the most tragic. Maybe there was something to Allora's rigid opposition to the Constabulary.

"Why, I was once confronted by a gang in an alley but a masked figure saved me. When the cops showed up, they tried to shoot her instead of thanking her. That is something I never had the chance to do either." Auran added, giving me a pointed look.

I squirmed under her look, recalling the incident. Fortunately, Auran must have read the troubled expression on my face and decided to change the subject, "I saw you race at the Munsa Classic. You were good. You should have made the cut for the Major League. It's good the Church is sponsoring you for it."

I suppressed a sigh, "Yeah, it's going to be an interesting challenge."

"But now you'll have Akzad on your side." Auran said with an earnest expression. "You can't lose."

I smiled politely. We had swung all the way back around to where our conversation had started, and I took that as an opportunity to leave. I thanked her and then left the Church for the garage. It felt good to have at least this much freedom again.

At the garage, I found a quadcyler parked out front, with my racing cycler in the cargo bed. Inside, Nerpi was pacing around the garage. He had removed his sling sometime in the past few days and he now raised his hands up in exasperation when he saw me.

"You're late."

I shrugged, "I had to eat breakfast."

"We need to go. The cycler is already loaded." Nerpi grabbed my arm and pulled me outside toward the quadcycler.

"Yeah, about that. What's with the quadcyler? Why aren't we just riding down to the arena?"

"Because Grant loaned it to us for the day. It's a racing cycler, not a street cycler. We need to keep it in pristine condition for the race."

I raised an eyebrow. "We always used to ride it over there before."

"Well, now we're professional racers. We must do things properly." Nerpi said primly.

"Uh huh."

I climbed into the cab of the quad, letting Nerpi take the wheel since it looked sized for an eowian. I wasn't that much taller than Nerpi, but my legs were a lot longer as eowians had a much bigger torso. Before he started up the engine a hand pushed me from the doorway. I looked over to see Allora trying to shove me over, so I scooted to the middle of the cab.

"What the hell are you wearing?" Allora asked.

"My uniform." I said with as much contempt as possible.

"Hishu's decision I assume?"

"Indeed."

We rode quickly through the empty streets until we neared the arena. There crowds had already started to gather and we were forced to slow. For the first time, I looked at the surge of people converging on the giant arena. There were a lot. Tens of thousands could fit inside if I remembered correctly. Granted there were only two large arenas in a city which was home to most of our world's population, but it was still a sizeable percentage. And they would all soon be watching me.

Once through the gates Nerpi parked the quad and I rolled my cycler inside. We were far from the first group of racers there and I had to weave the heavy, unpowered cycler through the throngs. It wasn't the hardest thing to do but I often had to stop to make small talk with fellow racers.

"Well, well, well, looks like you found a way to race against me up here in the majors after all." Hann said as he approached. Unlike our previous meetings, he didn't have his usual friendly smile. We had always been on good terms, so his look of distaste felt extra uncomfortable.

"Um, yeah, I guess. How are you doing, Hann?"

"I'm good. Certainly not as good as you though. Ms. Acolyte. Church's new golden child." Hann sneered.

I cocked my head, "The Church's what?"

Hann gestured up and down and I looked down at my uniform. My cheeks paled and ears quivered in embarrassment. "This wasn't my idea."

"But you're wearing it. I thought better of you than this. You scoffed at the Church and how they were worming their way into the sport. You raced hard. I thought you deserved a place in the majors and would earn it someday. But you sold out to the Church for a quick ride to the top."

I shriveled some at his lecture. What he accused me of wasn't even true. But that didn't mean it didn't hurt. If Hann, who normally thought the best of everyone, thought this about me, then everyone would surely feel the same, or worse. I could try to explain to him why I was doing it, but that would involve a lot of details about my life that I didn't feel like sharing. I wanted to keep that Knightshield nonsense as far away from my life as possible.

Instead, I just looked down, not meeting Hann's eyes. Maybe he would think me chastised and let up. To his credit, Hann did stop and unlike many of the others would, didn't look pleased with himself.

"Yeah, well, good race." He mumbled and walked away.

I pushed my cycler the rest of the way to my holding slot without any more confrontations. If Hann had turned against me, I was not looking forward to meeting Mallis, who had previously stated he would never let a woman into the majors. But he was also super devoted, so that confrontation might actually be more fun.

The racers around me nodded but didn't approach. They were all long-time major's racers who I had heard of but never met. Their nods weren't hostile, but nor were they inviting. I couldn't be sure if that was because I was racing for the Church or was a woman. Or uvoy. Not a lot of us raced.

I stood there alone long enough that I started to wonder if Nerpi and Allora had gotten lost. He had never had to park a quad before and might be finding it hard to find a spot. Given this was a cycler arena there wasn't a lot of room to park other vehicles nearby.

"Pardon me, my lady. Are you not new here?" An imperious voice said behind me.

I turned to see a human man in a well to do suit with a big rose on his lapel. He had a bushy beard down his cheeks that didn't go down to his chin, which looked rather ridiculous. He leaned away from me with his gut sticking out and his arms resting on his hips.

"Um, yeah, first time in the majors." I said.

"Capital! I do say, it is most exhilarating to see a new racer to the game. Especially one as lovely as you."

I let out a disgusted sigh and turned away, hoping he would get the hint. I didn't think the Church would like me decking anyone before the race even began.

"I hear you're one of the fastest, most bestest racers ever though." The accent changed to the man's voice to a far more yokel dialect. Then it changed again to a laid back droll, "Whose a bit of a badass sometimes."

I swiveled back to the man and looked at him again. This time I looked past the posture and the distracting beard and at his eyes. "En!"

"Well, I guess you know now, that's not my real name." En said and his imperious posture slouched.

"We always suspected. Your last movie was being advertised before every race. Plus there were posters everywhere." I said.

"Oh. Yeah. I never thought about that." En said, with that same confuddled expression he had often worn.

"Am I glad to see a friendly face." I said, "The attitude around here has not been the friendliest. But what are you doing here? We tried to reach out to you but were rebuffed."

"Yeah, my dad wasn't too thrilled when he had to bail me out of jail. Said my little stunt of rebellion was over. He never got that it wasn't rebellion. It was practice. I had to live like a commoner in order to become that role."

I raised an eyebrow and said flatly. "How enlightened."

"See!" En said exasperated, "It's so easy for his condescending attitude to just leak into everything. I didn't think common people were stupid. I had to get away to learn."

"So, you decided to slum it with us?" I asked, my previous elation slipping toward annoyance.

"Yes. No. Maybe." En said dejectedly and my annoyance evaporated. He had never told us what he was doing working in Nerpi's garage despite being a big name actor but he had never acted like a rich asshole. A regular asshole sometimes but so did we all.

"Well, it's good to see you. Have you talked to Nerpi or Allora yet? They should be getting here. They should have been here by now. It looks like the opening ceremony is about to start." I said, glancing out the rampway toward the central stage. The minor league racers were already starting to line up on the track.

"I'm not sure they'll want to talk to me."

"Nonsense. Like I said, we already knew about your other life. You might just want to stick to 'researching a role' as an explanation. Keep it simple."

Behind me, the speakers boomed to life and the opening music played. The board of commissioners came out onto the stage, accompanied by Hishu and to my surprise, Benthic. While he had been coordinating this venture into racing for the Church with Hishu, he had made clear his distaste for the idea. I wondered why he had agreed to go out on stage.

I stood with En in companionable silence while we listened to the usual opening day drivel. Good clean fun. Racing for glory and Akzad. Etc. etc. Before the commissioner turned the microphone over to Hishu for a prayer, a grunde man stormed onto the stage and shoved the commissioner aside. He held a large staff in one hand and took the microphone in the other.

"Nobody move! This arena is now under the control of the Grunde Liberation Front! Remain calm and no one gets hurt!"

At his words, two more grunde appeared inside the garage, each sporting rifles and pointing them at us.

Chapter 20

I glanced between En and the two armed grunde. I had faced off against armed thugs many times by this point. But I had never been in a hostage situation before. Nor had I fought anyone since getting shot. I no longer had my shield, both metaphorically and literally.

Outside on the stage, the grunde there planted his staff down hard against the wooden floor. The jewel at the top of the staff flashed a brilliant blue light and a melodious ring sounded throughout the arena. The crowd of spectators that had just begun to surge in sudden panic stopped moving. All eyes fell on the grunde who leaned into the microphone and started monologuing to the filled arena, "Long have we been oppressed by the entrenched powers in the city. A city that is supposed to be a united home for all of us on this planet. But is it? Why are there no grunde on the city's ruling council? Why no uvoy or nudra either? Why are we confined to the outskirts of the city, living in dilapidated buildings, slaving for poverty wages? Most of our people live outside this grand city of unity, in small towns working dangerous jobs, but still controlled by the powerful members of this city. Long have we been subjugated, but no longer!"

The grunde turned slightly and I lost sight of his glowing staff. "Damn it." I hissed.

En whispered, "What?"

"I'm not sure I disagree with the hostage takers."

"Well, yeah, of course you agree with the hostage takers. They have a point." En said with a nonchalant shrug. I looked at him with a look of surprise and he continued, "People don't do something big and showy like this unless they want attention. They aren't going to get any money out of

145

it. As a member of a similarly oppressed social class, you would naturally be more inclined to agree with their stance."

"Are you saying I should support these guys?" I asked.

"Nah. They're just going to invite a show of force by the constabulary and a bunch of people are going to get killed. That's something you're against. I think. You usually beat people up so it's a little uncertain what you really think about violence, but I don't think you hurt people for the fun of it. I know you hate guns." En said, some of his more familiar attitude slipping in.

I growled at the realization En had a point. A month ago, I would have argued with him, imagining the professional manner my father would have handled this. But after my recent encounters with the Constabulary, Allora's frank opinion, and my conversation with Auran just this morning, I wasn't sure they would handle it the same way. If the Constabulary did show up, they might very well come in guns blazing. It wouldn't matter that these hostage takers had a point. Or that they had, as of yet, not actually hurt anyone. They would probably see grunde with guns and there could be only one response to that. Shoot first.

"I guess it's up to us then." I said.

"What's this 'us' nonsense?" En squeaked.

"You think I should take on all of these guys on my own?"

"Sure. I've seen you fight more. Besides, you don't need to take them all down. Just enough to open a way out of the arena. There're far too many people here for these guys to contain if they start moving."

"Quiet!" One of the armed grunde shouted. He gestured with his rifle toward En and me. We sheepishly put up our hands and stopped talking, which seemed to mollify him.

Was En right? Could I, by myself, do something about this? I didn't see how. Sure, he had a point about the numbers. Taking down the two guarding us might be possible, but there were a lot of people who could die if these guys starting shooting.

The real question was whether or not I thought I should do it. Every time I had tried to do something, I had only made it worse. Avenging my mother had gotten my father killed. Going after ECG had gotten a bunch of innocent people killed, including a child and an old sandwich maker.

While I still wasn't a fan of the Church, I couldn't fault all of their lessons. And I had been subjected to a lot of them in recent weeks. One that stood out was that intention mattered. "If your heart lies with Akzad, your actions can not be truly evil". There were some interpretations of that quote I found troubling, the bit that stuck with me was that you had to have compassion and understanding for others. If someone did something wrong, but with good intentions, they could, at least, attempt to rectify their mistake. Those that did good but had evil intentions, only did good by accident.

Would my good intentions make any difference to the people who died as a result? Would that be any different than the actions of the Constabulary? Some of them would rush in here eager to kill some bad guys but at least some of them would be shooting with the intention of saving people. Was there a difference between those assholes and what I had been doing?

As I warred with myself and my uncertainty, En took away my choice. He stood up and strode cockily toward the exit. The two grunde shouted at him to sit down and they both moved toward him to force their point. For a moment, they both had their backs to me. My indecision vanished in the face of opportunity. If I did nothing now, En was going to get beaten and or shot.

I pulled my wraspisa off my head and hurled it toward the grunde furthest away from me. It wasn't my shield but it was still a circular metal object. As it was a bit heavier than my shield, it would probably hurt a lot more to get hit by. The wraspisa wobbled through the air, its shape less even, and almost missed the grunde, but did clip his shoulder, causing him to drop his rifle with the sudden numbing of his arm.

While it flew, I leaped up, springing across the distance to the other one in a burst. I landed on his back, knocking him down. We both tumbled to the ground, but I was ready for it and sprang back to my feet immediately. I kicked out with my foot, sending his rifle sliding across the floor into his companion's rifle, causing both to jumble up together and move further away from either grunde.

I pivoted from that kick and slammed my booted foot into the back of the grunde I had landed on. He grunted and scrunched up. I kicked again for good measure, using the motion to propel myself into a backflip over top of the second grunde, who by now had turned to engage me. He spun around to follow my motion but misjudged my position and swung his fists over the top of my crouching form. Being small has its advantages.

I kicked back and landed a blow into his exposed torso and then rotated. As I did, I smacked one foot across the grunde's face and grabbed his outstretched arm with both my hands. I continued my spin, pulling him along with me. Again, we both went down to the ground, but he had a lot further to fall than I did. I continued to twist his arm and felt the socket pop and he let out a roar of pain.

With him down, and probably out with his arm now disabled, I stood up. The whole action had taken only a handful of seconds and most of the assembled cycler racers were still staring transfixed at the grunde on the stage. The rest of them were staring at me wide eyed. Their shock lasted only a second before a few rushed forward to grab the downed grunde and ensure they wouldn't be any more of a threat.

Two of the racers picked up the downed rifles. "Now we take out the rest of these scum bags!"

This time I didn't hesitate. I crossed the distance over to them and yanked the rifles out of their hands. I quickly expelled their magazines and then disassembled them, before tossing the pieces to various corners of the room. The two racers looked at me incredulous.

"What the hell did you do that for? Now we're unarmed! How are we going to protect ourselves?"

"By leaving. Guns have one and only one purpose. To kill." I ordered.

"Sometimes that's the only way to protect yourself." One sneered at me.

"Sometimes. But now is not one of those times. We're not going to get the rest of the people out of this by killing anyone. Lead everyone down here and out through the garage."

Hann stepped forward and imposed himself between me and the two angry racers. "Getting tens of thousand of people out through one exit is going to take forever. They are going to be able to respond and stop them."

"They won't. Their attention is going to be on something else."

"Yeah, you mean that staff? I couldn't help staring at it."

I smiled, "No. Me."

I turned back to the open door that led to the arena and the center stage. "Oh, and one more thing. Start praying."

"For what? Salvation?" Hann asked.

"For fruit."

I looked across the wide expanse of space between me and the central stage. Unfortunately, today's race was to be one of speed and endurance rather than obstacles. The track had been laid out as just an oval, no switchbacks or mounds to traverse. That left nothing but open space between me and the hostages on the center stage. There was no way I could get close without being noticed.

I tried to gauge the distance but could only conclude I couldn't leap that far. If I got a running start, maybe they wouldn't notice me right away. Maybe I could get close enough that a final leap would get me inside their line of fire. A whole lot of maybes.

I stood at the edge of the garage watching for what felt like an eternity. I had retrieved my wraspisa and hefted it in my hands. During my leap, I would be vulnerable and they would have time to react. Either shooting me or one of the hostages. I needed something to distract them, hopefully remove their weapons as a threat. Normally, I would toss my shield. But this was far too heavy to use for that. Midflight, I wouldn't have any leverage to throw it far or fast enough to arrive much before me.

That's why I wanted Hann praying for fruit. Despite my failure to Manifest the fruit bowl during training, it was the only thing I could think of doing. In theory, I could Manifest the fruit midflight, meaning I wouldn't have to carry the weight during my leap and summon as much as I needed. I could hurl fruit at a good clip, even while in the air, yet it would be heavy enough to hurt or at least distract. I just had to actually do it.

I closed my eyes and concentrated. Unlike in training, I could feel something this time. It wasn't like during a worship service. I had felt that energy before and this was similar but different. I suppose, with their lives threatened, a lot of people were praying, but not specifically for fruit.

Hishu claimed that didn't matter. Regardless of what people prayed for, opening themselves up to Akzad provided the power acolytes could use. It was up to the acolyte to mold the power of faith. They needed to take the power and to exert their will on it.

Maybe that didn't mean I had to make fruit. He had demonstrated by making a golden ring. Maybe I could make a shield. Benthic said that Relics were Manifestations that persisted beyond forever. So far, the only thing the current crop of acolytes could make that did that was the fruit. Hishu's ring had evaporated before the end of class. But I didn't need a shield to last forever. Just until I had saved those people.

I concentrated on what I wanted. A shield like mine. I ran through the mantra Hishu had taught. I was the vessel of Akzad. I was his instrument on the physical plain. The power of the faithful was mine to shape. I deserved this power because my faith was stronger. My will was Akzad's will.

I needed this to happen. Despite failing at first, I kept trying. I kept repeating the mantra. The power swirled around me, drawn to me, but just out of reach. What was I doing wrong?

A gunshot and screams of panic brought me back to the present moment. All around the arena, the crowds were moving. A surge of people were pushing toward the exits. Panic hadn't quite set in yet, but it might soon. Behind me, the flow of people out the exit filled the space. The gunfire signaled either the hostage takers had noticed and were trying to regain control, or the Constabulary had arrived. It was now or never for me to act. The people in the arena outnumbered those threatening them. Their sheer numbers would protect them. Those in the center didn't.

Without another thought, I pushed forward across the racetrack. Hopefully, they would be distracted and not notice me. I continued to recite the mantra in my head. Part way across the field, my luck ran out and one of the grunde pointed at me and lifted his rifle in my direction. I was still further from the stage than I had ever leaped before, but I didn't have a choice now. I pushed off with my tight, springy muscles and launched myself into the air. I had to save these people. To give up was to deny who I was.

As I sailed into the air, the rifle cracks sounded, and puffs of dirt exploded from the ground near where I had been. That saved me from the initial barrage, but I could no longer accelerate while in the air so would only get slower the closer I got to the grunde. Maybe I couldn't make a shield appear, but some fruit might be enough to save my, and everyone else's, lives.

To my astonishment, an apple appeared in my outstretched hand. I blinked at it for only a second before cocking my arm back and whipping the apple forward as fast as I could. I had the advantage of my biology behind me. The same dense, springy musculature the let us uvoy leap great distances, also gave us one hell of a throwing arm.

The apple rocketed across the distance and hit the grunde firing at me directly on his shoulder. His arm must have gone numb because he immediately dropped the rifle and his arm now hung limply at his side. His face contorted in pain, and he grabbed for the dead limb with his other.

I shifted my attention to another of the grunde and felt a second apple appear in my hand. I threw this one across a shorter distance but with the same powerful throw. This time I hit the grunde in the chest and he toppled backwards, probably more from the shock of the painful impact than the force, but it did bring a smile to my face.

By this time, I had almost completed my leap and I came in hard, tucking into a somersault as I landed to help bleed away some of the force. I would have bruises tomorrow. Hopefully, that would be all I had to heal from.

I rolled across the stage and came up next to the central grunde, the one who had given the speech. He looked at me, his mouth agape, one hand on the staff. I wasted no time in ripping the staff from his hands, twisting around to smack the final grunde standing on the stage in the head with it, and then all the way back around to knock him down.

My swing had lost a lot of power after hitting the first, so the leader was not badly hit by my blow. He lay on the ground, cowering but alert. His eyes looked betrayed more than angry.

"Why would you do this? We were fighting for your people as well." He asked.

"Your goals were good but your methods not so much." I said. "Threatening a stadium full of innocent people wasn't going to win you any friends."

"It was the only way to get anyone's attention. Everyone is so beaten down, overworked, underpaid, they don't have the time or opportunity to learn about the chains that hold them back. We had to get that message to them."

"Not through threat of violence. There are other ways." I insisted.

His face twisted into a snarl, "Like you do? Wearing the clothes of our oppressors and doing their bidding?"

I blinked down at him unsure how to respond. It was only then, in the silence that I noticed there was silence. Hesitantly, I looked up and saw the crowds had stopped fleeing. They were all watching me, standing over the grunde who had threatened them. It was only then I realized the microphone, which stood right next to us, was still on and our entire conversation had been projected to everyone in the arena.

My eyes bulged and I felt my blood pressure drop. I felt cold and trapped, despite standing in the middle of a wide-open area, hundreds of meters away from the stadium seats. I stood there paralyzed.

Behind me, a gentle hand touched my shoulder and I jumped. I didn't react like I would in a fight. I moved back, terrified of whatever it was that had touched me. Fortunately, it was only the kind face of Benthic who smiled at me. He squeezed my shoulder and nodded to me.

"Breathe, Kali. It is okay." He said.

I nodded absently and made no move to stop him when he stepped forward, taking the staff from me in one hand and the microphone in his other. "My fellow children of Akzad, rejoice. Your moment of terror is over. Akzad has sent his champion to protect you. An acolyte of his church. His Knightshield."

Around me the arena erupted in cheers.

Chapter 21

Unsurprisingly, the race got rescheduled for the following week. Not only was everything a mess, with half the attendees still fleeing from the arena, and the Constabulary trying to swarm in through the crowds, many of the racer's cyclers got banged up in the fleeing crowds. I had suggested they leave that way, so it was kind of my fault, which earned me a few disgruntled looks from some of the racers.

Hishu and Benthic took charge of speaking to the Constabulary, which allowed me to leave the way I came, with Nerpi and Allora. I had some questions for Benthic regarding his little speech at the end but that could wait. For now, I was relieved to find my friends had gotten through the incident unharmed. En hadn't stuck around but he had had a way out, so I felt he was safe.

"How'd he fair?" I asked Nerpi when I made it to the racer garage. Nerpi was bent over, inspecting every last detail of the cycler.

"Everything looks to be intact. Some scuff marks, a small dent in the tail pipe where it smacked into the floor. But no signs of major damage." Nerpi said not looking up. He waved his hand behind him, "We were lucky. I heard a few had their front tires bent and some throttle control wires snapped. Who knew mad rushes of people could do so much damage."

I cringed a bit at this news. Now those dirty looks made a bit more sense. We weren't just talking about cosmetic damage. But at least they would have a week to make repairs.

"I saw En." I said and this prompted Nerpi to finally look up.

"Here? When? Where?"

"Before the race. Well, before the incident. He was pretending to be some big race sponsor. Or maybe that wasn't a costume." I said, thinking about En's fancy suit. He was a rich actor in truth, that was probably closer to his usual appearance than what he had worn at the shop.

"Maybe he's not too good for us after all." Nerpi said.

"I got the impression staying away hasn't been his choice. Though why his father gets to decide for him I don't get. He's older than I am. And has his own name to trade on."

Nerpi shrugged, "We can't know what's going on with his life or understand the relationship between him and his father. I am going to take it as a good sign that he came to see you."

"Speaking of which, do you know where Allora is? I've been meaning to talk to her but haven't had the chance to really talk to her since I went into the church."

"She's getting the quad. With the crowds and everyone else trying to pack up, I expect you'll be able to catch up to her. It's parked a long way down to the left." Nerpi gestured.

I nodded and headed out of the garage, trying to remember what the quad looked like. There were so many in the parking area and were all big and ugly. Fortunately, there was a long line of them stuck attempting to all move at once, so I had no trouble dodging traffic. I walked down the line of them, glancing into the cabs at the driver. About halfway down I found the one with Allora in it.

I climbed into the cab through the passenger door and suddenly didn't know what to say. I had had so many questions since my training began that I had wanted to get Allora's take on. Now that I finally had a chance to speak with her, I didn't know where to begin.

"Where'd you get the apples?" Allora asked, breaking the silence.

"I Manifested them." I said with a big grin. "It's the first time it worked."

"Were you repeating the mantra?"

I sighed, "Yes. I found it creepy at first, but I finally decided to give in and use it. And it worked this time."

"Well, you should stop." Allora said bluntly.

Her vehemence shook me. My excitement floundered. I had assumed she would be excited for me. This was the one part of church nonsense I found valuable. Well, this and Relics but they were kind of the same thing.

"Why? I finally got it to work."

"That mantra will turn you into an asshole."

I shrugged, "It is fairly cringey. But if that's what it takes..."

Allora turned in her seat and held a finger up to me, "That's how it starts. I used to think that way. But the longer I've been out, the more I've seen the harm the church does without any of the benefits."

"Then why did you send me in there?" I blurted.

"You hated the church. I thought that would protect you. Now look at you. Defending their selfish ritual."

I felt my face boil with heat, and I directed a murderous look at Allora, "I am not some sort of church stooge. You told me to go there and not get myself kicked out. I can't do that and fight them on everything."

Allora let out a heavy sigh, "I know. I shouldn't have said it like that. I just hate that mantra so much. The church is supposed to be a force for good. And it still is in a lot of ways. I try remind myself of that. But that mantra undermines everything."

I still felt anger boiling but I kept my mouth closed for a minute until my brain could do the talking. "If you don't like the mantra, how do you manifest?"

"I don't. Technically, I am not supposed to while on sabbatical, but I also didn't when I was there." Allora said.

"But you do some kind of spooky magic. You healed me super-fast after mumbling something. Don't think I didn't notice." I said pointing a finger at Allora. "But then, I guess, that's not really manifestation? Unless you summoned new skin or something."

Allora let out a chuckle, "No, I did not manifest new skin for you. Your healing baffles me. Yes, I do pray for injuries and sometimes my patients recover quicker than normal. But not like that. A knife wound healing over night? That's never happened."

"Never? If I heal super-fast then why was I in the hospital for weeks after getting shot?" I asked.

"There's a big difference between a stab wound in the shoulder and a gunshot to the lungs. Without medical care you would have died. And two weeks in the hospital and another few with some discomfort IS fast. You should still be healing now, not racing cyclers or beating up terrorists."

I thought about my time healing and could only recall the pain and discomfort. I found it hard to imagine every day I had spent since leaving the hospital being like those days. "So, are you better at this magic healing thing than you think, or do I have some kind of magic healing?"

Allora scoffed, "It's not magic. It is related to Akzad and Manifestation. I just don't know how. I wish I did. I wish I had more direct control over it. I could help so many more people if I could control it better. Medicine can only do so much."

We lapsed into silence. My hopes of getting answers from Allora died in that silence. She didn't know much more than I did. I would have to continue to rely on the elder acolytes in the church to learn more.

It took an agonizing amount of time, but we finally were able to pick up Nerpi and get the quad headed back toward the garage. When we got back, we found a surprise waiting for us inside. En sat in his usual seat at the reception desk. Aside from the fancy clothes he had been wearing earlier, he looked much the same as he used to, sitting in the chair with his feet propped up, snoring loudly.

Nerpi walked right up to him and shoved his feet off the desk, "I've told you to keep your feet off the desk."

En jerked awake and tumbled out of the chair. He stood up, his face blinking with sleep, "You weren't open."

"Which raised another question, how did you get in here? I changed the locks." Nerpi said.

"I picked them. It wasn't hard. You need better ones." En said, his accent was again moody and dopey like it had always sounded before. This contrasted with his fancy suit and instead of giving the impression of a bored slacker, he came off as a whiny rich boy. Which, I supposed, was probably closer to the truth.

"You're late for work." Nerpi added, "But I suppose, you never needed the job so I won't feel bad for firing you."

"Actually, I did need the money. I was here entirely on my own, I didn't have access to my family's fortune." En said.

"You're a big movie star, apparently, what about your own money?" Allora asked.

En shrugged, "It all goes into a trust. I don't get to see most of it. For my own good my father says. Keeps me from blowing it on drugs and women."

"He may have a point." I said with a teasing smile, "You did blow most of your pay on coffee."

"Something I haven't had today, hence my sleeping." En said.

We all migrated up to the second floor and to what had been our communal kitchen before. It must be very roomy up here with just Nerpi and Allora now, though having spent the last few weeks at the church and its massive buildings, I recognized just how tiny the place was. With all four of us squeezed in again it felt almost suffocating.

After the coffee had been made, En gestured around, "You all must be wondering why I have called you here today."

"Not really." Allora answered.

"This is my house, I invited you here and I'm beginning to wonder why." Nerpi added.

En continued without acknowledging them, "Well, it is time I told you the wonderful news that is going to change your life. I am back."

We all sat there, silently watching En. He glanced between all of us, clearing expecting some kind of response but as I didn't quite understand what he meant, I didn't know how to respond. "What, you want your old job back? Nerpi just fired you."

"He didn't mean it."

"Yes, I did."

"But no, I don't want my old job back. I am back now, as myself, as you requested. I will be your team's spokesman."

I leaned back in my chair and tilted my head, "You said your father wanted you to have nothing more to do with us. You told me this just a few hours ago."

"Yeah, well, then you went and saved a bunch of people from terrorists, in front of a large crowd. Things have changed. Now he wants me mooching your fame for myself, instead of you trying to mooch some fame from me."

Allora shook her head, "You need to work on your sales pitch."

En waved his hand, "Obviously that's not what he said. But that is what he wants. I don't care though. It gave me cover to come here."

"You know, En, you're a grown up. You're allowed to come visit anytime you want." I said.

"This way will be less suspicious."

"Less suspicious than what?"

"Then me coming here without an excuse."

"I mean why would it be suspicious? Who would care? Your father? Why would you care?"

En just shrugged without saying another word. We moved past it and for the first time in a long while, I had a pleasant afternoon.

Chapter 22

When I returned to the church, I was fortunate to find the apprentice rooms empty. I didn't waste that opportunity and went straight to sleep. Falling asleep in a room alone was a luxury. I hadn't thought to get more than a nap, but it wasn't until the chimes for dawn service that I woke up. Either I had been more exhausted than I thought, or my bunkmates had shown some curtesy when they had come to bed.

Groggily, I stumbled behind the privacy screen that had been set up for me in order to get dressed. My being awake but out of line of sight apparently was the go signal because immediately Mateto started calling out questions to me. He wasn't shy about asking questions most times, except before I dressed in the morning.

"Did you really beat up some terrorists at the race yesterday, Kali? They had a hundred grunde with swords and machine guns who vowed to kill everyone? And then you called upon Akzad to bless your hand and you rained fruit on them from the skies?"

I sighed but not loudly. "That's one way of putting it. But there were only like a dozen guys, just with regular rifles, and spread out. I only fought four of them. The rest ran when the crowd stopped being afraid. Why so many questions? Weren't you there to see it?"

"Why would we have been there? Cycler racing is an excuse for hicks to get drunk and waste their money. No offense." Jensen said with a sneer I didn't have to see to hear.

Instead of engaging him in an argument, that he was definitely trying to provoke, I feinted, "I'm surprise is all. I figured you would be a big racing fan now that Brother Hishu is leading the efforts to get the church involved in racing."

"Brother Hishu agrees with me." Jensen scoffed, "Racing is for the low brow. Which is exactly the people the church needs to reach out more to save their souls, hence this initiative. But that doesn't mean we need to watch the monotonous sport. How can anyone enjoy watching people ride around in circles?"

"There's a lot more to it than riding in circles. Only some of the races are endurance races. Many are obstacle courses and there are skill challenges." I snapped at him, feeling defensive, though, to myself, had to admit I had thought much the same thing at first.

"Semantics." Jensen said with a dismissive wave.

"Regardless," Claren said, verbally interposing himself between us, "We will be late for morning service if we don't get moving. We have community service to prepare for after that."

As much as I detested these services, I welcomed the opportunity to stop talking. I didn't want to argue with Jensen that racing was actually cool nor did I want to answer any more of Mateteo's questions. As I came out from behind the privacy screen, I could see the questions bubbling inside him, so I followed Claren out the door and quickly to the chapel.

I sat through the normal morning routine, intoning the responses and songs as required. I'd gotten pretty good at being able to do that without having to pay attention. But today I did focus on the words. Maybe there would be some other insights to how this magic worked in something besides the mantra.

No revelations came to me and when the service ended, the High Acolyte stood up. As this was a service day, all of the acolytes were in attendance this morning. He would make assignments for the service before we all dispersed. Us apprentices typically did all the dirty work to prepare and then hid in the basement. So, I was surprised when the High Acolyte called me out by name.

"Apprentice Kali will join us on the dais today for the Manifestation." All eyes shifted to me and I shifted uncomfortably. The room felt very crowded with all the acolytes here, even though it could still comfortably hold a few dozen more people.

"Um...uh...thank you...your excellency." I stammered, unsure how I was supposed to respond. It did the trick though, as everyone turned back to the high acolyte and he finished assigning tasks. I breathed a sigh of relief at no longer being the center of attention, but it didn't last long. I would have to spend the entire service on the central dais with the senior acolytes, watched by the hundreds of attendees.

When the meeting broke up, I turned to face my fellow apprentices and ran into a wall of disapproving glares. They had never been exactly welcoming to me, they had had started to soften. This morning's line of questioning, even Jensen's sneers, had been friendly and showed some camaraderie.

"What?" I asked.

"Now we see it." Jensen snarled, "You're the new golden child. Becoming the poster acolyte for the racers could make sense. But this stunt with the terrorists and now getting to participate in the worship service. What's your game? Which brother are you sleeping with?"

I felt dumbfounded by the hostility. I looked at Claren, who had been the kindest to me and even he frowned at me. "What are you talking about? How does that even make any sense? You think I'm shagging an acolyte in order to earn the right to fight terrorists at a racetrack?"

"No, you're doing it to get special permissions. We've been trainees for months longer than you and only Claren has been honored with a chance to participate in the Manifestation. And he knows how to do it. You've never succeeded before."

"I did. Once. In order to throw an apple at the guys with guns." I said defensively and threw up my hands, "I don't want to do this. You're right. I can't reliably Manifest anything. I don't want to fail in front of a crowd. I don't even want to be in front of a crowd."

The three of them continued to stare at me but their expressions did soften a little, if only for a moment. Jensen turned his into a sneer. "You expect us to believe that? You don't want the prestige? You? The glory hound slut?"

I pivoted to Jensen, and before I could think, my arm was pulling back to strike him. But a sharp voice brought me up just before I could release. Benthic's voice called out my name.

I kept my eyes on Jensen and held my fist for several seconds. Now that I had a moment to think, I didn't want to hit him and felt bad that I had reacted that way. My father had always taught me that violence was a tool of last resort. We should never hesitate to employ it when necessary, but we should never relish in its use, and always regret the necessity. Jensen wasn't an actual threat to me. He had just pissed me off. I felt that regret now. Yet I also felt powerful at the look of sudden fear in his eyes.

Lowering my fist, I turned around to Benthic. Most of the acolytes had dispersed by now so almost no one had seen what had been about to happen amongst us apprentices. But I knew that didn't matter. Benthic had seen. And if I cared about anyone's opinion among the members of the church, it was his.

When I reached Benthic, he spoke quietly, with a firm but kind tone, "Things are about to get a lot harder for you, young Kali. You became a public figure yesterday to a much greater extent than just another racer, or just another acolyte. Your actions will be judged and emulated. You must strive to set a good example. Something we all must attempt but now you must work twice as hard."

"Why?" I asked impulsively and when Benthic frowned, I attempted to clarify, "I mean, why am I a public figure? So, I fought some thugs with guns yesterday. I've done that a bunch of times before."

"But never in the open. You wore a mask and stopped crimes in the darkness of night. You wore no mask yesterday. You wore the banner of the church. So now, everything you do reflects on all of us. Brawling with your fellow apprentices is not you. What kind of message does that send?"

I sighed, "The wrong kind."

"You must work harder to make sure your every action is the correct one. You cannot react on instinct or emotion."

"That's what I did yesterday." I said.

Benthic smiled, "What you yesterday was to be led by Akzad's will. He used you as an instrument to save everyone in that arena."

"Felt a lot of like an emotional reaction to bullies."

"Think about that emotion. Did it not feel very similar to what you just felt toward Jensen when he insulted you? Anger. Contempt. The need to lash out." Benthic asked.

I shrugged, "Maybe. I don't know."

"The emotions you cannot control. You can only control your actions. They cannot be your guide. Only Akzad."

I let out a grunt of frustration, "I didn't sense Akzad guiding me yesterday either. Or any other time."

"Nevertheless, he did. Otherwise, you wouldn't have been able to Manifest the fruit."

The mention of the fruit reminded me of what had precipitated the argument with Jensen. "I don't know how I did that either. I can't do it on stage, in front of everyone. Why did the high acolyte pick me to participate?"

"It was Hishu's suggestion. He wants to capitalize on your actions yesterday before the people. Grow your popularity among the people. If they know they can see the famous racer and hero during services, they'll be more likely to come."

"Something I don't think you disagree with." I said flatly.

"Not entirely." Benthic admitted, "But I think it was premature to get you participating in the Manifestation. I think that was also deliberate. If you fail, he wants it to be publicly and soon. Then his stance that women shouldn't be acolytes will have more weight. This is a win win from his perspective."

"What do I do?"

"Trust in Akzad. Practice what you have been taught. Channel the people's faith. You may find it easier seeing them and their faith on display then when you practice in the basement. You will be able to harness and direct that power. It will not feel as wrong when you see how freely it is given by the people."

I returned to my pre-service duties after that, working silently with the others. The tasks were simple, if monotonous. Bookmarking prayer books, lighting candles, setting out pamphlets, preparing the bowls. By the time we finished, it was almost time to open the doors to the church.

We all headed to rectory to don our ceremonial vestments before the full acolytes. Before I went through the door, I reached out and touched Jensen's shoulder. He flinched at my touch, and I felt like I had taken a solid kick to my gut.

"Jensen, I'm sorry I threatened you earlier. What you said was horrible but not an excuse to hit you."

A perplexed expression crossed Jensen's face. It sat there for a moment but was soon replaced by his usual disgust. "You expect me to believe that? You who beat people up on the streets for fun before coming here to avoid jail? You think I believe you didn't want to hit me?"

I flinched, "No, I did want to hit you. But it wouldn't have been the right thing to do. Yes, I have done far worse than just punch people. I only do those things to save lives. To help people. Violence is terrible."

"You really are a hypocrite."

"Maybe."

My admission left him staring at me, a response hanging unsaid on his lips. I continued, "You might be right. I might be a hypocrite. I don't think using my fighting skills to stop others from hurting people is the wrong thing to do. But then, do the people I stop think what they are doing is wrong? Sometimes, I wish I could believe as strongly as you do and trust my actions were guided by Akzad's will. But I can't help but feel that every time I throw a punch, Akzad's will has already failed. He failed to teach a scumbag that rape is wrong. He failed to teach a corrupt boss that his employees are actually people. He failed to not oppress those grunde and beat them down so much that they felt their only options for life to get better was to threaten a crowd of people."

I threw up my hands. "Yes, I think violence is wrong but use it to stop more violence. I am a hypocrite. But that doesn't mean threatening to hit you earlier wasn't wrong. And I apologize for it."

Jensen looked at me for a long moment. He finally nodded his head and turned away, going into the room. I don't know what the nod signified. Acceptance of the apology. Acknowledgement I had offered it. Or just that he was done talking to me. But I couldn't force him to forgive me. Nor could I force him to admit his own faults.

We changed and then gathered at the doors to guide people into the worship center. The acolytes all stood at the doors to offer blessings and receive people's prostrations. Something I felt glad I didn't have to participate in that. The idea of people bowing to me turned my stomach. Despite that, I received my fair share of attention as I guided people to open pews. Far more than I had before. Not from everyone but if I had received any acknowledgement before, it would have been dismissiveness.

When the service began, I took my place on the dais with the senior acolytes. We didn't have much to do until the Manifestation. Just intone the prayers like everyone else. Except this time, I had to say them. I knew it would be trouble if I did my usual half-hearted mouthing of the words.

I watched the gathered crowds as I had very little to do except stand there. The place looked packed. Fuller than I had ever seen it. People were standing in the aisles and in the back rows. Everywhere I looked, eyes were on me. Benthic had been right. People had come to see the little uvoy girl from the stadium.

My heart started racing and I felt a growing need to run away. Anything to get away from those eyes. The ceilings were high, fortunately, so that provided me some relief. I glanced up at the towering statue of Akzad on the ceiling. I could probably leap up there. Hide in his outstretched hand. That would certainly give them a show.

My roaming eyes landed on Nerpi and Allora, sitting near the back. Nerpi gave me a happy little wave and I smiled. Allora nodded to me and I tuned the rest of the crowd out. I focused on my friends. This was just like any other church service. We sat through it. It wouldn't last forever.

When the Manifestation began, I at last had something else to focus on. I turned to my bowl on the central altar. The High Acolyte began leading the crowd in the ritual incantation. I tried to focus on my bowl and the mantra I was supposed to repeat but I couldn't help but hear the words the crowd said.

"We are the vessels of Akzad. We are his instruments on the physical plain. The power of our faith will shape the world. We give this power because together we are strong. Our will is Akzad's will."

I listened to that mantra for the first time. I'd heard it hundreds of times before. Mumbled it to myself most of those times. But I had never truly listened to it. The words were so familiar but understanding so out of reach. I thought about the mantra I had been taught to tell myself when doing a manifestation. The words I knew the other acolytes around me were repeating.

"I am the vessel of Akzad. I am his instrument on the physical plain. The power of the faithful is mine to shape. I deserve this power because my faith is stronger. My will is Akzad's will."

The mantras were so similar yet so different. One was power given, one took it. Neither felt right. What had I done when I finally called up that apple in my hand? I had been saying the one I had been taught. Hadn't I?

I mumbled both mantra's to myself but neither caused fruit to appear before me. Around me, the other acolytes looked locked in concentration. I had never noticed before how much it seemed to strain them. Only Hishu and Benthic looked relaxed. Both clearly believed this. Which, truth be told, surprised me a little. The fact they had the most fruit already appearing in their bowls suggested why I kept failing.

I didn't believe in any of this. Not really. I knew there was magic here. I wasn't skeptical it existed. Just that any of these rituals mattered. It was no surprise I continued to fail. And yet, I didn't fail yesterday.

I repeated both mantras to myself. I could feel the power hovering in the room. The whole place felt charged. Alive. I reached for that power as I said the words. It was being given freely. Most of these people did believe, even if I didn't. Despite the way the secret acolyte mantra made me feel, it wasn't wrong, right? I was using their power, but it was given to me. I was using it to feed them. To help them.

An apple appeared in the bowl before me. I smiled and repeated the words again. I was helping them. More fruit began to slowly appear. Hishu wasn't going to watch me fail. The old men weren't going to laugh at my failure. I could sense this power too. I could use it. I could show them.

I deserved this power.

It was mine.

Chapter 23

"**I**'m sorry, you want me to what?" I stammered out.

I was in Benthic's office with Hishu standing behind him. It had been a few days since the events at the arena and I had finally thought I was going to be able to put that behind me. That's when I was called in here.

"We want you to join the constabulary. How was that not clear?" Hishu said.

I ignored Hishu and looked to Benthic. "I thought the Church had to remain separate from the government? That was one of Akzad's laws. He formed the Church to unite everyone but not to rule them."

Benthic smiled. "I see you have been paying attention during classes. That pleases me."

"Sometimes." I mumbled. Church history could be monotonous but was my second favorite part of classes. The history of our time on Akka was rife with holes and inconsistencies, especially from before the Cataclysm, but the Church featured prominently in everything since then, which made them a good, if heavily biased, source for the story.

"You are essentially correct." Benthic continued, "No member of the Church can serve in the government. But this is a bit of a grey area. As you are not a full member of the Church, nor would you be a full member of the Constabulary."

"You would be a representative of both, but member of neither. All perfectly in keeping with Akzad's decrees. He does not want us to rule, as is proper, but we should be involved in all things to see the needs of the people in all aspects of life." Hishu said.

I frowned, unsure how to respond to that. I wasn't sure what I thought about any of this. Two months ago, I would have broiled at the idea of the

Church gaining even more influence. But now, I saw things from the other side. Hishu was a creep but most of the other acolytes weren't so bad. The Church had genuine magical powers, yet did not use them for evil. That had to count for something.

"So, if I wouldn't really be a full member of anything, what would I actually be doing?"

"You would be helping to restore order to the city. I am sure you have noticed the rise in crime, violence, and disorder in recent years." Benthic said, "You fought against that before joining us. It is the reason you came to us, in fact."

"No, the reason I joined was because I would have been put in jail for doing exactly what you're asking me to do now." I said with a roll of my eyes.

"Watch your tone, apprentice." Hishu snapped. I sighed but looked forward impassively.

"I recognize the irony." Benthic said, "But you can look at this as a chance to rectify that mistake. By working with the Constabulary, you can help to keep them on Akzad's path and help the people of this city."

"I don't know if that's possible. I've started to wonder if the police aren't part of the problem."

Hishu took his turn to roll his eyes and paced behind Benthic. "That's dangerous talk. Disrespect for the authorities is part of the problem we are facing. If people would learn their place, the constables wouldn't have to remind them of it."

"Learn their place?" I said, my voice growing heated as I leaned forward in my chair.

"Yes. That is what is causing all this trouble. People complaining about their wages, or their working conditions, or whining about some made up slight. If they would just recognize Akzad looks out for us equally, they would know they are already saved. By trying to break out of their place in society, they are causing the troubles they complain about."

My mouth hung agape at Hishu and fortunately, Benthic stepped in before I could reply and get myself into trouble. "Brother Hishu may wish to reconsider his words as I feel they are misrepresenting his point. The truth is unrest brings disorder and disorder causes harm. We want you to be the voice of the Church in curtailing that harm. Save people as you did before. Frankly, I am a little surprised you are so resistant. Was not your father a constable?"

My cheeks flushed and I nodded. "He was."

"And was not he and your mother killed by violent disorder?"

My mind flashed to the last family dinner and my father holding the dead corpse of my mother and the family in chaos. I saw my father drop dead before my eyes as a gunshot echoed, drowning out the rest of the world. That became my existence and it threatened to drag me back down into itself again. I forcibly shook my head, locking away those memories again.

"My mother was killed by corporate thugs trying to take over my town. My father died trying to stop them." I said, hiding the worst truth in this simpler version.

"You would be fighting that same fight." Benthic said, his voice reassuring, "You would be preventing violence by anyone who seeks it. Whether that's terrorist radicals or corporate greed. You would be saving people. Like you did before as the shadowy vigilante. But this time you would be doing it in the light of day."

I considered Benthic's words. Would this be any different than what I had been doing before? I would be working with the Constabulary and with the Church rather than on my own. But that would only make things easier, wouldn't it? I could try and curb their excesses rather than fear their reprisals. I would have access to official records. Maybe then I could finally track down the people who had really wrecked my town, rather than just their stooges like Venti.

"Okay, but why now? There have been problems in this city for a long time now. Why does the Church want someone working with the cops now? The arena thing was showy, but no one actually got hurt."

Hishu reached behind him and revealed the staff that the terrorist leader had been holding. He slammed the butt of the staff down against the floor and the crystal at the top flashed with light. "Because of this."

I stared transfixed at the staff, mesmerized. I felt ready to agree to anything Hishu wanted me to do. After a moment, Benthic picked up where Hishu had stopped, adding some details. "This is the Staff of Jundon. Legend says it has mind control powers. While I believe that to be an exaggeration, it clearly does have some power as I cannot take my eyes off it."

That comment broke my fixation on the staff. I turned angrily to Hishu, "This thing can control people's minds? You just used it on me!"

Hishu scoffed, "That is nonsense. As Benthic said, it cannot control your mind. We have only begun to explore what it can do though. It is mesmerizing. The idea of some ruffian using it to manipulate people goes against everything Akzad stands for."

"This is a very dangerous Relic to be in the hands of unsavory people." Benthic added, "There have been increasing rumors of powerful Relics turning up in the city, being used by criminals."

I thought about the candle Venti had used to start the fires on this street. I hadn't mentioned anything about that to anyone but then, I had been fairly distracted at the time what with being shot and all. "I've seen a few out on the streets. And no, I don't mean my shield. That had been in my family for generations. They can't all be like that to now suddenly show up, can they?"

Benthic shook his head. "We don't think so. Someone must have found a cache of Relics from the days of the Cataclysm. Tracking them down would be your primary goal while working with the constabulary. Who knows what else is out there."

I thought about the damage Venti had already caused with just his candle. What would that grunde have been able to do with this staff if I hadn't stopped him? Take over the city? Even if it wasn't that powerful it was not something I wanted to see in the hands of anyone, much less a radical terrorist. Even if I kind of agreed with their motives.

"Okay, I'll do it."

That was how my days went from jammed full of Church lessons, duties, and cycler racing to also being full of policing. I had experienced nights with little sleep before. While working at Nerpi's garage, I had gone out most nights patrolling for crimes to stop. But my day job hadn't been very demanding. To say I became exhausted wouldn't begin to describe it. I don't tell you this as an excuse or to forgive my actions. Only to put them into context. I don't deserve your forgiveness, for what I was about to do or what I had already done to my father.

I arrived at the constabulary precinct dressed in my apprentice robes and following Hishu. He had wanted me to wear the gaudy race uniform to convey the message of who I was representing. None of my objections had carried any weight with him save one. Constables didn't dress like that and I was supposed to be some kind of hybrid. While I may have won this first round, I feared I had another uniform in my future.

"How can I serve you, Excellency?" the desk sergeant asked.

"I am here to see Captain Jundel. I have his new recruit." Hishu said. The desk sergeant peered around him and stared dumbfounded at me. I couldn't blame him too much. In the bulky, oversized robe I'm sure I looked like a child.

We were directed toward the captain's office and the grey-haired human behind the desk stood up and extended his hand to Hishu. "An honor to meet you in person, Acolyte Hishu. I have enjoyed your sermons. Very inspiring."

I frowned at this. I couldn't recall the last time Hishu had given a sermon during service, though admittedly I had rarely paid attention to who said what before joining the Church. Nevertheless, Hishu appeared to appreciate the praise as I recognized the self-satisfied smile he wore. It was the same one he had when he belittled one of us during lessons.

"So, this is the Knightshield everyone's talking about?" Jundel said, "Not much to look at."

"You may be correct, but I will remind you that you are talking about a servant of the Church, Captain." Hishu said a rebuke in his tone. He had never defended me before, so I was actually impressed, though the fact that he had also insulted me in the same breath balanced that out.

"My apologies, Sister." Jundel said, though his tone didn't keep up with his words. "I merely wished to convey that the legends of your exploits conjure up a picture of someone much larger. Many of my constables have taken reports regarding your, er, activities. There were lots of stories."

"Yes, I've met a few. Almost all of them tried to shoot me." I said, trying to keep my voice neutral. I was still quite sore about that incident. I'll admit, more than a little part of me was excited at the idea of working directly with the constabulary. But Allora had gotten into my head enough that I could no longer just wave away that incident as a single bad apple.

"That is unfortunate but not unexpected. From all accounts, you wore a mask and attacked people in dark alley ways. Hardly a situation to inspire confidence in your peaceful intentions."

I bit back a retort. Getting into an argument with the captain was not going to make things easier for me here. He did have at least a little bit of a point. Masked figures in dark alleys wouldn't put anyone at ease. Maybe that was all it had been.

"History aside, we are now all going to be working together." Hishu said diplomatically. "Sister Kali is here to help the Constabulary track down the outbreak of Holy Relics that have been turning up in the hands of criminals. She comes bearing the will of Akzad and his wisdom."

Jundel let his disapproving glower rest on me for a moment longer before turning and bowing his head to Hishu. "A wisdom I always strive to follow. I welcome her assistance."

"Excellent. If you will give us a moment alone to say a final prayer, she can then begin work immediately with your officers." Hishu said.

Jundel looked blankly for a second and then recognized that he had been dismissed. If it had been anyone else kicking this entitled copper out of his own officer, I would have smiled. But since it was one entitled asshole kicking out another, I wasn't sure where I stood on the matter.

When Jundel had left, Hishu turned to me, "You must be on your best behavior. Remember, you represent the Church now. You are not a vigilante seeking justice. You are a member of Akzad's Holy Order seeking to bring his word to the people."

"Of course." I said.

Then he slapped me.

It was so unexpected that I didn't react. I've blocked and dodged many blows aimed at me. But you can't block something you don't expect. It didn't hurt all that much, beyond the sting to my pride and the shock of it happening. I blinked at him dumbfounded, unsure how to respond.

"That kind of flippant attitude is going to be the death of you, Sister. You are here to show the people and the Constabulary their place. But you must also remember your place. I have extended you a lot of latitude because Akzad has granted you the potential to deliver his word. Do not screw it up or there will be repercussions." Hishu growled at me.

As he spoke, I felt my temper flare and I was seconds away from returning the slap and showing him what would happen if he ever did that to me again.

Fortunately, he stood up and opened the door to the office, so we were now in full few of an entire building full of constables.

"May Akzad bless your work, Sister." Hishu said and then departed down the hallway.

Chapter 24

Still fuming from my encounter with Hishu, I found myself directed to a meeting room where about a dozen constables had gathered. A chalkboard dominated one wall and a corkboard another. The constables sat in small groups, mostly human but with a few grunde, evians, and a single nudra. They all cast glances at me, but no one approached. Which was fine with me, I didn't feel like making friends right then.

After a moment, Captain Jundel came in and took a position in front of the chalkboard. The constables all sat down and turned to face him, so I took a seat myself, all the way in the back. This gave me a view of everyone there and the door.

"All right you lazy sacks of meat, we have a tough job ahead of us. This group of subversives terrorizing our city has really upped their game. They took over an entire sports arena and we never saw it coming. Fortunately, the Church had Sister Kali Estuta there to save the day and has generously volunteered her services to aid us in finding the rest of these scumbags. So, please, join me in welcoming Sister Kali to our task force." Jundel said.

All eyes in the rooms were turned onto me. Jundel gave a perfunctory clap just in case I had missed the sarcasm in his tone. To my surprise, everyone joined in with a far more enthusiastic round of applause. A couple of them let out whistles of appreciation. They all turned to me, and several talked at once.

"Now we're talking."

"Did you really leap across the whole arena?"

"Nailing that scumbag right in the face with an apple...damn that divine retribution right there."

"Maybe now we can take the gloves off and bring these subversives down."

I wasn't quite sure how to respond to the attention but fortunately Jundel reasserted his control after only a moment. "Yes, yes, Sister Kali has shown admirable skill. Many of you may have heard of the good sister in her other persona, that of the legendary Knightshield. Carter and Bruneski got a firsthand view of her capabilities."

My gaze followed everyone else's toward two coppers sitting near the front. One was middle aged, and the other young. The young one flushed pink the way humans do when embarrassed. The other grew red with anger, an emotion he made no effort to direct anywhere else but at me. It took me a moment to recall where I had seen them before but then it clicked. The night I had been stabbed in the shoulder, these two had shown up and shot at me, after I had taken down the bad guys.

"She's the giant that took you two down?" One of the constables asked with mirth.

Jundel let the ribbing go on for only a moment before saying, "We've been able to track down an address for the thugs we captured at the arena. Unfortunately, most of their compatriots got away from us then. But not this time. This time we're going to bring them all in."

One of the constables tacked up an architectural drawing to the tack board behind Jundel. He took a metal pointer and indicated parts of the image. "Their building has three main entrances. Our targets are located on the fifth floor. Fortunately, this building hasn't been updated with the fire stairs. We'll go in in three teams..."

The rest of the briefing passed in a blur. While I had previously chastised the city constabulary for poor training, I couldn't fault them in their tactical planning. Even the part where I was designated to breach the door made sound tactical sense. I would be the best person to deal with unexpected Relics and I should be protected by an impenetrable shield blessed by God himself. The fact that I no longer had my shield, nor certain it would work even if I did couldn't be blamed on them as I hadn't wanted to admit this during the briefing.

The raid was planned for the middle of the night so I returned to the church. I debated who I should talk to about getting my shield back.

Technically, Hishu was in charge of the Relic office. He also was the one who seemed most interested in optics. I thought I might be able to convince him on the basis of it being a good look to have a church figure protected by a Relic. But, then I would have to talk to him, which I just didn't want to do.

I found Benthic in the garden as the sun was setting. He looked up from a book and beckoned me over to the seat beside him. "How did your first meeting with the constabulary go?"

I shrugged, not sure what I wanted to reveal so I went with a truthful platitude, "It could have been worse."

Benthic smiled, "So many things in life could be. It must have been hard for you to be there. With what happened to your father, and what has happened to you. I am grateful Akzad blessed you with the strength to see it through. Retrieving the lost Relics will be a great benefit to all of us."

"Yeah, about that..." I stammered. "They were kind of under the impression that I would have my shield with me when we went after these guys. I didn't know how to tell them it doesn't work anymore. Or if I should."

"What makes you think it doesn't work anymore?"

I gestured to my chest, "The hole that appeared in my lungs?"

"We have talked about that. The shield's failure that day stems from your lack of faith and training. You have used other Relics since coming here and have even Manifested. I have no more doubts about either of those things from you."

"Does that mean you'll give me my shield back?" I asked.

"That depends, do you think I should?"

I sat silently in response. I had come here to ask for the shield. Benthic had told me he thought it would work again for me. He had just offered it to me. Why couldn't I say anything?

Benthic let me sit in silence for a long time. He didn't look impatiently at me or go back to his book. I kind of wish he had though. Then I could have sat, stewing in my insecurities without observation.

Finally, quietly, I admitted, "I don't know."

"An honest answer if there ever was one. Facing death again is a scary prospect. For anyone. Especially for someone who has faced it before. But I suspect, there is more that you don't know beyond if you're ready to face danger. Are you worthy of the shield? Are you worthy of this role you've been asked to take?"

My anger flared and I stood abruptly. "What right do you have to ask if I'm worthy to do this?"

"I am not the one asking."

I paced around the garden while battling my thoughts. I wanted nothing more than to leap over the wall and get away. It was barely taller than Benthic, I could easily make it. My breathing became harder as I remembered the struggle to breathe. After getting shot. But also when I had beaten Jermain to get information on Rady. When my father had died.

"My father was a sheriff. He was a good man. He stood up to bad people. And it got my mother killed." I said quietly. "A corporation came to our town and bought up everything. They were supposed to revitalize us. Instead, they tried to subjugate us. My father was the only one to stand up to them. They threatened him, but he wouldn't back down. They attacked us during dinner. Unloaded whole clips of ammo. Killed my mother, my grandfather. Crippled my cousin. But again, my father wouldn't be cowed. He went to face them. Alone because his deputies were too scared to go with him."

I had never told anyone this, not completely, but now that I had started the whole story came out. "He told me to stay home. Revenge wasn't a thing to pursue. But I didn't listen. Those bastards had killed my mother. I followed him. Even then I was a trained fighter. It was something my father and I had done together since I was a child. I took out their guards. And then I took their guns. I went to kill the man, Venti, who had led the attack. But I missed. I wasn't very good with a gun. My father never carried one. I hit my... someone else.

"I ended up getting arrested for involuntary homicide. Finished my teen years in prison. But Venti and his thugs got away. The new sheriff never even investigated them. When I got out, I came here to pursue them. Venti pulled the trigger but ECG was the company that caused it all. I never found them. Until the day I got shot. Venti was there. He had a Relic he was using to burn down my neighborhood. He was the one who shot me."

Benthic looked shaken for a change. His usual calm demeanor showed cracks. "Venti was here? In the city? With a Relic?"

I nodded. "I tried to bring him down. Again. And again I failed."

Benthic breathed in a long, slow breath and his normal passive benevolence returned. "Why did you confront him that first time?"

"To get revenge for my mother."

"And this second time, why did you confront him?"

"To stop him from burning down the street." I said then paused, "No, that's not quite true. I fought to stop them, but Venti had given the Relic candle away. I fought him for revenge."

"And that is why the shield failed." Benthic nodded his head, "You understand that vengeance is wrong. Your father told you as much. Seeking it out corrupts your true self. Akzad withdrew his blessing from you for that."

I snapped my head up. "Because I wanted revenge?"

"Yes." Benthic said quickly. "You need to let go of this mission against Venti and ECG."

"I don't know if I can do that." I admitted.

"It will not be easy. But you must only take it a step at a time. This raid tonight, is it done out of vengeance?"

I shook my head, "No, these people threatened an arena full of people. They have dangerous relics."

"Then I would not fear the withdrawal of Akzad's blessing from you tonight. You do his work. When you confront them, you will have his protection."

Chapter 25

As I suspected, Hishu demanded that I wear my racing uniform for the raid. I wanted to tell him where to shove it but since the outfit I had worn on my nighttime patrols had been destroyed by the hospital staff, I didn't exactly have a ready alternative. This costume was demeaning and gaudy, but the form fitting part at least gave me plenty of freedom of movement. It would be terrible for sneaking in dark alley ways but since I was leading a raid, stealth wasn't part of the agenda.

I did wear my usual plain apprentice robes on top, despite it being a warm night. I had a long walk to get to the rally point and didn't want to draw any attention to myself. For a time, with my shield back on my head in place of my wraspisa, and the cover of darkness around me, I almost felt like my old self. Almost.

When I reached the rally point a few blocks from the target building, I was overwhelmed by the number of constables in attendance. Jundel had estimated the potential number of hostiles as high as fifty, though I thought it closer to twenty. Several had been captured during the event and they had been well spaced out through the arena. Assuming there was even anyone in these apartments. It had been a few days already. Plenty of time for them to flee.

"All right men, listen up!" Jundel shouted. The crowd of constables slowly quieted down and turned to face Jundel perched on the steps of a building. "We're going to do this fast and professional. These scumbags aren't going to know what hit them. No mistakes, no casualties. I want you to all go home to your girls when we're done. Do not let these assholes get the drop on you."

The men around me nodded solemnly. I saw the look of worry on many faces. I wondered how many of them had done something like this before. I'd been in quite a number of fights but the closest I'd come to a raid like this had been the night my parents died. But then I hadn't been thinking much. I'd just attacked.

"But do not fear, men, Akzad is with us. Sister Kali, blessed by him, will be with us. His blessings will protect us from harm so that we can do his work to bring those misguided to justice."

All eyes turned toward me, and I felt glad I was so short. Only the ones closest to me would be able to see. My shield still sat on my head, and I wondered if I should hold it aloft to show them. Then I remembered the perfect bullet hole in the center. That wouldn't inspire a lot of confidence.

"Form your teams. Let's get it done."

I had been assigned to what had been called 'alpha team', which would be the main one entering the building. The others would be surrounding it to prevent anyone from escaping. As it turned out, my team was led by Carter, the constable who had previously tried to shoot me.

When we gathered, I felt the eyes on me more intensely than before. This time they weren't contemplating their mortality but my role. I was the only woman and much smaller than all of them. I could see that thought play across each of their faces.

"Carter, what's this girl doing here?"

"Yeah, is she really going with us?"

"We're going to have to protect her and ourselves?"

Instead of Carter, the younger one who had been his partner that night, Bruneski, spoke up. "Hey, she can take care of herself. She took down a whole gang of thugs, then both of us down after stopping bullets with her shield."

"That's not much of an endorsement." One of the constables joked. "My sister could take you down Bruneski."

While they laughed, I punched him in the back of the knee. He stumbled forward as his leg gave out and would have fallen if we weren't so packed together right then. I know I shouldn't have done it. Hell, I knew it then. My father had always tried to teach me that just because you had the power to do something didn't mean you should. But damn it did feel satisfying at the moment.

At the front of the group, Carter snorted. "Well, I guess that answers that question. She is clearly a master fighter. And Bruneski's right. Her shield is a Relic, blessed by Akzad. She'll go in first to protect us all from any bullets."

My satisfaction quickly evaporated. Despite Benthic's confidence in me, I still wasn't convinced my shield would work. I was in too deep now though. I just had to show that I was strong enough to stand with these guys. Now I had to prove it.

We marched the few blocks from the rally point to the target building. It towered above me, decayed and dirty façade blocking out the nights sky. Only a few lights were on in the windows, and those looked to be the flicker of candles rather than the steady glow of electric bulbs. I hoped that didn't lead to yet another fire.

I didn't have much time to think about that though. Now that we had arrived, we had to move quickly. Dozens of constables would never be stealthy. We rushed through the main doors and up the stairs, me in the lead. I was in good shape but even still, running up five flights left me a little winded.

Behind me, Carter pointed to the closest apartment on our list. He sent groups of constables ahead to stake out each of the others. I couldn't be the first one in on all of them. As we got into position I turned the constable beside me, who turned out to be Bruneski.

"Why are be barging in? Why don't we knock first? They may open the door and surrender."

"But they might also just start shooting. We can't give away the tactical advantage." He responded immediately, repeating the mission briefing.

"They also might not. And then no one would have to get hurt." He stared at me dumbly for a second and then cocked his head as if finally attempting to contemplate it. I don't think he had ever given it any thought before.

Carter didn't give him much time to do so though. He raised his hand up high so everyone could see it. He extended three fingers and then exaggeratingly counted them down. When the last one dropped, the two constables beside me rammed down the door and I rushed in.

I was not prepared for what I found. Instead of a group of armed grunde thugs, I found a uvoy woman and a child. As soon as the door burst open, she pulled the child in close to her and stared at us with wide eyes. Since we were in her home, she didn't wear a wraspisa and I hadn't seen another bare headed uvoy since I'd left home. The slightly wrinkled skin patterned on her head reminded me of my mother.

I came to a halt a few meters inside the door unable to move. If there had been any thugs in other rooms, they could have easily shot me in that moment. The constables behind me fanned out, kicking down each door in the small apartment. It did not take them long to search the place and come back to the main room.

"There's nobody here." Carter fumed, ignoring the poor woman desperately clutching her crying child. He stalked out to the hallway, and I heard the other teams report the same thing. No group of grunde thugs with guns. Several apartments were empty but most had families in them.

I recovered myself and slowly approached the woman. I knelt and pulled my face mask down and put my shield back on my head to cover it. This wasn't my home and going uncovered would be incredibly rude to some uvoy. Even if I thought that tradition a little silly, I didn't think now was the time to make a statement about it.

"It's going to be okay." I said quietly. "We were looking for some criminal grunde. How long have you lived here?"

The woman glanced between me and the constables still milling about. "I just moved in yesterday."

"Do you know anything about the people who lived here before?"

"No. I never met them." She said emphatically. She considered me closely for a moment and hesitated before speaking again. "You're her, aren't you? The Knightshield?"

Inwardly I sighed. What did I expect wearing this stupid costume? There had been lots of photographers at the arena. My picture had appeared in the papers. But for the woman, I forced a smile onto my face.

"That's what people have decided to call me."

She studied me intensely for a minute before glancing nervously between me and the constable. Then she leaned in close. "They say you're a hero. Why are you working with the coppers? You're supposed to be protecting us from them."

I should have expected this kind of question. Given Allora's and Nerpi's general sentiment toward the constables, I knew a lot of people weren't fans. My experiences with them so far hadn't been all rainbows. But I had grown up the daughter of the sheriff in a town where everyone liked my dad. It still felt uncomfortable every time I ran into this sentiment.

"We're looking for the people who held up the arena. A lot of them got away."

That appeared to satisfy her as she nodded her head. "What those boys did was not right. Threatening all of those people. You say they lived here before me?"

I nodded. "Some of the ones who were captured did. What records we could find on them suggested the others would too. I guess they figured they would be located and left."

"Well, they didn't do a very good job of it. Landlord rented me the place as 'fully furnished' which turned out to mean those guys left all their crap behind. The furniture is okay but most of the rest of it was junk. What wasn't actual garbage is in that box by the door."

I smiled, "Thank you. Maybe we'll find something useful in there. And we'll get out of your home very soon. I promise."

The box by the door sat unnoticed by any of the constables. I picked it up and then turned to Bruneski who had moved beside me. "This stuff belonged to the people we were looking for. Can you get these guys out of this poor woman's home so we can look through it?"

He pursed his lips uncertainly before turning to survey the small room. Two of the constables had dropped down onto the woman's couch and one was rummaging through her cabinets. Bruneski's face shifted from bored to disturbed.

"Come on guys, we found some evidence here. Let's go through it and get out of here." The other constables didn't move at first and then he added. "Fine, let the girl get all the credit then."

It left me torn between relief and my blood boiling that this succeeded in getting them up and out the door to join me in the hallway. Once they started going through the box, I turned back and tried to close the woman's door. Unfortunately, the latch and frame were busted so it only partially closed. I cast one final look of sympathy to the woman before closing it the best I could.

I stood aside and let the constables look through the junk box. I doubted they'd find anything useful and if they didn't, I wouldn't know how to look for it. From what I'd seen there were just some clothes and bits of paper. I doubted the thugs had taken the time to write down their forwarding address and left it behind.

Someone from one of the other teams could be heard angrily shouting. I made my way toward the sound and looked into a room very similar to the one I'd just left. Instead of a poor uvoy woman, a frail old eowian man cowered before two constables. One of them, an eowian surprisingly, had his billy club raised and was about to bring it down onto the man.

I darted in and yanked the club out from his hand before he could bring it down. The constable looked dumbfounded at me. "What the hell are you doing?"

"What the hell are you doing? Beating a poor old man?"

"I was conducting an interrogation.

"Your first instinct to learn more from people is to beat them up and you wonder why no one will talk to a copper." I sneered.

Another constable, a human this time, moved to stand beside the eowian copper. "You're one to talk. I've seen your handy work. You've left some people barely able to breath."

Indignation flared but then was quashed as I recalled my meeting with Jermain. I had beaten that poor man quite severely. If Talesh hadn't called for help, I'm not sure how far I would have gone. Now they were both dead, and I bore most of that responsibility.

I didn't say any of this to the constables looking at me. I doubted they would care even if I did. Instead, I reminded myself Jermain had been the exception, at least I hoped he had been.

"I've hurt some people, sure. But only people who were hurting or about to hurt others. I never busted into a random man's home and slapped him around until he told me whatever I wanted to hear. Which is what you're doing."

"Don't talk like you have any idea how to do our job, kid." The eowian constable said. "Our lives are constantly in danger. There is a menace out there, and as far as I'm concerned, you were part of it. You may be dressed up as a sister now, but that doesn't change what you are."

"And what is she?" a new voice said.

The constable clamped up as Captain Jundel came into the room. His eyes didn't meet mine, but they did take in the scene. He didn't say anything else but stared pointedly at what I wore. I don't think Jundel liked me, but he did appear to have genuine respect for the Church.

The constable stepped away from the old man and I helped him up. He smiled at me gratefully and went through the bedroom door as quickly as he could manage. Before anything more could be said, Bruneski came into the apartment behind Jundel. "Captain, we found this among the stuff left behind by the terrorists."

Jundel took the paper Bruneski handed him but only glanced at it. "I'm not surprised. This kind of thing is the reason these thugs even exist. When is this?"

"Tomorrow, sir."

"Then we'll have to round them up. Hopefully catch a few of them."

"A few of who? What is that?" I asked.

To my surprise, Jundel handed the paper to me. Black and white text spelled out 'RALLY! Let your voice be heard! Unite with your fellow workers and join the PEOPLE's UNION!' and then gave tomorrow's date and a location. I'd seen similar flyers around a few times but never paid much attention to them.

"You think these guys are going to attack a political rally?" I asked.

Jundel scoffed, "They're not going to attack it. Their running it. Or at least recruiting at it. Now we have a reason to round the whole lot of them up."

"Wait a minute, you're going to round up people attending a rally? People who haven't done anything?" I demanded.

"Haven't done anything yet. They are attending a meeting about overthrowing our government." Another constable sneered.

"It's a rally. About elections. I admit, I haven't paid all that much attention to the city's leadership, but there are elections. Right?"

"This is clear evidence the terrorists plan to attend this meeting. It is our only lead." Jundel said.

"And you'd be throwing it away." I snapped but then tried to moderate my tone. Getting into a shouting match with the captain, after he had kind of backed me up a minute before would not be good. "Look, this suggests these guys might be there. But probably not all of them. And we don't know who they are. You arrest a whole bunch of innocent people, it's not going to look good or get you very far. Send some people instead. Have them observe, just in case it is a target rather than a recruiting ground."

Jundel shook his head. "I'm not going to subject any of my men to an evening listening to that drivel. People trying to blame all their problems on others. Besides, the first sight of a uniform and they'll run. If we're not bringing overwhelming force, it's not worth bringing any.

"But...you may have a point. You could attend. You're not a constable. You're a member of the Church. And their hero. You come and I bet they'll share all their secrets with you."

I frowned, "It sounds like you want me to spy on people."

"This isn't spying. It is gathering intelligence. These scumbags have already held hostage an entire arena of people. If you're not willing to help here, our only alternative will be to arrest the lot of them. We cannot be unprepared for their next move. Next time they act, people are going to die." Jundel said.

I fumed silently for a moment. I felt trapped by Jundel's argument. I didn't disagree with him about the potential consequences if this group acted again. Holding an arena full of people hostage was not the act of rational thinkers. They would only grow more violent. Even if I agreed with their goal, their methods were trouble. But spying on regular people? That didn't sit right with me.

"If it helps, this is a public gathering." Jundel said, softening his tone, "All we are asking you to do is to go and get to know these people. They'll be more accepting of you than any of us. So, in a way, you're helping them. Wouldn't our presence make things more tense for them?"

I sighed, "Fine, I'll go."

Jundel ended the impromptu meeting without addressing what had been happening to the old man. The constables spread out leaving me and Bruneski the last ones. He glanced at me but then looked sheepishly away before stammering, "I'm...um...I'm sorry."

That was something I hadn't expected and I looked up at him not sure how to respond, "Sorry? For what?"

"Almost shooting you."

I blinked at him. A lot of people shot at me. Despite the constabulary considering me a menace, I hadn't had very many encounters with them, at least the kind that had gotten them close enough to shoot at me.

"You had just taken down a group of Blood Daggers who had been harassing a woman. I thought you were one of the bad guys. It wasn't until after, when I talked to that poor woman, that I learned what had happened and what you had done."

I nodded, recalling the incident and subconsciously rubbed my shoulder where I had been stabbed. "Honestly, I'm surprised to hear you talked to the woman rather than just arresting her too."

Bruneski grimaced, "Actually, I did arrest her. All of them. It was procedure. But I let her go later."

"She was human if I recall." I said, looking at him pointedly.

"Yes."

"Would you have listened to her story if she had been uvoy?" I asked.

He started to deny it immediately but then stopped himself. I saw him engage his brain for a moment and my opinion of this constable went up a notch. Not sure it was enough for me to forgive him shooting at me, but it was at least worth considering.

"I'd like to say yes." He said hesitantly.

I stepped up next to him and our relative heights meant I had to look up at him. "Well, next time, be sure you could answer yes afterwards."

Chapter 26

The next evening, I followed the flyer's address to a community hall, which proved to be a rundown building in an area near Nerpi's garage. Which didn't say much as most of the buildings were fairly rundown. Several windows were broken and there was only one working light over the entrance. But there were streams of people slipping through the doorway, so I had clearly come to the right place.

The inside proved a lot better maintained. There were cracks in the walls and water damage in the ceiling, but the floors and tables were clean. There were even a few plants around the room giving the space a little bit of life. The lights all worked too.

The space turned out to be well packed. I don't know what I had expected to find but a packed house hadn't really been one of them. People didn't care enough to attend political meetings. At least, I hadn't.

I recognized a fair number of people in passing. People who lived in the area or who attended the church. I didn't know most of their names and fortunately, they didn't know me any better than I did them, so I only got a few nods of familiar greeting. I managed to get out of wearing my apprentice robe or that stupid uniform, so in my usual overalls I blended in with the crowd. It had been a big debate, as I wasn't sure if not wearing it would make me more or less of the spy the constables wanted me to be. In the end, I didn't wear it because I hated it, and this was an excuse to get out of it.

I stood by myself near the back, thinking I would be able to escape talking to anyone. They sent me here to get to know people so if I didn't talk to anyone, I wouldn't get to know any of them. Then I wouldn't have any secrets to pass on. I could just tell them what the meeting was about and just focus on anyone who suggested a violent uprising.

Unfortunately, someone called my name and I turned to see Anisu and Auran approaching me. I smiled at them, even if I hoped to avoid talking to people, I did like the both of them and it would be nice to talk to some fellow uvoy. I was initially surprised to see them together. Though, now I did recall that Auran had said she knew Sanja, Anisu's grandfather.

"It's good to see you again, Anisu. How is your family doing? I'm sorry I couldn't attend Sanja's funeral."

"We are well." Anisu said stiffly.

"Are you going to reopen the shop?" I asked.

Anisu's eyes dropped, "No. The building is not going to be rebuilt the same. We talked to the owner and the rent will be far too much for us to afford, especially since we already need to replace everything."

"I'm sorry." I said.

"Do not be sorry." He said, looking directly at me for the first time, "You and your friends saved my life. You stopped those thugs from burning down even more of the neighborhood."

My stomach twisted at his words. He didn't know I was probably the reason they had burned those buildings down in the first place. But how did I tell him that? Could I? Should I?

"I must admit, it is odd seeing you here, dressed like a regular person." Auran said. "I am not sure how to address you."

"As I've told you, just call me Kali."

"I can't do that. The senior acolytes would fire me." Auran said.

"Okay, maybe not at the church. But we're not there now. By the way, the soup you made last night was excellent. I didn't get to tell you."

She beamed and our conversation turned to more mundane things. As we talked, a few more uvoy gathered around us and I was introduced to them. Fortunately, no one mentioned that I was an acolyte apprentice nor did anyone say the words Knightshield. I felt lucky none of them were cycler fans.

A hush started cascading through the room as someone stood up onto a table at the center. This place hadn't been designed for speeches so there was no stage and in its rundown state I wasn't surprised it didn't have an electric speaker system. We all had to quiet down to hear the person. They were standing with their back to me so I couldn't make much out about them, other than that they were human.

"Thank you all for coming. I know it's hard to find time to get away from work and family to gather for something like this. So again, thank you. Now, my name is Arron Papadopoulos. You may remember me from such films as *It Came from the Trees* and *We'll Always Have That Kiss*. And you might be wondering what I'm doing here. Rich kid like me speaking at a meeting about the troubles you are facing."

The voice sounded familiar and then the name finally clicked. "Fuck. Is that En?"

The speaker turned enough that I could see his face, but I didn't immediately recognize him. But then, I had seen how good he was at slipping into a role several times now. The man I knew as En was not a public speaker. This man, this role he was in now, was.

"And you would be right to ask that question. For a long time, you have had rich people like me telling you what to do. What to buy. Where to work. How to live your lives. I'll admit right now, my father is one of those people. And I have been too. I sold you things in ads and with my movies. Things you didn't need. Things to keep you poor. But I spent some time living here. Amongst you. For the first time in my life, I saw the other side. And it's not an easy life.

"My dad, he, he would always complain about how much of a slacker he thought the crew on our movies were. Or brag about how fortunate they were for what he paid them. I never questioned it. Until I had to work at that same wage in order to feed myself. Then I got it. And I had a pretty generous boss. Nerpi is one of you too. He paid me what he could afford.

"But even then, I never quite got it. Not until the Lesshon Street fire. That fire took many lives. It ruined many more. People out of homes. Work. Their entire livelihood. And it wasn't the first one either. Other fires have happened around the city. Doing the same thing. The buildings, they're being rebuilt. But not for the people who lost their homes. These new places are too expensive. The structures of the city are being restored but not the soul, the people.

"Where were the governor's fancy new fire departments when these fires occurred? Where was the Constabulary when violent criminals started them? In my Dad's neighborhood. Protecting people like me and my father, who could afford to rebuild our home a dozen times if it burned down. Not protecting those that couldn't.

"That fire showed me how broken this city is. And it made me mad. And depressed. I'll admit, I fell into a bottle for a few weeks. But that was nothing compared to what happened to all of you. Even those of you who didn't lose anything in the fire, you still lost. You lost friends. Neighbors. Customers. Now you'll have to compete with fancy new giant corporations to be able to afford to feed your kids. I'm amazed at how much stronger all of you are than me. I fell into drink with just the realization. You still have to live with it.

"But then my eyes were opened again. This time, to hope. This doesn't have to be the way things always are. They may suck now, but they can change. When the Lesshon fire started, it wasn't the constabulary or fire department that responded. It was one of your own. She stepped up and stopped them from taking even more from you. When more thugs threatened you at the cycler arena, it wasn't the constabulary who stepped up and stopped them."

"Oh shit." I whispered to myself and started looking for the door. There were too many people around me. I wasn't going to be able to move without creating a disturbance.

En continued, "You all know who I'm talking about. The Knightshield. The protector of the innocent on the street. One of you. Not one like me. She stepped up. And you can too. I'm not going to be a solution to the problems you all face. But I am going to stop being one of them. It's time for the working people of Akka to stand up for themselves. Follow the Knightshield's example. Rise up."

En knew how to deliver a speech, I had to give him that. I could feel the energy of the crowd. It was a similar feeling to what happened during a Manifestation, yet different. I'd almost call it more whole but that didn't really make sense.

A few other people spoke after En, but none of them had the same effect. I focused mostly on trying to keep from being recognized. It wasn't until a grunde started getting a reaction from the crowd that I really started paying attention again.

"Papadopulos may be a rich boy telling us all how to live our lives, same as they always do, but he was right about one thing. The time for action is here. For too long we have meekly taken our lot in life. All while being lied to every week by our religious 'leaders'. They force submission down our throats and use their power to hide the truth about how we all came to this world. We need to get the truth out there. We need to take down those who have oppressed us!"

Both he and En were a bit vague about what action they were calling for, but the grunde definitely had a more dangerous edge to it. The crowd were far more mixed at his speech. Some booing openly and others looking very eager.

I leaned over to Auran. "Who's that?"

"Temrok. He leads the Grunde Emancipation Party."

"The ones who attacked the arena?" I asked.

"No. But word is they are associated. The ones who did that got impatient with his more reasonable approach."

"That's more reasonable? He sounds like we should be hanging any rich person we can find."

"It holds appeal for some people. We need to do something." Auran said. The casual way she spoke sent a chill down my spine. Auran was not someone I could ever see as part of a violent mob but she clearly didn't hate the idea entirely.

I watched Temrok throughout the rest of the meeting. When it ended, I tried to extract myself from the crowd as quickly as I could in order to follow him but there were too many people. By the time I realized I'd lost him, most of the rest of the crowd had dispersed. This also meant I never got a chance to talk to En after the meeting broke up. In truth, I wasn't all that disappointed. What was I going to say to him?

Jundel and Hishu were waiting for me to make a report the next morning and I couldn't think of a way to avoid it, short of running away. It would be better to get it over with sooner rather than later.

I met them at the constabulary precinct and ran through the general outline of what had happened. I left off any details that I could get away with ignoring. Especially names. I wasn't going to rat on people for doing nothing wrong. But I couldn't leave off En's name. I couldn't pretend I didn't recognize him, despite his unique way of feeling like a different person when he got into a role.

"This is disturbing." Jundel said.

"It is indeed, Captain." Hishu said. "I assume you are reluctant to arrest Mr. Papadopoulos?"

Jundel nodded, "He is a public figure and has powerful connections. That shields him from a lot of what we can do."

I frowned, "What is that supposed to mean? If En wasn't rich, you'd just pick him up off the street and throw him in jail? He hasn't done anything wrong."

"Not done anything wrong?" Hishu balked, "He is calling for violence in the streets. Riots. The overthrow of the government."

"What? That's what you got from what I told you? He did nothing of the kind. He's calling for people to stand united. Something the Church should be supporting."

"This is rabble rousing of the highest order." Hishu said.

Jundel sighed and shook his head, "It is. But until he does something more direct or calls for people to do something more direct, it would be problematic to bring him in. Who else is among the rebel's leadership?"

"Rebel leadership?" I asked, "These aren't rebels. These are citizens of this city. Members of your church. They just want their lives to suck a little less. For some of the injustices they deal with to be addressed. You should be on their side, helping them, not talking about arresting them."

The two men fixed disapproving glares at me. I didn't back down and stared right back. Hishu broke the silence. "Child, we do sympathize with them. But they can address their issues to the city council. Our concern isn't with the people after all. Just the leaders. The ones who staged that incident at the arena. Those who would hurt people."

"Right, so why the concern with En? He's harmless. Temrok is the only one of interest there. And even then, I'm not sure about it. He was more agitated but also didn't directly call for any violence."

"But he does appear to be connected to those that did. You must learn more." Jundel said.

"What? Me? How?" I asked.

"Through Mr. Papadopoulos. You have a connection there. He has connections to Temrok and any others. Someone will lead us to the dangerous ones. Hopefully before they can hurt any more people."

I wanted to refuse but he had a point. This was a dangerous business En was involved in. I would have to talk to him about it eventually no matter how uncomfortable the idea felt. Whether or not I was asking on behalf of the constabulary or not was beside the point.

Chapter 27

The next few days passed more normally. Days full of lessons and chores. Fortunately, aside from trying to use me to infiltrate these 'rebel' groups, the Constabulary hadn't quite figured out how else they wanted to use me so I didn't have much to do there. But I knew that wouldn't last. At some point, they would tout me out publicly.

The highlight of my week was practicing racing with Nerpi. We went out to some roads outside the city where I could get up to speed without the risk of running into anyone. I had scoffed at practicing before, as I hadn't cared much for racing. It had just been a thing I did to keep a roof over my head. But now I found a sense of peace in it. For a few hours, I could escape the pressure of the church and the city. The lonely dirt roads felt more like home than the towering trenches of the city.

So, I was in a good mood when I rounded the corner from the path, headed back to where Nerpi waited with the side car. As I got closer, I saw several figures with him, and I immediately tensed up. We were quite a way outside usual traffic as these roads were just routes to long dilapidated farms. I sped up more than was strictly safe on the terrain in order to get there as quickly as possible, even though Nerpi did not appear to be in any immediate danger.

To my relief, as I got closer, I was able to identify the two figures with Nerpi as En and Allora. I hadn't seen either of them since attending that meeting where En spoke so I knew this would be an awkward meeting. But at least we hadn't been beset by bandits or something.

I pulled to a stop near the group of them and they all turned to look at me. No one said anything and my short period of relief vanished. I felt like a kid called to the principal's office. I climbed off the cycler. After removing my helmet, I immediately reached for my wraspisa even though it was no longer my father's shield. Hishu would only let me have it for official duties.

"So, this is weird." I finally said to break the silence.

"Did you attend a rally recently where En spoke?" Allora asked.

I let out a breath, appreciating Allora's bluntness and getting right to it. "I did. Thought it was a bit weird to see him there. You never told us you were involved in this. But then you lied about your name for months, so I guess that's not surprising."

"Hey." En said with his familiar drawl. "I'm not the one we're yelling at today."

"What is that supposed to mean?" I asked.

"Why were you at that meeting, Kali?" Nerpi asked.

I looked between the three of them feeling ganged up on. I hadn't done anything wrong by attending. I didn't like where this was going.

"Why was I there? Why was En speaking? Why is he friendly with those goons who tried to take the arena hostage?"

"We're not talking about En." Allora said, her tone cold and flat.

"No? Then what are we talking about?" I locked eyes with Allora suddenly angry. We held the stare for what felt like forever until I finally blinked.

Allora let out a heavy breath and when she spoke again, her tone was much friendlier. "We've heard some disturbing reports that you were attending the rally on behalf of the constabulary. That you are now working for them."

I opened my mouth to protest but shut it. I couldn't outright deny it. Instead, I said, "Working with. Not for. And it wasn't my idea."

I knew that sounded lame and was a weak equivocation, but it was all I had to defend myself. I needed to say more so I added, "But all I did was attend that meeting. They thought I could fit in better than a constable. And I agreed. Would you have preferred armed constables there?"

"Yes, actually." En said. "We had nothing to hide. It was a public meeting."

"Which is why you going, on behalf of the constables, and hiding it is so concerning. What else are you doing for them?"

"Nothing." I mumbled.

"You didn't help them raid an apartment building?" Allora pushed.

I sighed, "Those were supposed to be where the thugs who escaped from the arena lived. That's where we learned about the rally."

"Why are you working with the constabulary at all?" Allora said, "Why would the Church approve this?"

I snorted, "It was their idea! They want me to track down Relics. Meanwhile, the Constabulary want me to help them track down the group responsible for the arena attack. Which, by the way, I don't feel particularly bad about. Those guys threatened a lot of people. Including all of you."

En cocked his head, "Wasn't it you who took those guys down specifically because you thought it would be a blood bath if the constabulary showed up?"

"Exactly." I said.

"Wait. I'm confused."

I sighed and started pacing around the group. "If I help the constabulary bring these guys down, I can do it without getting anyone killed."

"Do you even know why these guys are doing what they did?" En asked.

I shrugged. "I heard their speech at the arena. I also heard yours. I sympathize. But holding a bunch of people hostage isn't going to get them anywhere."

"Neither is being a pawn for the constabulary. We're not going to see change happen by playing by the rules. I thought you understood that. What with the whole Knightshield thing you do. You became a symbol for people. You should be working with us. Be that symbol for change and standing up to oppression. Working with the constabulary is going to undermine all of that."

"Working with the church is bad enough." Allora added.

"That was your idea!" I shouted turning back to her.

"Joining the church to avoid getting arrested. But dressing up and parading as the church's puppet defending the masses wasn't."

"I was just there to run a race. I didn't exactly have time to change out of that stupid getup when terrorists threatened everyone."

"Enough!" Nerpi shouted. Hearing him shout brought us all up short. I had never heard Nerpi raise his voice before. We all turned to him, and I felt a bit embarrassed. For a moment I forgot why I was even feeling irritated. I didn't exactly disagree with what En and Allora were saying.

"We're not going to solve anything by yelling at each other." Nerpi said. "Now, can we all talk like friends instead of enemies?"

I remained silent for a moment, exchanging glares with En and Allora. Finally, En gave one of his customary nonchalant, 'whatever' shrugs and then I nodded. Allora's expression remained fixed for a moment before she too nodded.

"So, if I'm understanding this all correctly, En is leading a rebellion and Kali is working for the oppressors?" Nerpi asked, his tone suggesting he was trying for a joke.

"Maybe?" I said with a shrug, trying to play into his lighter tone.

"Yeah, maybe." En said. "I dunno. I just want to make things better. I never realized how bad things were for people. I want to change things. Whatever it takes."

"Whatever it takes? Even gunning down a stadium full of people?" I asked.

En sighed, "Okay, I guess not whatever it takes. I just don't want to be on opposite sides from you, Kali. You were my inspiration to get involved."

I blinked in surprise at this admission. I didn't know how to respond. "I shouldn't be. I never did anything to change society. I was just out for revenge. Hell, I still don't understand why anyone even cares. I stopped a few thugs trying to mug people."

"And cops abusing their power." Allora added. "That's why we were so upset about you working with the constabulary. You became a symbol for people. A symbol of standing up to abuse. I had hoped you could influence the church by joining them. I am terrified by the idea that it's working the other way around."

My spine stiffened, "What is that supposed to mean?"

"Just a fear." Allora said quickly, "Something I would hate to see happen. The approval of the senior acolytes. That damn chant for Manifestation. It can mess with a person's perspective."

I nodded. "Okay, then help me find the ones responsible for organizing the attack on the arena. I know they weren't all arrested that day. We bring them in, together, find out where they're getting their Relics, and I can be done with the constabulary. Then maybe I can quit the church without having to complete another two years of training."

"We don't know who's responsible." En protested. "I haven't been involved with these people very long."

"I hear Temrok does." I insisted.

"That guy? Nah. He's just full of hot air." En said with a dismissive wave of his hand. "He talks big, trying to rile people up but he would never hurt anyone."

As En spoke, I glanced over at Allora. She wouldn't meet my eyes. I continued to stare at her and she began to fidget. I had never seen her anxious before.

"You know something, Allora. Temrok is involved isn't he?" I pressed.

Allora shook her head vigorously. "No, I don't think he is. In fact, I think he's trying to keep that kind of thing from happening again."

"But?"

She clammed up for a minute and I thought maybe she would be her usual stubborn self but finally she sighed. "He has met with people who are probably involved. But they were dumb kids and he tried to convince them to not do anything else violent."

"Based on his speech the other night that sounds like the opposite thing he would be telling people." I said.

"He wants action. He's not afraid of violence, if necessary. Which, I'll remind you, neither are you. But he is opposed to senseless violence like that stunt at the arena."

I nodded. "Okay, suppose I believe you about Temrok. I don't know him, so I'll take your word for it. But what aren't you telling me?"

Allora hung her head, "The boy we met with, the one he tried to convince, mentioned a name."

The hairs on my arms stood up and I shivered. Somehow, I knew what she would say next.

"Venti. The boys have been meeting with him."

My eyes went wide, and I lost all ability to speak. I just stared open mouthed at Allora as I processed this news. And I wasn't the only one as both Nerpi and En stared at her with the same look of shock and betrayal I felt.

"You knew about Venti being involved and you didn't tell me? I told you what he did. You saw what he's capable of when he burned down our street. Why in the name of Akzad are you protecting him?!"

"I'm not protecting him!" Allora shouted back. "It's those boys. They haven't done anything. Yet. At least not all of them. I only found out about this after I learned about your involvement with the constabulary. I wasn't sure what you would do. If you tell the coppers, they'll arrest everyone, no matter what crime they've committed. You know this."

I roiled with anger and started stomping in a circle around my cycler for something to do. I felt the urge to smash something. I needed to smash something. I deserved to smash something. The air around me tingled with energy and I sucked it in. It felt good and I concentrated on a rock nearby, projecting a big squash to manifest on top. I imagined Venti's face where the squash sat. Viciously, I kicked out, causing the squash to explode into gooey bits.

The rain of squash innards and seeds landed everywhere, including my face. The disgusting feeling startled me as my mind briefly imagined those innards being Venti's brain. The thought disturbed me, and my anger vanished in an instant, replaced by disgust. Not at the image so much as at myself.

I took a deep breath and turned back to my friends. They looked at me in shock. But more than their expressions, they all looked slightly drained, as if they were all suddenly tired. I thought about the Manifestation ritual. It took power from worshipers and maybe not so willingly given.

"This is what I have been afraid of. You're using the power to feed your own selfish whims. That's the same kind of twisted behavior that has corrupted so many other acolytes. You must do better." Allora said, but her tone wasn't condescending or full of rebuke. Instead, I only sensed sadness.

"He shot me. He killed my mom." Was the only thing I could say in reply. The words came out quietly and far more pleading than I would have liked.

Allora stepped forward and rested her hand on my shoulder. "I know. And we're going to bring him to justice. Him and the people he works for. But we can't have innocent kids suffer in the process."

I nodded in reply, though, at that moment, I didn't agree with her. To hell with anyone who interacted with that man.

Chapter 28

I managed to get a vague promise from Allora and En to get me a location where the Blood Daggers might be meeting in exchange for a promise not to share any of this with the constabulary. As they hadn't really given me anything, I agreed readily. Once they found something, I didn't know what I would do. I found it doubtful I could raid their place on my own. Telling the constabulary may be my only option for getting to Venti.

The next day of classes left me distracted. I wanted to be out there doing something instead of sitting in a classroom listening to theology. Fortunately, the morning passed without issue, as I always had a hard time paying attention, so no one noticed anything out of the ordinary.

At lunch, I sat at my usual table with the apprentices, ignoring their banter. They were no longer actively shunning me, but I still found it hard to engage with them. Shunning had given way to just accepting me sitting there quietly. On the surface it might look the same, but I can assure you it isn't. Looking back, I am far more appreciative of that transition.

All through lunch, I only wanted to go back to the kitchen and talk to Auran. She had been the one to tell me about Temrok. Maybe there was more she knew. But I stopped myself. I didn't want anyone to make a connection between her and the dissidents. It could cost her job, or much worse.

When lunch ended, we headed to our manifestation lesson. As he did every lesson, Hishu called on me to recite the mantra and to summon an apple for him. The last few lessons I had been able to do it and the lessons had been getting better. I opened my mouth to begin and then closed it. I didn't want to say it. Suddenly, the whole idea of the mantra turned my stomach.

"Apprentice, is this too hard for you?" Hishu said condescendingly. "I thought we had finally gotten past your female weakness and you were starting to do real work."

Hishu's words went right past me. I barely heard them. I remembered the joy I had taken in summoning that squash. I felt the triumph when I had manifested the apples to use against the terrorists. But I also saw the smashed squash that I had imagined being Venti's head. Then it became my father's head.

The walls of the classroom started to collapse around me. My chest tightened and air became scarce. What was happening? I needed to breathe. But I couldn't. I could only see my father's dead body before me, his face one of perpetual disappointment at how I had done this to him.

"Kali, are you all right?" Claren whispered to me.

I glanced over at him and saw a look of worry on his face. Beside him, the other two apprentices also shared the look, even Jensen. What must I look like to cause that level of concern? But I couldn't speak so I just shook my head.

"Uhh." Hishu sighed melodramatically, "Is it girl stuff?"

Again, the exasperation I normally would have felt after a comment like that wasn't there. Instead, I only felt a small ounce of relief for an excuse. I nodded weakly. Hishu waved a dismissive hand at me.

"Go, take care of it. You're distracting the rest of the class."

I rushed from the room and into the hall. As soon as I left the room, I felt the weight that was crushing me lift and I collapsed to the floor. Air flowed into my lungs, and I greedily gulped it down. Slowly, my heart returned to beating instead of a single constant hum. Eventually, my awareness of the world around me returned and I noticed I was on the floor of the corridor and two acolytes were standing over me.

I blinked and managed to make out their faces. One was Benthic and when I stood up, a little woozily, he said something to the other acolyte who continued on his way down the hall. I let Benthic lead me to his office and sit me down. He handed me a cup of tea and I took it, just to have something to hold and sip at, even though I didn't like tea much.

After we had sat there in silence for several minutes, sipping our tea, Benthic leaned forward across his desk. "Would you like to talk about it, child?"

I considered his words. I didn't like talking about myself. Especially to old churchmen. But Benthic had never been anything but helpful to me. Maybe it would help to talk about it. I wasn't sure going to Allora was something I wanted right now but I needed someone who understood this power acolytes had.

"I manifested a squash yesterday." I started simply. Benthic's face remained impassive but kindly, which I appreciated. I would have turned that start of a story into a joke.

"I was angry and I wanted something to smash. So, I manifested the squash. Then I imagined it belonging to someone as I smashed it."

I paused long enough Benthic decided to say something and he gave me a comforting smile, "That is nothing to be ashamed of. We have all had feelings like that at some point in our lives. Especially when we were young, such as you are."

"Not like this." I said stubbornly. "You know I went to prison for killing someone."

Benthic nodded, "Yes. It is my understanding that it was an accident."

"Yes, but only because I killed the wrong person. The person I imagined smashing was Venti, the one I previously tried to kill."

"You must hold a lot of hatred toward them. We have talked about letting go of pursuing him."

I felt my emotions flare and I stared my vehemence into my tea. "He killed my mother. I tried to get revenge but my shots missed and...and the person I killed my father. I killed my own father."

Benthic didn't say anything in response to that which I was glad for. What could you say when someone confesses to killing their own father? Nothing good.

"When I imagined smashing Venti's face in that squash, it changed. I saw my father's face. Then today, when Hishu asked me to manifest again, I couldn't do it. I had draw on my selfish desires to make the squash, and those same desires got my father killed. Every time I manifest something, I have to draw on those same feelings and desires. If using the power requires such selfishness and hatred, how can it be good?"

"I understand that it feels like a contradiction. Thank you for sharing your story, I know that must be hard. What happened to your father was an accident. A terrible one to be sure. But I think I understand now. Your desire to pursue this Venti person wasn't selfish revenge. It was to create justice. You said he killed your mother. Not an accident I presume?"

I nodded my head, "He led a group of thugs who shot up our home during dinner. Injured several of my cousins, killed my mother, and my grandfather died from a heart attack as a result."

"What those men did was evil. Desiring to stop them is not evil. Manifesting is all about forcing your will upon Akzad's gift. He has granted it to you for a reason. You have his blessing therefore your goals are his goals. Using that gift isn't selfish. Getting justice isn't selfish. It is your right, your reason for being gifted."

I looked up raising an eyebrow, "You say it like whatever I want is okay to do."

"If it is in pursuit of Akzad's will. But that doesn't mean you're infallible. What happened to your father is proof of that. What happened to you as well. Your control over the gift caused your Relic to fail and allowed you to get shot. I expect both happened for the same reason."

I shrunk back on myself, not wanting to hear what he said next, but needing too. "And why was that?"

"Because you lacked conviction. The purpose of the mantra is to remind us not to falter. You told me you debated pursuing Venti that night. You allowed doubt to color your will and your power over the Relic failed. I expect you did that night. You doubted your right to end Venti's life and it colored your will, causing you to miss."

Benthic leaned forward and rested a hand on my shoulder. "Tell me, was your goal to kill your father?"

I shook my head. Benthic continued, "Never lose sight of your goal. Never question that your actions are the right ones. Believe in Akzad's will."

We sat in silence again for a while. I found some comfort in his words, though I couldn't say why. It hadn't changed what I had done, and I didn't find trying to manifest any more appealing. But maybe that at least wasn't my fault if the power was up to the whims of a fickle god.

"Now, I hate to bring this up after our conversation." Benthic started.

I looked up and gave a wan smile, "But you will."

"But I will." Benthic said back. "Mr. Grant has sent word that he will meet you at the precinct this afternoon for some photos."

My brief moment of relative calm shattered. "Why is he going to meet me at the precinct?"

"For photos. I do not know the details. But he wants you in your uniform. Which I know you don't like but it does send a certain message. Especially after the events at the arena."

"But why the precinct? I thought he was a racing promoter? What does that have to do with the Constabulary?"

Benthic nodded slowly, "I can see your confusion. Mr. Grant has been taken on as the Church's promotor. In all things. His goal is to help us bring people back into the fold. That's the whole reason you on racing on our behalf. It's not about winning races. It is also one of the reasons you are working with the Constabulary. Did you not expect the two to cross paths? You can't be a symbol to improve the image of the Church and the Constabulary from the shadows."

I slouched back in my chair. "I thought I was tracking down Relics."

"And you can do that. But it is also about brand recognition, as Mr. Grant would say."

I nodded reluctantly. Based on how my friends had reacted to rumors I was working with the constabulary, I didn't want to find out what they would think about me doing it openly in church costume. Unfortunately, I couldn't think of any way of getting out of it.

Instead, I set my mind to finding a way to make it work for me. The Church wanted to use me to make them look good. The Constabulary wanted to use me to make them look good. What did I want?

I wanted revenge on Venti. I wanted to find out who he was working for both when he took over my town and when he burned down my street here in the city. I wanted to get justice on them once I found them. Now I just needed to make them help me do that. As Benthic had just explained to me, it was okay to do what I wanted. I was Akzad's vessel.

Chapter 29

It wasn't hard to decide what I wanted. Justice for my family and my town. Venti was on the hit list already. But he wasn't the mastermind, just the weapon. I hadn't made any progress toward finding out who they were since coming to this city. I did have a lead though, I just needed to be strong enough to use it.

Fortunately, my target had requested a meeting with me, which would make tracking him down easy. I arrived at the constabulary precinct to find chaos outside. A quad sat on the street and a group of people were unloading it. They had an array of big light bulbs on tall poles and were running cables to a generator. Right outside the precinct doors stood an odd metallic device on a tripod.

Wandering through all of this was Grant. He shouted orders to people, some of whom were coppers standing on the steps leading to the precinct, while moving everywhere with manic energy. Every few seconds, he looked at his wristwatch and then up into the air.

I stood there trying to assess what was going on, when he noticed me and threw up his hands. "Kali, there you are! Finally! Places everyone! We don't have much sunlight left!"

"Grant, what is going on?" I asked nervously.

"Only the most exciting thing ever!" Grant said. "We're going to make you into a movie star!"

"I'm sorry, what now?"

"I managed to get a hold of footage of you taking down the terrorists in the arena. With that and some new stuff of you raiding their stronghold, we'll make a movie so everyone can see your heroics on behalf of the Church!"

"A movie?" was all I could say in response. I didn't want to be in public wearing Hishu's stupid outfit or seen working with the Constabulary. I definitely did not want to do it repeatedly on a movie screen. My last bits of reservations about what I had come here to do evaporated.

"Grant, we need to talk."

"In a bit. We're losing the light. First, we're going to get a shot of you walking up the street and greeting the constables." Grant gestured to the group of surly looking coppers.

"No, we need to talk. Right. Now." I emphasized. "Privately."

My tone must have gotten through because Grant looked at me with a new light. He gestured for everyone to stand by and then led me down the street a bit, away from the chaos. When we were out of sight, he folded his arms and looked at me displeased.

"Okay, what? This is my big chance to make a movie and I want to do it right. Mr. Papadopoulos loaned me the gear but we have to return it in a week. Tell me you're going to raid the bad guy's lair before then?"

"En gave you this stuff?"

"En? Whose En?"

"Arron Papadopolous."

"Oh. No, this is from his father's studio."

Well, now I knew how En found out I was working with the constabulary. Not that it mattered. I leaned in close to Grant so I wouldn't have to shout. Plus, I always found a fierce whisper more intimidating.

"You're going to tell me who hired you to work with Nils Rady."

Grant's enthusiasm vanished instantly. He stared down at me with a look like he'd just eaten something that disagreed with him, and it was about to come back up. I was trying to be intimidating so I guess I had at least some success.

Grant gulped. "I already told you; I can't reveal my clients. Confidentiality."

"You also said you would comply with requests by the constabulary. I work for them now. And I'm asking again."

"Working with the constabulary. Not for them." Grant hedged, using my same argument against me.

I bit back a sarcastic reply, knowing I had to remain tough here. "You can either tell me now. You can tell me after I break your arm. Or you can tell me after I haul your ass into the precinct and throw you in a cell. The choice is yours."

He stared down at me, his nervous expression now replaced by one of stubborn resistance. "No. I don't believe you'll do that."

Moving quickly, I grabbed his arm, spun around behind him and pushed his body forward while bending the arm toward me. He let out a cry of pain so I let up slightly so I could lean back in close.

"If the next sound out of your mouth isn't what I want to hear, the arm breaks and we go inside." My stomach churned at this, partly reveling at the power I felt over his quaking form, part of it ready to vomit at what I was doing.

"Okay! Okay! Just let go!" Grant cried.

I released his arm and he dropped to his knees holding his arm close and rubbing his shoulder. "I don't know who hired me. It was all done through post. I was paid by a company called ECG but it was just a front."

Well, I had a confirmed connection now, even if it didn't tell me anything new. I needed to press for me. "You just took money from an obvious front to do what exactly?"

"To promote a racer who could win and attribute all his victories to Akzad and the Church. It was a little weird but who am I to question rich eccentric people? Besides, the Church decided to do the same thing eventually so it must not be that weird, right?"

That was the same reason Hishu had wanted me to become a racer for the Church. Could he be the one behind ECG? That would be too convenient I thought. One asshole behind all of my problems. I wouldn't be that lucky.

"Come on, you're telling me you didn't look into it further? I did that when I got to the city. ECG is a post office box. But I was just a kid from the hinterlands. You have to know more." I don't know if Grant heard the note of desperation that slipped into my voice, but I certainly did.

"I did, a little, after what happened to Rady, but I didn't learn much. Just enough to know I didn't want to look any further. Whoever is behind them has their hand into a lot of shit. Shit I don't want to get involved in. That's why I took the job with the Church. Safe. Or at least it's supposed to be."

I studied Grant's face, trying to determine if he was lying. Unfortunately, I was sure he lied about everything. He would twist anything he said to make it sound better for him. But that didn't mean he wasn't telling the truth. He did not seem the type to actively work with the kind of scumbags I was looking for. Unknowingly and if there was plausible deniability, absolutely he'd take their money. But out in the open?

"You said everything came via post? I want to see what they sent you."

"I destroyed it." Grant said immediately.

I narrowed my eyes, "Bullshit. You wouldn't destroy evidence until you know if it could help you. If you only did what you claimed, then nothing they asked you to do was illegal."

"But then they started doing illegal things and I burned everything I ever got from them. I didn't want any evidence I was ever involved."

He might be telling the truth here. I could press him harder, but would that change his tone? I needed something otherwise I was no closer than I had been before.

"Money." I said as an idea occurred to me. "They hired you via post, presumably they didn't send you envelopes full of coins?"

"No, they paid via check."

I smiled, remembering the first clue I had found in Radys account books. Follow the money. His books were gone now, presumably destroyed in the fire. But Grant wouldn't destroy his financial records.

"I need that account information. Where the money came from to pay you."

Grant opened his mouth, undoubtedly, to issue some kind of lie, denial or other obfuscation so just raised my fist slightly. I didn't threaten him directly but he hadn't lied yet either so I didn't even feel bad about it.

Grant sighed, "Fine. But it's not going to tell you anything. The bank won't open up their records, so I don't know what you're going to learn."

I smiled, "I'll know if someone else is giving or receiving money from that same account."

With Grant's promise to get me the pay stubs, I agreed to do whatever nonsense he wanted me to do for this camera. I wanted him to remain friendlyish at least until I got the information. The most annoying part was having to change into my stupid racing uniform because that is what I had worn in the arena.

I emerged back out onto the street wearing the stupid getup and joined Bruneski on the steps. The young constable gave me an overly eager smile. "It looks good."

I frowned at him. "Why? Because it shows cleavage or my hips?"

"Um..." Bruneski stammered. "Both...neither?"

I sighed, "Never mind. So, what do they want us to do?"

"They're going to have you leap in and we're going to salute each other."

"Salute each other?" I asked.

"Yeah."

"Do coppers salute each other?"

"No. Not really. I don't get it either. Maybe it's to show we respect each other?" Bruneski gave a shrug.

"But I don't respect you." Bruneski's shoulders slumped and I cursed myself. "Not you personally. That's not what I meant. The Constabulary. As an institution. It's so corrupt and only protects the powerful. Coppers lord their power over people instead of being there to serve them. And they're far to trigger happy."

That last part I said looking directly at Bruneski who flushed. Despite our first encounter involving him shooting at me, I was starting to like him. He didn't have the same air as most constables. Or at least not yet. He could still recognize mistakes and learn from them.

"Kali, over here, please!" Grant called. I glanced at Bruneski and gave him a little smile, trying to convey friendliness. He at least tried to be kind, unlike most of the others, so the least I could do was return it.

When I walked over to Grant, I got a small jolt of excitement seeing what he held in his hands. My shield. He handed it over to me and my excitement died. The circular shield was far too heavy to be my original Relic. Which made sense, I doubted the Church would hand it over to Grant for this performance.

What followed was a mind-numbing stretch of time. I'm sure it wasn't more than an hour but it felt like forever. I can't fathom how En endures doing this for long enough to make an entire movie. Maybe that's why he had started hiding out at Nerpi's pretending to be a receptionist.

When Grant finally let me go, after I gave him a final reminder to drop off the account information to Nerpi's, I went inside the precinct. Bruneski told me Jundel wanted to see me as soon as we were done. When I went into his office, the old man did not look please. Granted, he had never looked pleased to see me, so this wasn't new.

"Are they finally done with that circus outside and we can return to actual policing?" He grumped.

For once, I could sympathize with him about something. "They're done. Trust me, no one more's pleased to have that over with than I am."

Jundel harrumphed, almost in friendly agreement. "Now, about taking out these scumbag terrorists. We have a few leads but our best source of information, the leader of the failed attack, still won't talk. At least to us."

I kept my expression flat, not wanting to start an argument, after our first tiny hint of cooperation. But I could imagine how the constables had attempted to get the man to talk. It probably involved a lot of bloody knuckles. I had a brief flash of guilt at the thought of what I had threatened to do to Grant to get what I wanted. That was different though. I hadn't actually hit him. Plus, I was the vessel of God himself, so what I wanted made it okay. Right?

"However, he has said he would talk to you, Ms. Knightshield."

I jerked my head, startled at the statement. "Me? Why me? I stopped him."

Jundel threw up his hands, "I have no idea. Who knows how pig minds work? They're subversive trash. I don't care to understand. But what I do want is to know where his companions are."

Our moment of connection vanished at Jundel's display of casual racism toward grunde. "Maybe you should try. Understanding others might help you do some actual good for this city."

"I'm not here to be lectured by you. I'm here to give you an assignment. Speak to the prisoner. Find out where his friends are."

I drew my lips into a thin line. Arguing with him about this wouldn't get me anywhere. But maybe I could turn it to my advantage. I had gotten Grant to give me something. Now it was the Constabulary's turn. I would definitely feel far less guilt about this.

"I'll talk to him. But I need you to do something for me."

"This isn't a negotiation."

"You're right." I said leaning across his desk. "It's not. I have information connecting a man named Venti and the Blood Daggers to a shell company called ECG. I need the Constabulary to gather any information they can about this company."

"What does this have to do with these terrorists?"

"Maybe nothing. Maybe everything. My sources suggest Venti is the one who encouraged this group to attack the arena."

Jundel sat back and rubbed his chin. "Who are these sources?"

"The confidential kind." I said, "Look, you wanted me to use my status to get to know people. It's paid off. So, use this information."

We sat in a tense standoff for an eternity. Jundel drummed his fingers on the desk, looking up at me. I half expected him to call for constables to arrest me at any moment. Finally, he nodded.

"Okay, you get this scumbag to talk and I'll look into this ECG link. But it might not matter. If this pays off, and this Venti chap is involved, we'll likely find him at the lair with the rest of the trash."

I doubted that but I could hope. And maybe pray?

Chapter 30

Bruneski led me down a dark corridor. The stark cinder block walls and poor lighting had a depressing, intimidating effect. I could imagine how this walk would mess with the minds of anyone arrested, making them feel closed in, hopeless and scared. It probably played a role in how easily constables got confessions, even from innocent people. It was messing with my head and I wasn't the one about to be interrogated.

I glanced beside me at Bruneski. He seemed like an alright kind of person now that I had gotten to know him. Yet, on our first meeting, his first action upon seeing me had been to try and shoot me, then arrest me, before talking to me. For the first time, I started to wonder just how much of an effect the bleakness of this place had on the constables as well. When you spend all your time in a place of oppression, even if you are the oppressor, can you avoid having it mess with your head too?

As we reached the interrogation room door, Bruneski opened it for me. "I'll be right outside if you need anything. Captain Jundel will be observing through the mirror. It's a little hard to hear through the wall so try and have the prisoner speak up as much as possible."

"Yeah, I'll be sure to do that."

Bruneski's lips lifted in amusement as he stood aside to let me enter the room. Inside, the walls were even more stark and depressing, if such a thing were possible. The only source of illumination was a lone, weak light bulb suspended from the ceiling. The bulb wasn't centered in the room but hung over a chair with chains attached to it. I had a feeling, if anyone had resisted switching to electric lighting, it would have been the constabulary. Flickering torches would have fit the aesthetic far better. I remembered well the spooky effect they had on our home when I was a child, before our town had power.

The door slammed shut and I was alone in the room. It felt smaller the instant the door closed and the air I breathed in felt staler. I closed my eyes and began to relax my mind and body. That was one thing I could appreciate the church for. All the time 'praying' had given me time to practice the meditations I'd learned as part of my martial arts training. If I caught those anxious feelings early enough, the meditations could help stabilize them, so I didn't end up a shaking mess like I had outside the classroom the other day.

By the time I got my breathing back under control, the other door to the room opened and two constables led a chained grunde in. I barely recognized him from our encounter in the arena. He had lost a lot of weight and bore several half-healed bruises on all his exposed skin. I couldn't stop myself from gaping openly at the sight of him.

The constables roughly shoved the grunde into the chair and linked his manacles to the ones on the chair. They nodded to me, almost respectfully, and then exited through the door they came in from. I glanced at the mirror on the wall behind me, knowing I was being watched through it.

We stood there in silence for a long time. The grunde watching me intently. People watching me through a pane of glass. And me just standing there, frozen, not in panic this time, but with uncertainty.

I swallowed to clear my throat and then said, "I never got your name."

The grunde blinked and then nodded his head, "Hanmish."

"I'd say 'nice to meet you' but neither of our meetings have been under very nice circumstances."

Hanmish chuckled, "You could say that."

We almost fell back into silence, but I pressed forward, "Why am I here? I don't exactly know what I'm doing."

"I wanted to speak to you. I felt our conversation the day you captured me ended abruptly."

I kept my mouth closed but then felt the need to say something. Our conversation had ended abruptly, but that was because I froze in response. I hadn't known what to say to him. I still didn't.

"The constables expect you to spill the beans on where to find your compatriots." I said instead.

"I might."

"You're just saying that to make sure they don't shut this down and throw you back in a cell."

Hanmish shrugged as best he could with his arms shackled. Seeing how he had been treated, I couldn't blame him for being reluctant to go back. Though, I expected if he didn't give me what they wanted things would get much worse for him. Bullies didn't like it when they didn't get what they wanted.

"I was inspired by the stories of you." Hanmish said. "Taking down some coppers to save an innocent woman. That's a hero. When I heard that story, I didn't believe at first. But then I heard more. You were fighting back. I thought, maybe I should do the same."

"The stories you heard weren't accurate. I saved that woman from some of your buddies. Blood Dagger thugs. I did fight with some coppers too, but they weren't the ones chasing her."

"Only because they didn't get there first. Coppers are known to do that when they see something they want. That's why it breaks my heart to see you working for them."

I bristled, "With. Not for."

"Is there a difference? They like to use kind words and pat you on the back. But it's all just to control us. We're just resources to them. Only worth what they can extract from us."

"Maybe. But is threatening to kill a bunch of innocent people any different?"

Hanmish's cheeks flushed and he looked down at the floor. There was some guilt there, so I had something to work with. "You've heard about the Lesshon and Durmal Street fires? Those fires killed a lot of people and left even more homeless. They were set, not by cops, by buddies of yours."

Chains rattled as Hanmish stiffened and tried to stand. "They were not!"

"I was there, Hanmish!" I shouted, "I saw the Blood Daggers set the fires. I saw them shoot at me. I know their leader. And I know he's involved with your people. So don't play innocent!"

I was riled up now. I had been accused of a lot of uncomfortable things. Some, I wasn't sure were truly inaccurate. But that didn't excuse Hanmish from what he had done. I needed to know where Venti was and he was the only one who could tell me.

"Venti was the one to suggest the stunt at the arena, wasn't he? Did you know, in addition to leading thugs in burning down people's homes, he also works as muscle for big corporations looking to strip mine away entire towns? He's a front man for the same people you're fighting. That Relic you used? Came from him didn't it? That one only distracted people. He has others a lot more dangerous."

Hanmish stared a look of pure hatred at me. I could feel his betrayal and anger as if they were physically pressing into my chest. But I don't think all of the hatred was for me, personally. He, at least on some level, thought I might be telling the truth.

I glanced behind me at the mirrored glass. I thought he might be close to telling me something, but he'd still be reluctant with the constables listening. I looked back at Hanmish and his manacles. Even with them on, he had some range of motion. If I got too close, he would be able to grab me. While he might not be a trained fighter, the raw power in his hands could crush my throat with ease if he got a hold of it. But I had to take the risk.

I strode right up to Hanmish and leaned in, so we were almost touching. I looked him right in the eyes and barely whispered. "Tell me where I can find them. They are going to hurt more people. I don't want your friends, those that think like you. They are just being used. Eventually, they are going to be manipulated into doing something stupid, like you did. But it might be worse. You didn't hurt anyone. They might. And it won't be coppers who suffer. It will be people like us."

Hanmish stared back at me, but the hatred had already burned out. I saw him at war with himself. Helping me, helped his enemies. But not helping me still meant helping his enemies if what I said was true. I just had to hope he believed me.

"Will it only be Venti's thugs that get arrested?"

I shook my head softly, "I can't do that. The constables are going to be gunning for anyone involved with the arena. A lot of them ran after I took you down. Coppers already raided their homes but they were already gone."

Hanmish sighed, "Okay. Just the ones who got away from the arena? Promise me all the boys who haven't done anything aren't collateral damage?"

I nodded even though I had no idea how I was going to pull that off. But it was enough for Hanmish. "They'll be in the worker housing by the old river textile factory. But Venti isn't always there. That's just where Temrok is set up."

"So Temrok is involved." I hissed, thinking about how my friends had insisted he wasn't.

"He opposed this plan, but he didn't stop us. Ever since he met Venti, he's become far more radical. Insists that our entire society is built on a bed of lies. But even still, he didn't think this would accomplish much. And he was right." Hanmish slumped down in the chair.

With a flash of sympathy, I patted his shoulder, "It hasn't accomplished nothing. You got your message heard by at least one person."

I left the interrogation room and found Captain Jundel waiting for me in the hall. He looked furious. I smiled at him, knowing this would only antagonize him more, and then started down the hallway back toward the entrance. He stormed after me.

"You were instructed to have the prisoner speak up. We could barely hear half the interrogation."

"It's hard for him to speak up after his throats gone raw from screaming in pain during your previous 'conversations'." I snapped back, not keeping any contempt out of my voice.

We reached the main room of the precinct office. Jundel stopped yelling and turned toward his office but I remained where I was. He glowered at me and poor Bruneski beside him looked like he wanted to be anywhere but there.

"We'll continue this in my office. You can give us a full report on what the prisoner told you." Jundel said, his tone sharp but his volume more normal.

"I need to verify some of it first." I smiled wickedly, "You wouldn't want to look like a fool by raiding the wrong place? Twice."

Jundel narrowed his eyes, "Of course not. But tell me anyways and then I'll decide how to proceed."

"If I tell you, you'll send a whole strike team in with guns blazing. A lot of people would get hurt. I'm only going to risk that if I'm sure those people aren't innocents."

"You seem to be misunderstanding me. That wasn't a request, it was an order." Jundel said.

I straightened up to my tallest and held Jundel's gaze. "I don't work for you."

"I could have you arrested. We still haven't dropped all the charges against you for the wide stream of crimes you've committed. The Church can't protect you from everything."

"You could." I admitted, "It would look great for those cameras."

We both turned to look at Grant and his filming crew still working at the entrance to the building. I doubted they were actually filming anything right now and Jundel could have all the film seized and destroyed. But he couldn't arrest the entire crew, not without risking the ire of some powerful people.

I moderated my tone some. Not because I thought it would be diplomatic but because I really didn't want to get arrested. If I challenged him too much, I know he would do it no matter what. People like Jundel did not react well when you challenged their little corner of power.

"After I check this information out, I'll let you know. It could be the hideout for the entire gang. But it could also be a hot bed of lies. If it is their hideout, I can't take them down alone so we're going to need to work together."

Jundel looked like he might still refuse but then Bruneski spoke up. "Sir, wouldn't it be better to verify it's not a trap without risking any of our men?"

I glanced at Bruneski, annoyed at the idea of being used as disposable, but saw him giving me a hopeful look. He was trying to help in his own way. It turned out to be an effective tactic because Jundel nodded agreement.

"Fine, be back tomorrow. I don't want to let those subversive pigs remain out there any longer than we have too."

My blood boiled and I decided to add another condition. "When I come back, I'm going to need to speak to the prisoner again, either way. If he's been touched at all between now and then, I won't say a word about what I found."

I didn't give Jundel a chance to say anything else before turning and leaving the precinct.

Chapter 31

The next day, I caught a break. I had been wondering how I was going to get out of my duties at the Church to investigate Temrok, when Allora showed up outside one of my classrooms. She exchanged greetings with the acolyte instructor and managed to get me excused to speak with her.

"I thought you were trying to avoid this place?" I asked once we were alone in the corridor. With just us in the empty stone channel I had to work extra hard to keep my voice from echoing.

"I am." Allora left a pregnant pause hanging in the air.

"So why did you come?" I asked.

Allora opened her mouth as if to speak and then stopped again. Finally, she shoved an envelope at me, "This turned up for you from Grant. I thought it might be important based on how eager he was to see that you got it."

Greedily, I tore open the envelope and took out the papers. At first, they made no sense to me as they were full of numbers in cramped text. I hadn't had much exposure to bank checks so deciphering what all the numbers meant turned out to be harder than I had anticipated. I knew enough to know that people had accounts labeled with numbers to identify them but couldn't tell which set of numbers that would be.

"You look confused." Allora had a small smile on her face.

I glared at her half-heartedly, "Nerpi needed to pay us by check at least once so I would know what I'm looking at now."

"But you don't have a bank account."

"Well, then maybe I would and I wouldn't be broke."

Allora sighed and reached her hand out for the papers. I handed them to her, "What are you trying to figure out?"

"The account number of who ever paid this money to Grant. It's the account ECG was using to pay him to support Rady's racing. If I can find that out, I can know if they paid anyone else, or better yet, if anyone paid them. Such as, possibly, the people behind the curtain."

Allora gave a small nod of her head, "That's not a bad idea. Though, you'd have to gain access to other people's bank records, which isn't going to be easy. Of course, the harder part is going to be figuring out whose accounts you'd even want to look at."

She paused and then let out a heavy sigh. "I might have an idea one in mind for who you might want to look at."

"Who?"

"Temrok."

I blinked uncertainly, "I thought you were certain he wasn't dirty."

"I was. But then I found out Venti is hiding out the same place as Temrok."

I stiffened, "The old housing by the abandoned textile factory?"

Allora nodded, "How did you know?"

"Hanmish, the guy who led the assault on the arena, confessed to me that Temrok led his group. Introduced them to Venti, who suggested the arena event. Told me where I could find them. I've been looking for an opportunity to check it out."

"Temrok has spoken openly against what happened. He wants action, yes, but direct action against the Church or the Council. Not innocent people. I couldn't believe he would be involved with this. But now I don't know what to think."

"We can ask him after we arrest him." I said.

Allora shook her head emphatically, "No. No constables. We need to talk to him, but I don't want constables shooting him and asking questions later."

"But you said Venti is there. Now. We have to take him down."

"After we get Temrok and his people out. They're just kids. Then you can send whatever you want after Venti."

I fumed in silence. Finally, I nodded in agreement.

"One minute. I need to talk to someone else first." I said holding up the banking documents she had delivered. I trotted down the hallway until I caught up with the group of apprentices who were just leaving the classroom, headed toward lunch.

Mateto smiled at me, "What was that about, Kali?"

"Super-secret police stuff." I said cryptically, knowing it would get his attention but also keep him from asking more questions. "Claren, I need to speak to you for a moment."

"Okay." Claren said uncertainly.

"Privately." That earned a suggestive eyebrow wiggle from Jensen and I rolled my eyes.

"Okay." Claren said even more uncertainly.

I pulled him down the corridor a little, just enough to be out of sight from the others. "You're doing work for Brother Tremel, right? On the accounting books?"

"I am."

"Good. I need you to look through the books and see if anyone in the Church has paid or been paid by this account number." I showed him the number Allora had pointed out.

Claren's uncertainty had shifted to concern. He glanced around us as if someone was watching us. "Kali, what's this about?"

"It's part of my investigation." I said, deliberately vaguely.

"You think someone from the Church is funding those terrorists?" Claren asked his eyes widening.

I bit my lip stopping myself from saying yes right away. I needed to think about how I worded this. Over the past weeks I had come to trust Claren but he was very devout. I wouldn't take an accusation against the Church lightly. But I couldn't exactly lie to him. I wasn't good at it.

"I don't know." I settled on, "I know this account is linked with some bad people. And I know a lot of money flows through the Church. They might be using it to launder the money. Donations or something. It may not show up. But it's something we need to know for sure, wouldn't you say?"

Claren nodded in agreement to that "Then why are you coming to me? Instead of the Constabulary speaking directly to Brother Tremel or the High Acolyte?"

Now I had to lie. I held my face as impassive as I could. "In case it's nothing. I'm the liaison with the Church and Constabulary, right? This is why I'm here."

"So why ask me? Why not look yourself?"

"Because I'm not an aid to the accountant. You are."

"Yeah. I suppose. But this is going to take a while. Looking through all the records for one particular account number will take hours."

I smiled at him, "I'll help you when I can. Right now, I have to go look into something else."

I almost left immediately after that but stopped as I neared Hishu's office. I knew where Venti was. This was my opportunity to take him down. I had promised Allora we would confront her friend without constables. If I waited until after that he would get away. But if I was able to pass a message along to the Constabulary now to have a team meet me there, Venti wouldn't have time to flee. I knocked on the door and went in to speak to Hishu.

After, I avoided making eye contact with Allora as she led me into an even more depressing part of the city than our street had become. Work at least had begun to tear down the burned-out buildings on our street, but here buildings that had burned in other incidents were left crumbling wrecks. Most windows had been replaced by boards and everything was covered in soot that drifted out from the nearby power plants and factories.

I had been depressed at the state of the city when I had first moved here. Growing up in a border town, we didn't have electricity but we did have space. The city always felt so cramped and rundown. But the areas I usually spent my time were open and magnificent compared to this. You could have barely gotten a cycler down the street the buildings were so close together.

We went inside the decaying building. This was more familiar to me, as I had been in several buildings that were falling apart. They were common throughout the poorer parts of the city. Temrok resided in a room on the second floor. Two young tough guys, a nudra and a grunde, stood outside his door. They unnecessarily cracked their knuckles when they saw us approaching and started to saunter over. The dim lighting must have kept them from seeing very well because once they recognized Allora, their whole mannerism changed. They visibly relaxed and they smiled offering her affectionate greetings.

I stayed behind her, trying to remain as unnoticed as possible. I wasn't sure how I felt about this development. On the one hand, it was good they recognized Allora and we weren't going to have to fight them. On the other, it meant Allora was very involved with these people. Temrok had goons outside his room which didn't make me feel very confident about his peaceful intentions.

We were let inside, the guards remained in the hallway, and Temrok sat at a desk with a typewriter. He swiveled in his chair to look at us but when he saw Allora he turned back and continued typing something. I surveyed the rest of the room while he ignored us but saw nothing of interest. A rundown apartment, cracks in the walls, water damage in the ceiling. The floor and countertops were clean though.

After an interminably long time, Temrok let out a huff of air. "What do you want Allora? I'm working."

"I brought someone to meet you. We have some questions."

"She'll have to come back."

"It's the Knightshield."

"So? I have no time for a Church stooge."

I cringed at Allora's use of the fantasy title people had given me but Temrok's dismissal of it left me feeling uncertain. What he said was exactly what I felt about the whole thing. So why did it hurt to hear it out loud?

Allora continued her argument, never losing her calm demeanor. "I'm a Church stooge too, if you recall."

"Yes, but I don't hold it against you. We were all dumb in our youth. You've seen the light."

"She's no older than I was when I joined. I was hoping you could show her the light too."

I scowled up at Allora. "I'm not here to listen to your propaganda. I'm here to find out about Venti and for you to convince me you had nothing to do with the assault on the arena."

Temrok finally stopped typing and spun around in his chair. He lowered a pair of reading glasses that rested on his tusks and fixed an intense stare at me. "Or what? You'll arrest me? Yes, I am also aware you are not only a Church stooge but police bootlicker as well. Care to become a corporate shill and get the trifecta of class traitor?"

I held his glare with one of my own. "At least I'm not threatening to shoot innocent people who just wanted to watch some cyclers race on their only day off. Or burning down entire neighborhoods."

Temrok's response grew cold and quiet. "That wasn't my people."

"That's not what Hanmish said."

Temrok's glower faltered. A look of concern and hurt crossed his face, "Hanmish said that? How badly have you beaten him? I'm sure he'll say anything you want now."

The genuine pain in his voice brought me up short. I had been convinced this was the real mastermind behind the attacks. Venti had always been a hired stooge. I didn't think he was capable of running a cause, even if that cause was mayhem.

"How do you know Venti?" I asked, trying to get a handle on all that I didn't know.

Temrok looked back at his typewriter. "I was just a simple historian back then. He brought some text to me to translate. Old script, pre-unification. That changed my life."

I glanced at Allora about to roll my eyes, but she only nodded solemnly. I looked back to Temrok and moderated the sarcasm that had been about to come out. "How did old text change your life?"

"I learned the truth about our origins on this planet. The Cataclysm wasn't some disaster on our home worlds that Akzad saved us from. The Cataclysm was when we weren't brought here by Akzad to enslave us. Unification was when the slaves rose up against him."

It was my turn to stare openmouthed. I'd had my beef with the Church and disagreed with a lot of things they did and taught. But this was on an entirely different level.

"Some old papers said this?" I asked.

"Not precisely. It was instead an unedited version of founding Church documents. The Church taught we got our power from Akzad. Which is true. We learned the old magic by emulating him. Learning how to Manifest and many other things. That was how we overthrew his army. The tribes united for the war and then almost immediately turned on each other. The Church evolved as a way of ending that infighting. That much of doctrine is true. They just left out the part where they suppressed knowledge of the magic so only they could use it. Somewhere along the line, Akzad went from the thing we were uniting against to the reason we were united."

"And you have these documents?" I asked.

"No. I was only given them to translate."

"By Venti?"

Temrok nodded. "He had been tasked with retrieving them and wanted to know what they were before turning them over to his employer."

"Who was his employer?"

"I don't know. He never said. I didn't care at the time. I only wanted to know where he got them. Dug up from a mine in the border towns."

I slumped back against the counter behind me. "My town. Or one like it. They took over my town to dig up some old texts? What else did they find? Is this where the Relics are coming from?"

"I do not know. Venti has provided us with a lot of things but the first thing I heard about Relics was the arena incident. At least, I assume Hanmish got his from Venti."

"Okay. We'll pretend I believe that. You said he had you translate it. Who was he digging it up for?"

Temrok shrugged. "I don't know exactly. But based on the content, I assumed the Church. Who else would want this suppressed?"

I shook my head, "Why would they pay scum like Venti to dig it up only to suppress it? Just don't dig it up."

"If they are the ones to dig it up, they can control who knows about it." Allora pointed out.

"Sure. But honestly, would anyone even believe some old texts? We've all been taught about Akzad our whole lives. I've never been religious, despite my current occupation, and even I'm not convinced Temrok's not just lying to us." I pointed to Allora. "I assume you've never seen these texts. Because you've never mentioned them. And it seems like kind of a big deal."

Allora nodded, "You're right, I've never seen them. But I can't say I don't believe him. What he has said matches what Church documents I have seen. It's not as preposterous a theory as it sounds at first. This is one of many reasons my sabbatical has gone on for so long."

I fumed and paced around the little room for a moment. There was a lot potentially going on here. How much of it was important? I needed to find the ones behind all of this. But everything kept pointing back to Venti as my best lead.

"Where is Venti? If he's really the one behind the arena attack, and not you, then we need to bring him in so we can prove your innocence."

"Prove my innocence? Now I must prove it?" Temrok snarled.

"The one who carried out the attack claims it was your idea. So far, it's your word against his."

Before Temrok could respond, the door to the room burst open. A young evian child rushed up to Temrok and pulled on his sleeve. He sighed but stared down at them good naturedly.

"What is it child?" he asked.

I didn't hear their response because my world narrowed as I recognized the child. I dropped to my knees beside them. "Talesh?"

They turned to me with a wide smile. "My knight!"

"How are you here? I thought...I thought..." I stammered unsure how to tell a child I thought they had died. "Your apartment burned down."

They nodded. "Yes. It was very scary. But Mr. Temrok took mummy and papa in so we live here now."

Allora and Temrok were staring at me uncertainly. I had never told Allora about my encounter with this child and didn't feel like now was the time to explain I wanted nothing more than to grab them in my arms and hold on. Not everyone I had failed was dead.

Still kneeling on the floor, I looked up to Temrok. He looked at me as if expecting something and I realized I had missed why Talesh had come in here. I glanced between him and Allora.

"Why is there a child here?" I asked.

"There are lots of children here." Temrok said with a shrug. "I have taken a lot of refuges in."

"You keep children in a terrorist camp?" I balked.

Temrok growled, "No, children live in an apartment building. Because they have no where else to go. As you seem aware, their homes were destroyed."

"By Venti, the very man you're working with!"

"Nonsense." Temrok responded but his tone lacked conviction.

I gestured to Talesh, "His Blood Daggers burned down their home. And almost burned down ours. So when I learned he was here, I summoned the Constabulary to come take him down. But now you're telling me this place is full of children!"

Temrok growled, "The coppers are coming here? Because of you?"

I looked at the child, now shaking in fear at our raised voices. This would be the second home they lost because of me.

Chapter 32

I can't say I was a fan of the accusatory looks Allora and Temrok cast me. Even if they were completely justified. I couldn't meet their eyes but nor could I avoid it for long.

"How long do we have?" Allora asked flatly.

I shrugged, "I asked Hishu to pass a message on to the Constabulary. Then we came here. Depends on how quickly the messenger arrived and if they took it seriously."

"They'll take it seriously. Any opportunity to bash some skulls in." Temrok snorted. Then he looked down at Talesh still standing there uncertainly. "Run along to your mother, child. It will all be okay."

Talesh looked at me and smiled. "Do not fear. My knight will protect you."

That seemed to reassure them and they dashed back out the door. I stood up, took in a deep breath, and faced Temrok. "I'll wave them off. Tell them I was wrong and neither of you are here."

Temrok laughed, "You truly believe that, don't you? They don't care who they arrest. All they care about is cracking some skulls and keeping us in our place. If they arrest the real terrorists or anyone who has reason to be opposed to their power, it doesn't matter. They'll have spread fear. Even if you succeed in slowing them down, they'll still have driven us from our home. They'll have spread their fear."

I thought about the constables I had met and the ones I had grown up with. I wanted to argue with him. There were good ones. My father. Probably Bruneski. But were they enough?

"I don't want that to happen either." I said almost begging. I glanced at the door Talesh had left through. "I don't want these people to suffer more. I only want to help them."

Temrok smiled and shook his head. "You had started too, I'll admit. A lone person, standing up to those in power to protect those without. A shield against corruption and evil. You had some power as a symbol. If you wanted to do something, you shouldn't have let them take that symbol from you."

I felt the still unfamiliar weight of my replacement wraspisa. I missed my old one. Not only for its function as an actual shield. Nothing had felt right since it had been taken from me. I know Temrok wasn't being so literal with his statement, but it drove the point home even more.

I nodded slowly. "I think I'm beginning to understand what you've been fighting for. You're right. I shouldn't have let them take it from me. But then, what choice did I have? What choice do any of us have? Just those over our own actions. I'll go and try to stop the constables. I might fail. But if I do nothing people are going to die. There is no way Venti is surrendering without a fight. I was fine with that, eager even for that confrontation. But that's when there weren't a bunch of innocent people who would be caught in the crossfire."

I turned to the door but then Temrok grabbed my arm. "Wait. I'll go with you. If you can turn me in, it might be enough for them.

One of the guards standing by the door shook his head defiantly. "Don't do this. Don't give in to them. We'll fight."

"No, Lasin, that is what I am afraid of. Violent uprising is the last resort. It may be necessary someday. But we're not ready. Not enough of the people are behind us. Not enough even know it's possible for life to be different. I will go and confront the constables. It will be up to you to spread the message now."

The guard, Lasin, looked as if he were going to argue more. A tense moment passed between the pair of them before Lasin finally nodded. He embraced Temrok and then let him go as I led us down the stairs.

The approaching constables were a lot closer than I had been expecting. A good dozen of them were riding in the bed of a quad, all armed with rifles and billy clubs. The quad was only a short way down the street from the apartment building. If people started trying to flee now, they wouldn't make it far.

As I approached the constables started hopping out of the quad. They were led by Carter and Bruneski. I wasn't sure if I should be thankful it was constables who knew me or not. Carter sneered down at me. "I see your meeting with the terrorists went well. You've captured one already."

"He's the only one. The rest have already fled here, just like the last place. Unfortunately, by the time I sent you the note to meet me here, they must have already been running. Sorry to make you come all the way out here for nothing."

"What about the other one?"

I said and gestured to Allora, "She is with me. She's an acolyte of the Church."

Carter sighed, "Oh fine. Just arrest the pig. Then surround the building so we can round up the rest of them."

I stepped forward to get right up next to Carter. "The others aren't here. Just him. The people that live here are just people. They have nothing to do with this."

"And you've talked to all of them? Even if you're right, they are trespassers. No one is a tenant of this building but they're living here anyways. Without paying rent, the lazy vagabonds. So even if I believe you, which I don't, they'll be coming with us."

I gestured a hand at Temrok. "We have what we need. He can tell us where to find the others. But if you hurt the people in this building he's going to clam up."

Carter shrugged, "We'll get him to talk, just like the other one."

"Because that worked so well. He only agreed to talk to me. Your torture got nowhere. Take this win and walk away."

"Got nowhere?" Carter laughed, "He told you how to find this place. This one will as well. Whether he wants to or not. Now stand aside so we can round up any others hiding among the riff-raff."

I glanced back at the building. Venti was within reach. These constables could help me take him down. Maybe we could do this safely. It would save more people in the long run if Venti and his Blood Daggers were taken down. So what if a few people got hurt now to prevent infinitely more later?

"They're not here." I said, surprising even myself.

"What?" Carter asked.

"Any other terrorist. Temrok was the only connection. And he can tell us where to find the others. But only if we walk away. There are a lot of innocent people here."

"They're not innocent if they're harboring terrorists and illegally squatting."

"They're just people! Trying to survive. Walk away."

Carter waved a dismissive hand. "Arrest him and then take the building. Move!"

One of the constables started to move up the building's steps. As soon as he opened the door, Venti's thugs would respond, I felt sure. They had to have noticed the squad of constables on the street by now. People would be killed in the crossfire. Venti may be one of them, but would that be worth it?

Without any more hesitation, I took off my wraspisa and flung it. It took a lot more effort but the extra weight paid off. The metal disk embedded itself into the building's door handle, preventing it from opening. It wouldn't stop them for long, but it did stop them for now.

"What are you doing?" Carter exclaimed.

"Stopping you."

He snarled. "You've gone too far. I don't care what the captain thinks, you're interfering with a police investigation. You're under arrest."

I smiled broadly at him. "You'll have to catch me first."

The constable nearest me lunged at me from behind. I dropped as soon as I sensed him move and rolled into a reverse somersault, tripping him as I did. Another one swung his billy club as I stood back up, but his swing was clumsy. I easily dodged and then pushed him on his follow through, knocking him into another constable.

I grabbed their two rifles, ejected the magazine and then cracked the weapons against the engine compartment of the quad. It wasn't a hard blow but fortunately, my time with Nerpi had taught me a few things about engines. The muzzle of the rifle penetrated the weak grill and punctured the radiator. Steam and water billowed out from the engine.

"You've got a choice, Carter." I said. "You can raid this building, with three men already down and no vehicle to transport any prisoners back in.

You can shoot me, a member of the Church, in broad daylight. Or you can withdrawal."

Carter looked ready to act on the idea of shooting me when Bruneski put his hand on his arm. Carter cursed but waved everyone off. "Fall back. We'll need more men."

To me he snarled, "As for you, run while you have a chance. The Church won't be able to protect you after this."

Chapter 33

As the squad of constables retreated down the street, leaving their disabled vehicle behind, I turned to regard my too companions. I couldn't fathom what to say now. Nothing about this encounter had gone at all like I had anticipated this morning. I walked in silence back up the steps to the building to retrieve my wraspisa. It was wedged tightly into the door handle and frame and took some leverage to pull out. Once I did, the door swung open lazily, no longer able to latch closed.

"Sorry about your door." I said.

"Well, the constable was right about one thing, this isn't my building."

"But you live here, so it should be."

For the first time, Temrok smiled, "I think you'll have better luck convincing the Church I'm not a heretic than you will of convincing the ruling class of that. But, either way, it's not my home now. Those coppers will be back. And in far greater force."

"We need to get everyone moved. But to where? These people were already made homeless once. They have nowhere else to go." Allora said.

"While you two figure that out, I'm going to go see the man responsible for that." I said resolving myself to this confrontation. The last three times I had encountered Venti, someone I cared about had been shot. I didn't relish the idea of seeing who was next but I liked the idea of letting him go even less.

Allora rested a hand on my shoulder. "Kali, you just sent the constables away specifically to avoid a confrontation with him. Why are you going to do it now? At least wait until we get everyone else out of here."

"If we do that, he'll get away. The difference is I'm not going in with a bunch of trigger-happy constables. I'm not going in with a gun of any kind.

That's why it wasn't safe. Constables start shooting, the Blood Daggers start shooting, everyone else in the building gets shot. But this is just me, no gun."

"That's suicide, Kali." Allora demanded.

"Only if I fail." I winked and started to push my way inside.

"Is that what your father would do?"

I froze halfway through the door. My blood boiled and I didn't turn, unable to look at Allora. "What did you just say?"

Her voice quiet and gentle, "You don't talk about your past much. But what you have said has been about your father. How he taught you everything you knew. How to fight. Right from wrong. How to make good choices. He sounds like a wise man. Would he confront a group of thugs alone and unarmed?"

"You don't know anything about my father. He, and my mother, are dead because of this asshole."

"You're right. I don't. But you do. Would he want you to do this?"

"I know what he would do. He would do exactly what I'm going to do." I snarled and then my anger dropped, replaced by sadness. "And it's what got him killed."

I had never told Allora everything that had happened. That I had been the one to pull the trigger that killed him. I realized at that moment that it hadn't mattered. The moment he had decided to confront Venti alone, he was dead. He'd never take a pay off but he was too scared his deputies had. Going alone had been suicide. What's worse, at that moment, I realized I think he had known that but done it anyways. Despite having me to still care for.

I'd hated myself for years for pulling the trigger. I told myself the hatred was for my missing Venti and hitting my father, but it was for picking up the gun in the first place. The only reason to do that was to use it to kill. I hated Venti for killing my mother and ruining our home town in the first place. I hated the people who had sent him there. The ones who used their influence in the City to override our rules against having guns in town, which had made the townsfolk too scared to oppose the takeover.

Now, I realized, I also hated my father for confronting Venti that night. He had left me alone. Even if I had never followed him, he would have died that night. One person alone wasn't going to change anything.

I finally allowed myself to look up. I saw Allora with her usual look of compassion. A few paces behind her, Temrok stood silently, but not unkindly. This was all affecting him and everyone else in this building too. They were homeless because of Venti and the people he worked for. They had been tricked into taking him in. I didn't have to confront him alone.

"Get everyone out of the building. I'm not going to confront him alone this time."

The evacuation of the building went far smoother than I would have anticipated. I guess that said something about why these people had come here. This wasn't the first time they were being forced to flee their homes. At least this time the place wasn't on fire.

As expected, Venti and his group of Blood Dagger thugs slipped out in the midst of everyone else. They didn't brandish any obvious weapons, but I was sure they were all armed. Undoubtedly, they had been aware of the arrival of the constables and were weary of a trap but also just as eager to not still be here when the constables inevitably came back. Now they were out in the open, I had to figure out how to confront them without it turning into a standoff. I had positioned myself on a second story overhang so I could leap in or away as needed.

As luck would have it, this decision was taken from me as Temrok pushed through the crowd and planted himself in front of Venti. Why Allora wasn't yelling at him about doing something stupid I had no idea. Especially since she was standing right beside him.

"Get out of my way, Temrok." Venti demanded. It was barely audible over the general hum of the confused and fleeing crowd of people. The people around them sensed the tension and immediately spread out, making the next words easier to hear. "We need to get out of here now that you've sold us out."

Clearly not expecting to be on the defensive, Temrok stared open mouthed and only managed to stammer out a weak, "What...it's you who've..."

The initiative lost, Venti pushed past him and I knew I had to step in now. I sprung from my resting place and landed in the small bit of open space in front of Venti, blocking his progress yet again. In my rough apprentice robe, I doubted I looked very impressive, but he and his group did stop. I almost wished for the racing uniform I had, as much as I hated it, it did draw your attention.

"You're not going to get to just walk away from me this time, Venti." I snarled.

To my eternal chagrin, Venti showed not a single bit of concern and he actually chuckled. "Third times the charm, eh, kid? Good luck. I've let you live because, believe it or not, I felt sorry for you. Shooting your own old man? Getting shot when you think you're invulnerable? You just have the worst luck. I mean, here you are rushing to confront me while surrounded by a mob of people who are homeless because of you."

Unlike Temrok, I was ready for Venti to go on the attack so I was prepared to fire back, "I bet these people would be real interested in learning whose really responsible for making them homeless. Who started those fires that burned down their homes. Why did you do it, Venti? Money? Just a desire to watch the world burn."

"You mean the fires you started?" Venti shot back. "You and your friends burned down my bar and that spread to the whole neighborhood."

"That happened the day before that fire. What made you go back and set a new one? Some rich investor decide he could make a quick fortune on insurance fraud? Or make more money rebuilding pricier condos?"

"Or how about the second fire, that occurred after you broke in beloved racer Nils Rady's garage in order to sabotage him? Or the most recent one that burned down almost every other shop but your pal Nerpi's? Did the poor sandwich shop owner slight you in some way so you burned his shop down in revenge?"

The brutality of his assault left me unsure how to respond. I had been expecting him to deflect but he was good. The smile on his smug face made me want to punch him. I knew that it would be over if I did. His men would butcher me and the crowd wouldn't help me. I had to turn things around.

"Why don't we start at the beginning?" I stood up as tall as my meager frame would allow, "How you were paid by someone to take over a remote village in the Outskirts. You came with lies about rejuvenating the town when all you wanted was access to the old mines. To find what? Some old Relics and church documents. Relics that convinced a few scared kids they could be used to sway everyone in the Arena to their cause but only resulted in scaring a bunch of people and getting those kids arrested.

"That's why you are here. These people are desperate. Driven there, in part, by you. Someone wants them desperate enough to do something stupid. Something like take over an arena. Or anything else that results in a blood bath. That way, everyone ready to stand up for a change is turned away for fear of being associated with that. Everything you do is at the behest of the highest bidder and you don't care who gets hurts along the way."

I knew I had gotten somewhere close to the truth by Venti's lack of an immediate response. A few of the goons in his group bore looks of uncertainty which said even more. I realized then, this wasn't about confronting Venti, it was about those he had following him. Undoubtedly, some of them just enjoyed violence. But the recent recruits, like those he'd convinced to storm the arena, were disillusioned kids.

"Have you been working for the same person this whole time or switching masters? It's been my goal to find out who paid you to ruin my hometown. Is it the same person who paid you to burn down neighborhoods? Or was each time a different person? First rich guy saw how much money his buddy made and hired you to do the same? What do they have planned for you next? Something bloody I'm sure. Something to get all these kids killed and to allow the constabulary to crack down hard on anyone acting out of their place."

Around me the crowd stirred. Most were probably just confused, responding to a change in mood. But a few, the closest few had heard. Some of those were part of Venti's entourage and they didn't look happy. Sensing the shift in mood, Venti decided to change tactics.

"Those are some mighty fancy accusations coming from a stooge of the constabulary and the church. So whose working for the highest bidder here? You'll suck the cock of anyone in power for a pat on the head."

Then Venti got slapped in the face. To my eternal surprise, it wasn't my hand that did it. Instead, an old grunde woman in the crowd near me did it. Everything went silent for a moment as everyone looked in surprise at the old woman. I didn't recognize her but had to appreciate her form. The slap had clearly had some power behind it, despite her frail body.

"You speak to the Knightshield with more respect. You're the reason my grandson sits in prison. She may have arrested him but if she hadn't, he would be dead. You talked him into going to that damned arena. You're a bad, bad man."

Sometimes, all it took was a sharp word from grandma to turn things around. The mood in the crowd rapidly shifted now. Those that had been just curious now looked with hostility at Venti.

Sensing this shift in mood, he decided it was time to act. Fortunately, this was what I had been waiting for the whole time. Venti reached under his coat and drew out a gun. Before he could bring it up though, I snapped out, grabbing the barrel and twisting it from his hand. I had gotten quite a lot of practice at this maneuver. I had him disarmed and the magazine ejected before Venti could even blink.

Unfortunately, he wasn't the only one armed. Several of his thugs responded, drawing far more deadly weapons than a simple pistol. The crowd gasped in fear and took a collective step back. The thugs twisted nervously, covering the whole crowd with their barrels, but several of them had guns trained on me.

Venti rubbed his cheek with one hand, and shook the stinging one I had disarmed, but he still managed to let out an amused laugh. "Thought for a second there you'd get the upper hand on me, didn't you? But you should know by now, the person with the bigger gun always wins. Now, get out of the way before anyone gets hurt."

He wasn't prepared for the smile I returned to him. "You've always been free to leave here, Venti. You've revealed your true colors and now everyone knows you for what you really are. A man who'd threaten an innocent old lady. A man who must rely on a big gun to get his way. A man who retreats from an unarmed little girl."

Venti looked uncertainly at me when I stepped aside. He walked slowly forward and then looked back. Only a few of his group followed him. Several others had lowered their rifles, looking ashamedly at the old woman. Seeing so many of his followers stay behind, Venti picked up his pace and fled from the scene.

Chapter 34

I watched Venti run down the street. A part of me ached to chase after him. I had been so focused on taking him down today. To make him face justice for all he had done. But I was no longer certain what justice looked like. The constabulary's treatment of prisoners couldn't be called justice. Even for someone like Venti. In an odd way, this almost felt better.

Stepping up beside me, Allora voiced the same thoughts, "You're letting him go?"

"I still don't know who's responsible for sending him to my town. But he was never going to tell me unless I threatened his life. That just doesn't feel right anymore. I'll find them though. For now, we have a bunch of people to help."

I turned around to survey the growing crowd of people. A few hundred had already emerged from the building and they were now being joined by more from the neighboring building. The narrow street quickly became crowded with confused and scared people.

"Why are there so many people?" I asked.

"A lot of people lost their homes in those fires. But a lot more were here before that. Squatting in these abandoned buildings because they had nowhere else to go. If the constabulary is coming back, they're going to come for everyone nearby."

"So they have nowhere to go and it's my fault. Again."

Allora shrugged. "Maybe. If you hadn't intervened they probably would have just arrest Temrok and Venti, a couple people would have died, and then maybe they wouldn't have come back for the rest. Now they're definitely coming back."

"They were here in the first place because of me."

"Yes."

I felt the weight of that simple answer press down on me. Then it lifted slightly when Temrok joined us. "But it is also my fault. I knew working with people like Venti was wrong. But I did it anyways. What he revealed to me about the Church made me want to tear the whole system down. You don't do that without bloodshed."

We stood in silence for a moment, taking in the growing crowd. His words swirled around in my brain. I didn't like them. "Why not?"

"I'm sorry?"

"Why can't we upend the system without violence?"

"Because those in power won't just let their power go without a fight. Every effort at change is met with fierce resistance. Small, but noticeable, improvements are undermined, fought, and outright stopped. This makes people bitter and hopeless. Soon, the only way to make change is to force it through violence. I had nearly gotten to that point. Hanmish and others clearly had. More and more people will. Soon it won't be a few people holding up an arena threatening bloodshed but an actual massacre. Once that happens, there's no going back. We'll have open war in the streets. Which, I think we'll lose. The people are mad and desperate. But they have no focus, no direction. I've tried. Even your buddy En is trying. But people don't want to listen, and they're so spread out and divided."

Something that Temrok said sparked inside me. At first, I didn't know what. I felt a solution hovering just outside my reach. I knew it was there, but I couldn't find it. It taunted me.

"Maybe En might have the answer." Allora said. "You think he's rich enough to buy these buildings so these people aren't trespassing?"

Allora's words poked at that feeling but I couldn't get the idea to coalesce into solid form. I clapped my hands together in triumph. "I feel like there's something there. That En is the answer!"

"I'm sorry, what?" Allora raised her eyebrows at me, "I was joking. There's no way he could afford that. His father maybe. But even if they're willing, they couldn't do it fast enough."

"No, not that. I don't know. We need some time. A place. Big enough that won't be immediately raided by the constables."

"The Church!" Allora snapped her fingers. "We'll take them to the church! I'm an acolyte. If I bring them there and they can't turn them away immediately."

I frowned, "Temrok is a heretic in their eyes. They're as likely to burn him at the stake as shelter him."

Temrok looked like he wanted to object but just shrugged. I continued, "You really think the Church will take all of these people in?"

"No. not long term. But it buys us time at least. They won't turn them out immediately and the Constabulary won't raid and arrest them immediately. We will need a next step soon though."

I sighed, "Let's see if this first step will even work first."

Despite my pessimism, the arrival at the Church did not meet with instant controversy. The doors were open to all or so the saying went. We herded the people inside the main worship area and had to spill over into the reception area to accommodate them all. By the time that happened, we gotten the acolytes attention.

"What is the meaning of this?" Hishu demanded when he stormed into the worship hall.

I bristled at the tone and was prepared to respond but fortunately, he directed his anger at Allora. Being a lowly apprentice had its advantages, I was easier to ignore. For her part, Allora stood her ground and made Hishu come to her. I silently applauded her composure.

"The meaning of this, Brother Hishu, is compassion for those in need. Unity and aid for the people of Akza."

"All of these people can't just come in here and take over the Church!" his tone got nastier but also quieter. I had to strain to keep listening in to them.

"Are not the doors open to all?"

"Yes but...that is for worship...not whatever this is."

"I don't think that's your call to make."

"Neither is it yours."

Allora smiled wickedly, "Then we are agreed."

"You will answer to the High Acolyte. He will decide. And after he does, you will remove all of these...people from this holy place."

The pair of them stalked off toward the high acolyte's office, leaving me to oversee getting everyone settled. I looked over the mass of confused and scared people and felt that familiar rising sense of panic coming. I closed my eyes and remembered the meditation ritual my father had taught me. We had done it every morning after our sparring practice. While I'd kept up the practice, I hadn't kept up the meditation.

I slowed down my breathing and piece by piece, relaxed every muscle in my body. The panic feeling didn't vanish, but it did lessen. By the time I completed the ritual it had receded to a manageable level. When I opened my eyes, I felt an eternity had passed but it must not have been that long.

Around the room, various members of the clergy poked their heads in to see what was going on, but most turned away. Few were as confrontational as Hishu, and those that were had undoubtedly accompanied him to the high acolyte's office. That left a few members of staff and apprentices.

"Kali, what is going on?" Claren asked when I walked over to where he, Mateto and Jensen were standing.

"All of these people are homeless. Their homes were burned and then today were kicked out of the buildings they had been using as shelter."

"Using as shelter?" Jensen said, "It sounds like you mean were squatting in."

"Technically. But only because there was no where they could afford to live after they lost their homes."

"That sounds like they need to get jobs."

"Most of them have jobs. They just aren't paid enough."

Mateto spoke for the first time, "Then they need to get better jobs. Pull themselves up rather than blame their problems on others."

I stared dumbfounded at Mateto. He had suffered almost as much abuse and disdain from the mostly human acolytes as I had because he was nudra. That he was now parroting something I had heard many senior acolytes said left me speechless. There were just as many nudra among the homeless people here as there were uvoy and grunde.

"Do you really think it is that simple?" A new voice interrupted us and I turned to see Auran approaching. "I am the head cook here at the Church. Would you not say that should be a good job?"

Mateto looked stricken. I had seen that look before in class anytime Hishu questioned him. I realized then that he had been parroting what he had heard but didn't have the actual disdain and self-confidence in his position that the acolytes who said it had. But I made no move to defend him. He had to hear what Auran had to say.

"It is prestigious, is it not, to oversee feeding the great men of the Church? Yet, here I am, living among these very people. My home was burned. Everything else is either full or charging more than I can afford to pay to live there. Especially as my former landlord is insisting I keep paying him rent for the remainder of my lease. Despite no longer having a home. I have been walking over an hour every day from these abandoned buildings where I had least had shelter for my children. So, tell me again how I am supposed to fix that by getting a better job? What better job is there?"

I let Mateto stand there cowering, unsure how to respond. I knew he had a good heart in truth. I saw similar discomfort from Claren and Jensen. That's when I realized I had misjudged all of them. They had never been my friends. But they were just as much victims of abuse as I was. As all of the people around us were.

Instead of letting Auran continue to berate him, I rested a hand on both their arms. "Is not the Church supposed to be about bringing people together? We need to learn compassion to do that. The people here aren't poor because of a moral failing. In order to see that, we have to think beyond what we've been told to see and look at what is actually there. People without hope, desperate to survive. Some by living wherever they can. Others, by repeating what powerful people say in a hope of avoiding the same fate."

I only let silence hang there for a moment, not wanting to let the urge to fight back rise up. "Now, Auran, we need to get these people food. As a member of the Church, I am ordering you to go to work and prepare a meal for them all."

Auran looked taken aback at first but then she smiled, "Of course. Right away."

She headed toward the kitchen but did not get far before Jensen called after her, "I will help."

When Mateto started to follow as well, I stopped him. "We could use some blankets. It gets cold in here at night."

Mateto nodded, "We have many empty beds. I'll see what I can find."

"I'll help you. But give me a minute, I'll catch up." Claren said. He gave me an appraising look that made me shift uncomfortably. I wasn't sure what he was looking for or what he saw but I didn't like the idea of it.

"What?" I finally asked.

"You surprise me."

I pursed my lips but said nothing. Claren looked down and scratched the back of his head, avoiding my eyes. Finally, he said, "I was debating telling you this. Because I don't know what it means or what you'll do with it. But I found that account you were interested in."

"Already? I thought you said that would take days. It's only been a few hours."

"Well, as it turns out it was easy to find. That is the account used by the Relic office. It's a Church account."

Everything I had suspected fell into place. Temrok got his heretical text from Venti who got his Relics from the old mines near my town. Temrok had assumed the Church had funded it to hide the texts. Now here was definitive proof. They had done exactly that. I had hoped this would be true because that meant Hishu, the head of the Relic office, would be responsible for everything bad that had happened. It felt convenient but I couldn't argue with evidence.

I didn't say any of this out loud though. But I must have shown something because Claren took a small step back and he grew concerned. "Are you all right, Kali?"

I forced a smile and said, "Yes. That was very helpful. Why don't you go help Mateto?"

"What are you going to do?" He asked nervously.

"I need to see how Sister Allora's meeting with the High Acolyte is going." I lied.

Claren studied me intently and for a moment I thought he was going to argue with me, but then he nodded and left the worship hall. Whether he decided I wasn't going to do anything stupid or that he'd rather be very far away when I did, I don't know. It might have gone better had he pushed me more. If I had had to explain my intentions out loud, I might not have followed through with them.

For the moment, at least, I did do exactly what I told Claren I would do. I paced outside the high acolyte's office for an unseemly long time waiting for the meeting to end. No one raised their voices, so I had no idea what was going on inside. When it finally ended, everyone who emerged looked unhappy. Benthic, Hishu and a few other acolytes dispersed down the halls without saying a word to each other.

I almost followed Hishu but Allora got to me first. "Well, they can stay."

"That's good. Right?"

"They can only stay until Restday. Then they are all going to be arrested for trespassing unless they leave."

"That doesn't give us a lot of time. Are they going to do anything to help find them a place to go? The Church owns a lot of property. There must be some place they could go."

Allora snorted a derisive laugh. "You've hit the matter in the heart. The Church does own a lot of property. Who do you think bought up all the lots on this street that burned down?"

"The Church, I assume from your tone."

"Precisely. So, they're the ones rebuilding and pricing all of these people out of their homes."

"Well, while that does suck, none of those buildings are livable yet."

"No, you're right about that. But those aren't the only buildings the Church has bought in recent months. There are several that are currently sitting practically empty because they can't find tenants who can afford to live there."

"What? Really? And they're still refusing to help?"

"According to Brother Hishu, Akzad will provide what you work to achieve. And the other old snakes agree with him."

"All of them? Even Benthic?"

Allora shrugged, "Maybe not. He did support me in there some. He at least didn't dismiss everything I had to say just because I'm currently a woman. But it didn't make any difference."

If I had had any lingering doubts about pummeling Hishu until his face broke before, I certainly didn't anymore. Now, at least, I would have a purpose other than revenge for my family. I could force him to change his mind about the refugees. Just like I had done to Grant. Use my power to make things the way I wanted.

First, I needed to get rid of Allora. She could complicate things. "I sent Auran and Jensen to the kitchen to start preparing food for everyone. My ordering Auran to do it is rather a flimsy cover. It might help her out if a full acolyte gave her the order."

"You're probably right. We can discuss what to do next after we get everyone settled at least." Then, either sensing my plan or just her usual meddlesome self, she asked, "What are you going to do?"

"I have some investigation stuff to follow up on. Claren was looking into something for me." It wasn't a lie, so I felt I did a good job of keeping my face neutral. It must have been enough because Allora just nodded and headed off for the kitchen. That left me to take on Hishu.

I doubted he had gone down to the worship center to tell everyone they had to leave soon. He wouldn't want to be seen as the one delivering bad news. Nor would he go there to help out. That left his room or his office. I chose office for the simple fact he kept my shield there. Either he wouldn't be there, and I could retrieve it, or he would and I wouldn't have to hunt around for him.

I debated kicking the door in and rushing him immediately but decided against it. He might not even be here, and it would make a lot of noise. Besides, it was a fairly heavy wooden door, and I was still a tiny little uvoy girl. People bigger than me could be unbalanced and had vulnerable body parts. Doors were just heavy.

I knocked politely and was rewarded with an annoyed, "Yes?" from inside. I took a big, slow breath before opening the door and going inside. Hishu sat at his desk, fidgeting with a pen. His lips curled at the sight of me which I felt appropriate. I didn't return the gesture only because I had already suppressed the feeling to keep him unsuspecting.

"What do you want, apprentice?"

"I thought you would want an update on the investigation into the Relics that have been turning up." I closed the door behind me and sauntered as unobtrusively as I could around the office. I saw my shield propped up against the wall behind his desk. Getting to it without drawing attention would be difficult. But then, I didn't have to have it in order to smash his face in.

"Oh, are you still doing that? I thought you had switched sides on us."

This caused me to stumble. "Switch sides? What does that mean?"

He gestured vaguely toward the worship center. "You are supposed to be helping us bring order to this city. Instead, you've sided with the riff raff and soiled the Church with them. These are the enemy."

"What sides? They are people. Hopeless people. I thought we were all one people. That is what the church claims to teach isn't it?"

"Don't be naïve." He snarled, "We're all Akzad's children, yes. But there are those blessed by him, and those not. Those of us who are blessed are the ones willing to work to earn his love. Those lazy miscreants created their own fate."

"Is that all they are to you? Miscreants?" I asked.

Instead of answering right away, Hishu sighed. "That does come off as a bit harsh, I'll admit. No, you are correct, we are all Akzad's children, so I do care for their plight. I just know seeking handouts is not the way to earn his blessing. They are damning themselves with their laziness."

"Needing help is not laziness." I snapped back, more irritated at his waffling. It was much easier to see him as a monster if he had just admitted to hating everyone else.

"The need, no. But asking for handouts is a morale failing. The church has programs to help those in need."

"They just can't ask for that help?"

Hishu waved a dismissive hand at me. "I am not going to debate you child. Didn't you come here to update me on the lost Relics? Tell me what you learned and get out."

I stared daggers at him, but I kept my rage in check. I would tell him what I knew and then I would make him admit what he had done to my town and my family. Then I could punch him.

"The Relic used in the arena and to set the fires on Lesshon street came from a cache found in an abandoned mine in Gofferd's Crossing, a small town on the Outskirts. A group of mercenaries took over the town and dug up the Relics."

"Yes, yes, we suspected that already. It is not new."

"But what is new is who hired those mercenaries." I paused, watching for his reaction. He did peak up but not how I would have expected. Instead of squirming in guilt he just looked curious. I continued more uncertainly, "The money came from an account owned by the Church. An account used by the Relic office."

Hishu stared blankly for a second and then flushed red. He slammed his hand on his desk and grumbled something to himself. It wasn't the reaction I was anticipating but I pressed forward. "So you admit it! You paid the Venti to take over my town and kill my parents!"

This time Hishu twitched as if startled. "What? This was what, five years ago?"

"Um, yeah, about." I said uncertainly.

"I only took over the Relic office last year. Benthic was the head of the office then. And the old bastard lied to me."

The floor dropped away from me, and I felt cold. I must have misheard him. Benthic couldn't be involved. Out of all the old bastards here at the Church, he had always been the kindest, most reasonable among them. He couldn't be the one I had been after all these years.

Hishu carried on, completely ignoring my world collapsing around me. He grumbled for a moment and then snapped his fingers. This time he looked pleased and his flush of anger changed to pleasure. "You have proof of this?"

I didn't respond at first, so he repeated himself, "Apprentice, you have proof of this?"

Slowly, I looked up. Technically I didn't. I only had the records from Grant, which showed the Church had paid him and Rady. But I knew Venti had been involved in that plot as well so it had to be the same account. Hishu didn't need to know all that though.

"Yes."

"Then come with me. We're going to take that old bastard down."

Hishu shot up from his chair and strode from the office with a renewed energy. I watched him uncertainly. I had come here to beat the living crap out of Hishu for all he had done but instead I had learned he might not have been the one to do it. Instead, a man I thought I could trust had been responsible. I let my confusion and doubt grip me for a moment but then I snapped myself out of it. I had to know for sure now.

I glanced at my shield and paused only a second before grabbing it and following Hishu.

Chapter 35

I followed Hishu and for once I had no idea what I was going to do. For years I had been focused on bringing the man responsible for what had happened to my parents down. Now, to find out it had been one of the few people in this shitty place I kind of liked left me reeling. It had been easy to believe Hishu had been the root of all evil. I had felt no guilt about ending him. Benthic being involved made everything messier.

When we arrived at Benthic's office, Hishu barged right in without knocking. Benthic had been pouring himself some tea and the door flying open made him jump and spill the tea over his desk. My first inclination was to feel sorry for the old man, but I stopped myself from offering to help him clean it up. Had he been playing me with this kindly old man routine the whole time? Was he secretly a real bastard just like Hishu? That would certainly make things easier.

Hishu ignored Benthic's efforts to clear up the mess and set right in on him. "You lied to me. You said Venti was reliable but you left out the part where he is the one blackmailing you."

Benthic glanced between Hishu and me uncertainly. "Are you sure this is something we should be talking about now?"

Hishu turned and seemed to notice me for the first time since leaving his office. He had told me to follow him, so I assumed the frown was directed at me holding my shield, which he had not told me to take. His lips curled and I felt the scolding hang in the air but instead of releasing it, he turned back to Benthic.

"She's how I found out about this. You've also been sloppy. She found the account. Knows you used it to pay him."

Benthic sighed. "I doubt very much she had any kind of proof. But now that you've just admitted it."

Hishu froze in the middle of whatever tirade he had been about to unleash. He looked back at me, and I gave him a little smile which prompted him to curse. Despite all his flaws, that is not something I had ever heard him do. It just made me smile broader.

Through gritted teeth, Hishu said, "It doesn't matter. What matters is you assured me Venti was reliable when he clearly isn't. He's the one who lost the book. So why did you send him to me?"

"Hasn't he done exactly what you've asked of him? You have your excuse for a crackdown. People are flooding back to services. I told you he could be relied upon to do your dirty work."

"But he's also the one who turned on you. What's to stop him from doing the same to me?"

"It appears he already has. If Kali knows about the account, he must have been involved." He stopped mopping up the tea and stared down at his desk before turning sad eyes bad at me. "I am sorry for what Venti did to your family, child. It was never supposed to go down like that. He was only there to retrieve some lost texts we believed had been buried in the old mines. Things must have gotten out of hand."

"Out of hand!?" I shouted. "To take things from the mine didn't require taking over the town. You could have gone down there, and no one would have noticed. Or cared. But you got the people's hopes up for better jobs. You turned the people against each other by only giving jobs to people who were 'religiously devout'. You flooded the streets with guns and encouraged people to use them against 'sinners'. All to retrieve some old texts that prove you're nothing but a bunch of hypocrites."

A heavy weight descended on the room after my rant. Benthic and Hishu exchanged a look that wasn't anger. I felt something shift and I realized my temporary alliance with Hishu had ended. Which suited me. While he wasn't the one who got my parents killed, it sounded like he might be the one behind everything Venti had done in the city recently. That turned him back into my enemy again, which felt far more comfortable.

"You have seen the text then, child?" Benthic asked quietly.

I froze. I hadn't seen it, just been told about it. Would it be better or worse if I had? I decided to err on the side of truth. It was usually the better choice. "No. Just heard about it."

"Heard about it from who? Venti?" Hishu asked.

"Don't be daft." Benthic snapped. "She hates that man. She would sooner sleep with you than have a conversation with him. It must be Temrok, His speeches have been blasphemous. Which you have used Venti to encourage."

"How was I supposed to know he was the one with the lost text? Temrok spewing hearsay would help me turn the people against him."

"Only if he can't support it."

As they bickered, I started edging forward. A quick blow to the back of Hishu's head would drop him. Benthic wouldn't be a threat, as old as he was. Then I could drag the pair of them down to Allora and Temrok and reveal they were responsible for all our problems. The crowd would overthrow the rest of the clergy and live happily ever after. I didn't really believe the last part, but it felt like a good lie to tell myself. I would have my revenge against these greedy bastards at least.

"What do we do about the girl? If she hasn't seen it." Hishu asked, a strange note of reluctance in his voice at the implied threat.

"We'll have to contain the danger." Benthic said flatly. "I thought Venti would be content to blackmail us and would never actually release the book as long as we kept paying him. Clearly, I was mistaken as he has shown the book to others."

My blood ran cold, and I narrowed my eyes at the pair of them. "What do you mean, 'contain the danger.'"

Benthic sighed. "I am sorry that this has all happened to you, child. Your life has been one series of misfortunes after another. But soon you will be in Akzad's eternal embrace." Benthic words were heavy with regret. Didn't stop me from recognizing the threat in them though.

I snorted out a laugh. "You're threatening me? I trusted you, which was my mistake I admit. All of you are the same. You care only about your power, not all the people you hurt. But in truth, you're just an old man. And I am going to end you."

I sprang into motion and smashed my shield into Hishu's face. His nose bled profusely and he collapsed in a heap to the floor. I hopped onto

Benthic's desk, and for once, towered over him. I smiled savagely down at him, conveying in that look all the terrible things I had ever dreamed of doing. I let that look linger for a moment so it could really sink in what was about to happen to him.

I lifted my shield, prepared to bring it down on him again and again. But it felt heavy and as if I was moving through molasses instead of air. My knees then felt weak, and my legs trembled. Then Benthic shoved me and I fell, my back landing hard on the floor.

Benthic held his place behind the desk while Hishu stood up above me, holding his bloody nose. I tried to get up, but I felt so weak. Drained and cloudy.

"This has always been your trouble, child. You set out on a quest that is against your very nature. You never had a true killer instinct. Or the will to do what you must. You thought you were at war with others, but you've only been at war with yourself. Despite your potential, you never would have had what it takes to truly use Akzad's power."

That's when I recognized the feeling. I had felt it during Manifesting classes, when Hishu demonstrated. I had felt it from the other side when I had summoned that squash to smash. They were draining me to fuel themselves. But it was more than that. I had also felt it when I had tried to beat Jermain for information. A poor, innocent man asleep in his bed.

Manifestation, according to the mantra, required you to be committed to what you were doing. To believe you deserved it. I had felt guilt in what I had did to Jermain. But didn't I believe that about getting justice against Benthic? My rage had fueled my manifestation of the squash. I had felt power when I had threatened Grant, unlike when I had threatened Jermaine. Was that the difference?

I tried to channel my rage at everything that these two had done. I deserved to bring them to justice. I deserved to get my revenge. A felt a flicker of my strength return. The drain Benthic had on my weakened. But only slightly.

Benthic shook his head. "You really do have so much potential. But you won't grab it. You're too softhearted. Compassion can aid you, but it cannot control you. Those of us with power must use it to guide others. For their own good."

"What the ever living fuck is wrong with you?" I snarled. "That has to be the most twisted bit of logic. Who are you to decide for anyone else what they should do?"

I felt my strength returning. I still felt Benthic's drain on me, but something had changed. I doubted I could manifest an apple right now, but I pulled myself up onto one knee. I didn't need magic to defend myself from two old men.

"We are the Church. It is our holy mission to care for the souls of the people of this world. That means guiding them away from sin and blasphemy."

"I thought you actually cared about people. Unlike this asshole." I waved my hand toward Hishu who still held his nose.

"I do. I do not want to see them suffer. Unlike some of my colleagues, I don't think blessings should be distributed based on species or gender. All are equal under Akzad's eyes."

"Just so long as they bow to you."

"Not me. The Church."

Benthic stretched out his hand and a revolver materialized in it. It was a massive weapon that I had no doubt could deliver an ugly wound. That he could hold it steadily impressed me but it probably didn't weight what a real one would. Just like my shield was lighter than it should be.

I raised my shield to cover my body, though I wasn't sure if it would even work. I had yet to get shot at since it had failed me. Then there was the question of whether a Relic could even stop a Manifested bullet. How would that magic interact?

"Unfortunately, child, as you've just shown, you are too dangerous to be allowed to leave. You know too much and while we can contain your gift, the constabulary wouldn't. Sadly, that leaves me with no other choice."

My mind raced. Drained as I was, I didn't think I could move fast enough to disarm Benthic before he could fire. Could I power my shield somehow to ensure it worked? The thought of the Mantra made me queasy and feel weaker. Was it even necessary?

I needed my shield to work, not just for me, but for all the people I had agreed to help. All the people these men meant to take advantage of. All the people they had hurt. It wasn't just about me.

The crack of the gun firing shattered my thoughts. The world slowed. I heard the shot but not the clang of the bullet deflecting off my shield. I also didn't feel the impact of the bullet on my body. Had he missed? I looked around, between Benthic and myself. There was no way he could have missed at this distance.

Then I saw it, the second hole in my shield. The bullet had gone through. The shield had failed. But why wasn't I dead? I dropped the useless Relic to better check my body for a bullet hole. As I did, I gaped. Hanging in the air where my shield had been was a blue shimmering shape that looked exactly like my shield. Embedded in the center of the glowing phantom was a bullet. We all watched as the bullet disintegrated to nothing before the blue phantom shield also vanished.

Benthic and Hishu looked as uncertain as I felt. But I recovered quickly. I didn't quite understand what I had done and didn't want to stand around and see if I could do it again. If I attacked Benthic again, I didn't know if he would be able to weaken me like he had before, so I decided living to fight another day was the best choice.

I did a reverse somersault back out of the room, leaving my shield behind. As I moved, I heard more gunshots follow me. I rolled out of the doorway and out of Benthic's line of sight before bouncing to my feet. The further I got, the stronger I felt. I don't know how much my weakness had been him and how much had been my own guilt but now I could move almost as well as normal.

I dashed to the nearest exit, which opened to the garden. Without looking back, I leaped over the wall and away from the Church.

Chapter 36

Safe for the moment, I struggled to figure out what to do next. Benthic had just tried to murder me. He had also been the one I had been hunting for years. I guess the attempted murder made it easier to think of him as a bad guy now.

My immediate needs were more pressing. The constabulary was eager to come after me and I doubted I would have the protection of the Church now. The cities revolutionaries, who a day before would have been eager to have me join them, were now at the mercy of the Church, thanks to me. They probably didn't like me much either.

With nowhere else to turn, I headed to Nerpi's for now. He could warn Allora and I could take my cycler, letting me get through the city much faster. Naturally, I found Nerpi on the ground, underneath a quadcycler, whistling his usual tune.

"Nerpi, I need your help." I said without preamble.

"Oh, hello, Kali. I also need your help." Nerpi said, sliding out from under the quad. "I can't seem to find my 10mm wrench again."

"Why ask me? I can never find it. I look and I look but it's always you who finds it in the end." I said, annoyed to be diverted from my quest.

"I do, don't I?" Nerpi reached into his toolbag again and rummaged through it. I felt a slight tingle across my body. He pulled his hand out of the bag and grinned triumphantly. "It seems you were right. Here it is. Right where I need it to be."

He crawled back under the quad, and I stared transfixed while he worked. I recognized that feeling now. I had felt it before but never thought about it. How had Allora never noticed it?

With some difficulty, I waited for Nerpi to finish, knowing he would never be able to concentrate with a half-finished job sitting there. When he finally emerged out from under the quad, I watched his hand intently. He put the wrench back in his bag, but I kept my eyes on it while he went to go wash his hands. I never took my eyes off the tool. That is, until it vanished.

"Temrok was right."

"I'm sorry, what was that?" Nerpi asked coming back into the room.

I smiled but put the revelation behind me. "I need your help. I'm, uh, kind of on the run. Again."

"From the constabulary?"

"Them too."

"You get kicked out of the Church?"

"Something like that." I said and I related the events of the past few hours. "I need you to go to the Church, pretend to be looking for me. Talk to Allora. Tell her Temrok needs to get out of there and if there is any chance they think she's working with him, she does as well."

Nerpi frowned but didn't ask any more questions before leaving the garage. I took the opportunity to change, I wouldn't need these apprentice robes anymore. I put on my usual overalls. Despite my impending doom, it felt comfortable and more right than the robes ever had.

Once I had changed and washed up a little, I climbed to the roof and bounced across to the neighboring building, one of the last remaining original constructions between Nerpi's and the Church. Already, the burned-out husks had been torn down and new frames were going up. I wondered how many of the construction crews would be able to afford to live in the buildings they were helping to build.

As I feared, a short time later I saw Nerpi returning back down the street, escorted by Allora, Hishu, Benthic, and a pair of constables. I had no worry that Nerpi had turned me in. But the list of places I might go after fleeing the Church was short. They would have come here eventually. Hopefully, they would look, not find me, and then leave.

I almost got my wish. After a quick search, Benthic and Hishu left, but the two constables remained behind. They took up positions at the corner where they could see the main entrance and the side stairs to the apartments.

That would complicate things for me, as it was always easier to use a door, but I had slipped in through the upstairs window before. I could do it again.

Once inside, I settled down to wait. I hoped Nerpi and Allora would think to come up here as I couldn't access the garage without being seen. While I had just been up here to change, I hadn't given myself much time. I sat down at the small dining table with its mismatched chairs. None of us had been good cooks. But we had some nice meals together. I hadn't realized how much I missed those. They were much like my family meals back home. Something that had ended the night my parents died. Or, at least it ended for me.

After getting out of prison, I'd returned home just once, to retrieve some clothes and my father's shield. No one had seen me. I didn't want to subject them to that. Or, at least, I didn't want to face them. I would rather not know if they hated me than find out for sure that they did.

Finally, the door opened and Nerpi and Allora came inside. Allora just threw out her hands in exasperation. "Kali, what the hell is going on? I knew the constabulary might be after you, but why is the Church actively aiding them now?"

"You know that thing I had to do before we went to speak to Temrok?"

"You did more than just summon the constabulary?"

I sighed, "Yes. The people who paid Grant to help Rady were the same people who sent Venti to my hometown. I bullied him into giving me his bank records and then had one of the other apprentices look through the Church records for that same account. I thought I might find a connection, that maybe the Church was funding them or had given the similar goals of promoting worship. But I found a lot more than that. The account is the Church's Relic account. Benthic and Hishu have been behind funding all of this."

Allora stared at me open mouthed. Then she shook her head and started pacing around. "My opinion of the Church has declined in recent years, but I never thought them capable of this. And Benthic. Not in a million years. You have proof they're involved with the fires and terrorism?"

"Not exactly. They admitted it me, but I doubt that would convince anyone else. I know they paid Grant to help Rady. And that same account paid Venti to look for Relics in my town. I can't prove they are still paying

Venti now. But that should be easy to trace if we look at the actual bank records."

"Maybe, but don't we have a more immediate problem?" Nerpi asked. We both turned to him and he gestured to the door. "Those people at the Church? You said they were going to be kicked out, probably just outright arrested, come Restday. Proving the Church is corrupt will take time and I doubt it would help those people."

Of the three of us, despite Allora being a full acolyte, I think Nerpi was the most devout. I could tell he was bothered by all of this. He might be trying to avoid thinking about the implications by focusing on the homeless people, but he also wasn't wrong. That was a more immediate problem.

We sat there in silence for what felt like a long time. My mind kept drifting back to Grant and how he had to know more than he was saying. Some faster way to get more proof. He was probably making that movie about me, the hero of the church right now. It would be canceled as soon as Hishu thought about it. Maybe then he would be more willing to help me since he had been very excited to be making it.

Then it clicked. I smiled and looked at Allora and Nerpi. "We need to get in touch with En and Grant."

After explaining my plan, Allora headed back to the Church and I sat astride my cycler, with Nerpi in the attached side car. I revved the engine and took off down the street heading for En. Nerpi directed me to an area of town I had never been to before. The buildings here were cleaner, newer and fancier looking. They looked a lot like the newer buildings that were being built to replace the ones burnt down. Which meant they would have electrical wires and the newer indoor plumbing integrated into the design, rather than tacked on. It also meant they would be expensive to live in.

Past the apartments we came to an area of lower buildings that almost looked like warehouses but were sturdier designs. They didn't have any windows but did have streams of people going in and out. Some of these people were dressed in very unusual clothes and a few even had on wigs and masks.

"So, this where they make movies." I said as I parked the cycler.

"Apparently." Nerpi said. "En told me his dad was making him go back to work on some movie. It was the only way to keep him in the dark about his latest scheme as a revolutionary."

"His dad doesn't know about that?"

Nerpi shrugged. "I get the distinct impression En's father is the type of person who would have a heart attack if he heard the kind of things En says in his speeches."

"Well, I don't want En's dad to die so let's make sure he doesn't hear about what we're about to ask En to do."

We found En sitting in a chair in front of a mirror. An older uvoy woman flittered around him, applying bits of makeup all over his head. She'd pause, study him in the mirror, frown and then continue her work. Her lack of wraspisa struck me as odd and I had to remind myself not to stare at her.

When we got close, she frowned at us, "You'll block my light with that big thing."

I realized she meant my wraspisa and I took a step back, even though I couldn't see how it would be affecting here. There were lights everywhere in this place. She resumed her work but still gave us a cold tone.

"Mr. Papadopoulos is very busy and cannot be disturbed for autographs. Go back to your jobs."

"Mr. Papadopoulos is going to be disturbed whether he wants to be or not." Nerpi said.

"Now, you see here!" the makeup artist started but then En opened his eyes for the first time.

"It's okay, Alyic. These are my friends. Why don't you take a break?"

The woman frowned and gave En a disapproving look. "You are due on set in thirty minutes. I haven't even begun to do your hair."

"I have a feeling we're going to have to postpone the shoot for today." En said with a mischievous grin.

"Mr. Depaul is not going to be happy." She insisted.

En waved a dismissive hand and then tore off the cloth covering him. Alyic let out a huff of annoyance and then stormed off. I felt sorry for her, we had just interrupted her hard work, but I put that aside and focused on En.

"So, what brings you lot to see little old me? Do we have a caper? A job? A score?"

Nerpi started to object but I cut him off, "Yes, yes we do."

En took us to another sound stage. This one had plywood structures that had been painted to look like roof tops. A bunch of grunde stood around wearing blood makeup, at least I assumed it was makeup, while Grant talked to a uvoy woman and some humans. The humans all wore constable uniforms and were all fit and handsome looking. Not like regular constables at all. But the uvoy woman made me stop in my tracks. She was gorgeous. I'm not one to usually care much about looks, but this woman made me feel very inadequate for some reason. And she was dressed in my costume.

"What is all this?" I demanded.

Grant gave a start at my tone and jumped back slightly. On second thought, his reaction might have had less to do with surprise and more to do with how I had nearly broken his arm the last time we had met. I felt bad about that, but I didn't soften my expression.

"Uh, Kali, this is, uh, unexpected."

"Is she supposed to be me?"

"Uh, yeah, I needed a stand in. Didn't want to have to disturb you for every little scene."

"She looks nothing like me. Her skin's the wrong color and she had far too much cleavage. If she jumps around like I do, her boobs are going to be flopping around. They'll be sore for hours."

"They are a bit." The woman agreed.

"What do you mean the wrong color? She's green. You're green."

"Wow. Just wow." I said and shared a look with the poor actress. She just rolled her eyes and I suspected she had encountered this type of thing more than once. I sighed and decided there were more important things to focus on right now. "None of that matters now. We're here to change your movie."

Grant sighed, "It's not a movie. Just a news reel."

"Even better. Because that's what we need it to be. Short but direct."

"Wait, you said change." Grant looked between me and En, "What do you mean change?"

"It's going to have a different message than the original script."

"Did Brother Hishu approve this?"

"Let's pretend he did." Nerpi said.

Grant frowned and shook his head vehemently, "I can't change anything without his approval. He's the client. It's his money. Well, the Church's money, but he's in charge of this. I'd get fired."

"As you said, it's the Church's money. And I work for the Church. And I am here, Hishu is not."

"Are you going to threaten to break my arm again if I refuse this time?" He snarled. I felt the stares of everyone else at his words. I deserved that. Would it be best to just lean into that to get him to agree? He was already scared of me.

Instead, I let out a low sigh. "I'm, sorry about that. I shouldn't have done that. What we're asking you to do is part of my penance. Instead of some cheap Church propaganda, we want you to make a masterpiece."

"This is my masterpiece." Grant's face drooped.

"Let me ask you something," En stepped in, walking slowly around the room. As he spoke, his skin appeared to shine and he even looked like he got taller, "How do you want to be remembered? For a man who told people to go to Church? A man who helped those with the loudest voice be heard even more? Let me tell you, there are a dozen directors who do that. How about, instead, you had the chance to be the man who gave a voice to those without one? A hero."

As En talked, Grant perked up slowly. Around us, the actors and crew had all turned their attention to En. As they did, I felt the radiance from him increase. His face sharpened. It wasn't different exactly. It was just more. More beautiful. More commanding. I didn't need to feel the familiar tingle of power this time to know it was there.

"The people of this world are in trouble. They need a hero. They need someone to step up and give them their voice back. Can you do that? Can you be their hero?"

"Yes!" Grant shouted and then his cheeks flushed red.

En clapped him on the back, "Good man. Now let's get started. This needs to be edited and distributed before Restday."

"What? That's crazy, there's no way we can get it all done by then."

"My good man, Heroes don't have the luxury of choosing their timeline."

Chapter 37

I stood among the bustle of the cycler crews as they prepared for the day's races. Techs and crew chiefs rushed about doing final checks. Racers stood among them, masking their nerves each in their own ways. Some yelled needless instructions. Some joked with their comrades. Others stood quietly. I tried to blend in with this last group.

Despite the season's warmth, I wore a long coat. Underneath, I wore the hideous racing uniform Hishu had designed. Grant had insisted he already had a lot of footage with me dressed like that and if we changed how I was dressed in the newsreel part way through it might confuse people. I had been prepared to argue but En had backed him up. Then I hadn't wanted to come here wearing the damn thing, but Allora of all people had insisted. It may be awful, but it was what the people at the arena had seen me in, and then only from a distance. If it did anything well, it was noticeable from a distance.

So, I wore it, but also covered up. In theory, no one would need to ever know I was here. They would see the movie and they would either listen to it or ignore it. My presence shouldn't make any difference.

I fidgeted with the edges of my coat. It wouldn't be long before they played the pregame newsreel. There hadn't been time for me to see the whole thing from start to finish back at the studio. The timeline had been tight in order to make copies and get them to all the theaters around the city before this morning. It was Restday, arenas and theaters would be packed. I just hoped the High Acolyte's deadline had been by the end of the day rather than this morning. Otherwise, this could all be for naught.

"Haven't seen you here in awhile. Thought, after that last race, you had given up."

I jerked when I realized someone was talking to me, but I breathed a sigh of relief when I saw Hann standing there. The big grunde had a curious look on his face that I couldn't decipher. It wasn't exactly unfriendly, but it wasn't his usual good natured grin.

Uneasily, I said, "I can't quit until I beat you, old man."

"Not till the day I retire. And I'm not retiring today." He grinned and I let out a sigh of relief. Whatever was bothering him, he could still joke. If even he lost his good nature I don't know what that would mean for the world.

"I'm not racing today though. Just here for the pre-game."

"You normally hate the pre-game."

"Most of it. But not the movie. It's normally the only one I get to see."

Hann shrugged, "The newsreel? I normally ignore it. Just some nonsense propaganda about some commissioner and some ad for something."

I panicked for a second. It was true, most of the racers ignored the newsreel. I had assumed the audience watched but now I wondered if they ignored it too. "You'll want to pay attention to this one. And get the others too as well."

"Why?"

"Um. You'll see."

Hann frowned and studied me. "Kali, does this have anything to do with the rumors I heard? That you're wanted by the constabulary?"

"You know you shouldn't put much stock in rumors." I said with a smile even I didn't believe.

"Uh huh."

I wanted to say something else to alleviate his suspicions but then I saw someone else approaching us. "Shit. It's Mallis. If he sees me there will be a scene."

Hann clapped me on the shoulder and moved to intercept the fussy eowian commissioner. I heard the shrill voice and knew I owed Hann big time. With his bulk, he would completely block line of sight on me and I took the chance to move.

It had been my mistake to stay in one place for too long. I had been spotted. I slipped out of the racer area and up the stairs to the stands. If I kept my coat on, there wasn't much chance of anyone recognizing me. I sighed as I acknowledged to myself En and Grant might have been right.

I was so wrapped up in my thoughts and looking for a spot to blend in, that I didn't notice that the newsreel had started. The fanfare of trumpets that Grant had insisted on including at the start caught my attention. It grabbed more than just my attention as the people around me turned to watch the giant screen on the center stage.

The trumpets were followed by an exciting musical piece I had heard before in many other ad reels. There hadn't been time to record something unique, which Grant had complained about endlessly. But I wasn't paying attention to the music as I saw myself projected larger than life. Larger than anything. For a small uvoy, to see myself suddenly bigger than the biggest grunde, was quite the sight.

There were a quick series of action shots of me leaping about, beating up pretend bad guys. There was no film footage of any of my actual confrontations. In truth, I couldn't tell which of these scenes were me and which were done by that actress, they moved by too fast.

The music faded and En's voice, deeper and more commanding than usual, replaced it. "In a world full of dangers, her name gave you the courage to face the dark streets. When constables abused their power, she was there. And when your arena faced attack, who stopped it? The Knightshield!"

The music swelled again and I shrunk. I couldn't bear to watch so I averted my eyes and saw the usual commissioners on the stage, ready to give their remarks after the film ended. But this time, they weren't idly chatting. Hishu was among them, and he was arguing animatedly with them. To my dismay he held the Staff of Jundon and the commissioners each stopped arguing when they turned to look at him. I didn't know exactly what he was demanding but I expected it had something to do with stopping the movie.

Without thinking, I leaped over the railing separating the stands from the raceway. I had made it down and across the first part of the track before the movie cut out. It hadn't gotten to the important part. The part that implored everyone to act. Without that the whole thing was worthless.

Once again, I found myself running across the track toward the center. I let my coat fly loose. I had to give Hishu this, as soon as I did, I heard the crowd notice me. The costume was gaudy and demeaning, but it was noticeable. Well, they wanted action, might as well oblige. I sprung up, landed on a course obstacle, and then leapt again before somersaulting to land beside Hishu and the racing commissioner on the stage.

A hush fell over the audience as, once again, all eyes were on me. This time, no one was threatening them. Hishu backed away from me and grabbed the microphone, holding the staff aloft. He gave me a dark look and smiled wickedly.

"Children of Akzad! The Knightshield has betrayed your Church and attacked your holy acolytes. She spits at your faith, your way of life! Now she has come for my life and our holy relics."

I could hear the collective gasp from the crowd and I cursed. This was the opposite of how things were supposed to be going. I needed the crowd on my side, not his. I took a step toward Hishu. I felt that familiar rage. The same rage I felt any time I confronted Venti. Any time I was alone with my thoughts. I hated Hishu. He was just as responsible for what was wrong with this city or what had happened to my family as anyone else. I could break him like a twig and take the staff. Then, the people would be forced to listen to me.

I stopped. I hadn't come here to force anyone to do anything. The movie had been meant to inform. It told the people the truth about the Church. It told them the truth about those in power. And it asked for their help to make things right for all the people homeless and desperate at the Church right now.

Hishu looked confused that I had stopped. I think he actually wanted me to attack him. His eyes flicked away from me to something else and his smile returned. I whirled around to see a group of constables coming up the stairs, guns drawn. They had evidently increased security after the attack.

I was exposed out there on the stage. No shield, no cover. I had somehow blocked Benthic's manifested bullet but didn't know if that would work on real bullets. Or even how to do it again. The look on the constable's face told me I had only a second to figure it out. If I didn't surrender now, they were going to shoot me.

I thought of the tool Nerpi had made. The way En changed his appearance. Neither of them knew the Mantra but had manifested power. The way Allora healed people felt the same. She hated the Mantra and refused to use it. The fruit I had used at the arena. I had been repeating the

Mantra but then I had stopped. At the time I thought I had used the power of the crowd and my will to force it to appear. What if it was something else?

I hadn't been trying to use the power for myself that day. I had been using it to save others. The squash had been about me, and it had drained my friends. Benthic's gun was about himself, and he drained me to make it. There was more than one way to use this power.

With a slow breath in, I focused on my purpose here. To help people. Not for revenge. Not by force. My father had kept the peace and never carried a gun. He learned to fight, to train his body and to defend. Not for coercion. I had forgotten that when I bullied Grant and Jermain.

I looked at the group of constables and I saw the determination in their human eyes. The glee. They were going to take down a subversive and they were going to enjoy it. They were going to force me to submit.

I grinned back and raised my arm. A blue glow appeared and hovered there, forming the shape of my old shield. At the same moment, the constables fired. No satisfying clang answered, but the bullets all stopped in midair, embedded in the blue glow. Everything froze around us.

I concentrated on the glow, willing it to solidify. It brightened and then the blue traces were replaced by a metal framework. I felt the weight on my arm and couldn't suppress a giddy grin. The constables recovered themselves and fired again, this time the reassuring clang echoed through the arena as each bullet smashed itself against the metal.

When their barrage finished, I moved. I dove to one side to avoid any more fire. As I dived, I grabbed the shield with my other hand. When I came up from my roll, I tossed the shield with a flick of my wrist. It sailed through the air, striking the first constable's gun hand, making him drop the weapon. Then, defying all physics, it turned and did the same to the other three before clattering to the stage floor.

For a second, I watched it sitting several meters away from me, the constable's guns at their feet. Granted their hands would all be stinging and possible unable to grip anything for a few minutes, but they were closer to their weapons than I was to mine. But it didn't have to be.

I twisted my hand and the shield vanished from the stage and reappeared instantly back on my arm. It wasn't a real piece of metal but a manifestation of the world's magic. I could hear Nerpi's arguments in my head, but it didn't have to make sense.

Then I turned back to face Hishu. The constables could go for their guns, but I didn't think they would. They were as transfixed as the crowd in the stands. This time, I approached Hishu not with threat but determination. He cowered in front of me but had nowhere to run without falling off the stage.

I stood beside him, in front of the microphone, and realized the movie may have ended but I still had a chance to address the people. I felt a rise of panic as I recognized the eyes on me. With difficulty, I held a shield up to it in my mind. I would decide what I did, not fear.

"Tell them what that is." I said.

Hishu glanced at the staff in his hands. I was careful not to look directly at it but focus my eyes on his. I saw him consider his options. He raised the staff above his head. "This is the Staff of Jundon. A lost Holy Relic. The Knightshield has come to destroy it in blasphemy."

It was almost clever, but I didn't let up. "Tell them what it does."

"It draws all eyes to Akzad's blessing."

"It draws all eyes to the holder. It makes them susceptible to the wielder's words."

"It shows them the truth! Akzad's truth."

"You mean the Church's lies. How Akzad was the slaver who brought us here. It's true, we rose up to free ourselves. It's true the Church united us to stop the civil war that followed. What they don't tell you is they cover up the true source of their magic. It's not a blessing from Akzad. It was what he used to control us. It is what they continue to use to control us. But it's not rare or something only they can wield. Any of us can use this magic."

To emphasize my point, I made my shield vanish and then return in a flash of light. The crowd remained silent around us, still enraptured by the staff. Seeing this, Hishu grinned. "They aren't listening to your apostate. My words are the only truth. I hold the staff."

"So do I."

Hishu glanced down and saw my hand on the staff below his. He gasped and started to yank it away, but despite his height, he lacked my strength. I pulled the staff from his grip and then brought it down onto my knee, breaking it in two. Murmurs rose from the stands as people shook themselves from their trance.

"This was but an example of the Church's efforts to control you. They tried to usurp me to better manipulate you. They fund racers to deliver their message of worship. They support council members who think the way they like. They take funds from rich businessmen and they preach messages praising these men's business. All to keep those in power at the top. And to keep you down and desperate enough that Akzad, your ancestor's enslaver, is your only beacon of hope. But it doesn't have to be this way. This power they have, you have. And more. You have the power of the people. They suppress us but only because they fear us. Right now, people whose homes have been destroyed due to the rich's greed, are about to be kicked out of the Church. A place they thought they could go to for shelter. After all, it's here for us all is it not?

"You have a chance to change that. Come with me to the Church. Demand the Church return to what it was founded for. Unifying and caring for the people. Demand the council do the same. Demand the constables serve and protect you instead of treat you like a threat. Together we are strong."

That last line reminded me of the Church's Mantra. The people declared they give this power while the acolytes quietly announced they deserved that power. It was time for something different.

"We are the people of Akza. We are united on this physical plain. The power of our union shapes the world. We share this power because together we are strong. Our will is the people's will."

Chapter 38

I didn't look back as I marched from the arena. There had been movement from the crowd as I left the track. The audience was doing something. I wouldn't let myself feel hope that that something was them following me. It would be very anticlimactic to arrive alone.

About halfway down the first street, I heard shouts and honking and so had an excuse to turn around. Behind me were people, so I wasn't alone. Being shorter than most of them, I couldn't tell how deep the crowd was, but there were enough to stretch across the street at least. At first, I couldn't see what the commotion was about until the people spread apart to let a cycler squeeze through. I didn't get a good look at the driver, but clinging to his back was Hishu. Obviously trying to get to the Church ahead of me.

I considered racing ahead. I could take to the rooftops and have a slight chance of beating them by being able to take a straight path. But then I would leave all these people behind. They were the point of all of this. What could I do by racing ahead?

I resumed my walk. I had thought the uncertainty of whether anyone had followed me was tough, but it was nothing to the full knowledge that at least two dozen people were behind me. All watching me. Well, I had endured it when several thousand were watching and listening to me. I could endure a few dozen walking with me.

I had never actually made the journey from the arena to the church on foot before. We'd always taken the cyclers or a quad to the arena for races. It wasn't that far in truth; closer than many other places I'd gone. But I wasn't leaping across buildings now, nor was I being followed then. These combined to make the journey feel like an eternity.

When we turned onto Lesshon street, one of my other worries lightened. There were some people ahead of us outside the church. I hoped that meant people at the movie theaters had seen the newsreel and heeded the call. Of course, it could just be all the refugees being kicked out of the church.

I picked up my pace a little, eager to be done with this, however it turned out. I could sense the crowd's anticipation building. For the first time, I started to worry about what I had set into motion. A massive crowd could turn into a riot just as easily as a protest. That would inevitably end in bloodshed.

But there was no turning back now. They were here. I was here. And, based on the flashing lights ahead, the constabulary was here. Had Hishu summoned them, or had they already been here?

As I approached, the crowd that had already gathered parted as if by magic for me. I don't think it was any actual magic, aside from the magic of the movies. Like it or not, I was well known by everyone here. Anonymity was going to be tough in the future. If there was a future to look forward to.

Once at the front, I saw several constabulary quads. People from inside the church were in the process of being loaded into the enclosed backs. Had they seriously been arresting these people?

Evidently, the arrival of the crowd, and then the large group following me had given them pause. Captain Jundel stood at the top of the stairs next to Hishu and Benthic. Other acolytes and apprentices were poking their heads out from windows and other entrances. The high acolyte was nowhere to be seen but then, he normally visited an estate outside the city on Restday. Apparently, this had been no exception, leaving the consequences of his decision for others to face.

Arrayed at the bottom of the steps leading to the church doors were a line of constables, billy clubs and pistols in each hand. I made eye contact with Bruneski among them, but he blushed and looked away. Well, at least he had the sense to feel embarrassed by what was going on. The others I didn't know well. I couldn't tell eagerness from worry or regret.

It wasn't until I pushed completely through to the front that I saw him. Waiting just inside the church doors, with a rifle strapped to his back and casually twirling a dagger, stood Venti. Apparently, Benthic had given up all pretense and summoned his lapdog in as a second layer of defense for the church. I couldn't see more, but assumed there were more of Venti's Blood Dagger thugs inside. He's lost some followers after our last confrontation, but he had no end to lowlifes who thought as he did.

He saw me watching him and gave me wink before tossing his dagger up in the air and catching it. I glared at him for a second longer before looking away. This wasn't going to be solved by focusing on Venti. He deserved justice but I had let him go once for the greater good. I could do so again if need be.

"Captain Jundel, what are you doing with those people?" I came to a stop about halfway between the crowd and the line of constables. It wasn't a large distance from either of them, but it was enough to leave me feeling like I was alone between two dangerous forces.

"Ms. Estuta." Jundel emphasized the miss, "Thank you for presenting yourself for arrest. Saves us the trouble of tracking you down. Carter, take her into custody."

I turned my look down to Carter who stood just far enough away we could both reach our arms out and just not touch. He glared at me but only momentarily. His eyes kept shifting to the crowd of people behind me. His hands tightened on his weapons as he watched them, but he made no more toward me.

"Captain, there will be no arrests today. Unless you're prepared to take Brother Benthic and Hishu into custody. For sowing discord in the city. Abuse of power. Murder. Arson."

"The only one sowing discord is you, child." Benthic said with his usual calm, friendly tone. "Turn away from this path. Return to the light. There is still time for redemption in Akzad's arms."

"Yeah, what with recently revelations, sayings like that take on a whole new meaning." I said.

Benthic stiffened. "You refer to blasphemy and heresy. Do not believe the lies these degenerates have filled your head with. Akzad's love is eternal."

"I wouldn't call kidnapping people from half a dozen different worlds and taking them here as slaves is what I would call love. Greed. Sadism. Evilness. Those seem more appropriate words to describe Akzad."

"I see you have fallen further than I had imagined." Benthic said and he appeared genuinely saddened.

"But none of that really matters. It happened hundreds of years ago. Let's focus on now. Those people you are arresting, are in need of nothing more then shelter and assistance. They've committed no crimes."

"They are squatters, vagarants, and trespassers. If they're so desperate for shelter, they can shelter in our jail cells." Jundel said.

"You can't have enough cells for all those people. There are hundreds of them."

"Then we'll build more." Jundel sneered.

"Why not build more fucking homes instead? Or better yet," I turned and gestured to the new construction going up behind us, "Let them go back to where they lived before."

"They are welcome to move in when construction is done. Nothing's stopping them."

"They can't afford it. They could barely afford what they paid before. These new places are charging triple. And half of them sit empty because no one can afford the rent. Pay them more."

"Child, your naivety is showing. We cannot change how much people are paid. It is the will of the market." Hishu joined in.

"It's the will of rich, greedy pricks." I snapped. "The Church employs a lot of people around the city. Pay them more. That would at least be a start."

"If we paid the servants of the Church more, we would have less money to do our good works."

"What good works? It looks like the only good you're doing these people, who came to you for help, is having them arrested."

"You clearly have not paid attention during your lessons to all the Church provides the people of this city."

"I have paid attention to all the rich foods you eat and the expensive luxuries filling your rooms. And don't think we all haven't noticed the high acolyte's absence today. He's not off feeding the poor. He's at his giant villa. From what I hear, its big enough to house half these people."

Hishu started to retort but Benthic grabbed his arm. They stared at each other for a second before Hishu backed down. Benthic took a step forward and spread his hands, sweeping his gaze over the crowd.

"We will not solve these concerns by yelling at each other today. Let us adjourn for now. When the high acolyte returns, we will conference with him about changes the Church can make to better the lives of you, our children. We will make recommendations to the Council."

I could feel the resolve of the crowd behind me start to waive. To many of them, especially those who had thought about these things for the first time today, this might sound like a victory. But I saw it for what it was. Empty words. He had promised nothing concrete and specifically left out any mention of what would happen to the people in the church right now.

"Empty words aren't going to cut it this time." I shouted, hoping I could be heard by everyone. "We're tired of promises that are never followed through. We're tired of neglect and lies. Show you're serious. Let these people go. March with us to the Council Hall. Show the Church supports immediate action."

Relief flooded me as I heard echoes of approval from behind me. I hadn't lost the crowd yet. For the moment, at least, I'd turned us back to the immediate problem. How far were they willing to go?

"We cannot do that. Those that violate the law must face its consequences. Without it, we would face anarchy. They must face justice."

"It will be a cold day in hell before I let you avoid it either." Jundel added. "I will keep peace in this city. Through force if necessary. Ready, arms!"

There was a moment's hesitation from the line of constables but they all eventually raised their weapons. Even Bruneski, though he did it reluctantly. Surprisingly, Carter also did it with evident hesitation. It might be my words were getting through to him. It might be because the crowd outnumbered the constables twenty to one.

The threat was not lost on the crowd behind me, especially to all of those up front. They would be the ones absorbing the barrage of gunfire if it came. Things were quickly spinning out of control. I glanced behind me, looking for Allora, or Nerpi, or En. Some familiar face to tell me what to do. But if they were here, they were lost in the masses.

Lost in the masses. That was part of the problem. I had been directing my words to Benthic, Jundel and Hishu. The ones at the top, with all the power and the most to lose if anything changed. I had forgotten all the individuals around them.

"Think carefully here. What you do next could have long lasting consequences." I walked slowly along the line of constables, deliberately putting myself directly in each ones line of fire in turn, "You hold the power of life and death in your hands. Never forget that. Jundel is telling you you're defending order here. That your gun is for defense. But we're not the ones threatening your lives. You won't be killing these people to defend yourself. You'll be doing it to defend the power of the men standing above you. The men who are less like you than the people you'll be shooting. They want you to forget that. To think about order and law. But look at their faces. The people you're about to shoot. The people. They didn't come here to hurt you. They came here to help other people. Other people, that those powerful men behind you, also want you to hurt. But you don't have to. You could join us."

Silence fell over the scene as I reached the end of the line of constables. Their aim was shaky and their resolve, at least in a few, wavering. I just needed one to make a choice. I fixed my eyes on Bruneski, hoping he'd be the one. But he wouldn't meet my eyes.

As it turned out, it wasn't a constable who broke the line first. Instead, Mateto walked down the stairs from a side door and crossed the gulf between groups. He then turned and stood among the crowd, facing up to Hishu and the others. After that, Claren followed only a few steps behind. Jensen gaped at them but didn't move to join.

That must have been enough though. Bruneski lowered his gun and stepped away from the line. As he approached the crowd, holstering his gun, they cheered him on. Behind him, the rest of the constables looked more and more uncertain. Carter, watched the cheering crowd with envy. He lowered his pistol and I thought he would follow when the crack of a gunshot rang out.

The cheering turned to screaming. The people who had been cheering Bruneski now backed away in horror as he collapsed to the street, blood flowing from his back. I followed the line from the wound back up the stair to Jundel, his pistol draw and aimed at Bruneski. He sneered at me.

"Traitors who turn their backs on their duty die like the rats that they are."

Now I spotted Allora as she pushed her way through the crowd and rushed over to Bruneski. I didn't know what she would be able to do, as she didn't have any of her medical gear with her. Before she could reach him though, Jundel shouted again.

"Back away, lady. Let him bleed out. It's what he deserves."

Besides Jundel, Benthic and Hishu both looked alarmed. Technically, Allora was like them, a full acolyte of the church. She was also helping those who opposed the church. I didn't envy them their predicament but hoped it might get them thinking more carefully.

I leaped from my place at the end of the line of constables, to land right beside Bruneski. I nodded to Allora who continued approaching. Then I turned back to face Jundel and materialized my shield. We stared at each other over the rim of it. He'd never seen this trick and I think it unnerved him because he lowered his pistol.

Behind him a new voice joined the fray, "Don't be an idiot. She can't protect them all."

Venti had emerged from the doorway. He raised his rifle and pointed it at the crowd, well away from where I stood. There was no hesitation from him, and another crack echoed through the streets. One of the people in front of the crowd dropped. I could tell this one wouldn't be getting back up from the sight of blood flowing from his head.

The crowd behind me shifted. Screams sounded. They weren't all terror though. They were also angry. Either they were going to flee, or they were going to surge forward and tear anyone who got in their way apart.

I had to do something. I could throw my shield at Venti and hope he didn't shoot me in the time it took to get there. I could charge at him, but knew if I did, the crowd would follow. Things were unraveling too fast for words to make any difference now.

Before I could find a solution, one was found for me. Hishu and Benthic must have sensed the dangerous shift in the crowd. They both turned and grabbed Venti between them. He was much stronger than either of them but hadn't been prepared for it. He dropped the rifle in the struggle and then the pair of them threw him down the stairs. Venti rolled roughly and came to rest at my feet.

"He is the one responsible for all the unrest in the city. He killed your family. We hand him over to you for justice. You may stand down, Captain Jundel. We will not be pressing charges against the people here at the Church today."

I didn't miss the final word of his speech. It was a concession though. They backed down from the arrests and sacrificed Venti to the rage of the crowd. It might be enough to avoid further bloodshed, aside from Venti's, but what else would it do? I looked down at the startled man who had caused me so much torment. I had missed him when I tried to murder him. He had shot me when I tried again. Then I had let him go. Now he was at my feet.

"Sergeant Carter." I shouted, loud enough to regain some attention back on me. "You wanted to maintain order. This man, and Captain Jundel, both murdered people in broad daylight."

Carter froze for only a second before turning to the constables beside him. He directed two to grab Venti and then he walked up to Jundel personally. To his credit, Jundel made no effort to fight. He handed Carter his pistol and then walked stoically down to the waiting quad.

Venti put up more of a fight, drawing his dagger and turning it on the approaching constables. This time I didn't hesitate. I kicked out, hitting the back of his knees and then slamming my shield into the side of his head. He offered no more trouble as he collapsed to the street, dazed.

Before the constables hauled him away, I leaned in close, "You're not going to avoid facing justice this time you son of a bitch. But, I know you're a survivor. I assume you have evidence on the role Benthic and Hishu played in what you've done?"

Venti smiled, "Of course."

"You just might avoid the noose then." They hauled him away and I didn't regret the idea of him avoiding that fate. If he could save himself by turning on those that would otherwise avoid repercussion it was worth it.

The rest of the constables lowered their weapons, uncertainly at first, then a few of them went over to check on the dead man in the crowd. The tension was ebbing but I couldn't let the momentum end here.

Chapter 39

As the constables stood down, the crowd looked on. The ones in front were still in shock from the bloodshed and the near miss of more. The ones in back probably didn't have any idea what was going on. I felt a bit overwhelmed. We had accomplished what I had set out to do, the people in the church weren't going to be arrested. But now I had thousands of people expecting more from me.

I looked up the stairs at the remaining constables, who looked more uncertain than I felt. "Sergeant Carter, if you have any men to spare, we could use an escort to the Council Hall."

He looked uncertainly at me. I know he didn't like me. He also didn't really agree with me. But he was the kind of opportunistic asshole we needed now. We had the upper hand, and he knew it.

"Very well. Men, get officer Bruneski to the hospital and then the rest of you form a line to escort these...people to Council Hall."

As the constables vacated the stairs, I advanced up them. Benthic and Hishu remained, along with the other acolytes watching from the sidelines. They had turned on Venti, probably hoping to save their own asses from the wraith of the crowd. I stared at them, feeling all my hatred and anger swelling inside me. I wanted nothing more than to bash each of their heads in.

I had let Venti go. The man who had pulled the trigger. These men had been behind everything. They had to face justice. I reminded myself Venti would turn on them to save himself. Justice would come. If I acted now, there would be no stopping the crowd. It would be the signal for a rampage.

I wanted to say something, but all of my words felt stupid. Instead, I turned to the other acolytes. "These two men are responsible for the fires and unrest in the city. I expect some of you are fully aware and complicit in that as well. But right at this moment, I don't care. You're going to find them guilty in whatever sham trial the church likes to do. Then you're going to absolve that stupid rule that acolytes can't be tried for their crimes like regular people."

"That's ridiculous. The church must stand apart." Hishu spluttered.

"That's part of the problem. But things are going to change." I waved my hand toward the watching crowd. "You need to be part of them. Not separate from them. The truth about Akzad is out there. I'm sure not all of you knew about that. If you want the Church to survive as an institution, you need to be part of the change too."

Brother Joh stepped forward from one of the side doors. He was one of the eldest acolytes and had taught the history course for apprentices. It had been a boring class, but he had never treated me poorly. I joined the course late, when history was all about different church leaders and their petty differences in doctrine, rather than the events that formed our world. The events that were now in question.

Joh studied me closely as if looking at me for the first time. Then he nodded, "I would very much like to see these documents you have spoken of. Some of the parts of the official history have always felt too convenient."

"I'll see if I can arrange that. For now, would you come with us to the Council Hall? Having a member of the church stand with us will help avoid further bloodshed."

Joh nodded and I returned the gesture. Then I turned back to face the crowd. They had been watching all of this, but we hadn't been speaking loudly. I'm sure they had been expecting me to do something more dramatic. I hoped some words would suffice.

"We've won our first victory!" I shouted to the crowd. They cheered, even though it was clear a lot of them didn't understand it. I had to press on, "On to the next! From here we go to Council Hall and demand changes! We demand a better life!"

Again, they cheered, "I need En and Nerpi! Then on to Council Hall!"

I had to repeat myself a few times before I finally found them. En sauntered out of the crowd, dressed like I had seen him every day at Nerpi's shop. Despite him probably being the richest one here, he didn't stand out among the rest of the crowd, even though they mostly consisted of workers who had been out for a day of fun. Nerpi just looked overwhelmed.

As they approached, I clapped them both on the shoulder, "Are you ready to come out of the shadows and speak publicly on behalf of this, um, whatever this is?"

En raised an eyebrow at me. "I don't think I should be the one speaking on their behalf. I was happy to encourage them, but I can't speak for them."

He surprised me with that statement. Once again, I had underestimated him. "You're probably right. But that's not really what I meant. We need someone articulate who the rich assholes on the Council aren't going to dismiss."

En looked doubtful, "That seems dismissive of everyone else here."

I sighed, "Maybe. You'll have Nerpi there with you.

"You know I can't give a speech," Nerpi said.

"But you can give some authenticity. We don't have time to interview everyone and find someone else who has the knowledge and ability to speak. We've got to move now before we lose the crowd."

"What about Temrok?" En suggested.

"He'll be there too. If we can find him. But again, after the arena incident, you think they're going to listen to a rabble rousing grunde? We need someone who speaks their language."

En sighed, "Fine. Of course, I'll do it. What about you though? You have a way with words better than I would have thought."

I felt my cheeks blush, "Maybe in the heat of the moment. But if we actually sit down in a meeting with people, I'm more likely to hit them than convince them. And I'll be there if you need me to do that. But even I know that wouldn't be very effective."

Their arguments ended there, and I got them moving along with Brother Joh. Mateto and Claren approached me next. I looked at them uncertainly. I liked them most out of all of the people I had met at the church, but their decision to cross the line over to the crowd had surprised me. I didn't understand why they had done it, but I also didn't know how to ask.

Instead, I just smiled at them. "Thank you."

Claren shrugged. "When something is right, it just is."

I nodded, accepting that as good enough. I told them that Brother Joh was coming with us, and he might need some assistance. They both went off to help the elder, leaving me at the trailing end of the now moving crowd. The only ones remaining now were Allora and a few constables waiting to take Bruneski to the hospital once he could be moved.

"How is he?" I asked as I squatted down behind Allora.

"Not good. He was shot in the back, but I think the bullet missed his spine, so that's good." Allora said as she worked.

"You'll save him. You have the skill, and you have that Gift for healing. It's not Akzad's gift, but it is a gift. Don't be afraid to use it. The Church is going to change. Be the start."

Allora turned to look at me then. I don't know what she was thinking but she studied me for a long time before nodding. She went back to tending to Bruneski and called over her shoulder. "Don't you have someplace to be?"

I stood up, watching the departing crowd. I didn't know what was going to happen. Revolutions rarely went off without bloodshed. But I could only do my part. I could be their shield.

Also by Wayne Basta

From Grey Gecko Press
Aristeia: Revolutionary Right
Aristeia: A Little Rebellion
Aristeia: Tree of Liberty
From Many Worlds Fiction
Seraph's Gambit
Seraph's Bind
Seraph's Break

Don't miss out!

Visit the website below and you can sign up to receive emails whenever Wayne Basta publishes a new book. There's no charge and no obligation.

https://books2read.com/r/B-A-DTNS-RARWG

Connecting independent readers to independent writers.

Also by Wayne Basta

Seraph
Seraph's Gambit
Seraph's Bind
Seraph's Break

Standalone
Knightshield

Watch for more at waynebasta.com.

About the Author

Wayne Basta is a lifelong science fiction fan. Reading and watching it proved not enough, so he turned to creating his own universes. Aside from writing novels, he also loves games and works as the editor for d20 Radio.

Read more at waynebasta.com.